# Two Novels

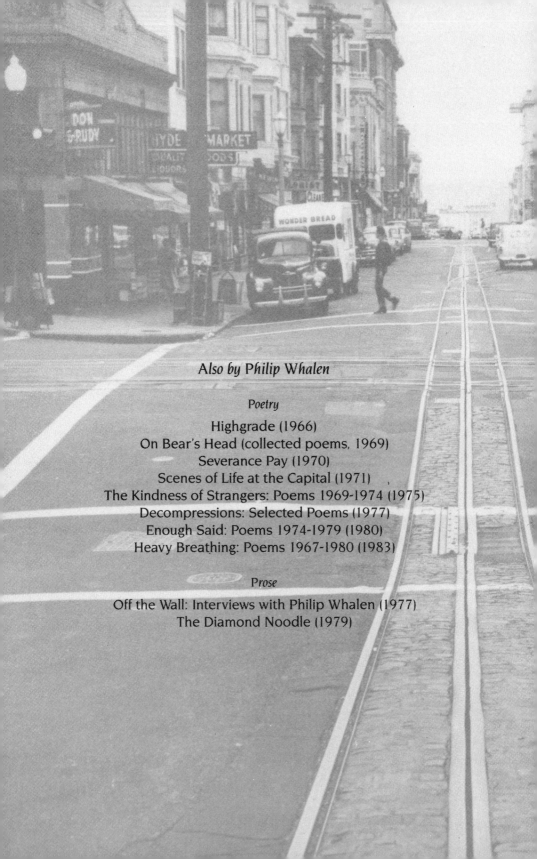

**⊷ Philip Whalen ⊶**

# Two Novels

### You Didn't Even Try

### Imaginary Speeches for a Brazen Head

**⊷ Introduction by Paul Christensen ⊶**

Photographs on cover, title page, and page 1 are reproduced by
permission of the San Francisco Archive. Photo on page 121,
"Philip Whalen, 1965," is copyright 1975 by Larry Keenan, Jr., and
is reproduced by permission. The jacket photo of the author
is by Tom Girardot, and is reproduced by permission.

Design by Ed Hogan.

*You Didn't Even Try* originally published by Coyote Books, 1967.
*Imaginary Speeches for a Brazen Head* originally published by Black
Sparrow Press, 1972.

*Publication of this book was assisted by a grant from the
Massachusetts Council on the Arts and Humanties*

ISBN 0-939010-06-2 (paper)
ISBN 0-939010-07-0 (cloth)
Library of Congress Catalogue Card No. 85-51335

The paper used in this book meets the minimum requirements of
the American National Standard for Permanance of Paper for Printed
Library Materials Z39.48-1984.

ZEPHYR PRESS
13 Robinson Street
Somerville, Massachusetts 02145

# Introduction

Every life has a few important seams in it, things or events that change destiny; one in Philip Whalen's life was meeting Gary Snyder and Lew Welch while he was attending Reed College in Oregon. Here were a couple of young men with ambitions to become serious artists; with deep reserves of talent and discipline to draw upon, already they seemed well on their way to writing effectively. Like Whalen, both were caught up in the awakening of youth that rumbled like thunder across the nation in the post-war years. The three men lived in a boarding house together near the Reed campus, shared their convictions about writing and invented a dadaistic game for composing poetry. Choosing a difficult, "unpoetic" word at random from the dictionary, each would develop a poem around it, writing without calculation; few of these experiments were ever published. But when William Carlos Williams visited the campus on his western reading tour in 1950, he was impressed with the writing of all three men: "Good kids, all of them, doing solid work," he noted in his *Autobiography* (1951).

Whalen was older than Snyder and Welch by a few years and had served in the Army Air Corps (1943-46) before going to college on the new G.I. Bill. His own ambition had already taken root during the war years, when, as an instructor for radio operators in B-17 bombers, he had the leisure to try a novel in the manner of Thomas Wolfe. Like Jack Kerouac, who had written *The Town and the City* (1950) in the passionate, lyric style of Wolfe, Whalen was also trying to learn style from one of his generation's literary heroes. But he destroyed this effort and went on to try another novel when he lived with Snyder and Welch in 1950, a "dotty period" as he has called it, in which he wrote in obsessive nine-hour jags each day. That manuscript went up in smoke as well.

If Whalen's abortive novels were about friendships in the Army and at Reed which had educated him and precipitated changes in his life, they would hold with the pattern of his two published novels, for they are careful reconstructions of circles of friends and of the circumstances which precipitated new directions in his career. In a sense, Whalen's two novels are self-prophecies. In *You Didn't Even Try*, published originally by Coyote in 1967, we are treated to the elaborate social life of the San Francisco intelligentsia during the years Whalen lived there, on and off from 1959 to 1964. The novel's protagonist, Ken, is reminiscent of Whalen, with some discrepancies—Whalen has never married, for example. The friends are portraits and composites of actual figures. Ken is introduced to us as married to Helen, a petulant but beautiful woman with a keen mind whom Whalen describes with zest. At the novel's end, Ken is divorced and chased after, not only by Helen, but by two other women, each infatuated with his independence and whimsical nature. Instead of choosing a second wife, Ken promises to create a "work" which will bear the weight of his love and to "distribute it to the rest of the world"; he vows to be an artist.

Like the novels of Thomas Wolfe, *You Didn't Even Try* is about the making of an artist, beginning with the moment at which the hero is freed from domesticity and made to face life alone, when he chooses to follow a deep-seated though unnamed calling. After completing his final draft of this novel, Whalen received a grant from the National Academy of Arts and Letters (with the help of Allen Ginsberg) which paid for his move to Kyoto, Japan, in early 1965; there, he began writing his mature poetry. So in its own way, the novel parallels Whalen's life.

In *Imaginary Speeches for a Brazen Head*, written during Whalen's second sojourn in Kyoto (1969-71) and published in 1972 by Black Sparrow, the plot and its outcome are similar to those of *You Didn't Even Try*. The protagonist, Roy Aherne, another character reminiscent of Whalen, is a poet who has enjoyed wide reputation and awards for his writing, and he is welcomed into the same sort of intelligentsia which populates the earlier novel. As social life wearies Roy, he is slowly pulled away from his ties and commitments and made to choose a new path. In a parallel occurrence, shortly after completing work on the novel Whalen attended the Zen Center in San Francisco at the suggestion of his friend Dick Baker; a year later he requested ordination as an *Unsui*, or Zen monk. In 1975, Whalen was appointed *Shuso*, head monk, at the Zen Mountain Center in Tassajara Springs, California.

In one way, the two novels connect in their self-prophecies; the move to Kyoto in 1965 exposed Whalen to Gary Snyder's conversion to Buddhism, and may have started the psychological process that is completed in 1971 with his attendance at the San Francisco Zen Center. Both novels bring their protagonists wearily to an end of material pleasures, which have grown tediously repetitive; in both cases, a compelling alternative lies ahead. The novels break off just as Whalen's life takes the next step toward this alternative, and so might be viewed as imaginary rehearsals for the author's forthcoming decisions.

These are not novels strictly predicated on escape from conformity. Far from it, they make the society and terrain of San Francisco so inviting that only the most resolute quester could think of quitting it. But they are novels which spring from a literary tradition of flight from convention. Many male-authored novels about visionaries and artists—and there have been many in the mid-century—put up an easy foil to the dreamer longing for release. Dingy households where parents bitterly eke out a life, small-minded communities that scorn ambition or artistic goals—all that drabness could be easily left behind, as in Kerouac's first statement on the theme, *The Town and the City*. It was only what one was fleeing *to* that appealed to most of these authors: the urban landscape of bohemian life, where casual sex and serious conversation floated in the same night currents, as in Norman Mailer's *Barbary Shore* (1951), John Clellon Holmes's *Go* (1952), and Chandler Brossard's *Who Walk in Darkness* (1952). Each one takes off from Wolfe to invent a disaffected but gifted rebel.

The dim surroundings darken even more by the next round of escaping heroes, as in the grim absurdity of Yossarian's service in *Catch-22* (1961) and Ken Kesey's asylum captivity of Chief Bromden in *One Flew Over the Cuckoo's Nest* (1962), and they turn completely mad in the novels of Barth, Vonnegut and Pynchon. A long hatred for domestic entrapment and dead-ended employment builds up the drear landscape from which the dreamer bolts in modern male-authored fiction. In Whalen's novels, the flight from home is already behind the protagonist; he has arrived at his urban destination, where he finds great pleasure and enrichment but discovers it is not the end of his quest. Something lies beyond the city to complete his fulfillment as an artist and he seeks it out.

Whalen's two portraits of San Francisco give us the minds, the glittering personalities, the eccentrics of human excellence in an otherwise drab America. These gems jut out at odd angles from the conforming silhouette of the average citizen. Ken, Whalen's first protagonist, and the poet Roy Aherne of *Imaginary Speeches* both trawl the waters of this society in constant curiosity of what might turn up from its depths. The women are brash, smart, and keenly witty, of an independence that tortures some of their husbands; they are stately, willowy people looked at almost with the longings of a voyeur, though Whalen gives to both his heroes strong charms that attract a variety of these heady females to their beds. The men are powerful, stubborn, aloof in their thoughts, of convoluted personality that often irks their wives, who stay with them through the thin years because of their cranky, gifted intellects and interesting lives. This is what cements Whalen's social microcosm: a love of intelligence, the freedom it brings, the sweetness it confers on daily life; without it, nothing.

Another focus of this swirl of humanity is the city of Berkeley, headquarters of the University of California's preeminent campus, a magnet for high achievers who are gathered together in a new culture that is by turns Viennese, Parisian, Oxonian—with a dash of American. Whalen lavishes attention on the high culture of the West Coast and on the beautiful landscapes too, especially Mt. Tamalpais, a haven from the madding crowd celebrated in both novels. But the most remarkable aspect of Whalen's two novels is this core of humanity gifted with sight, powered by a consciousness that will not permit of mere survival.

Whalen's portraits are complex, a social commentary on American life. Equated with elements found in postmodern poetics, the social interactions of his characters dramatize the dynamics that Charles Olson and Robert Creeley worked out as the dynamics of a poem. Whalen applies these heady notions from physics and poetics to his fictional characters, partly in jest, partly in earnest. At one point in *You Didn't Even Try*, Ken compares his friends to phenomena of a force field:

> ...It was strange to spot them, rising above the fairly regular Riemann surface he looked out upon whenever he sat still and looked. There were these discontinuities in it, sudden multidimensional warpings that indicated the presence of a field of action or force which was operating autonomously.

The plot places such figures of power into a field of relations; they affect one another much the way perceptions affect the ongoing course of a poem, in which, Olson would say often, the awareness is being widened and enriched. The figures of intellectual power who move in Ken's orbit warp the field by their own dynamic influences. Indeed, their influence on Ken throughout the plot may be the catalytic agent delivering him to higher consciousness at the end, because of which he ironically more or less abandons them.

Ken remembers the best things said by his gifted friends, but no one collects them more assiduously than does the novelist Marilynn Marjoribanks. Her husband Travis

> rigged up a tape recorder so that it would pick up whatever came over the telephone as long as Marilynn kept her foot on the treadle-switch. She'd give the switch a kick whenever one of her callers got going on a particularly poignant or self-revelatory theme. Marilynn had a nice ear for turns of speech and colorful expression, a great sense for recognizing the dramatic, intriguing bits that people throw away in conversation.

Ken's friends are sources of open consciousness, the alert sensibility that is at the heart of postmodern poetics. Whalen gives to Marilynn Marjoribanks the methodology he himself uses as a poet; her treadle-switch phone is the equivalent of the many journals in which he has recorded the *bon mots*, *apercus*, brainstorms and other delights of daily consciousness. From them a poem is drafted, not in a sudden frenzy of lyric outburst, but carefully, built up as in mosaic, in which bits and pieces of the journals are juxtaposed into a single, high-velocity streak of perception that implodes years of rambling and digression.

Here is how Whalen expresses his poetic through Marilynn:

> She edited the tape at the end of the day, transcribing onto paper the phrases and anecdotes she believed she might use. For, very slowly, she was taking all these words and little homey incidents and breaking them down, boiling and smelting them into the fabric of an enormous novel. The final composition and editing of this vast collage were a little more than half done.

The friends are the natural phenomena of the field; the artist Marilynn is the concentrator of the perceptions and brilliant phrases that have been uttered and then forgotten. Like an alchemist, she compresses them into a frame; by "smelting" and laborious mixing, she comes up with something like gold, a filament of purity, a rarified instance of human consciousness at its fiery best. Only then, is the implicit argument, is an artistic work made. This view is expressed by the full range of the arts at mid-century, many of which are governed by a single goal: to reach for the center of human awareness, to find its molten core of understanding and to reproduce it in some medium where its original force is not lost.

In both of Whalen's novels, San Francisco is an intellectual Eden where a few good minds are able to have great perceptions and many others are able to live at a high altitude of talent and intelligence. The rest, of which few are noticed, are of that dull, even Riemann surface of the grid, the humble clerks and go-fers who also serve. Brooding over the paradise of San Francisco are forces which threaten to undermine it—government and big business, whose alluring contracts can seduce free spirits into drudgery and deceit. Work is not in and of itself redeeming in Whalen's cosmos, especially work by contract, by the clock, wherein many dull efforts accompany the one or two good things achieved.

The most admired members of Whalen's cast are those who have retained their intellectual independence. Travis is one of them:

> He was much consulted by the Government (for whom he declined to work), by other physicists, and by such vast invisible corporate beings as the General Dynamics organization. He could, if he chose, take a week off to work on the electronic organ which he was building at home, and nobody would complain to him or try to fire him from his job.

Stanford, where Travis is employed, pays him vast sums "to sit around discussing [why] the current theories were all wrong."

Clifford Barlow of *Imaginary Speeches* is another independent thinker. He too likes to play the organ, has a well-rounded, powerful intellect, but is the more artfully drawn of the two characters; he embodies a subtle freedom that permits him to contradict his own personality and still retain the preeminence and self-confidence of the true free spirit. He stays apart by living outside the country, and when he has to take employment, limits it to teaching for nine months. The distinction made in both characters is between an interest and a career, a capacity and an obligation to perform it routinely.

Both men are measures of achievement to their friends; they are like pinnacles thrust up out of the grid to remind everyone of the reach a human being is capable of making. They are each necessary to the others as an inspiration and, at times, a goad, but there is a significant shift of interest between the two portraits of genius. Travis, a speculative scientist, is a contentious, daring theorist willing to take a leap or risk in thought. Clifford is earthier, more interested in human beings and their cultural and anthropological unities; his gift for language allows him to decipher the underlying patterns that link ages and cultures. The portraits of Travis and Clifford in part parallel a change of interests in Whalen, from the grand program which Olson had set out for poets that Whalen early admired, to the concern for the small, the simple, the plain, a unifying principle of everyday life to be found in Snyder's poetry, and increasingly in Whalen's.

Much of the rollicking humor and complaint of the poems in On Bear's Head (1969)—a large selection of Whalen's best poems, in which he portrays himself a "laughing Buddha," an impractical but brilliant hanger-on in the social scene of San Francisco—are found in the character of Roy Aherne, popular poet and social boor. Alice Lammergeier complains to her husband in an early scene of Imaginary Speeches that "He talks too loud. He dominates the room. It's like having a sound truck in the house." But her husband Max defends Roy and even insinuates that his wife is attracted to him. Whalen is clearly amused by Roy and gives him sex appeal, enormous intellectual powers, and a flat-footed manner. Roy is a little too forthright with his student admirers, as in an opening scene at a bar, or too thoughtful and slow on the draw with the imposing figures of higher San Francisco society. But more than anything, Roy is a wanderer enjoying the drift of fate or folly.

In Roy's characterization, as in Whalen's persona as poet, is an old paradigm of the beggar poets, those mountain bards of India and China who taunted their fellow villagers with sly verses of seeming madness in exchange for a little food and drink. Whalen's dependence on friends (as noted in his book of poems, The Kindness of Strangers [1976], the title taken from Blanche Dubois's famous line in A Streetcar Named Desire), is an inverted arrogance of sorts, wearing in time but charming and nevertheless potent. But below the smiling mask of the bard is an ideology intact from the start—the conviction that the artist must remain free to be good and should be paid tuppence for the pleasure of his company.

In certain ways, Imaginary Speeches is a better novel than You Didn't Even Try. The prose glistens with intelligence, is smooth, flexible, deft and precise, never prosaic or labored. It is obviously from the pen of a craftsman, a poet who has written verse for long years and who knows how to prevent the rhythm of a long passage from flagging. He can turn on a dime when attention seems to wander or interject wit that lifts up a long, perhaps flabby digression or deflate his own drift toward some abstraction not entirely intended. The point of the prose is pleasure first—in the sound of the word, the chemistry of sound in a phrase, the overlap and harmony of inner-rhyme, delicate nuance, shading. These all make entirely forgivable the sometimes soap opera plotting of the novel, for what powers the imbroglios and subplots is a pure, limpid language springing from a master.

The doctrines of postmodernism are present in subtle form; the

ideas are ironed out, digested, placed in the exposition and characterization. The three-dot section break that marks off scenes is one manifestation of postmodernism, a subtle way of noting the discontinuity principle
of the work, present in all of Whalen, present indeed through much of the
art of the period. The rivulet of prose overcomes each of the seams, flows
through and around its impediments, but the section break, like particles
of a hexagram, floats there to remind us that nothing is seamless, everything is made up out of the vastness of things and chosen, juxtaposed,
by hand.

The colors are vivid but less obvious in *Imaginary Speeches*. The San
Francisco social world is muted, the extremes not so widely placed.
Dorothy, a character similar to the first novel's Helen, dramatizes the new
mean. She has been sharing the love of two good men, Roy and Clifford,
and has known the agony and pleasure of their fine intellects. Only after
having that experience can she willingly accept less in her new lover, Tom,
and appreciate him more. In *You Didn't Even Try*, fame, notoriety, crowds of
admirers may have intrigued Ken and might have precipitated a change
of life, but in *Imaginary Speeches*, Roy grows weary of them. His drinking has
become habitual and boring, his nights lost in a boozy haze. Whalen himself was the figure of much attention in the press, as were all the members
of the San Francisco Renaissance. From the start, at the poetry reading at
the Six Gallery in San Francisco, in 1955, when Ginsberg first read his
poem "Howl" in public, the group was hounded by the media and a certain flamboyance of style was reinforced by the attention. Whalen looks
on this celebrity with a jaundiced eye in his treatment of Roy as he steers
him to the edge of the city. In one scene late in the novel, Roy wakes up
in a stranger's apartment, repairs himself like a rag doll, and leaves wondering who has kept him for the night. It is the tattered end of one stage
of a poet's life.

Roy's change of heart takes something of the form of Ken's in the way
he expresses his new detachment from the social whirl of San Francisco:
"I don't really love them, I love their beauty. The trouble is that I don't
love just one single person. If I really loved one, I wouldn't be interested
in the judgments of all the others, nor would I be seeing all the others as
judges." He is chafing to be let free; "We are all such fixtures here," he tells
Dorothy. When he implies he wants to travel, Dorothy tells him to get a
job. But for the first time he calls *writing* his job: "I haven't got time to work
for anybody else." The story closes a little later, but it is obvious Roy must
now find shelter someplace where his work comes first.

Soon after finishing this novel, Whalen visited the Zen Center and dis-
cerned in the religious order the possibility of a new life. There is no clue
what Roy will do, of course, but for Whalen the Center was a kind of
uncontaminated university of the spirit, without corporate sponsors or
government interference, where one could contemplate the imagination,
much as he had all along, and be secure in the fact that it was the duty
expected of him. This was the one meaningful employment Whalen had

searched for throughout his life. It was a place where mind was given its unfettered freedom. In *You Didn't Even Try* and *Imaginary Speeches for a Brazen Head*, Whalen gives us the progress of poets making their way to this spiritual and artistic fulfillment beyond the city of first dreams.

*Paul Christensen*
*Bryan, Texas,* 1985

# You Didn't Even Try

"The sick and sleepless man, after the dawn of the fresh day, is fain to watch the smoke now from this and then from the other chimney of the town from his bed-chamber, as if willing to borrow from others that sense of a new day, of a discontinuity between the yesterday and the to-day, which his own sensations had not afforded."

—S. T. Coleridge, *Notebooks*, 1811-1812

# I

Although Helen and Kenneth had been fairly happily married for almost three years, each of them had begun to think, privately, of divorce and the pleasure of living independently. They were nearly the same age (a little more than thirty), reasonably intelligent, reasonably healthy. But Ken was beginning to be afraid that any minute now he might realize that his learning and feeling, his whole being, may have reached a level kind of plain of a very definite size, shape, and color, in the midst of which he would remain until he died—afraid of hearing a voice that would soon be telling him, "This is all there is to your life, just this: this is all you have, this is all you are, all that you're going to get."

For the past year and a half they had lived in San Francisco. They liked the city, they had many friends there, they had left all their in-laws in another town. It wasn't hard for Ken to make a living in the city. He could work as a statistician, he could operate certain kinds of computers. Sometimes he might take a job for a short time in market research. He never worked longer than four or five months at a time; he preferred to stay at home and read philosophy. If he ran short of money, he'd collect unemployment insurance for a month or so. He'd continue to read, sometimes he'd go with Helen to the museums where he'd argue with her about pictures; she had several degrees in art history. But if, one day, Helen wanted to buy an expensive art book and there'd be enough money to pay the light bill but not enough to pay for her book, too, she'd complain gently about being poor and Ken would go to work again. Helen would be most apologetic and truly sorry, but he would assure her that he had no real point to his reading, no real project, he might as well be working.

Ken remembered how they had both felt a kind of rejuvenation during the first year of their marriage. They were able to see the world as if they were much younger people who took a great delight in it, in that sense of having the world to do with as they pleased. Perhaps this new entity which they made, this "couple," really was a young and eager creature whose intelligence might be represented by a number less than a quarter the total reached by adding her IQ to his. This new, dumber, social entity was perhaps dragging them down or hauling them apart, which was it? Ken wondered whether he himself were not quite simply regressing. He couldn't work on other people's problematical numbers and machines very long without becoming very distracted or disassociated, or at least very tired and cranky. When he'd come home from work he'd have a few drinks and then drink quite a lot more after dinner.


"If there's a logical sequence to your thoughts," Kenneth said, "I don't see it. But why should I expect there to be one?"

"One what?" she inquired. "Thought, logic, or sequence? And is it important to you that it be logical? Why do you have your eyes shut?"

"We must keep trying to face up to each small matter as it arises," he said. "Otherwise the chances are greater that we shall be overwhelmed by problems of larger magnitude, those more serious and profound. The former, I will admit, often appear bigger and more troublesome than the latter. Our judgment of these matters is affected, of course, by the state of our health and by our emotional condition." He kept his eyes tightly closed and carefully put his glass to his lips and drank.

"There's hardly an 'issue' involved here," she replied. "Anyway, I supposed that the 'issue' comes after whatever occurrence or fact— I never can remember which is the former and which is the latter."

He had to open his eyes in order to put the glass back on the coffee table without spilling it. Not, he thought, that I care about this particular table which has repeatedly taken untold square inches of skin away from my shin bones. "All you have to do is pay attention. It isn't that difficult."

"How do these things get started, anyway? I suppose you'll say I bring it on myself, although anyone can see that I'm only a victim of circumstance." She dropped her cigaret into her glass in order to put it out. Then she saw what she'd done and picked up his glass and took a drink. "I shall take the little car."

"There won't be enough room for the luggage," he said. "And the right front tire is down to the cord."

"Well, what do you suggest we do?"

Ken thought about it. He took the glass with the cigaret in it and very nearly drank out of it before he carefully returned it to the table. "I don't know," he said. "I suppose that I could leave you a check for ten dollars. You could cash it at the corner store. I— What day will it be?"

"The twenty-ninth is Thursday."

"I'll give you a check and deposit money to cover it on the thirtieth, when I get paid."

"Will you remember, though?" she asked.

"The last time I forgot, the bank sent me a nasty letter."

"Yes. Now tell me which is the former and which is the latter."

"Oh, I don't know," he said. "It just seems that there's always a thing that has to be moved first before I can reach what it is I'm really after—I

6

must move the chair away from the table in order to get at the sugar-bin."

"We could move the table to this side of the kitchen," she suggested, helpfully.

"I just meant it as an example," he said.

"An example of what?" she asked, peering at him through the smoke of a match that she kept trying to put out but which smouldered and fumed.

"Why don't you pay attention?"

"Why do you get mad and shout all the time? I'm sorry. I try to pay attention. I love to have you talk to me and have you explain things. We never have a chance to talk any more since you got this damned job."

"That's what I mean," Ken said. "I have to have this job in order to pay for this house for us to live in so I can be with you. I did marry you, after all."

"I trapped you into it," she replied, contritely. "But are you going to have Thursday off? Marilynn and Travis want to know if we're going to the party and will give them a ride. Their cars are broken or in the garage or something."

"My God! Is that thing happening this Thursday? I can't hardly get a minute to sleep in the little time I get off work. I've got to go to these insane entertainments and listen to all your creepy friends and their zithers and banjos."

"It's not MY creepy friends this trip, Buster. It's Joan's party, remember, YOUR best friend in the whole world and happy college days. You always enjoy yourself well enough at her place."

"Yeah," he said.

"Hah!" she replied, "Now you better get out some more ice and a clean glass."

"OK," he said, "I lose." He went into the kitchen, imagining the shadows of leaves and branches falling across his head and back as if he were walking in Golden Gate Park, as if the sun were shining as he knew that it was, on the other side of the earth, inhaling part of its atmosphere with his every breath along with the fumes of this inexpensive gin.

"We ought to get another bottle of gin for the party, I suppose. I hate to go places empty-handed."

"I want those olives with other things inside them than pimentos," Helen said.

"Pimenti?" he amended, uncertainly.

She ignored him. She asked, "Are you going to wear those pants tomorrow, too?"

"I don't know," he said. He looked at his pants and saw that they were middling filthy. "Did you pick up my slacks from the cleaners?"

"I haven't had TIME," she cried.

Ken wondered idly whether ultrasonic waves might cause flower buds to open prematurely.

"You could wear the blue ones," Helen said.

7

"Did you fix the cuffs?"

"Oh, God. Mother was going to do it and she forgot and I left them."

"That's all right. We can get the other ones from the cleaner tomorrow."

Helen said, "Uh-huh," as she lighted a fresh cigaret. "Tomorrow's Sunday," she said.

Ken looked at the buds on the begonia plant. The smaller ones would be nearly colorless inside. There'd be no point in having them opened now. The larger ones, just about to burst, would open if one turned a supersonic generator in their direction. Or the buds would fall off completely? Would it knock the dirt and spots out of these trousers without shredding the fabric? "Don't worry about it," he said, "We can put these in the washing machine tonight."

"It's awfully late," she said. She went into a long recitation of the inconvenience of living in a building where everyone else retired at nine p.m. and complained to the landlord if anyone so much as flushed a toilet after that hour.

While she was talking, Ken tried to remember the new euphemism for *leprosy*. He wondered about the word "Michigan," meaning a card game, or one of the United States, doubtlessly a French name unless, by analogy from "Waukegan," it was an Indian one. Neither had any connection with "Oregon" or "hooligan." He thought of his father, who had a fair tenor voice, trying to sing "Rocked in the Cradle of the Deep," a song for basses. How long had it been since he heard anyone use the term "basso profundo"? He had learned in high school to say "counterbass," meaning the lowest voice range of men in the Don Cossack Chorus. "Hansen's Disease," he said to himself. He felt quite pleased. He could remember if he tried, drunk or sober.

He looked so pleased, Helen thought. She wanted to touch him. He seemed miles away. His hair stood up in a cowlick at the crown of his head and he didn't realize that it made him look both absurd and endearing to her. She wanted him to answer her, to tell her what to do. She could feel herself begin to get afraid of being nervous and silly. She must stop herself before she started. It would certainly bother him, more than usually, if she were to start talking too much now. "When Marilynn called, she and Travis were thinking of coming over today. I told them no and made excuses. We'll see them at Joan's party, anyway."

He didn't answer. She knew that Marilynn and Travis made him nervous. She hoped that he'd appreciate the fact that she had not carelessly invited them to come today, although she loved gossiping with Marilynn. Ken wasn't attending. He said, "What about Marilynn and Travis?"

She explained it all again.

"That's good," he said. "We can go together for dinner before the party at Joan's."

"For God's sake, let's eat someplace other than Chinatown," Helen pleaded. "The last time we were there you made such a scene I can't possibly face going back. Not for a while, anyway."

"Why not? I paid the bill and they didn't tell us to stay away. I've been there for lunch a couple times since we were there that time. They had a chance to tell me to scram if they wanted to. You like black mushrooms in oyster sauce as much as I do."

"We could go to a different restaurant this time, I suppose. But what I'd really like to have is eggplant Parmigiana, I haven't had any Italian food for so long and I love to eat it so much, can't we go to some cheap place on the Beach?"

Ken was saying something like "I guess so," when she really let loose with a steady flow of babble, all about the beauties of Italian cookery, the delight of preparing and eating it. She spoke of the various dishes and the provinces of Italy where each one is supposed to have originated. She talked about the various meats and vegetables, about the color and weight of olive oil, about the varieties of onions and hams and sausages.

Helen spoke for seven minutes by the clock; Ken was watching the second hand go around, thinking of the different kinds of mechanical, optical, and musical toys which might be powered by the same gear train which drove the second hand...articulated figures of people, animals, angels, historical personages, all of them engaged in varous erotic activities. He was thinking of such a clock as might be especially designed for sale among the caucasoid-Methodist-transplanted Iowans of Southern California when Helen shouted at him.

"Hah? Don't you think so? Ken?"

"I suppose so," he said. He knew it was something about saffron, he hadn't completely blocked her voice from his consciousness. He said, "In any case, I'm going to retire for a while. Come on to bed."

"Why don't you pay attention to me when I talk to you?"

"I pay lots of attention to you. I propose to pay you even more, if you will kindly step this way."


They lived in a four-room flat which had once been painted in decorator colors: chartreuse, charcoal, olive, and ochre. The original plaster ornamentation, the seraphim which upheld the corners of the window embrasures, the female masks (bodiless Caryatids) which faced each other beneath the lintel of the arch between the living room and the dining room had been left white. The high ceilings were white, as were the decorative roundels of plaster fruit and flowers from which the lighting fixtures hung. Ken had painted all the walls white. He had visited San Francisco enough times in the past to know that a part of almost any day is foggy, and he wanted his house to be light.

The plumbing was falling to pieces, the floors in some of the rooms had a pronounced slope towards the outside wall, and the whole place tended to be damp. There was a fireplace in the living room; Ken had thought it was only an ornamental one since it was very shallow and had

9

marble jambs and mantel. Bruce Chadwick, who claimed to have exactly the same kind of fireplace in his own living room, told Ken he could use it for heating. He demonstrated by burning a sheet of newspaper in the tiny grate and then hustling Ken up onto the roof of the building to show him the tin chimney from which they could see a puff of smoke and a few cinders of burnt paper drifting down. "There you are, a fireplace," Bruce told him. "You're lucky. Now all you have to do is find packing crates and cardboard boxes to burn and you're in business. You'll have lots of fun carrying out the ashes twice a week."

No matter how long and how well the fireplace kept its fire, no matter how long the gas oven in the kitchen operated, no matter how long the gas-burning wall heater with its Moorish-looking fire tiles (which glowed red hot) roared and whizzed, no matter how many electrical fuses blew out on account of the portable electric heater used alternately in bedroom and bath, the flat was always a little bit cool, just the least bit damp.


Helen said she couldn't stand Bruce Chadwick, he was too much of a smart aleck. The combination of Bruce and Kenneth in the same room was almost intolerable to her; they talked too extravagantly.

Bruce once told her that nobody except art teachers from Methodist normal schools in the backwoods of Missouri could take Berenson at all seriously. Helen took issue with this; she felt that Bruce was badly mistaken. B.B. was one of the most civilized, profoundly wise and charming of men—nay, perhaps the nearest she might ever come to seeing a really enlightened one.

Chadwick said, "Charm, yes, OK, lots of illuminations—but not much more. B.B. invented Lorenzo Lotto out of his own hat—and if he didn't personally paint the pictures attributed by him to Lotto, they were prepared and executed directly under B.B.'s close and expert supervision."

Helen was completely enraged by this. She came very near to screaming at Bruce and driving him from the house. Kenneth persuaded her to be calm, Bruce apologized for upsetting her and went away. She never forgave him. He was Ken's best friend, they had been friends for years; Helen had to reconcile herself to seeing Bruce in her house quite often, but she hated him.

Chadwick had been living in San Francisco for some years before Kenneth and Helen arrived. He was a little older than Ken, quite thin and tall, with a deeply lined and leathery appearing face. His hair was still more black than grey, but it was white around the temples.

He had been involved in a number of theatrical projects. He designed sets for the avant-garde theaters, he had made several experimental films which were much admired by other film-makers; sometimes he acted on the stage. He made sculpture that showed lights through prisms, lenses, crystals, and mirrors. He made sparkly machines that did no work. He described himself at different times as an alchemist, a vegetarian, a wastrel, a genius. He was always making things and some of them were always being shown in galleries, museums, theaters, bars, or restaurants. The public and the art critics alike ignored him.

Quite a lot of the time it seemed that Bruce was drinking in North Beach bars. Women of a certain age, beat chicks, waitresses, sewing machine girls, pursued him. He allowed himself to be caught regularly but never permanently. He had once been married to a woman called Joan who still lived in San Francisco, but she moved in quite other social circles, so they seldom met. They had been divorced for some years.

Ken had always been intrigued with Joan—Ken had known her as long as he'd known Bruce. She was a big woman with huge black eyes and long black hair. Her skin was very fair. She had, some time after divorcing Bruce, inherited an importing firm. She traveled. She told funny stories to Ken about everyone they had ever known. She saw many of their old friends who were then living abroad, and her descriptions of their lives and times were extremely diverting. Ken loved to go to dinner at her house, or invite her to his, where they could sit and talk and gossip for hours. Helen was jealous of Joan, but she felt, intuitively, that Joan had no real interest in tolling Kenneth away, and that Kenneth didn't seem to be giving off his peculiar kind of sex vibrations when he was in Joan's company, so that she, Helen, was willing to complain relatively little about the attentions Ken paid to Joan. It seemed that they were only friends, after all.


Helen was talking. Ken listened for a while, but it was only a repetition of an incident that happened in her childhood, about a pet dog who had eaten all the chocolate Easter eggs. She was describing the kinds of sugar flowers, their colors and flavors, which had adorned each egg. He said, "I expect I would have stomped that dog into little bits." He stood up from the table."

"Not CROOTIE," she replied complacently. "He would have taken your leg off right at the shoulder. He was a chow dog, I told you. What your friend Chadwick would call a *mean* mother."

"Have you seen my pants hanger?" he asked.

She immediately became confused and apologetic. "No, I don't know—maybe it fell down behind the shoes—I'll go look..."

"Don't bother, I'll find it." He went into the bedroom and she followed him, talking about how many postmen Crootie had torn and maimed in his long career of crime, vice, and ill temper. "But what I was going to tell you was—is—it's all in my head. The doctor says I'm not the least pregnant."

"That's good. We can try lots more times. We'll probably have the record baby of all time if we concentrate on it a little. I don't think we've been concentrating."

"What do you mean, 'we'? You aren't the one who's got to get all swollen up and funny-looking."

"I'll look funny enough," he said, looking at himself in the mirror above the sink. She put her arms around him, pressed her cheek into the hollow between his shoulder blades.

"No, you don't," she said. "I think you're the handsomest man I ever saw, I love you."

"Don't squeeze me while I'm trying to shave," he said.

She kept her hold on him. "Talk some more," she said, "I love to hear your voice through your back, it's so smooth."

"Cut it out, will you, I'm trying to shave! I'll cut myself."

"I hope you cut your throat, you conceited hog! I'm going to make another pot of coffee." She let go of him, picked up the bathmat and hung it over the edge of the bathtub. "Maybe we can have a baby a little later."

"I hope so," he said.

"I do want to have one," she said. "Probably next year we may have a little more money and it will be easier."

"What's money got to do with it? We'll get by all right, I think. People have been having babies without money for quite a few years."

"But you have to buy so many things—basinettes, baths, diapers, layettes, diaper service, bottles . . ." She went on with her list of what she considered the trouble and expenses of becoming parents.

Ken remained calm, finished shaving and washed his face. He said, "I expect we'll have what we really need when the time comes."

"I suppose that Mother and Daddy would help us once the baby got here and they saw their own grandchild. I want some more coffee," she said.

"I thought you were going to make another pot."

"There isn't any more coffee," Helen said.

"Go buy some—and get another fluorescent light to replace this one." The light on the left side of the mirror hummed and flickered and blackened in an irregular rhythm.

"I'm not dressed yet," Helen replied.

"Go get dressed."

"Oh hell, I can't win, I guess." She walked out of the bathroom and slammed the door.

She wondered why he wouldn't answer. Helen couldn't think what she had said that was wrong or upsetting. Ken wasn't anything like her father, who was jolly and articulate and was always aware of what he was doing, of what he wanted, always so sweet, except for sometimes in the morning.

"What?" she said.

"What shall I bring home in the way of meat?" Ken asked her.

"Oh, I don't know. What do you want?"

"I want baked lamb shanks with all the trimmings."

12

"I'll make a list," Helen said. "Just a minute." She found a pencil and a piece of paper.

Ken said, "I can remember all right."

"Well, we need a few other things for the house." She read aloud slowly as she made out a list of some twenty items.

He waited. He tried to be patient. He hated the way she wrote everything, labeled everything, lost or misplaced all the objects and the inventories that listed them with their true locations. She had a habit of writing notes that she'd leave for him to find, telling him she was out and when she'd be back and what it was she wanted him to do while she was gone, take out the garbage, scrub the toilet with scouring powder and bleach. Her notes never failed to infuriate him; on paper she sounded like a very snotty martinet, a megalomaniac, a shrew. She really believed that her notes were simple statements of what she wanted; she wrote them without the least intention of bullying him. She supposed, on the other hand, that once it was written down it was as good as if the job were actually done. She had quite a primitive feeling about language being an infallible magic. Ken wasn't sure why it was that her notes upset him. He knew that she wasn't a bossy type of woman. It only happened when she wrote and he read it. He must remember this.

> "A *kiss is but a kiss,*
> A *sigh is but a sigh.*
> *The world will always welcome lovers,*
> *High die dee die,"*
>
> Kenneth sang.

Helen smiled as she wrote. He was happy, she thought to herself. Then she said, "Oh, dear," and stopped writing.

"What's the matter now?"

"Oh, nothing—I just remembered something—we're out of bulghur."

Ken could see that she'd made up the word on the instant he asked her. She wasn't saying what it was. She was pleased to believe that he'd be annoyed if she told him what was bothering her. That's what she used to tell him. He believed that she was more used to his cranky sounds by this late date. She'd go on this "trembled with fear at his frown" routine for a while, then get bored with it and pay no attention to his growls.

She had remembered a saying of her father, "Sing before breakfast and you'll cry before night." Her father would whistle in the morning while he cooked breakfast. Sometimes he'd forget and sing, and after he'd sung a line or so, he'd remember his superstition, swear softly to himself and stop; however, he might forget again and be singing before he ate, and that would spoil his temper. Helen's father had taught her that superstitions are silly and sometimes evil. He had a number to which he was faithful, and Helen learned more of them from her mother and a few more from the girls at school. Everyone agreed that superstitions are neither good nor productive attitudes.

"I heard a white-crowned sparrow about two o'clock this morning," Ken said.

She finished the list. "I was thinking of my father a minute ago. You were singing and I remembered what he always said about singing before breakfast. I didn't tell you because you'd get mad and say it was a silly superstition."

"Well, it is silly, so what—it's probably true. I expect my mood will change a number of times in the course of the day. Did you hear the sparrow?" He refrained from telling her that her father was a hopeless nut.

"What sparrow?"

"Oh, never mind."

"Well, tell me about it."

"I heard a white-crowned sparrow, it must have been two this morning."

"Oh, yes, I always think of them as nightingales more or less."

"You must have heard real nightingales in Europe."

"Oh, yes, but I always hear these birds at night and think 'nightingale' whether it's right or not. I acted once in *Romeo and Juliet*. 'It was the nightingale and not the lark.' You know."

"Your memory works all right, my memory works all right, we don't have to bother with all these lists. Anyway, I haven't got time or money enough on me right now to buy all this plunder."

"I'm making it for you. You're the one who's always complaining about forgetting everything and your mind decaying away.

"I guess so," he said.


The smell of burnt toast lingered in the kitchen and was perceptible as a pale cold smell as far as the front hall. A fine dusting of carbonized bread-crumbs decorated the greasy dishes in the sink.

Helen could not regulate the toaster. She claimed that the control knob was too hard to turn. She had trouble with anything that required the slightest exertion of her hand muscles. She couldn't get her cooking pots entirely clean because it was too hard to rub them with steel wool. Opening a can of coffee, a can of sardines, was too hard. If she felt like it she could play a few complicated Bach fugues on a piano, but she claimed that her fingers had no strength in them.

She let the toast burn, not complacently, but more or less stoically. She would scrape the blackened crust away, spread jam on half a piece of the "toast" and leave half of that on her plate.

Wheat bread, rye, Russian bread, she said that all these were very good to taste but too much trouble, too hard to eat. She preferred the soft white bakery bread from the supermarket. She cut the crust away when she made sandwiches of this unwholesome confection.

Helen said, "I wish you'd take out the garbage."

Ken said, "Uh huh," but he didn't move.

"I sure wish that we had a disposal unit."

"They don't do anything about cans," Ken said. "Or bottles. Besides, everybody says you drop a knife or fork into it by mistake and ruin it. Or forget to turn the water on."

"I suppose," she said. "But some day when we have a house of our own I want one."

"By the time we get around to having a house of our own there'll be some new and interesting way of getting rid of garbage. Atomic disintegrators or something. Or there won't be any garbage to start with; they'll be making edible wrappings."

"Marilynn's works all right. Why don't you like them?"

"They cost lots of money and make lots of noise and do very little for you. They are like passenger airlines; they do their best to make you believe that they're doing you a favor and giving you a first class service. All they really do is take all your money, treat you like an immigrant just landed at Ellis Island, make a lot of noise, and about half the time, collapse and you go down the drain, ready or not."

"You like to fly, you told me."

"If I have to go on a long trip it saves time. Otherwise I'd rather take a train or walk."

Helen said that she didn't care if she never saw or heard another train as long as she lived. She went into a six-minute takeout on railroads. Her father had worked thirty years for one of them. While she talked it seemed to Ken that the second hand on the clock almost stopped running. Helen was talking about railroading, using all the railroad slang she could remember. She said that someone really ought to do a book about railroad talk.

"I expect that somebody already has," Ken said. "Lucius Beebe writes about railways all the time. No doubt there's a recording of old railroad men talking, a tape recording that can be ordered from the Library of Congress."

"Do you really think so?"

"You could write and ask them for a catalog."

"Why do you have to be so smart all the time?" Helen was a little angry. "Just because I didn't have time to read absolutely Everything while I was in college like Some People."

Ken laughed. "I'm being serious. Write to them."

Helen shouted, "Why are you laughing if you're serious?"

The telephone rang. Helen said, "Hello!" angrily, and then immediately happier, "Oh, hi, Marilynn. I was just screaming at Kenneth."

Ken retired into the bathroom with a volume of Plutarch. It wasn't long before the fluorescent tube opposite the new one began to flicker and buzz. He swore. When he returned to the living room Helen was still talking and laughing into the telephone. Ken waved at her as he stepped into the hallway, headed for the front door.

Helen screamed after him, "WHERE ARE YOU GOING?"

15

He shouted back, "I'm going to the store for another tube light."

"WHAT?"

"TO THE STORE!"

"YOU DON'T HAVE TO SCREAM AT ME LIKE THAT, I CAN HEAR YOU PERFECTLY WELL. GET ME SOME CIGARETS WHILE YOU'RE THERE."

"GIVE ME SOME CHANGE."

"WAIT A MINUTE—DON'T GO YET—OH, GOD."

Ken waited on the front porch, where the sun was shining brightly. He left the door open behind him. Urgent babbling and cigaret smoke wandled through the open door. The damned place smells like soft shit, Kenneth was thinking. He smiled up at the sun. Fuchsia plants were blooming beside the door.

Helen was talking faster and faster, trying to hear everything that Marilynn was saying and to tell her everything before Ken could get away to the store. It had made a great deal of excitement when Helen and Kenneth had first come to live in San Francisco. Ken had not met Marilynn before, he began talking to her at a party, they had not been introduced, he didn't know who she was, he simply took her into the garden and seduced her. Helen heard from Marilynn all about it, Marilynn made a full confession; she was Helen's oldest friend from college days. After weeks of trying not to think about it, trying to take it all in her stride, trying to be reasonable and understanding about the whole thing, Helen finally threw a screaming fit, threatening Kenneth with everything— murder, suicide, divorce, a suit for separate maintenance, pregnancy, lobotomy, and her eternal displeasure.

Kenneth listened to her story. He assured her that he'd found that Marilynn was a very unhappy woman and that he wasn't the man who was designed to make her happy. He admitted that he had seduced Marilynn, he claimed that he had done it in a fit of pure lust, instantaneous desire, he had been able to gratify that desire almost immediately, and there was an end to it. He didn't tell her that he had seen Marilynn from time to time after that event and that they had made love together on several occasions; he felt that since he had no real attachment to Marilynn, it wasn't worth having too much noise made about it.

"But what about ME," Helen demanded. "The insult to ME, and I've known Marilynn for years, the only other woman in the world that I can talk to, the only female I knew that I could trust—I just don't know what to think."

Ken told her, "I think you realize that you're the one I love, you're the one I married, I want to live with you. I'm not planning to leave you for any other woman. I still like Marilynn as a friend, and I don't want to break up the friendship between you."

"And what about Travis?" Helen continued, "I should think he'd be looking for you to kill you."

"Travis is too busy designing atom bombs to kill anybody."

"Marilynn hasn't told him. I might," she said.

That caught his attention at once. "Try it," he said.

Helen burst into tears. She forgave him a few days later; or thought she did or at least didn't choose to go on pestering him about it right then. She bought herself a new hair-job that even she could tell was hideous and Ken didn't complain, or at least not too loudly.

Kenneth went to Marilynn when he knew she'd be alone, and asked her what was the idea of spilling the beans to Helen. He threatened to do terrible things if she caused him trouble ever again. Marilynn was terrified; she found herself powerless to distract his attention. He began making love to her and she let him, not knowing much what else to do, and feeling almost persuaded that perhaps he was right, it was only pleasure and delight which nobody could say they didn't deserve.

The next time Helen lost her temper and lectured Ken about his habit of leaving his shoes in the living room instead of putting them in the closet, he went to see Marilynn again.

"What have you been telling Helen?" he shouted when she opened the door.

"Nothing," Marilynn said, feeling confused at the sight of him. "What's the matter? I've hardly talked to her on the phone."

"If I thought you'd been confessing things again I'd break your neck. No. I know, I could make an anonymous phone call to the FBI and say that Travis was for Wallace in 1948. You'd all be out in the street."

"You're insane," Marilynn whispered. She was terrorized, fascinated, and erotically aroused.

"Just be careful what you say to Helen."

"But we've been friends for years! We have the HABIT of telling each other Everything."

"Let's see if we can't get you into some new habits," he said. He began to disrobe. She was too busy trying to guess what the real situation was that had driven him to come around to her again to think of resisting his advances. She made, at least, the few gentle protests, arguments, and appeals to reason which the rules of polite behavior demand in such a case, but in the end she capitulated again.

Marilynn was not an apt pupil, however. It was her reluctance to learn any new thing which made Kenneth lose interest in her rather sooner than he might have done.

"I don't MIND doing it," she said. "I really can't stand the taste of that stuff."


Seen in her own home, in the daytime, Marilynn seemed to be a matron of quite definite years. If she decided to look like a movie star, she could do it with very little trouble. How she looked depended on where she was, what she was doing, what she wanted.

Many people detested her on sight. They said, "There is a devious and deceitful baggage who's up to mischief of some kind. Anything she says, any single word that she speaks, is bound to be false." Other people, as for example Travis her husband, or Kenneth, were instantly captivated by her.

She always said that she was very busy and that she just couldn't be bothered coping with many of the curious things that kept trying to happen to her, incidents and accidents that kept trying to divert her attention, to carry her away into somebody else's love life. She couldn't be bothered.

Ken noticed that she had a trick of casting her eyes upwards which made her seem to be looking up at him, although she was half a head taller than he was. She had, to his ear, a strange, exciting way of talking; it was as if she had some unidentifiable foreign accent.

She dyed her hair when it suited her fancy to do so. Ken thought that in some of these transformations she looked remarkably tough. In other colors and styles she was irresistibly exciting to him.

Travis seemed to pay little attention to her, but as far as anyone knew, they were a reasonably devoted couple. They had three children and the children looked clean and happy, quite intelligent enough for their respective ages. One boy, the youngest child, was a redhead. He sang a great deal of the time. The middle child, a silent and enchanted little girl, had long blond curls. She spoke very little to anyone except to her brothers, whom she ordered about rather severely. She would ask her parents' guests, "How do you do?" and then clam up tight. She did not giggle or squirm. She simply smiled at them tolerantly until Marilynn told her, "Very well, Dottie. You're excused." Dottie could then return to her brothers and take up the task of giving them orders for their part in whatever conspiracy or plot against the world Dottie had most lately invented.

The oldest son, Clancy, had straight thick chestnut colored hair that fell across his forehead, and he had a habit of tossing his head to one side in order to get his hair away from his eyes.

"We must get Clancy a violin to go with that gesture," Travis told Marilynn one day.

"Why don't you take him to the barber?" she replied. She didn't look up from the London *Times* crossword puzzle she was looking at.

"I like the color of it and it looks good that way. Do you suppose you might speak to him about shaking his head that way? But I suppose he can't help it. It is peculiar. Do we have any scissors? I might—"

"I don't know," Marilynn said. "It reminds me of a horse I used to have. But you're right, he may pop a vertebra or something. I'll take care of him."

Much to Clancy's humiliation his mother took him with her to see her own hairdresser, a stringy, fast-talking old lady with rhinestone glasses and bright hair. She fixed Clancy up most handsomely. He looked rather like Christopher Robin when she was finished with him.

"You didn't expect me to go into a barber shop, did you?" Marilynn said. "No lady could go into one of those places."

"I hope I don't have to go with you again at any rate," Clancy said. "She's made me look like Freddy Bartholomew in Captains Courageous or something."

Travis told him, "I'll take you downtown tomorrow and we'll get it fixed."

"I had to pay twelve dollars to get him into this shape," Marilynn complained. "I think he looks wonderfully continental."

"He looks like he could make his own living on Polk Street. I'll take tomorrow off and we'll celebrate, Clancy."

"Take me to Stacy's Technical Books," Clancy suggested.

"Delighted," Travis replied.

"I have done all that a mother can do," Marilynn declared.

Travis hugged her. "Little mother," he said.

"Git away, old man," she replied.

Travis was very busy all the time. He knew a great deal about theoretical physics and he had a lot of ideas about why the current theories were probably all wrong. He was being paid a lot of money by Stanford University to sit around discussing why he thought so with another two or three amiable eccentrics like himself. He was much consulted by the Government (for whom he declined to work), by other physicists, and by such vast invisible corporate beings as the General Dynamics organization. He could, if he chose, take a week off to work on the electronic organ which he was building at home and nobody would complain to him or try to fire him from his job.

He was a big, slow-looking man. He wore gold-rimmed glasses. He had deep-set small brown eyes. His flat, straight chestnut and silver hair fell down over his forehead. To keep it out of his eyes, he had the habit of holding his hair out of the way with one hand.

Marilynn suggested that he get a crew haircut or put hair oil on it and free one of his hands; he could probably get more things done not to mention that he would probably be more comfortable.

"I don't want to look like some Prussian, some Erich von Stroheim character," he told her. "All the kids now days cut their hair that way. I'm not an athlete or a soldier or twenty-two years old and afraid people think I'm a faggot. My hair is just fine. And I don't want to pour goop all over it, either. I hate the smell and feel of the stuff. And I'm not about to wear a hat all the time like Oppie."

"All right," Marilynn said. "You just go on holding it down. But don't keep on being surprised about how many people ask you what's wrong you got a headache or what."

Ken loved to look at Helen. He was fascinated by the color of her skin, what color he couldn't say, perhaps in the direction of goldy pink. Her hair, dark brown, had a natural waviness and she kept it long. She had

19

quit trying to keep up with the changes in style. She wound it in a coil at the top of her head. She had very large brown eyes and very white, regular teeth.

He loved the intensity she displayed towards everything that appealed to her. She complained a great deal about what she hated (including much of what Kenneth said and did). It was her enthusiasm that he loved. She had a genuine interest in painting and a real taste for history, not simply a bundle of romantic fancies about the exciting life of Rubens. He thought that she had a very interesting mind, but he was exasperated again and again by her seeming unwillingess to use her intelligence regularly in the conduct of life.

Once Helen went almost mad and tried to kill herself. She was in college, she had become pregnant, and she was afraid of what her parents would do if they found out about it. She ate a great many sleeping pills. She became very ill and had a miscarriage. She was in the hospital a couple of weeks. She told her parents that she was having the flu. She learned that suicide was only a temporary solution to any problem. She never tried again to kill herself. She had learned that there are worse things to endure than parental disapproval.


He wondered what it was about talking—her talking!—that caught between his teeth, that crept up his ass and twisted his balls like bad underwear, what was it? He had tried listening to discover what it was that she worked so hard at trying to say. Was it a cry for help, was she in pain—everyone is, to a certain extent. He realized, as any sensible person does, that incarnation has certain deadly disadvantages, and that yes we do all need all the help we can get. He gave her all the help and comfort that he was able to give her. He realized that there were more things he might do to please her. He knew that he could imagine more ways of communicating with her.

Helen talked. It dragged him. He stopped listening, but half the time he had to put himself into a kind of idiot trance, lest the rhythm of her speech invade his own silence, his own fantasy, so that he might as well have been listening consciously to what she was saying.

He wondered if women used their tongues like boys handle their penises, as often as possible and a little bit extra in addition. They flop and wiggle it pleasurably. Flopping the tongue, echolalia, lalling, in children learning to talk is a pleasure like sucking and feeding, so the doctors have said. Helen used her tongue, Kenneth imagined, to project herself, assert herself, like the exhibitionist in the city park flapping his naked dong at pretty ladies passing by.

*And yet I'll love her til I die*, Ken sang.

Helen took it as a personal compliment when he smiled or sang. "It's so nice to hear you sing again," she said. "You used to sing all the time. I wish that you felt like taking a few voice lessons again. You really sound very sweet."

"I'm generally admired," Ken replied.

"Really, I mean it," Helen said. "And I'm glad you've got over feeling so grouchy."

"Who's grouchy?"

"You were so cranky a while ago."

"I always feel better after I've had a great big healthy shit."

"I wish that you'd stop feeling that I ought to know about it every time it happens," Helen said. She lectured to him about her delicate sensibilities, about his grossness, about how she was sometimes nearly embarrassed to tears by his lack of good style. She went on talking.

Ken wondered more than once why it should bother him. It didn't hurt him, that she talked much or little. Sometimes it rang in his ears but what was the matter with his ears, with his perceptions, that simply hearing her talk would enrage him.

Sometimes, he thought, it was the subject of her discourse. She had been to a good school, she had been an exemplary scholar while she attended it. It sometimes seemed to him that she had the mind and vocabulary of a seven-year-old. Other times the simplicity of sense coupled with the minatory tone which she so often used made her sound like a grade-school teacher, one of the kind he knew as a child: narrow-minded maiden ladies with very little knowledge to impart, their minds and tongues scaled down to minute size; they were convinced of the absolute truth of what they were saying. Their constant repetition of that truth, their almost continuous association with it, gave these women courage to identify themselves with it. They became self righteous. They formed an elite group. They were at once the Company of Grace and God's Avenging Angels.

Helen might say, "It is raining," or some comparably simple sentence. Her tone might imply, to Ken, that there had never been any other meteorological fact, that this one was finally and absolutely established and unchangeable. Being so, it justified Helen all her words, opinions, and actions.

He wondered if Maugham was right when he wrote, "All women are constipated." He might have known, considering that he claimed to have studied medicine.

Helen said, "I thought you were going to the store."

"I am," he said. He was sitting on a hassock, gazing dreamily out the front window, looking towards City Hall, picking his nose with great concentration.

"Let me get you a handkerchief," Helen said, going towards the bedroom.

"I've got a handkerchief," he said.

"Well, I wish you wouldn't do it right in the front window, then."

"Why not? It's my window. Let people look at something else."

21

"Are you going to the store or not?"

"All in good time, little hollyhock."

The telephone rang. Ken picked it up and told it hello.

Marilynn's voice said, "Hello, Kenneth, can I talk to Helen?"

"She's not here," he said. "She just this minute went out the door."

Helen shouted, "Give me the phone! Marilynn! I am too here!"

"Would you like me to have her call you when she comes in?" Ken inquired.

Helen kept screaming, "Give me the phone! You brute, you monster. Not you, Marilynn, I'm here! HELP!"

"Oh, here she is," Ken said. "I was mistaken. I thought she was gone." He handed the phone to Helen, gave her a great hug and kiss while she kicked and struggled. Then he went to the store.

When Ken returned, Helen was washing the dishes. The radio feebly honked out Lalo's *Caprice Español*.

"I don't know why you feel that you can just go on amusing yourself at my expense," Helen said.

"It's quite economical," Ken replied. "Quite well worth the expense of keeping you." He took her in his arms and kissed her neck while she writhed and swore.

"Let me go. I have to get these dishes done if we're going to the supermarket."

He picked her up bodily and began carrying her off towards the bedroom while she kicked and screeched and pretended to cry.

"Sweet baby," he said.

"Let me go," she yelled. "What's the matter with you, anyway?"

"Oh, I just thought I might want to talk to you in an atmosphere uncontaminated with all these domestical chores," Ken said, unwinding her turban, unbuttoning her clothing, groping and feeling.

Helen bucked and bridled the whole time. "Stop it, I've got to keep my hair . . . will you STOP it. I mean it. I haven't got time to amuse you right this minute."

He let her up. "Very well," he said.

She returned to the kitchen. Ken followed her, rearranging his shirt-tail and resetting his trousers.

She asked him, "What are your plans for today besides going to the supermarket and to work? Please put it back in your pants, I'm sorry that I don't have time. Really, the people next door can see right in here, I know because when I was over there and she— "My God, what are you doing regressing right in the middle of the kitchen in—will you PLEASE STOP IT! YOU JUST AREN'T IN THE LEAST BIT FUNNY!"

"Bullshit. He wants a little exercise."

"IF YOU DON'T STOP THAT I'M GOING TO I DON'T KNOW WHAT . . ."

"I'm not going to get a haircut until tomorrow," he said, "and the library books are due. Will you have time to take them back? I won't have

22

much time, I'll be hung up waiting for the barber."

"Tomorrow is Sunday. But you really do scare me when you do things like that. You're so nervous and you keep doing these really insane things every once in a while. I have to see Dr. Stokes tomorrow, I'll fix it up so he'll see you too . . ."

"Again? What's he doing to you now?"

"Something about the allergy test, I asked about it before and I have to go in and have him see . . ."

"Damned quack. He appeals to your masochistic nature."

"Travis told us that he'd still be having sinus trouble if it wasn't for Dr. Stokes. He's a fine doctor and a fine man."

"He talks to you like you were a rather dull six-year-old child; how do you stand it?"

"I think he's an old dear. He reminds me of Daddy. Anyway, I'm tired of having my face and my whole head swell up and hurt every time the weather changes. I want something DONE about it."

"Oh, well."

"What do you mean, 'Oh, well'?"

"Nothing. Did you pick up the shoes I left to be half-soled?"

"I didn't have TIME!"

Ken said, "Try to do it next time you're downtown."

"But I have to wait to see Dr. Stokes, he's always so busy even though I have an appointment," Helen said.

"And the pants, if you think about it."

"Why don't you pick up your own damned things? Even after you get them home, you drop them in the middle of the floor for me to put away."

"How long will it take you to get ready if I start drying the dishes right now?"

"Oh, God," she sighed, craning her neck to see the kitchen clock.

"Two o'clock," he said. "I have to get ready for work at three."

"And there's nothing to make you a lunch. I'll finish the dishes later. I'll get ready and we'll go right now."


They had a long and almost bitter discussion about window shades. It seemed that Kenneth couldn't bear to have window blinds that roll up. He said that they reminded him of his plebeian origins. Helen couldn't bear to look at venetian blinds. Ken suggested jalousies for a compromise. Helen said no, it was even more Venetian than regular venetian blinds, jalousies would not do.

They settled on having match-stick bamboo blinds. Then Helen wanted big drapes on a traverse rod as well. She believed everyone outside could look right through the bamboo blinds. Ken didn't believe so. He went outside and looked while Helen turned the light on inside. He discovered that she was quite right. They got the drapes, or at least Helen's mother sewed the yards of oyster-white cloth that Ken hung from the thousand little hooks in the traverse rod. He thought that yellow was a better color but he decided to let well enough alone for the time being. He could persuade Helen to change the color later. He calculated that she'd be wanting a change in six months' time anyway. Spring would come, she'd be cleaning and hollering at him to move all the furniture into the same places.

"Marilynn told me the funniest thing that Dottie said." Dottie was three years old.

Ken looked at Helen without saying anything.

"She said that the balloon man at the Zoo was extraordinarily distinguished looking. Isn't that wild?"

"No," Ken replied, calmly.

"I think it's terribly amusing, considering that Dottie's only three."

"I'm tired of the brilliance of other people's children. After all, Travis and Marilynn are reasonably well educated people, they speak fairly clear English, they don't talk much baby talk with Dottie; naturally Dottie will talk pretty much in the language that she hears. She's still only a three-year-old. It doesn't mean that she really feels or has observed anything about the balloon man. She just made a grammatical sentence. I'd be rather more surprised if Dottie spoke like a stage Irishman or like Jimmy Durante."

"You make me tired, you're so smart," Helen said. "You never get a kick out of anything except your own awful jokes."

He laughed. "I think you're pretty funny."

"I'll tell you another thing. I'm getting tired of your making fun of me, too. Laugh at somebody else for a change. You don't have to be such a smart-ass."

"What did I do?" Ken inquired, rather disingenuously.

"You know what you do—and what you don't do. I wish you'd please take down the garbage."

Ken said, "I hope this isn't one of those days of confusion and disorganization."

"What do you mean by that?"

"I used often to look out the window, see that the sun was shining, and I'd decide to go out walking. But then I'd have to shave and the phone would ring and I'd find, a few minutes later, that I had actually accepted an invitation to go somewhere. Three minutes later I'd remember all the things I'd been thinking I might accomplish on the day for which I'd just accepted the invite. In a fit of rage, I'd notice next that the garbage was spilling out of the bucket onto the kitchen floor. By the time I got it outside, put a new lining in the garbage pail, and washed my hands, I was in no mood to see or do anything that day, it was late afternoon, and I was exhausted with frustration and rage. If I didn't go walking I'd stay inside and break things or wash things and talk mean to whoever might telephone."

"You seem so self-sufficient," Helen said. "You don't really depend on other people, you don't really like other people. I don't honestly know, sometimes, why it is you decided to marry me. I doubt that you're really interested in living here with me."

He said, "Don't be silly. You know me well enough by now to know that I'd walk out of here if I didn't want to stay with you."

"You know, you kind of scare me when you say things like that."

"Why?"

"Because you do funny things often enough as it is."

"I guess so," he said. "I'm about as funny as everybody else. But I'm here because I want to be. I love you. I want to live with you."

He didn't tell her that other people often appeared to him to be not very cleverly programmed automata. He knew very few persons who were aware of where they were and what it was they were doing. It was strange to spot them, rising above the fairly regular Riemann surface he looked out upon whenever he sat still and looked. There were these discontinuities in it, sudden multidimensional warpings that indicated the presence of a field of action or force which was operating autonomously. It seemed to him that on a few occasions it had been possible to seize an edge of that surface and give it a good shake, a flap, and resettle it to suit himself. He hadn't touched it, hadn't bothered for some time to inspect it with much attention. He felt himself beginning to get into a position where he might be able to look at it again.

He didn't say it. He didn't want to explain all that right then. He was in a hurry to get to the store and back so that he wouldn't need to hurry in doing other things later.

It occurred to him at last that what he wanted was a quality of life something like looking through a grove of trees at a creek tumbling down over the rocks. The ferns and moss are green, five p.m. early spring.

"Nothing will sustain me, my entire weight and being," he thought, "except the unexpected."


While Ken was looking at the fuchsias on his way to the store, carrying in his hand the volume of Plutarch he was working at—he could read it while he waited in the checkout line—Helen was talking with Marilynn on the telephone. Helen liked to stand up while she telephoned; she felt she could talk better. She could walk a few steps back and forth as she talked, and this made her feel more lively, more as if she were in the presence of the other speaker. She could address all her attention to that small black rubber microphone, that friendly tireless rubber ear that invited her to talk on and on.

Marilynn listened. Marilynn was a good listener, she said "uh hum" and "—oh?" and laughed when the jokes came along. None of her friends knew what Marilynn did while she listened ever so patiently and faithfully. Travis had rigged up a tape recorder so that it would pick up whatever came over the telephone as long as Marilyn kept her foot on a treadle-switch. She'd give the switch a kick whenever one of her callers got going on a particularly poignant or self-revelatory theme. Marilynn had a nice ear for turns of speech and colorful expression, a great sense for recognizing the dramatic, the intriguing bits that people throw away in conversation. She edited the tape at the end of the day, transcribing onto paper the phrases and anecdotes she believed she might use. For, very slowly, she was taking all these words and little homey incidents and breaking them down, boiling and smelting them into the fabric of an enormous novel. She'd been working at this for ten years. The final composition and editing of this vast collage were a little more than half done.

She told Travis, "I don't know what will happen if it ever gets printed. Probably nothing, considering that nobody reads novels any more—or if they do, they don't understand what's said in them. But if they read this, there'll either be an immediate bloody revolution in which I shall be tarred and feathered at the very least, or I'll very quietly get every prize there is. I feel it in my bones."

"The poet Yeats felt something of the sort in what he alleged to be 'the heart's deep core,' " Travis replied. "I hope that we won't have to leave town. I like it here."

Listening to the telephone as it rattled with greater or lesser intensity, Marilynn tapped the treadle-switch off and on. She drank large martinis very slowly and worked at solving the problems printed in the daily paper—the chess problem, the bridge problem, the daily cryptogram. If the telephone kept on talking, she began work on the crossword puzzles in the London *Times* and the Manchester *Guardian*.

Promptly at noon, Marilynn would excuse herself and hang up the phone, no matter who was talking, no matter whether they were being recorded. She would take a fast shower, get dressed, and either drive her own car or take a taxi to a restaurant for a substantial lunch.

She went to a different restaurant each day. She would eat meat or seafood, salad, coffee, and cognac. If she felt extravagant, she ate a big French pastry for dessert. She sat, while she waited for service, listening to people talk; sometimes she looked at each one of the persons sitting there.

She used to asked herself, "How do people look, what do they say, what has it got to do with what they do and what I see of them?" Then she stopped, after years of trying to record it all, driving herself almost crazy to write down each detail of each person's appearance and action in every kind of scene she witnessed. She stopped looking. She wrote it into three novels and stopped writing. Then she began trying to see the world in another way entirely. She looked now for persons she had met once or twice. She always remembered each one, and San Francsico is so small a place, it's possible to see almost everyone who lives there, sometime or other, somewhere in town, at the opera, in the courtrooms, on the buses, on the Ocean Beach. She did not want to be recognized, herself, but she wanted to watch these she knew a little about; they engaged her imagination, got it to thinking in words, in sentences.

Sometimes she might unexpectedly meet her husband or one of her friends in a restaurant. She would make pleasant conversation, but she'd seem to them rather preoccupied, and she would make an excuse to leave without having coffee or dessert. She would go somewhere that she was not likely to see any of her friends, where she'd see many people. There she'd continue thinking about how the way words go together does (or doesn't) have some connection with all these persons and the way they all were inhabiting the world as it happened to be right now: the main floor of the J.C. Penny department store.

There she'd stand, hearing it, smelling it, censoring out big areas of it, ignoring huge sections of it purposely, like a painter looking at pictures in an art gallery will make a screen of fingers before his eyes the better to see how the various parts of a painting go together. Later in the afternoon, she would drive to the nursery school to meet her children and bring them home.

Helen was talking to her on the telephone. The tape recorder was operating. The morning chess problem was moderately difficult.

"I just can't get through to him any more," Helen was saying. "I keep trying to tell him that I just can't continue to put up with his nonsense any longer. He just laughs at me. He won't believe anything I say. I don't think he hears much of what I say. I really am seriously concerned about Kenneth, you know that I am, after all, kind of addicted to him, but there's a limit. I tried to tell him to go see a doctor; I've even arranged an appointment with my own—our own doctor, Travis's and mine—hah!—but he won't go! He just keeps on getting more and more withdrawn. I'm really becoming just a little frightened. I don't suppose Travis might not kind of—you know—talk to him—or Bruce Chadwick whom I can't stand myself but he's Kenneth's best friend. Well, if you could ask Travis, or perhaps better, ask Travis to ask Bruce for me—well anyway, I'm just about at the end of my rope. I don't want to hurt Kenneth, but we just can't live like this and I've got to find some way of communicating with him in order to let him know that he's either got to get some kind of help or I'm getting out, or he's going to have to move out, or both, or all three—I'm getting so nervous myself, as you've no doubt observed, that I have trouble talking about it. He keeps talking all the time about how we need children, how much he wants children, as if that would help anything—it's almost obsessive—but good God, I don't see how I can have children by this man who's rather clearly got some sort of hereditary mental disorder, or anyway with a weakness in that direction that would be inherited by our own children and they'd all have two heads or mongolism or something. I just couldn't face it, and I can't seem to talk to him and I just really don't know what to do."

27

Kenneth said, "A great deal depends upon what you expect from other people."

"What do you mean?" Helen asked. She was still in a bad humor.

"You're sore at the man in the liquor store."

"He was rude to me."

"Why should he be polite to you? You were asking a favor and he refused to do it. What's wrong with that? These guys get taken several times a week on bad checks."

"He didn't have to be nasty about it. We buy enough booze from him."

"Were you polite to him?"

"What do you mean?" Helen said. "I'm polite to everbody."

"Well then. As long as you do what you're supposed to do, what do you care whether or not he's polite?"

"Listen. Anybody in business, anybody behind a counter HAS to be nice to people if he wants to keep his store open. Nobody's going to buy anything from somebody who gives them a bad time every time they walk into his store."

"Why do you imagine that you deserve anything else? People are running the streets while in the possession of every possible kind and combination of mental and emotional stress. Some of them are stark raving mad. More than you imagine. You ought to consider yourself lucky that you got back into the house without being robbed, raped or murdered."

"I don't see how you can be so cynical," Helen said. "I LIKE people."

"People are all right. I just don't expect them to be nice or polite or sensible when I see them in the street or on the bus, or at work, wherever. Life is too complicated, too goofy—and most of the people you see out there aren't trying to figure it out. They're just going. They're running around grabbing and shoving and tickling and stroking and hollering at each other every waking hour. But I figure I must behave properly anyway. I won't admit to being uncivilized. I may be as cuckoo as everybody else, but I try to treat them gently, with some kind of politeness."

"Why not just ignore them?"

"Because I'm responsible to them, for them . . ."

"You *are* cuckoo," Helen said.


He was in the bathroom but he could hear Helen talking. That was Helen, that's my wife, Ken thought. Sweetyface. She speaks. She is talking on the telephone at the moment. He could hear her say "drains." He surmised that she was addressing either the plumber or the landlord. He wished that he could stop listening.

He was sitting in the bathtub, which was very nearly full of cooling water, reading Plutarch's *Life of Aristides*. The translation was supposed to be the work of John Dryden but it had been emended by several hands.

28

Judging from the temperature of the water, he expected that Helen must presently come to pound on the door and scream at him to emerge from the bath and carry the garbage out of the kitchen into the big can at the foot of the backstairs. But her greatest pleasure was talking and she appeared to have an audience; consequently she would leave him alone for another few minutes. He wished that she had gone in person to see the landlord or whoever it was; it was a beautifully sunny day. He himself looked forward to going out-of-doors to inspect the world with some careful attention to details. He noted with a shock that Helen had stopped talking. Then he relaxed as he heard her dialing the telephone.


Ken wondered if he were simply afraid of Helen. Had he given her power over himself—or had she taken it—or did she simply have it without knowing she had it, without thinking of wanting it? How could he endure the tyranny of a person who could name a dog "Crootie"? He knew that she was actually quite intelligent. That few minutes she was in Florence, she had sense enough to break away from the tour long enough to introduce herself to Berenson, whom she saw and immediately recognized in one of the galleries. She even had had presence of mind enough to ask him a question about Lorenzo Lotto, which Berenson had been kind enough to discuss with her. Ken knew that he could never have been able to meet, say, A.N. Whitehead and ask him a question about philosophy. He would have felt too shy. It wouldn't be good form to have simply said, "How do you do, Mr. Whitehead, etc., I wonder if you would give me a hint about that serial universe etc." if he had met the great man in a bookshop in Harvard Square.

Ken was afraid she might leave him. The idea was, actually, absurd, he thought. She had no real motive for doing such a thing. Helen complained about many things but so, he felt, do I. He supposed that she might think it was fun to have a great dramatic quarrel, ending with a door slamming, but she didn't seem interested in that kind of theater. She spent a lot of time going to the doctor; however, she never seemed to be seriously ill. She spent most of her time shopping, going to galleries, entertaining her friends, and being entertained by them; and a great part of every day was occupied with telephoning. Every chance she got, she went to visit her parents in Seattle—why not? Sometimes she reread a chapter of Berenson or Pater, Ruskin or Morris. She read a great deal of Renaissance history at rare intervals. Mostly she read the San Francisco *Chronicle* and *The New Yorker*.

Where would she go if she left him? What would she do there? He knew that she had enough initiative to find a job, find friends, and keep herself amused if she were left to her own devices, but it seemed to Ken absolutely unlikely that she would ever do such a thing. She hated moving, she hated traveling, she preferred not to work for anyone else if she could avoid it. But she might do all that and more. He felt obliged to accept as a real possibility the idea of Helen's going away.

It would embarrass him. He would feel at once foolish and a failure. Here was this marriage, this system, this arranged world all set up with Helen and himself in the center, and all the rest of the world outside, some of it scattered in confusion, some of it in a useful pattern. Perhaps both of them had invested quite a lot more hope and pride in this engine than they supposed. It was awkward to think of its malfunctioning. It was working, it had been working, it wasn't perfect but it was operating in fair order. They were both surprised, he guessed, that it wasn't exactly the way they had planned to have it, this particular style and shape, but here it was...(or not quite "was," since it couldn't really be thought of as completed)...yet there were enough liberties and comforts within, around, and about it to please him.

Helen's departure would bother him. He was quite attached to her, although he found it hard at times to live with her. She seemed to grow noisier and harder to please all the time. She kept stalling him about whether they were going to have children. Maybe they were just not really as stable a combination as he thought. And there was the problem, still, of what he was to do about his own ideas, his own ambitions or fantasies—he wasn't sure any more what to call the sense he had of the potential he felt in himself to say something, create something. If he were alone, he might find out at last what it was he felt or thought he felt about philosophy or history. He might be able to study again, make a final try to plan and execute some kind of serious work, or produce a finely finished, possibly quite beautiful—what?

The discontinuities apparent in the visible world fascinated him. There was this fascination with surfaces, for example, his sharp awareness of the air being here, "outside"—then the break represented by the smooth glassy face of the agate—then the color-stripe world "inside." He could not describe even for his own benefit how life was before the war, how it was in those first chilly half-furnished years after the war, how it was three years ago. There were, to his imagination, four different colors; he sensed them, but not visually; he could not name them. Four colors, because what happened during the time he was in the army and in Germany was another kind of inclusion inside the agate, as it were a band of crystals, rough and brilliant and jagged. One second he was just himself, a cold man on a cold day in the open air that smelled of burning and kept roaring and clattering and irregularly blumphing, the next second his arm had burst open like a spoilt sausage, a mess of bloody meat. That was that.

He found that he was walking up and down the room, unconsciously wringing his hands. He looked out the window, not seeing, only feeling a terror, a horror more profound than reason or the interior monologue that ordinarily filled his mind, horror, HOW CONTAIN IT ALL? HOW KEEP FROM BURSTING OUT, FROM CURLING INTO OBLIVION, FROM DYING OF THE ABSOLUTE FACT OF THIS VERY INSTANT OF EXISTENCE—and

30

seeing very calmly and clearly at the same time that the whole thing "took its course," as we say, had its existence, within one or two microscopic cells of protoplasm inside his own skull.


He wished they had children. He wished for sons. He liked children and most children liked him. Talking to them, Ken found it easier to remember for himself the larger, brighter colored world, full of mystery and terror, which he had once inhabited. He had not been a happy child, he wanted to hurry and grow up, he wanted to be free. The world that was allowed to him by the government, by the society around him, when he finally did grow up, was a pale and tiny one, compared with what he knew he might have, with the one which he had begun to build, secretly, in his own imagination, in his own dreams, and which he was only now beginning to find ways of realizing, of literally making real.

Thinking of his father and grandfather, thinking of himself as a creature, as a set of peculiar genes, he awoke to a feeling of responsibility towards his own meat and flesh. He must preserve it. In order for it to survive and be preserved from the accidents of time and nature there would have to be more of it besides the few pounds of it he carried about on his own bone rack.

It was difficult to arrange and adjust his life with Helen, at first. In the morning when he felt energetic and lustful, she wanted to sleep. At night when she was feeling romantic and kittenish he was tired. He felt that she was rather prudish and old fashioned. She thought he was selfish and self-indulgent and really quite possibly some kind of sex fiend; she was a little afraid of him, he was so wild on certain mornings.

Helen had visions of herself in the shape of The Young Mother, beautiful, draped in heavy blue robes, holding a beautiful glowing pink infant, a tiny beautiful baby girl. She couldn't bear to look at pregnant women. She herself was always worrying about becoming fat.

She hated the idea of painful childbirth. Nevertheless she knew that she would be beautiful holding a baby all her own.

Ken thought about his children. There'd be three or four boys and maybe some girls. He could see that they'd be babies a little while, then they'd be in school playing ball, then they'd be jacking off and going with girls and going to college and marrying and having families, their own, but somehow his, a world of his own, his tribe from which he would yet be separate and apart, and they would go about doing as they pleased, buying and selling, carpentering, doctoring, playing horns and violins, it didn't matter what they did as long as they were strong and sane and as long as they were free to construct worlds of their own.


"I don't like to have you drive the little car unless I'm with you. You let it lug without shifting down," Ken said.

31

"Which way is down?" Helen asked.

"Down to a lower gear."

"I never can remember whether the lower gear has a higher or a lower number."

"It's just an expression about gear-ratios. They put that tachometer there so you'll know when to do it, no matter what you call it. All you have to do is remember to look at it and shift when the needle drops."

"But I have to look at all the other cars. They all want to run over me. The car is so little and everybody seems to hate it so."

"They won't bother you. The car will last a good deal longer if you're nice to its gears. Not that I don't want you to watch where you're going."

He was very fond of the car; he had made great sacrifices in order to obtain it. He doted on every spoke in each wire wheel. Most of all he loved it for its right-hand drive. He knew that when Helen drove it she rode the clutch; he could tell because he watched her and besides it was wearing out faster than it had been used to do.

She was talking. He thought about nasturtiums, he'd seen a great field on a sloping hillside in the park just for a moment on Saturday. It had been foggy. The ground was dry, the nasturtiums glowed, the round leaves not very intensely green. How he loved them! He could remember being very young when he first planted those wrinkly seeds—poke a hole with his finger into soft black dirt, put in the big pea-like seed and cover it up. Why should anything happen, following such an abstract occupation; the dirt is dirty, must be washed off one's clothes and hands right away. The seed is dry and round, hard and dead, unlike anything green or flowering. But sure enough, later on, there were nasturtiums, yellow broken trumpets with red streaks, solid orange, white-red and yellow, the flowers mysteriously imperfect, the leaves round, broad but enigmatic, small objects lost out of pockets appeared if you looked on the ground under those leaves, tipping them aside.

Helen talked about all the things that she was going to do tomorrow. There was a complete plan and now she was rehearsing it. She hadn't added or subtracted a single errand. She repeated the list of things that she intended to buy, each in its kind, each with a descriptive adjective. There were also a few things she intended simply to inquire about—were any to be had at all of the kind she wanted to be able to buy on some uncertain future day? She just this minute remembered that the coming Sunday was her father's birthday. She'd have to find something inexpensive to send him for a present.

"Just send him a card," Ken said, "He'll be pleased you remembered his birthday whether or not you send him anything else."

"Oh, I always try to find some little thing—I won't spend more than a dollar."

"I expect," he said.

"You always make a great fuss about your own birthday."

"The entire country used to observe three minutes of total silence at

32

11 a.m. on my birthday to remember me," Ken said.

"You've got your festivals mixed," she said. "I'm old enough to remember that particularly morbid one. Thank God nobody pays attention to it any more. Both Mother and Daddy used to go practically to pieces every year, being in the parade and everything. Later on I was a majorette myself."

"Good God! You never told me that before. I had no idea you had such a record."

"I got second prize once for twirling."

"You're kidding."

"Daddy has a trophy I won, it's sitting around the house somewhere. I thought I showed it to you the last time we were up there."

Perhaps he might tell her about the nasturtiums, he considered it, but there was no point to the story. He had told her before that he liked nasturtiums; it wasn't important whether she remembered. To tell her that he planted some, that they grew and blossomed, that wasn't a story, it had no interest for anyone else. If a hydrangea plant had come up with clumps of blue foam blossoms that would have been interesting and he might have told an amusing story about it, but it had not and wasn't about to happen; he didn't like hydrangeas well enough to plant them. He had nothing against them, he liked looking at ones which were already there, more or less, especially if they turned pink then blue and then white, although the colors were not intense enough to interest him. The change of color might or might not attract his attention, might possibly interest him if he was feeling liberated enough at the time he observed them. Otherwise he preferred almost any other flower. Who likes hydrangeas?

While he inspected this last idea, Helen was repeating for his benefit her description of the house where she grew up. What were the names of the rooms, what was their disposition, their decoration and furnishings. Which pieces of furniture were descended from what pair of her grandparents. What pieces of furniture were authentic, interesting, or just ordinary. Which pieces were "horrible." Helen knew that he had seen it all, and that he had seemed to listen with interest to her mother, who introduced Ken to each chest, chair, and bridge lamp.

He listened now without protesting. He supposed that Helen might be feeling temporarily homesick. He wondered whether she might begin pestering him about the vacation. Would he take her to visit her parents. He planned on going to the mountains. They had already had quite lengthy discussions of the question. Ken had made up his mind that he would go into the mountains whether Helen came or not. He told her as much, but she still didn't choose to believe that he wouldn't take her to Seattle to see her momma and daddy. Of course, he thought, if they went to Seattle, he could very well leave her with momma and daddy while he went into the Olympics or into the Cascades.

33

He listened for a moment to what she was saying. She was planning again, deciding exactly what to do. Ken wished she would simply choose to do or not do whatever it was instead of describing it in detail, and making up her mind about the hour and day that it might happen. He wondered when she would finally get what she needed and wanted. What would she have, in the end—it could be nothing less than the entire production of all the factories, mines, smithies, and looms of the entire globe. He wondered what she would be like on that day, when the last of her plans had been executed. He could think of no good reason why she should not have her heart's desire.

Helen's mother, Mrs. Beckwith, was a white-haired woman with the figure of a fashion model. She was in her early sixties, her face and hands showed it, but she was still very handsome, very active, a lively, hurrying woman. She devoted her time to keeping her house and garden in an almost painful condition of cleanliness and order. She had been a "career woman" for a number of years and she was tired of life in an office.

During the war, while Helen was away at school, her mother took a job with a real estate and property management firm. She had no pressing need to take a job; her husband had a good job with the railroad. She was worrying too much about her sons in the war, Helen's older brothers. She couldn't bear to sit home alone thinking of what might be happening to them.

Mrs. Beckwith worked for the firm only a few years before she was appointed office manager. It developed that she had a flair for organization, and she had a great deal of tact and imagination that she could use in getting along with other people and persuading them to get along with each other. In another few years she was an executive vice-president in the company. By that time she was tired of working. She resigned after having spent a couple of years on the board of directors. She said that she wanted to spend the rest of her life baking chocolate cake for her grandchildren. The firm gave her a vote of thanks and a very handsome new kitchen stove as a going-away present.

Helen surprised her. Helen married the wrong man. Mrs. Beckwith had somehow reconciled herself reasonably well to the girls whom her sons had married. It had been difficult for her but not impossible. Helen had, on the other hand, married a bum, a boy Mrs. Beckwith hated the first time she saw him. He was very polite to her, but she felt that there was something terribly wrong with him. He was supposed to be very intelligent, he had been to the best schools, Helen was absolutely in love with him, it wasn't a simple infatuation, but Mrs. Beckwith could not help herself. She didn't like Kenneth, and she warned Helen that he was the wrong man, that she would be making a hideous mistake in marrying him.

Helen told her, "I don't care. I love him, he's the only man I ever knew who was intelligent and fun to be with and virile. He loves me, he has no money, but he can always make lots of money when he does work. He'll be more settled when we have our own place to live. I'm not worried about that."

"Helen, the boy is disturbed. I can feel it. He doesn't seem normal in some way. I don't see how you can look into those impersonal, flat eyes of his and still be interested in him, love him."

"Who knows?" Helen answered. "All I know is, I very seriously, quietly, happily love him and I'm going to marry him. I don't want to be an old maid all my life."

Mrs. Beckwith felt that she had been entirely justified when Helen came to her, at last, on a visit—not just a visit, but a kind of flight—to see her, to ask for help. She tried not to feel too self-righteous about it. Helen was her youngest child, her baby; she hated to see her being hurt.

But after Helen told her story, she was perplexed and amazed. She said, "Helen, I don't want to make any judgements about your proposal. Everyone, nowadays, seems to be living for himself. The world is so risky we feel like running, doing anything to save ourselves. I feel that sometimes myself, even though I'm so old I can't expect to live much longer anyway... I ask myself why I should care if it all blows up. But I can't see myself giving you money for such a purpose if—well, if you want to go on living with Ken."

Helen was surprised. "What do you mean, Mother? I thought you hated him."

"Oh, Helen, I don't hate him. I just thought that he was the wrong man for you. I still think so. But if I give you money for the...the operation, I must make a condition. I'm sorry to put it this way, I know that it's almost impossibly difficult for you, but if I give you this money and you use it that way, I must insist that you leave Kenneth as soon as you can possibly manage..."

"Mother! How can you...you're being absolutely evil!"

"I don't pretend to understand anything, Helen; I just see what I think ought to be done, how things ought to be arranged in order to balance, to make an equity."

"What?"

"I mean if you want to stay married to Kenneth, you should bear his child. If you ask me to help you get rid of this child—"

"But it's not a child yet—why it's hardly there at all, only a clump of cells, little bubbly—"

"I don't care how you may have rationalized it to yourself, the fact remains that it is Kenneth's child, my grandchild—"

"Oh, mother!"

"Helen, I'm quite serious. I'm saying that you can have Kenneth and bear his child or you can have the money, but I won't allow you to have both."

Helen was frightened and angry. She couldn't look at her mother. The whole world was somehow a hopeless messy tangle around her arms and legs.

"I just don't know what to do," Helen said.

"It's a real problem, Helen, and it's up to you. I don't think there's any really conclusive answer to it, but I feel that I know what's fair."

"Mama, how can you babble on about abstractions like that at this late date? I can't imagine such a—"

"Listen, Helen. I'm getting tired of this. You're asking me for quite a lot of money for a purpose I don't approve of. It would please me, of course, if you were divorced from Kenneth, but I detest the idea of it happening under these circumstances. I hate the idea of killing my own grandchild."

"Why do you want to control my life?"

"Because you're going about it so carelessly. I feel responsible for what you're doing. I'll be directly responsible for this operation if you go through with it. From what you've told me, I believe I understand how much Kenneth wants a family, how strongly he feels about it . . . and what he'd probably think of you if he knew what you plan to do. I think it's time you were separated if you've come to the point where you can want to hurt him in this way."

Helen was weeping. "I don't know," she wailed. "I don't know!"

"I'm sorry about the whole thing, Helen. I've told you what I think and what I'll do, and what you must do in return. I love you very much, Helen, but I shall have to find the means of holding you to our agreement if you accept my terms."

"I don't know, I don't know, I can't think . . . you're so *mean*, Mama, how can I?"

"We'll talk about it later, Helen. I'm getting confused now, myself."


In exasperation, Helen said, "What IS it that's bothering you? Why are you so cranky?"

"Oh, I'm not mad at you," Ken replied. "I was thinking of the weekend, another two days of inescapable bother."

"But nobody said anything about the weekend. Your friend Joan's party is on Thursday night and even that's a kind of party you like, a small dinner. It isn't supposed to be a drunken brawl."

"Oh, on the weekend everybody and his dog feels free to come popping in, right about the time I've decided to sit down and read or take a bath or something."

"Sweetie, that's just nonsense. You know you love to see all your friends."

"I hate them on Saturday and Sunday, is all. I wish that people would stay home and amuse themselves. Then I could go to their houses."

"I don't know anybody who goes visiting less than we do. Since when were you interested in going about in society?"

"I hate society. All I want to do is to sit here and read Plutarch without being bothered."

"For crying out loud."

"By God, you wait and see. Saturday morning early I'm going to leave the house and not come back until Sunday night—or at least not during the hours when anybody might find me here."

"Well, that's charming. What am I supposed to do all this time? Piece a quilt?"

"You can come along if you're ready on time."

"Hah. Saturday morning, like every other Saturday morning, you'll be fast asleep in your own little trundle bed. The telephone will ring at ten a.m. and there'll be your friend Chadwick and all his dirty socks Bohemian friends wanting to rush in with a gallon of wine to spend the day, breakfast, lunch, and dinner."

"You can come along if you're quiet," Ken said.

"Go by yourself, if you can't stand to have me around." Helen looked as if she might cry.

Ken said, "I didn't say that."

"It certainly isn't the most cordial invitation I've ever received. You go by yourself." Helen had begun to cry.

"I didn't mean to hurt your feelings," he said. He tried to put his arms around her and comfort her.

"Leave me alone," she said.

"Very well." Ken walked towards the door.

"Where are you going?"

"I'm going to buy some coffee and a new fluorescent tube."

"Oh."

"Also the light bill is overdue. I'll pay it at the bank."

"Are you going to give them a post-dated check too?"

"I don't know. I'll have to look through the checkbook." He groped into several pockets. "Have you seen my checkbook?"

"No."

Ken wandered through the rooms moving piles of clothing, books, magazines, papers. He found the checkbook on the floor in the bathroom.

He was nearly out the door when she called him again. "Wait—you're forgetting the list."

"We'll go to the supermarket later."

"But I want some Kleenex right now."

"Is it on the list?"

"I put it there a minute ago," she said. She ran about distractedly, hunting for the paper.

"Holy God, I want to get to the store and back before sundown," Ken shouted.

"Well, you don't have to scream. You turned the place upside down looking for the checkbook. Here it is." She found the list under a record album.

"I suppose we ought to stay home on the weekend and . . ."

They were lying together without covers, the room was warm enough, for a change. They had been fucking. She was talking and fingering his body here and there. She wished that they could make it at night more often, she didn't like it so much in the morning when she either wanted to sleep or to be planning all the things that she intended to accomplish that day.

He lay feeling totally satisfied, totally at ease, enjoying the sensation of love drying on his naked skin and the near continuous touching of her. Ken didn't become so nervous and cranky if she talked a lot under circumstances like these. He wondered if he would feel the same lying next to just any woman. He thought of Marilynn but the recollection didn't much engage his attention. He didn't get the same thing from her. Being with Helen now was completely satisfying.

"Am I as good as Marilynn?" Helen asked.

Ken looked at her and smiled. "Almost," he said.

"Oh!" Helen exclaimed. Then she bit him. They struggled together, happily, for a few seconds.

"She looked good to me," he said. "I simply went and asked her and there we were."

"Just like that," Helen said. "It was just vanity on your part."

"Sure," he said. "I was pleasing myself."

"When are you going to try pleasing me?"

* *

* * *

They lay together quietly for some time.

"I must get up," she said.

He wrapped his arms and legs about her, silently.

She laughed. "I have to go. Let go."

He relaxed his grip and she slid away. He got up with a rush and chased her into the bathroom. She squealed all the way.

Ken turned aside in the hall and went through the house to the kitchen. He put the coffee pot on the stove, then went back and lay down on the bed. The sheet was splashed; he squirmed about to find a dry spot on which to lie.

Helen found him lying there looking up at her.

"You better get up," she said.

"Uh huh," he replied. He rolled over and propped himself up on an elbow, supporting his head on his hand. He watched her while she rummaged in the closet for clothing to wear. He was feeling happy, vacant, almost disembodied.

She said, "I wish you wouldn't look at me while I'm dressing."

"I like to look at you."

38

"I'm ugly."

He got out of bed. He stood behind her and hugged her and kissed her. "I'll go make the coffee," he said.

He made coffee in the kitchen. He opened the drapes in the living room but didn't move the bamboo blinds. He peered between the slivers and saw that the sun was beautifully bright. He searched about but couldn't find the volume of Plutarch he was reading. He looked at the bookshelves, reading the familiar titles. Helen found him in front of another bookshelf, his head cocked to one side, looking for what wasn't there. She thought how funny and young he looked without his clothes on.

She said, "You better get dressed, if you've finished admiring yourself. I don't know how you can get such a kick out of going naked."

"I'm warm enough," he said. "I'm going to take a bath in a minute. Have you seen Volume II of Plutarch?"

"It's in the bathroom."

"Uh huh," he said. He continued to look at the book spines while he absent-mindedly rubbed his genitals.

"Men are the absolute, final, and everlasting limit. You can't let that equipment alone for a minute, can you?"

"What?" he said, looking lost. Then he laughed and said, "That's what my mama used to say." He went into the bathroom and Helen trailed along, talking, telling him to wash his hair, to be sure and trim his toenails, to please not leave towels on the floor and to wash out the tub afterwards. The latter part of her instructions were somewhat lost amid the roar of rushing waters.


Helen kept on talking. She recited the names of things that she wanted, needed to have. She paused to tell him that it was really high time that he saw Europe. She herself had only been there once briefly, years ago. The trip was a high school graduation present, a very fast nine-day conducted tour for a group of American young ladies. She said that she must go again, now that she was old enough to know what it was all about. "You were lucky to see it during the war before it was entirely Americanized," she told him. "It was dirty enough, God knows, but you could get hamburgers, french fries, and Coca Cola on every corner."

She wanted a new gadget for cleaning the toilet and a new stink bomb to perfume the air. She wanted a new jar of cologne, too many of the wrong people were using Faberge. She wanted an Osterizer or a Waring Blender, whichever was better. She really needed one in order to make vegetable juice for her weight reduction diet. There was a new bottled Hollandaise sauce she'd read about in The New Yorker. Why, incidentally, didn't he write to renew their subscription? Marilynn loaned her their copies but reading them second-hand made her feel behind the times.

"Which times?" Kenneth inquired. "All about Broadway shows

nobody wants to see and expensive soap. Pages of fake-British prose...warmed-over H.G. Wells...I wish you wouldn't bring the damned thing into the house."

"What are you getting so excited for?" Helen asked. "It isn't hurting you any. You don't have to read it."

"I certainly don't. All I have to do is just sit here or go visit one of our friends in order to have the contents of each issue repeated to me verbatim, cartoons and all. Who wants his head cluttered up with all that froth and pretense?"

"It just happens to be the only readable American magazine," Helen said. "W.H. Auden said so."

"Everybody knows that Mr. Auden reads nothing but crossword puzzles. There are none in *The New Yorker*. He was really talking about the airmail edition of the Manchester *Guardian*."

"Kenneth, I'm really awfully tired of your being so stuffy. You're not actually that old and crotchety. Why don't you try to be a little pleasant?"

"You can go ahead and read *The New Yorker* until your head snaps, I don't care. I don't want to see it or hear about it. I will not pay for a subscription to receive it."

"Maybe I can get a subscription for my birthday. Daddy will get it for me if I ask him."

"I guess he will," Kenneth replied, rather quieter than before. He stood up. "We really ought to leave soon. We can only spend four dollars, though."

"Why?"

"Because it's all there is until Friday."

"Oh, no it isn't. I have ten dollars in my purse."

"Sweet frugal baby," he said, admiringly. "Let's go."

Helen loved to look at him. His skin was red and white under a haze of wiry-looking golden hairs. She was always surprised to feel the solidity of his flesh under her hand, the scratchy-looking coil-spring hair was almost impalpable. She loved the shape of his head and the whirling cowlick in the hair on top of it.

A long scar parted his fur almost the full length of his left forearm. A German boy whom he had never met sent off a mortar shell which exploded rather near to where Kenneth stood or crouched or whatever he was at that moment doing, he never seemed able to remember too clearly except that it was a very cold day in or near Remagen.

He had a heavy ridge of bone above his eyes like a helmet visor; his eyes were blue but they had minute black stripes from the pupil to the iris. He wasn't as tall as Helen. She knew that some of his oldest friends still called him "Shorty," although one of them told her that Ken had grown considerably since he was a boy. She had spent half a day in Florence looking at Michelangelo's *David*, and she had spent hours sketching from male models, but she thought that Kenneth was quite magically something else.

She said that she got great comfort from cuddling close to him at night, wrapping her arms around him in sleep. Ken couldn't endure this for any length of time. He felt too hot and sweaty. His arms and legs would grow cramped and he'd have to move them, but he'd worry that moving would awaken her. Being afraid made him impatient, and the impatience and indecision would make him angry with himself, and presently he'd be sweatier and more uncomfortable. At that point he'd slowly disentangle himself from her arms, get out of bed, and smoke a cigaret. He was afraid she would tell him, should she waken, "If you really loved me you'd let me hold you." Helen never said precisely that.

She woke up or at least she spoke, very slowly and clearly, he knew that she had her eyes shut. "What's the matter? Does your arm hurt?"

"No. I got too hot and wanted a cigaret."

"What time is it?"

"I don't know."

"Sit over here," she said. He was standing in front of the dresser where the cigarets were.

He sat on the bed beside her. She wrapped her arms around his waist and snuggled her nose against his hip. She didn't say anything.

He smoked. He wondered how anyone so beautiful could love him, put up with his curious whims and weaknesses.

She said, slowly but clearly, "Don't go away."

He stroked her shoulder. "Go back to sleep," he said. He wondered about the strange Englishmen who tramped all through central Asia in disguise, trying to thwart Russian Imperial Designs against India, about the tough Moslem tribesmen of that area who were mean enough to put a thumb in your eye just to hear it go Squitsch! and then laugh when they heard it. He thought of Colonel (later Sir Francis) Younghusband bluffing and blarneying his way to Lhasa in order to sell the Dalai Lama 19 million yards of colored calico, several tons of tinware, and the anti-Czarist line. Also a few thousand gross of bullets to keep down the bandit population.

He thought of how to compute the date of Easter by counting from the date of the Vernal Equinox and when they changed it from falling on the same day as Passover, or too near or too far from that day.

He wondered how to persuade Helen to go with him into the mountains, instead of going to see her parents in Seattle, although he'd win even if they did go to Seattle, he thought smugly, contemplating the Olympics and the Cascades. It would cost more money than would ever exist conveniently, but he couldn't worry about that any more. He put out his cigaret, gently eased himself up and over Helen's sleeping body and down the other side, under the covers, and fell asleep.


Ken kept thinking—actually, in an interior auditory memory—certain fragments of music: chord progressions and bits of melody out of a liturgical piece by Stravinsky. He couldn't decide whether it came from the *Symphony of Psalms* or the *Mass* or another later work. Trying to place it, to identify it positively, that wasn't his feeling. The succession of notes and rhythms, the instrumental timbres, the voices singing Latin words recurred to him at irregular intervals throughout the day. They pleased him. There were occasions when this same kind of obsession with a floating unidentified chunk of music would drive him to spending hours rummaging through miniature orchestral scores, more hours of listening to a few minutes of a vast number of phonograph records until he could positively identify the music he was remembering.

He knew that he should take the time to sit down and compile a commonplace book which would be a catalog of dates, quotations (musical, poetical, biographical) and other items or facts that he had difficulty remembering, as for example how to say "not just now" in French, the names of Lin Chi's teacher (in Chinese and Japanese), the English word "velleity." "But," he'd tell himself, "all I have to do is try to go on learning and practice remembering, and try to attend to what I'm seeing and hearing."

When Helen asked him, "Why are you so gloomy today?", he said he wasn't. "There, you see? What's bothering you so much?"

"Oh, I was just thinking," he said, "about how I'm not doing anything. I never write anything or paint anything or build anything any more. I don't even study."

"You read practically all the time," she said.

"Yeah...but not to any point, any conclusion. I wanted to learn harmony. See there on the bookshelf, there are all the textbooks—the *Harmonielehre*, Hindemith, Piston...you can see the manuscript paper sticking out of the top of Schoenberg, it has a couple of exercises written on it...it's wrinkled and yellow and crimped. I don't know anything about 6/4 chords."

"Well, why don't you do something? All you have to do is sit down and begin. I'm not going to bother you if you want to study."

"I guess so," he said.

"I ought to go out and get a job again," Helen said. "Then you could take a part-time job. You'd have more time that way to do whatever you want. At least you'd probably feel better."

"It isn't your fault, Helen. I just don't really have enough imagination, enough energy to produce anything."


Sometimes Ken found it was impossible to listen to any more of Helen's reminiscences, explanations, lists, or wishes. He'd tell her that he had an urgent meet elsewhere. She'd plead to go along. She'd promise, if he had, on the other hand, simply told her that she was making him nervous, that she'd not speak another word. She would promise to leave him alone, to occupy herself with the laundry, the dishes, the vacuum cleaner.

Having waited until she paused to take a breath, having refrained from kicking her out of the way so that he might run screaming out of the door, having refrained from falling on the floor and assuming the fetal position, having refrained from going back to bed, from slashing his throat with a razor, he would say goodbye and walk out. He would drive the car to Land's End to sit and look out over the ocean, or he might drive into the Park.

He'd sit in the car and read. If he did this in the park he'd soon fall asleep and awaken after sundown. Then he'd drive home, feeling miserably guilty. Why couldn't he face living with her, he loved her...or tell her that they must divorce?

He knew that if she didn't make much fuss when he was leaving, she'd be bound to make a scene of some kind when he came back. Sometimes she had a real reason for being upset...the electrical fuses had blown or the water heater had misbehaved. Or a great crew of his old friends might have arrived while he was out and he'd find them milling around all through the flat, hollering and drinking. The house would frighten him then. Had he come to the right one?

He very seldom went to bars alone. He didn't enjoy the atmosphere, he didn't like the people he saw there. If he did go he'd have one drink and then leave. Helen would smell him when he came home and make a few remarks about how they had no fresh tomatoes in the house. She bothered him a little too much on one occasion when he'd come in really drunk. He beat her. They both wept. He was a model husband for several days afterwards. He never beat her again. He knew that a tardy reappearance at home or a series of short, unexplained absences bothered her more than being beaten.

"Where were you?"

"I took a drive."

"Where?"

"Oh, just around."

"Around where?"

"What's for supper, Sweetie?"

"I don't know," she said angrily. "I couldn't drive to the market and get anything because you had the little car."

"It isn't far to the store."

"I can't carry all that stuff back here without help."

"It don't take more than you can carry in your tiny fragile arms to make a single supper."

"I hate you to death," she yelled.

"Very well. We'll go out to dinner."

"What shall I wear? My hair is all undone! Oh, wait for me!"

Ken wondered if all this might not be the "horrors of American middle-class experience" which he'd heard about in college. He hoped not. He wondered what ever happened to Henry Wallace.

Helen was talking. Kenneth was thinking about grapefruit. It had been something new and different that people had begun to eat for breakfast, one of his early memories. He remembered that he could not, at that time, pronounce the word correctly, and his parents made fun of him about it, "grate-thruit." It was seven or eight years later that people began to drink tomato juice in the morning; they had hangovers to cure, then, and tomato juice was supposed to do it, especially with Worcestershire or Tabasco sauce added.

Kenneth liked soup or stew or meat for breakfast. Helen liked to eat vitamin pills, fruit juice, and black coffee; she said breakfast made her nervous; she hated to get up in the morning. She said that she could bear it a little better on Sunday when there was a big edition of the newspaper to console her. To celebrate Sunday morning she'd eat half an English muffin, the kind that claims to be "the toast of San Francisco."

When he first knew San Francisco, before he was married, Ken used to eat breakfast in out-of-the-way places. He'd go in the middle of the morning to a bakery on Columbus Avenue for fresh pastry and cafe espresso, or into Chinatown for steamed meat-filled dumplings and tea. He never found a place where there was decent clam chowder. If he wanted that, he had to make his own. He made it in the New England style with milk; he thought the red, chili-flavored concoction which famous restaurants purveyed under the name of chowder was pure poison. Maybe they called it Coney Island chowder because it was used as a dressing for hot-dogs.


As usual, it was warmer outside than it was in the house. Kenneth went into the kitchen where he lit the gas oven and propped open the oven door. He lit the gas wall-heater in the living room. He hated the early morning—or early whenever he got out of bed—that trip down the hall and across the crummy kitchen linoleum barefoot. He seldom awoke in possession of enough sense to put on his slippers. If he was more completely awake, he was too impatient to stop and find the slippers and his robe; he wanted to dash out and start the fires and leap back into bed before he realized that he was cold. Soon the rooms would fill up with the stink of gas, the air in the house would lose a little of its chill, the windows would become nearly opaque with steam. Then he and Helen could have a short argument about who was going to have a bath first.

By swiping some of the steam off the bathroom window he could get a nice view down the hill to the Bay Bridge. To the left, the disproportioned dome on City Hall marked the Civic Center, while the taller buildings in the financial section were sharply outlined in the bright air. There was a nice view of the hotels on Nob Hill, and of the unfinished Cathedral where the nicer rich people went to church and were, doubtlessly, taught to be nice to each other. He sighed. It was fine now, but later he knew it would flatten; that is, the scene would set itself like a lantern slide, like a bar mural, fixed, exactly the size and shape of this bathroom window. Thank God for earthquakes.

It always surprised him that he saw a person in the mirror as he walked past it, the figure and face of a man who, he had been told, was "You, Kenneth." He was never certain that that was who it was. If he were thinking of something else when he saw that image, he didn't recognize it for his own.

Helen was talking. Nevertheless, she was extremely beautiful. He was watching her reflection in the toaster and comparing the real woman with that fluid, shifting but highly concentrated (the color of her face and hair, the colors of her clothing, the flashing of lights as she moved) image and the smooth, bright world which contained it.

"Isn't it so," she said.

"Which?" he asked. "The former or the latter?"

"You haven't the least idea what I said!"

"You asked if it wasn't so, whatever it was—the latter, I believe."

"Why do you have to be so unpleasant all the time?"

Without thinking, he replied immediately, "Why must you speak forty words with every breath you exhale? I've been trying to count the words, you go so long and so fast that I'm not sure whether it's forty or more."

"You certainly talk enough yourself," she said. She was growing angry. "I was only trying to discuss our plans for tomorrow so that we'll know what we're doing, so that we can arrange the day in order to get it all done."

"If things must be done tomorrow, I expect that you or I will do them, if we can. One at a time. There's no necessity for a long detailed discussion of something that hasn't happened. I don't think we have to discuss the purchase of a roll of paper towels for fifteen minutes." He hoped that he spoke moderately and not without gentleness.

Helen replied that he could take his delicate ears and his tangled up nerves and his fragile sensibilities and stuff them.

"Don't be naughty," Ken replied mildly.

Helen began screaming and pummeling him on the shoulder. "Are you alive or not? How can you just sit there? Listen to what I say to you!"

He hunched his shoulders and shut his eyes, his face set into a grimace. He tried to hide behind the morning newspaper. She left off beating him for a moment.

"What is it, exactly, that you're trying to tell me?" he inquired.

"We won't be able to do anything unless you get up early enough so that you'll have time to go down and pick up your paycheck and bring it to me so I can put it in the bank."

He looked at her and smiled. "Darling baby," he said. "You want to get that endorsed check into your grubby little claws so that you can run off with some sailor who'll be waiting for you in Blinn's on Market Street."

He seized her and sat her on his lap.

"You'd like that, wouldn't you," she said. "You'd be rid of me at last, wouldn't you. But I won't. I'm going to stay with you and make you suffer. I'm going to expose you for the fraud that you are. I'm going to get you in trouble with the police." She was all the while rubbing his head, pinching his ears and arms and ribs. "I'm going to tell them that I'm only fourteen years old, a statuesque rape, and they'll put you away in Napa and cut off your things."

Ken liked Travis. He didn't talk unless he really had something to say, and he was very intelligent. He didn't talk much to the guests in his house, but neither did he appear uncomfortably silent or smugly superior. If Travis had something to say, an observation, an anecdote to tell, he spoke very clearly, and often quite wittily, then he was silent. If the person Travis was addressing made some comment or asked a question, Travis would reply, "Maybe so, yes, can I get you another drink? Would you like some cheese? I must check the refrigerator." Travis would bring the drink, or the cheese, and go away. People who had not been guests there before used to ask each other, "Who was that?" Sometimes they found out.

Travis had patience enough to spend about an hour at one of his own parties. Then he'd disappear, go lock himself into his basement shop. He'd bought a kit which contained a piano keyboard, a loudspeaker, and many pounds of resistors, capacitors, and other electronic parts. Using nothing but a screwdriver, a soldering iron, and a pair of long-nosed pliers, he was assembling his own electric organ. He found before he progressed very far that he needed a volt-ohmeter, but he was able to swipe a very good one from the lab where he worked in the daytime. He told Ken, "You ought to buy one of these kits. You like music. Put it together and do E. Power Biggs imitations—a new show business career. Nobody knows that you're home on weekends if you're safely down in the basement building and tuning."

"I never could get a soldering iron to do anything except burn my initials into a workbench," Ken told him.

"I don't know how I'm going to tune the thing. I suppose I'll have to build me a signal generator. But let me get you another drink. Have you had some cheese? I must check the refrigerator."

"Come on, Travis, what have you got in that refrigerator that you spend so much time looking at?"

"I'll show you if you want to look," Travis said, looking about to see whether anyone else was listening or watching them. "Please don't say anything about it, though."

"Come on, Travis, I'm no cop."

"Okay, come and see."

Several days later, Helen asked him, "What were you and Travis having such a long talk about? He never talks to anybody."

46

"Travis is a great man," Ken said, smiling.

"Don't be tiresome. What did he say?"

"We were just talking about music. He and I both like Sweelinck. Also Buxtehude."

"You don't know Buxtehude from Dittersdorf. Don't try to kid me."

"I know what he keeps in his refrigerator that he keeps looking at."

"What?"

"His first wife."

"Why do you have to be such a smart-ass? I get sick and tired of your silly jokes. All I did was ask you a simple question and you have to make it into a whole comedy routine. When are you going to grow up?"

"The trouble with you is, your sense of humor has been ruined by reading nothing but *The New Yorker*."

"I'm really serious. It seems that it's becoming harder and harder for you to have an ordinary pleasant civilized conversation with any-one...not just me. I don't understand what's got into you."

"Don't you read the *Chronicle* every morning?"

"Of course. I'm no dumbbell, I know the world is run by a set of cretins who are doing their best to kill us all. I know that the air is so full of fallout that each time it rains the storm sewers light up like the Tunnel of Love. But that doesn't mean that you can indulge yourself in these fits of quarrelsomeness, silliness, and selfishness."

"Did you send in the car insurance payment?" Ken inquired.

"Yes, I did," Helen replied, triumphantly for once, "I sent it in a day earlier than it was due."

"Then I apologize. You win. You are a better man than I am in every way. Have a cigar."

"Kenneth, you're so hopeless I just can't talk to you any longer," Helen said. She then made a ten-minute speech, the main tenor of which was, that in her opinion Kenneth was becoming more and more alienated from any kind of social reality. She told him that it would do him a world of good to go talk to a good Jungian analyst.

"No. I don't think so," he said. "I might start saving cigaret wrappers so that I could build an orgone box on the back porch, but no Jungians. My brains are tiny enough now."

Helen talked on, rather too long, this time, perhaps a trifle too loudly; she went on and on about his habits, about the garbage, about her happy college days, about Bernard Berenson and Daddy and Crootie, and what Dr. Stokes had told her was probably the real trouble with Kenneth. Kenneth got up from his hassock beside the window and headed towards the front door.

"Where are you going now?" Helen demanded.

"I'm going out to get drunk, naturally enough."

"Take me with you."

"That's precisely why I'm going out to get drunk instead of sitting here to drink my own gin. I want to go out and get drunk all by myself. I'll be happy to see you later, but right now, I intend to go out alone."

"Do you expect me to be sitting here waiting for you? Go ahead and get drunk, but don't expect me to congratulate you about it. You're acting like a child!" Helen shouted.

"Sweet thing," Ken said, as he closed the door behind him. He heard something, possibly a shoe, hit the closed door with a thump.

Ken had not really intended to get drunk, not in the way he might have meant that phrase ten years before, when he was in the Army, when it was a kind of desperate and exciting act. He could no longer drink in the same way, he didn't enjoy it so much, he didn't become so disassociated as he was able to do then.

He went first to a steam beer tavern and drank a couple of glasses of that curious brew, but it didn't taste as good as he remembered it. He moved on to a place on Geary Street where there were quite a lot more kinds of beer and great sandwiches, but there were too many people and too much noise. He moved on down the street to the Scotch bar where it was quieter. He sat drinking half-and-half, watching an old man kidding the resident parrot into eating a few bits of fish and chips. It required much persuasion and flattery on the part of the old man. Ken found it difficult to follow the argument, and it came to him, suddenly, that he himself must be growing intoxicated. He tried to make up a problem in logic for himself as a test:

"If there's a question whether Europe is moribund, does it exist." He repeated this to himself in various ways, shapes, and forms. He noted with a shock, several minutes later, that the question or statement or whatever it was made no sense at all. He started over again, hurriedly.

"Suppose my name were Stephen Eubanks. Okay. Stephen EUBANKS, an old Scots family, Steven" (he wondered about the spelling) "Eubanks, well and good. If my name was Stephen Pepper I'd be a dead aesthetician. How about that. But I am...Harold Pringle, for example." He turned towards the man who sat next to him at the bar. It was so dark or Ken was so drunk and disorganized, he didn't recognize or he forgot that the man was his friend Bruce Chadwick. Ken held out his hand and said,

"Permit me to introduce myself. My name is Henry W. Standish, from Hartford, Connecticut."

Chadwick turned to him and gravely shook his hand. "How do you do, Mr. Hartford," he said. "My name is Wilfred Kubelik. I am a commercial traveler in tweed yarns from Waupakanetta Falls, Ohio."

Ken was temporarily very upset. The man had answered him, and had not tried to start a fight. The man was his friend Bruce Chadwick who was also pretending to be someone else.

"Allow me to buy you a drink, Senator...yours is getting cold," Chadwick said. He wondered what was the trouble with Ken.

"It's getting rather drunk in here, Chadwick."

"I've seen it worse," Chadwick said.

"I was trying to make it all orderly, if not logical," Ken explained. "Do you realize we knew three men—or boys—in college, all of them named Marshall? Marshall was their first names, their family names were different. None of them claimed to be related to Marshall Field or to the late General of the Armies."

"Cattlet," Chadwick said. "He was Secretary of State more lately than he was a general, but I don't know any more which is considered the higher rank. He was a cousin to Walter Cattlet in the movies. Very high society, no matter how you look at it."

"That isn't what I was trying to say," Ken complained. "Their first names was all Marshall. Two of them were heavy men, almost fat. One of these broke his leg while he was skiing, another of those two wanted a heavy velvet cape with a red satin lining, he was some kind of a political scientist, a Stalinist chess player. Two heavy Marshalls merry and bright, and the third one tall, thin, saturnine, much younger, looked like a movie star, he spent all his time down by the swimming pool. Three men or two men and a boy, three males all of them circumcised, some of them Jewish."

"You forget at least one other one," Chadwick said. "They called him something else besides Marshall, but Marshall was his first name. He was more nearly our age, his wife was in school when we were; he had already graduated at the end of our first year there. That beautiful girl who played the cello so well. They were great friends of Travis, later."

"The point is this," Ken said. (He had been struggling with this while Chadwick had been altering the number of possible subject cases.) "Who ARE Marshall? What is the quality that is 'Marshallness'?"

"I don't know," Chadwick said. "I never can tell which are the Universals and which are the Particulars or whatever those things are with toothpicks in them. How much does it matter?"

"A great deal. It is a question of whether you want fish and chips, whether you want them with vinegar and salt, or with tartar sauce or with catsup or give up and feed it all to the parrot and go eat a pizza."

"What's all that got to do with Marshall?"

"Marshalsea was a London jail, g-a-o-l. I want some fish and chips which are not far away before I collapse into this pretty sawdust on the floor and go to sleep."

"No kidding," Chadwick said.

"I have said," Ken replied. "Wait a minute." He went away to the men's room. He washed his hands and face. He combed the parrot droppings out of his hair. He looked at himself in the mirror and hated the way he looked—boiled, swollen, apoplectic.

Chadwick finished his drink when he saw Ken approaching. He stood up. "Let's go," he said.

"Yes, sir," Ken replied. They left the bar.

The air outside was warm and damp. There was a high fog that trapped the colors of the neon lights from the city below, then moved into blackness and made clear spaces where stars were more lights of the towns across the Bay. Chadwick was talking about Travis and Marilynn or something, Ken couldn't hear too well, and he was trying to be careful where and how he was walking. They found themselves in the fish store and gave their orders, not knowing they hadn't been there for several hours or some other lengthy, greasy, hot era of time.

"There's a secret in the Fellows family," Chadwick said.

"Certainly," Ken replied. "Mutual forgiveness of every sin, just like Blake says."

"I can't remember what it was. Somebody said that there was an ancient delicate history. I thought you might know."

"Sure I know. It's an open scandal. It's so public that everybody's forgotten about it, it was so many years ago. And now she's just Mrs. Travis Fellows, and nobody associates that name or that person with Marilynn Marjoribanks, the sensational teen-age novelist. People here in San Francisco think of her simply as Dottie's momma. She hasn't written any books since 1947 or 8, quite some time ago. One of them is still in print, a paperback. The other two are unobtainable, unless you spend a lot of time searching in second-hand shops," Ken said.

"No kidding. Marilynn Marchbanks. It does sound like somebody else."

"There have been three famous American women who were called Marilynn. Marilynn Miller, Marilynn Marjoribanks, and Marilyn Monroe. Marilynn Miller is dead, Marilynn Marjoribanks Fellows is a homemaker, an old school friend of my wife who is very likely talking with her on the telephone right this very minute."

"I know the real secret," Chadwick said. "I know what's in the refrigerator."

"I don't want to hear about it," Kenneth said. "I want more fish." He felt much better.


Ken sang in a quavery falsetto,

> A *kith ith*
> But a *kith*
> A *thigh ith*
> But a *thigh*

Helen said, "Why do you have to clown up everything? Can't you be serious once in a while?"

"I'm serious all the time," Ken said. "I never saw a world system yet that was so funny as this one. My laughing at it won't hurt it any. Just don't expect me to take it for what its label claims for it—officially, scientifically, legally real. The whole thing is a big hype."

"I used to think that you were at least intellectually honest," Helen said. "I know you're not terribly responsible in that area, and I don't expect you to be." She spoke thoughtfully, she was trying to be reasonable, trying not to lose her temper. "But you really haven't the right to criticize absolutely everything. You haven't been able, for all your intelligence and study, to come up with a better idea for the world, with any kind of rational, sensible suggestions about how we might make a more equitable, more reasonable life for people in general—much less with regard to our own relationship."

Ken said, "What are you recruiting for now, the DAR or the Great Books Program?"

"It's hopeless trying to talk sensibly with you," Helen raged. "You keep on behaving like a two-year-old!"

"You're the one who always gets mad," he said.

"You just better hope and pray that I don't really get mad one of these days: when I do, it's really going to cost you, and I don't mean maybe. You'll be one sorry smart aleck, I want to tell you!"

"Feel free," Ken said.

"I mean it."

"It'd be worth it at twice the price," he said, turning to look her in the eye.

"Just keep on! Just keep on!"

Ken laughed. He said, "That's what my momma used to say when she got mad at the old man. "Just keep on like that and there's going to be one less Swede around here."


She was talking. She was looking forward with pleasure at the prospect of going to Seattle when Kenneth got his vacation. She ran through the shorter one of her lists of recollections about growing up in that city.

Kenneth listened but without paying much attention.

"What would you do if I got pregnant?"

"I'd be delighted," he said. "I think we ought to have several children. We've talked about it enough."

"No—really."

"I told you, if it was a boy I'd breed him up to go into the Navy. If you had a girl, we could put her away in a convent school until she's nubile, then sell her to a rich and jaded old voluptuary. Then we can go to Europe. But you told me already Dr. Glotz doesn't believe you're pregnant."

"Not now, no. I just wondered, is all."

"You know I love the idea of having children. I think it'd be wonderful."

"We might adopt some. But not right now."

"I'd like it better if we had our own."

"I know, so would I, actually. Later. Are you watching the time?" Helen asked.

"Yes. We can still go shopping before I go to work."

"I wish we had a longer vacation. I'd love to go to Hawaii."

"You'll enjoy the mountains, once we get up there."

"I went up there once. That was enough," she said.

"That trip you took a couple months ago kind of set us back, but we'll have enough in August to pay our way into the mountains for a couple weeks. I want to get out of the city."

"Get Travis or Bruce Chadwick to go with you."

"I'd enjoy being there with you a great deal more."

"Well, I don't know," Helen said. "I'll think about it. But you'll have to promise not to be as surly as last time."

"Okay. Well, let's go. Have you got your list?"

"Yes. Let's be off. I want to fix you a specially good lunch when we get back."

"Darling Booboo," Kenneth said, and kissed her.

She let him hold her for a minute, then she turned away, hurriedly, saying that she must get her sunglasses. She eventually found them in her purse. They set out for the supermarket. As they walked down the street she raved about the weather, but she was wondering what Kenneth would say and do if she told him what had actually happened in Seattle when she went there alone two months ago.


Helen fussed with her hair, trying to make it look new and different, or at least look neat. It was hard for her to see, the bedroom was dark. She went into the bathroom, where Kenneth was installing the new lighting tube. "There," he said.

"Thank you," Helen said, "I'll be ready in a minute."

"You look good enough already," he said. He embraced her.

"Do you love me?" she asked.

"Exquisitely," he replied.

"Why? I'm so stupid, I can't take care of the house or of myself. I hardly have patience any more to read a novel."

"Because I love you," he said. "You are so beautiful."

"I look horrible. What am I going to do with my hair?"

"Your hair is beautiful."

"It looks like a condor's nest," she said. She was happy. "Let's go now."

"What do you know about condors?"

"He was a decadent painter. Ask me something else."

Ken laughed. He went into the kitchen and looked inside the refrigerator. The box was filthy and full of inedible leftovers in little covered dishes. It wasn't her fault, he knew. He had been a guest in her mother's house and he knew she had learned from her mother this habit of wrapping little dribs and drabs of creamed spinach, dead gravy, half-chewed bones of steaks, wrapping them up and entombing them in the refrigerator. There in the cold and dark they dehydrated, shrank, and became mummified; the essences of their one-time flavors haunted the flat dead air in the box.

Helen came into the kitchen and groped his crotch. "Ask me about Odilon Redon. Ask me about Francis Picabia. Ask me about Bebe Berard. Ask me what became of Genia Berman's brother."

"Hey! I told you about doing that gently. I appreciate your attention, but be careful."

"Why are you so jumpy? I hardly touched it. You're always fingering after me when I least expect it."

"I'll try to be brave," he said, "and gentler."

"You're so big and solid. It's hard to believe that you're so delicate right there."

"You are a little flower," he said.

"So are you if I tickle you a little. You spring up like a poppy."

"All it takes is a cold blast of wind, one little bacillus. Or pop a little blood vessel in my head and I'm done. I'm not so tough."

"I don't care too much, as long as you aren't so cranky. Shall we go?"

"If you're all ready."

"You better button your pants," she said.

"Sweet thing," he said. "When you die I'm going to have you pumped full of butterscotch syrup instead of embalming fluid. Then I'm going to coat you with chocolate and eat you."

"I hate butterscotch. Make it raspberry or strawberry goop. I can't stand butterscotch."

"You'll never know anything about it."

"Oh, yes I will. And I'll come and haunt you. But I don't really have to worry. Women live longer than men."

"If you say so, Cupcake," he said. He kissed her. They went out.

# II

Kenneth picked his time card out of the rack, read the bulletin boards, and waited with all the crowd for the hands of the time clock to jump a couple of points. The young men talked about the latest adventures of Huckleberry Hound, and about their cars. The older men talked about the stock market, their wives, and the possibility of having to work overtime today. Some of them drank coffee or Coca Cola from paper cups. Almost all of them smoked.

The air was faintly dusty. Fluorescent lights radiated too much brightness, the PA system scattered music that was only a trifle louder than the clatter and roar of the machines. The loudspeakers whistled and screeched, then a voice came on, dismissing the regular day people. The crowd around the time clocks became a howlng mob as the hands of the clocks entered the critical area.

Bruce Chadwick rushed past, shouting hello, gave him a whack on the shoulder. Ken hurried away to his regular station. He would see Chadwick later, at lunch or in the swing room. The loudspeakers were delivering music again, Morton Gould's *Pavane*. Someone in the distance whistled the tune. Behind him, Ken heard one man ask another, "Say, what's the name of that song? I never did know." The other man said, "Caravan." Kenneth winced, inwardly. He hated to have mistakes like that go uncorrected. He looked around to see who the men were. They were strangers; he thought better of intruding on their conversation. They wouldn't care one way or the other about the music. Presumably they preferred hearing it to the roaring of machinery.

Helen was gone, but a few times Kenneth was certain that he heard her talking as if she were in the next room. Once he was at a party, a very large occasion, many people, and he kept hearing her in the distance, from time to time, all through the evening. He became very drunk, and when he decided, early in the morning, to go home, he made quite a fuss hunting for Helen in order to take her with him. He shouted and staggered about, weeping, calling for Helen, falling down, vomiting. At last he collapsed entirely and his friends put him to bed.

In the morning he was confused, sad and ashamed. His friends told him not to worry about it, everyone still loved him.


After the fact, Ken was aware, he could think of himself as knowing that he was vulnerable to fits of disintegration, during which he was unable to do anything at all—such as getting out of bed, brushing his teeth, getting something to eat—without spending quite a length of time contemplating the action in advance. He would feel jailed. He felt as if the world was operating on a schedule he could not learn. These fits of quasi-paralysis were almost certain to occur if he was obliged to get ready for a long trip, or if he were, for example, making a visit of any length to his parents.

It required a considerable time for him to get used to the fact of Helen's departure. He couldn't, at first, do much of anything but rehearse to himself the long list of his own failings which always ended, "...and my own simple-mindedness, of which my present activity is the latest example...my inability to decide whether to stop and eat a sandwich or a bowl of soup or a milkshake or an apple..." He was conscious all the while that he was doing nothing, as if he were frightened of moving; he was examining with great care the design of curly flowers, leaves, fruit, and scrolls of the plaster roundel in the ceiling above the light fixture, the grooves of cherub wings and eyes and mouths in the window embrasure. He sat completely remote in his own living room; he knew only "remote from the past." He wanted no more from the world "outside," had no greater expectations than before; nevertheless it seemed farther removed and perhaps, very subtly, sealing itself from any further contact with him. He could almost feel it going faster and faster, away, and as it moved it grew to contain beauties and wisdoms and delights that he would never know. At the same time it was as if scornful eyes and fleering mouths regarded him over the coldest of shoulders as they were smoothly, swiftly, and silently borne off into spaces of many brilliant lights and gorgeous music.

He could remember, later, that all this had happened before. He was never able to meet it, to cope with it as it was happening, nor could he think how he might prevent its recurrence. He must endure these collapses. Their cost in terms of time, thought, possible love, possible creation—not to mention the quantities of exploded nerve tissue—was more than he could ever afford. He felt, quite exactly, that he was "ruined." At the same time he realized the absurdity of that expression, insofar as he was still alive, not in a hospital, a madhouse, or a jail, not deaf dumb blind or crippled.


Marilynn had been shy of Ken for some time after the divorce. She considered herself Helen's friend, after all. Although Ken pleased and intrigued her as long as he was physically present, the prospect of seeing him frightened her, repelled her. Then, one evening, she and Travis met Kenneth at the theater. They went out together for a drink. Curiously enough, Travis became interested in something that Kenneth was saying about music in the play; he invited Kenneth to come to their house for dinner sometime soon. Marilynn was annoyed with Travis. She repeated the invitation but used terms and tones which she hoped Kenneth would interpret to mean that he was not intended to accept it.

Ken heard what she said, and feeling about her as he always had, he said that he would be delighted to come for dinner. Marilynn hauled Travis away almost immediately. Ken could see her giving him quite a definite lecture as they walked up Sutter Street towards their parked car. No doubt the subject of her discourse was himself, something to the effect that he was a worthless object upon which to bestow their hospitality, considering that he had mistreated and betrayed Helen until she had eloped, in a fit of despondency, with an old friend of their happy college days.

Marilynn's cousin Kate arrived soon afterwards for one of her short regular visits to the city. She inquired after Kenneth, and Marilynn felt obliged to make a somewhat embarrassed telephone call to Kenneth asking him please to come to dinner. There would be a very small gathering, for drinks and a plain dinner . . . he and Kate would be the only guests.


Kenneth handed his time card to his supervisor, a fat popeyed man in a brown suit who shouted and waved his arms when he wasn't busy collecting time cards. He spent a lot of time shouting into the PA system microphone. His shouts were translated into ear splitting squeals and thunders of microphone feedback; he'd never learned how to adjust the controls in order to broadcast at a reasonable level. One of his assistants, hearing the howl, would rush to his side and adjust the gain control and the loudspeaker would deliver a reasonably clear message. Afterwards none of the workers could complain about not having heard a command, or not having heard the boss summoning one of their number. The supervisor was fond of calling for individuals to report immediately to his desk. He would shout and rave at those miscreants who had punched their time cards in the wrong columns, or those worse offenders who were goofing off the job, drinking coffee in the swing room.

Almost everyone did his own job regardless of the supervisor's shouts. An increasing flock of assistant supervisors, sub-assistant supervisors, supervisor-trainees, and supervisor-trainees-presumptive saw to it that everyone stayed busy and worked as quickly as possible. Ken thought of them as being like Army KP pushers. They had to take a lot of abuse from the boss and the people they were supposed to control made fun of them, hated them, appealed from their authority to the boss or to the tour chief, the man at the top. Men who had brains enough to pass the civil service examination for a supervisory position, and who had years of experience in the service, seldom bothered to work their way into a higher job. The raise in pay wasn't enough to compensate for the strain of meeting the tight schedules of operation set up by the head of the department, far away in Washington, D.C., or to help cure the busted nerves resulting from the continuous arguing and explanation and harrying of people who wouldn't follow directions, who made mistakes, who messed up the job so that the schedule was in continuous danger of being broken or of collapsing entirely.

Kenneth, working in his usual place, was daydreaming. He considered the job as being the act of printing numbers on his time card four times a day. The numbers on the card were read by a machine that printed his pay check. A great number of persons and written regulations governed the manner in which that card was handled. These people presumed that their fellow employees had taken jobs with the department in order to defraud the government of the United States in the amount of their regular pay. It was presumed that everyone had gone to the trouble of taking a long civil service test, had been interviewed by insolent and suspicious personnel and security officers, and had spent hours filling out literally pounds of official forms so that, once they were hired, they might shirk on the job, practice habitual absenteeism, drink while working, or take extended vacations at government expense. Not only that, but everyone would probably steal or destroy government property. The entire crew, from the Regional Director down to the man who fired the boilers, was constantly dogged by security checks, property checks, efficiency studies, time studies, and various schemes to speed up the entire operation. Every third man in the building was a secret agent working for the Treasury Department, for the FBI, for the department's own security office, or was a secret investigator sent out by individual senators or congressmen.


Bruce and Joan Chadwick had lunch together. Joan was just then newly returned from abroad; hardly anyone knew that she had come back. Bruce had made the appointment with her through her attorney, quite formally, as he had become accustomed to doing after their divorce.

They ate a very elaborate Chinese meal very slowly, chatting together quite amicably.

Bruce said, "I must tell you that I'm getting married."

Joan said, "I'm surprised. I wondered that you've waited so long. I didn't suppose that anyone would catch you after all this time. Is it anyone I know?"

"I don't think so. Her name is Alice Sedley and she works at Stanford with Travis's group. She's a real bright girl."

"How old is she?"

"Twenty-five, blonde, five-nine, a substantial girl."

"Well, you're not exactly robbing the cradle."

"No."

"How is Kenneth?"

"Oh, I don't know. He seems kind of blank all the time when he isn't being cranky. I guess he's all right, but he was pretty upset when Helen left."

Joan said, "I suppose." She took a sip of tea and carefully set the cup back onto the table. "You know, he wrote letters to me all the time I was gone. I sent him postcards."

"Good. Is it all right if I tell him—but then, he must know you're back, if you've been writing—"

"I didn't tell him exactly which day I'd get here. If you see him—yes. Say I'm here."

"You know, he's really quite a guy. He's always thought a lot of you."

"I know. I could never talk to him very well, but I always like to listen to what he says. He has such a strange view of everything."

"You two ought to get together."

"I don't know. I'm awfully busy and my nerves are awfully jumpy."

"Your nerves would be fine if Kenneth paid you a little attention."

"Lay off, Brucie. If he wants to see me, he'll call up."

"I think you'd make a great pair."

"Just don't trouble yourself with making any of your famous arrangements. I told you, I'm very busy."

"Are you going to give yourself a welcome-home party?"

"Fairly soon, I expect. I'll let you know."


The building where Kenneth worked had miles and miles of fluorescent lighting tubes and scarcely any windows. Once he was inside it, he very easily forgot what time of day it was; consequently he was often surprised to leave the place and discover that the sun was shining or that a fog had come in off the Bay.

"Working here is like working anywhere," he told Detweiler, a new man who had asked for a little help. "You learn which rules they enforce and which ones they overlook, and which ones they invoke periodically. It's like the traffic laws or like being in the Army. You learn how and when you can goof off, how much the boss will put up with."

Detweiler looked at him, rather blankly, having heard a great many words. Ken could see that Detweiler was having trouble following him.

Detweiler said, "What kind car you drive?"

"I haven't got one right now."

"Why not? A man can't do nothing without a car. I got a 1959 Buick sedan goes like a sonofabitch on the freeway." Detweiler proceeded to tell Ken the entire history of each automobile he had ever owned. "You ought to get you another car," Detweiler told Ken, "It don't cost so much. You get a car you can take all the girls out and screw them. You know any good girls?"

"Sure," Ken said.

"You married?"

"Not right now."

"You ever been married?"

"Yeah, but not any more."

"I wish my old lady would go away but we're Catholic. You got any kids?"

"No."

"It ain't so bad, then," Detweiler said.

"It's bad enough," Ken said.

"I got to move on. Old Shitface find me hanging around instead of working." Detweiler went away.

Ken tried to concentrate on what he was doing. He played a game wherein he tried to move his hands only after he had made a conscious demand upon each muscle and bone required to make the motion. It was very difficult, for as he watched them, his hands kept making autonomous minute adjustments in order to pick up objects, turn them in the air, and place them elsewhere. The supervisor was shouting as he sped in Ken's direction, otherwise he would have found Ken in a state somewhat bordering upon *samadhi*.

"All you folks in this row switch over to Station K as in Karmelkorn. All you folks in here, just put that stuff down, Mrs. Cluck, everybody goes, Station K as in Karmelkorn." An assistant chased the supervisor waving a sheaf of papers, repeating his orders. He caught up with the supervisor and led him away to his desk, where they stood and shouted at each other for a while, waving their arms.

Ken sat looking blankly before him. He was disoriented by the sudden change of position. A little grandmotherly lady, her squinched-up face bright with inaccurately applied makeup, asked him to trade seats with her. She wanted to continue a conversation with the lady on his left, who was waving and nodding at Grossmama, three hundred pounds of mama, aunty, big and little sister all in one person, a holy mystery. Ken traded chairs and the ladies went on talking about the latest crotcheting and surgical news. What ever happened to Liberace, how the weather is, has been, and will be, all out of kilter because of the atom bombs, what a prince is our supervisor. Then they shrieked with terror, as did a number of other women in the place. "My God, Edna, did you feel that earthquake!"

Ken looked up, and sure enough, the light fixtures, the locator signs and other paraphernalia that hung from the ceiling all were swaying to and fro and there had been a very quiet but definite subterranean rumble and thump. Ken sighed and wondered how long it would be before the entire San Francisco peninsula finally severed its moorings and began to drift slowly out into the Pacific where it would gently and majestically sink while everybody sang "Nearer My God to Thee."

59

He tried to remember who told him the story about the opera singer who was afraid of horses. She was singing Brünnhilde in *Die Götterdämmerung* and very gingerly holding, between two fingers, what was possibly the longest bridle rein in the history of opera as she mounted Siegfried's funeral pyre. The rein was attached to a great ancient fat beast who hadn't had a wicked thought since the spring of 1925. If the rein had been two inches longer the horse would have been completely off-stage right. The singer kept looking at it apprehensively, and trembling visibly, she bravely sang her part as she entered the flames of red and yellow silk. That would have been fifteen or twenty years ago, Kenneth reflected.

"You people can work faster than that," the Tour Chief shouted, as he passed behind them at great speed. "Use both hands and cut out the talking." These last words trailed behind him.

Ken sighed and put everything on a ledge in front of him. He told the silent, responsible appearing man on his right, "Watch my place, will you? I'll be back in a couple of minutes if they come looking for me." The man gave him a quiet stare from under a green eyeshade, nodded once, and kept to his own work.

Ken wandered up the alley to a main aisle. He could see the Tour Chief waving a long arm and pointing a finger while the supervisor explained whatever it was, shouting and waving both his arms.


Some days Ken couldn't stay on the job, he wanted to think, he wanted to sit down, he wanted to be alone, but he couldn't afford not to be at work. He took sick leave as often as he dared, but he had been warned not to push his luck too far. He had to find some way of getting out of the building and back in again without anyone knowing that he was gone. He had to be able to turn in a time card at the end of the day, and the card had to be marked in the proper places.

The doors of the building were guarded; other guards patroled the enclosed catwalks suspended from the ceiling. There was a double checking system involving the time cards which permitted the supervisors (and anyone else who was interested) to find out where any employee was supposed to be working at any time during the working day. If a man wasn't to be found in this manner, he was paged by a supervisor speaking over the PA system.

By carefully observing how the time cards were handled, by listening to older employees talk, and by watching what things the door guards chose customarily to see and what they ignored, Ken found a way to escape whenever he wanted to get away. He had to be very cautious and at the same time, decisive in his movements. He couldn't get up nerve enough to do it too often, but when he felt that he absolutely needed to get out, he could do it without being caught.

On such occasions he sometimes went up the street and around the corner to Flynn's. Its tawny wood 1930s "modern" interior pleased him.

The only time it was noisy was on nights when there was a fight showing on television. Ken knew only a few bars in town that he considered to be quiet enough, that had an impersonal feeling, a lack of "atmosphere."

Flynn's was a place where people went to buy drinks and talk to each other. It didn't pretend to be an old San Francisco institution from before the fire. They hadn't turned out all the lights, put a plush rug on the floor, installed an electric organ, and billed the place as a cocktail lounge. It was a filling station, a dispensary. There was enough light to read, the bar man and the waitress were good enough not to keep hustling all the customers to finish their drinks, and the prices were reasonable. Ken could sit and read from his paperback Hume and drink just enough to strengthen his nerves so that he could work the rest of the shift without feeling as if he might fall down on the floor and curl up like a caterpillar.

Marilynn said, "I don't see how you can stand to keep on working in that creepy place. Bruce is different, he has no nerves left, but I don't see why you don't work someplace pleasant, as long as you're going to work."

Ken had met her unexpectedly in the library of the Mechanics Institute. She had been reading about the latest discoveries in archaeology and wishing that she could go to Asia Minor to see the ruins for herself.

Ken said, "I figured that you'd be in Europe or something, by this time."

"Are you kidding? My book is still in New York and they're not saying a word. My agent called the other day—I may have to go back there myself to straighten everybody out. Are you going to be able to make it to my dinner?"

"I think I have that day off from work, but I never know for sure what they might do. I can probably call in sick, though. I want to see Kate."

"Who cares about that insane job of yours? Cousin Blowsibelle is holding her breath until she gets to see you again. Don't you like her?"

"We get along just fine as long as the gin holds out."

"I thought you LIKED her."

"We like each other just fine. We have lots of interests in common."

"My cousin cannot by any stretch of the imagination be thought of as 'common.'"

"I'll see you later, Marilynn. I have to go to work."

"I think it's affecting your brains," Marilynn said. She held her hand to his forehead. "You're kind of hot and sticky today."

Ken smiled at her. "Thank you very much," he said. "I don't think it's contagious. I just get a little sneezy because of the dust over there. The machines and all the people walking around keep the air full of it."

"Seriously, why are you doing this?"

"I have to. I go there every day at this time for eight hours or longer, depending on the time of year. I stay there, I work, I hate it. I still owe a little more on the divorce."

61

"Even after Helen's married to that goon-child and lives in another town. My land. What'd happen if you just went and told them you didn't have any more money?"

"I expect they'd attach my salary."

"Well, I think you ought to get a salary someplace else. I have to go now, too. You come to supper, we'll cheer you up."


Ken sat in his assigned chair, the machines roared, the fluorescent lights flickered and bubbled. He stopped working for a minute to light a cigaret. He didn't hear the small, toad-like assistant supervisor approaching.

"What's the matter, Ken, you slowing down?"

"Getting old, Monty."

The assistant peered up and down the alley, his eyeshade flashing. He lit a cigaret and picked up some of the work, pretending to be inspecting it.

"Everybody better look good tonight. Some kind of high mucky-muck from Washington is supposed to come through here on a surprise visit. The supervisor is all in an uproar, the Tour Chief's been twisting his tail."

Ken said, "Uh huh." He couldn't understand why Monty chose to bring him these bits of uninteresting intelligence. He knew that all the bosses were excitable men, that Monty and all the other assistants were both nervous and eager to please, were determined to make a home for themselves in the service.

"The chief says, 'I want you to get these people in shape. It's too quiet around here. Everybody's goofing off right here on the floor. Everybody else is in the swing room. We're behind schedule, it's past seven-thirty, see if you can't get this straightened out.' Old Hammerhead was sweating and choking and popping his eyes; I thought he was going to swallow his cigar."

"I expect," Ken said. "But I doubt if he's very scared. They've been hollering at each other for years. The chief has been running around and hollering but none of his wheels has dropped off yet. Old Hammerhead hasn't busted, either, although when I was first working here, I was expecting to see him carted out of here on a board almost any minute."

"Yeah," Monty said. "Well, try to look busy."

"Sure," Ken said.

Monty went away. He could hear people talking further up the alley, and went to silence them. Ken had learned years ago that if you're standing still on the job, keep your hands moving and be looking at them. If there's nothing to move or polish, then walk—not too fast, but decisively, looking pleasant but determined—on the longest and most circuitous route to the men's room, the stock room, wherever else in order to get out of sight. When there's nothing for it but to work, do it slowly and deliberately while looking very busy, earnest, and cheerful. Most

62

employers would overlook all kinds of inefficiency and loitering if they thought their slaves were cheerful, industrious, and loyal to the firm.

Ken stepped out of one of the back doors of the building, then walked on around the truck-loading docks where the confusion of men and machinery would mask his unauthorized departure from Government Property. The sun still shone, small foggy cloud patches blew by very fast, low in the sky. The air was fresh and at the same time, smeared invisibly by clouds of coffee roasting smell from the packing plant in the neighborhood.

He crossed the street and entered the Foster's cafeteria in the back of the Embarcadero YMCA. He had stayed in that hotel a couple of times during the war when he first visited San Francisco. The waitress gave him coffee and a hot butterhorn. She joked with him about joining the other refugees who were already seated at a table where they were having a serious argument about basketball and ice hockey. She was quite a handsome woman, large-boned and blonde; she spoke English quite well.

Ken paddled his fork in the melting butter on top of the pastry—not enough butter to wet the thing properly—then he devoured it quickly. He cursed himself for eating too fast and too often. Here was another pointless snack. His belly was feeling lumpy and sticky. But he wanted the taste, the action of chewing and swallowing, for pleasure, for comfort, to locate himself as separate from the insane screams and roars of the office, its rules, its invisible authority over him. He watched the men at the table nearby; they kept on arguing. Most of them were older men who knew they probably wouldn't be fired if they were caught, and there were a few very young men who didn't care one way or the other. Ken thought, irrelevantly, of Elisha the Prophet and the children who mocked him, "Go up, thou bald head!"—and of the enormous she-bear that God sent out of the woods to devour them.

He hated to be in this place stuffing himself with icky bakery goodies like a bored suburban housewife, and he hated the idea of going back to the office. Nevertheless, he returned to work. He had experienced a number of times in the past the excitement and delight of leaving jobs spontaneously, never to return. He couldn't do it again, or at least not now. He was stuck with his debt to the past. He wanted to get rid of it so that he might at last be free to be a completely uncommitted man existing today, *having*, being able to enjoy, the present. Right this minute his time and his life were shut away from him by the job. He couldn't see, much less actually use, the present day. He belonged to this time, instead of creating his own time by his own existence, by his own actions in the world.

There were days wherein the noise and senselessness of the authorities had him inwardly howling and beating his head against the wall. They would not let him alone, just let him work and then go home. They must pester him with new and more infantile rules, more complicated and time-consuming procedures to be followed in the performance of the simplest tasks. Ken felt beset, insane, and at last, moronic: he followed directions, kept his mouth shut, and knew nothing but hate and fatigue and frustration.

Joan Chadwick had been out of the country for a couple of years, making a survey of what was happening in Europe and Asia. She had to know, personally, what was available, what native industries had revived after the war, which ones had died out, what raw materials were to be had, how and where they were moving, what the prices were, what she could make on any of it legally, illegally, whatever.

Joan told Kenneth, "I enjoyed your letters. You've got a good eye for politics and the stock market. You could make a lot of money if you set up in business as a consultant—you wouldn't have to be in a brokerage house or a bank, just work for yourself as a private consultant to the larger firms, the bigger operators. Or maybe you could write up one of those secret insider dope sheets that go out to subscribers only."

"I'd go crazy trying to compose the first page of such a thing," Ken said. "Why don't we settle down together? You could spend your time cooking exotic and extravagant dinners for me."

"I'm too nervous. I like you well enough, Kenneth, but I have to keep up with my schedule. The business is in good shape now, but it's taking every minute of my time."

Nevertheless, she had invited him to her apartment for a drink of cognac after he had taken her to dinner and a play. They conversed as usual, they drank several glasses of cognac, and at last Ken arose to take his leave.

"You weren't thinking of going," Joan replied to his farewells.

"I thought you were probably tired."

"Let's have one more sip of cognac."

She told him, the next morning at breakfast, that he could see, at last, why she hadn't much time for sex, it was too exciting for her, it too easily took control of her thoughts, her consciousness. She said that she had to be careful not to indulge too often. She hoped that Kenneth would understand.

Ken said that he understood, but he felt the least bit hypocritical. She had seemed to him to be no more excited than any other woman he'd known. She was perhaps a little less demonstrative than some women. Her beauty still intrigued him, her curiously dim ardor added to her somewhat Pre-Raphaelite style of beauty.

There came to be an unspoken agreement between them to meet a couple of times a month to spend the night together. At first, it seemed to Kenneth to be an ideal kind of arrangement, but it quickly became a puzzle to him. Their meetings acquired a quality at once dream-like and mechanical.

The low roar of the machinery had floating above it, as an oil slick on the water above a mill dam, continous canned music playing on the PA system. The tunes were popular songs of the 20's and 30's played in elaborate pretentious or whimsical arrangements by large orchestras with lots of strings and horns. Ken could sometimes remember the words to some of these songs, and if he was working in a part of the building where not too many people were about, he'd softly sing the words to the music.

One of the younger men heard him one day and said, "What's that song you singing?"

Ken said, "It was 'All I Do the Whole Night Through Is Dream of You.' " It was in an old Joan Crawford movie about 1935 or so."

"Um-um. That was before my time."

"I guess so," Ken said.

Most of the younger men there were too young to have seen a Joan Crawford movie except on a late television show. Ken didn't feel any older or any different from these young people, but he imagined that they would know—that they already knew—kinds of living and feeling which he would never experience.


Ken worked quite steadily after he'd eaten lunch. When he became aware that he was making more mistakes than he usually did, he stopped working and looked at his watch. He was surprised to learn that he had only another hour and a half yet to endure of this work day. He lit a cigaret and set off on a tour of the office. He rode an elevator to the top floor, made a circuit through the main aisles, quite as if he were on an official errand. Then he walked down the stairs to the floor below and made a tour there. He repeated this procedure until he located Bruce Chadwick. He asked Bruce about his headache.

"I'm fine, now," Bruce said. "Listen, I want you to kind of hang around nearby at the wedding and remind me not to get too smashed. I don't want to get arrested on the way to Carmel."

"Have you got your reservations?"

"A friend of Travis's is lending us what he calls his beach cabin down there. It's actually a nine-room house with a patio, a pool, and a garden."

"Rich friends are the best kind."

"Ain't it the truth—people who've never been hungry or cold or without someplace to go—they make us poor folks feel more secure."

"As for living, the rich folks will do it for us," Ken told him, and laughed at his own misquotation.

"Something like that. I'll pay you the four bits on Friday."

Kenneth sang,

*She will toddle away, as all averr*
*With the Lord High Computationer!*

"How come you're in such a cheery jolly frame of mind?" Bruce asked him. "I'm the one that's getting married."

"I only have another fifty-eight minutes to work. I've already been married."

Bruce said, "Everybody's married, for whatever good it does."

"Better and worse, according to the script," Ken replied. "I got to reappear at my station, now. I'll see you later." He walked away, whistling the same few staves from *The Mikado*.

Helen had told him that she was tired of the uncertainty of life with him, tired of his really wild whims, his laziness, his warped sense of humor.

"Why do you suppose everything is going to be so cool with Ron?" Ken had asked her.

"I've known him all my life. I know his family, I know how he feels about me, and I know what to expect from him."

"You really enjoy the idea of life in the social pages?"

"Don't be silly. Of course life in Seattle is different—"

"Oh, there's still a few rich folks in San Francisco."

"It isn't the *money!*" Helen shouted at him. "I must do this in order to save myself from going crazy or from shooting you. Don't you understand? I have to."

"Well, don't holler about it. I wish you'd stay. I don't promise you anything, but I hate having you go away."

Helen sighed and shook her head. "I just have to. Ron and I understand each other, respect each other. We have the same kind of expectations, the same kind of background. He'll. . . we'll. . . well, anyway, I must."

"I still don't know what it is that's got you into this goofy affair," Ken said. He rubbed his head. "You sure got it all fixed up awfully fast."

"My God, this conversation has gone on for months! That's your idea of fast? I can't go over it any more thoroughly than we already have, day after day. I've made up my mind."

"I expect I ought to accept all that, but I don't," Ken said. "I ought to go find that guy and kick the shit out of him."

"Oh, swell. I can just see it now. 'IRATE PHILOSOPHER STOMPS WIFE'S LOVER.' I don't understand why you can't face this thing rationally. I think you'll be better off when I'm gone."

"I don't know what kind of simp you take me for. I want you here."

"Please stop it, Kenneth."

"I don't care. Sure I'm selfish. Sure I'm self-indulgent. How do you expect me to behave when my life is getting busted up? Just sit and let him, without saying anything, doing anything?"

"Listen, Kenneth, I want out of this house, I want away from you and your frenzies, I want a quiet normal life. I intend to have it. If you try to

66

stop me, if you try to beat me up or to hurt Ronald or anything like that, you'll be sorrier than you've ever been."

"What's all this magic incantation? Just exactly what are you threatening to do?"

"Just keep on and you'll find out. I'm warning you, Kenneth."

"Baloney. You may be a nut but evil isn't your kind of line. I know you better than that."

"Try stopping me."

"By God, I will!" Kenneth was shouting, now. "We'll have the loudest, messiest divorce trial the world has ever seen. I'm not going to be shat on by every flying elephant in the world!"

Helen calmly replied, "Very well." She proceeded to tell him about her trip to Seattle and the conversation she'd had with her mother.


One of the young men was working beside Ken. He worked very fast and was talking to Ken half again faster than he worked. He said that he would soon be out of college, then he would get married or go into the Air Force; he wasn't certain. He spoke of his father's wanting him to be a dentist. He talked about his car. He mentioned his admiration for General Eisenhower and Foster Dulles, and how they were so expertly thwarting the expansionist pretensions of the International Communist Conspiracy. He was pleased with the progress which J. Edgar Hoover and the FBI were making against the secret underground hard-core communist atheist subversives who lurk in our midst, very serpents in the bosom of Columbia. He spoke of the menace to young American manhood presented by the growing army of queers in San Francisco. He had read and admired the works of Mr. Herman Wouk. He had once been required to read a few poems of Dylan Thomas in a literature class. He said he didn't understand them but they were probably great writing, considering the feebleness and degeneracy of the present age. Now he was growing tired of reading, after four years of college, four years of high school, eight years of grade school, a year of kindergarten, and two years of nursery school (not to mention Sunday school, confirmation class, and the education in rugged manly outdoor living provided by his Boy Scout troop)—he felt that he was ready for other things. He wanted a fair income before he married. He wanted a power boat, he loved to water ski. He needed new golf clubs. He had just bought a second-hand movie camera and a new spinning reel for his fishing rod. How he admired Richard Nixon! What a great columnist was Mr. Earl Wilson! What a great and accomplished actor was Mr. Tab Hunter! What a beautiful, talented and infinitely desirable creature is Miss Tuesday Weld!

He asked Ken, "Say—what happened to your arm? You in an automobile accident?"

"No, I got it messed up in the war."

"Were you in Korea?"

"No, in Germany."

"I didn't think you were that old. My old man was in World War Two."

"I'm old enough," Ken said. It struck him odd that he might well have been the father of just such a funny looking young animal as this one, old enough to shave and talk about getting married and about what he would do when he finally inherited the world from Kenneth's increasingly feeble grasp. The kid was wide-eyed and skinny, but he looked strong. He was apparently stuffed to the gills with enough goofy notions and propaganda and "education" to keep him from taking any sort of a straight look at the world or at himself for perhaps forty years to come...perhaps never. Why should he.

"My old man was in the Signal Corps in the Pacific," the boy said. "He got a good job with the telephone company after he got out of the Army. I hope I've had enough science and math in school so I can learn something like electronics in the Air Force. I can make a good living when I get out, working in television or computers. Have a trade I can work at..."

"I thought being in the Army was a real drag," Ken said. "On one side we had all these insane rules and regulations and officers and noncoms trying to grind us down, and on the other side there were all these people shooting at us with live ammunition, trying to kill us. It seemed like it would never stop."

"Well, of course it's different now," the young man said. "A lot better deal."

"I expect it will be safer to be in some airbase in Turkey than to be living here in San Francisco when all these guys start pushing their buttons to blow up the world."

The boy laughed nervously. He said, "Maybe you're right, but that won't happen, I don't think. We're getting further ahead of them every day with our technology."

Ken said, "I expect." He worried himself for the rest of the day, wondering how he might have told the kid in a nice way that he was being bilked by the government, the newspapers, the world, that they wanted to kill him. How could he tell him so that he'd understand that he should grab his girl friend and head for the hills right now and let the governments of the world do without him. On the other hand, the kid might be an agent, some kind of cop, trying to sound him about his loyalty or some other idiot project.


His nose was full of black, his head hurt, his back was tired. The PA system was broadcasting a complicated latino version of "Blue Moon." Kenneth worked steadily but not too fast; his consciousness for the moment was confused with billowing clouds of trivial information reported to him by Detweiler, by Monty, even Chadwick had come around and told him some horror story about compulsory flu shots. Everyone in the government service was about to be inoculated, willy-nilly, with some dread antitoxin which produced a mild case of bronchitis and a number of bizarre side-effects.

Someone said that the Tour Chief was probably going to retire next week and be replaced by a man with a reputation for being the most hard-nose supervisor in the service. There was a rumor that everyone was going to be required to wear some kind of instrument on his wrist which would count the number and frequency of hand motions. Assistant supervisors were patrolling the swing rooms and toilets every half hour to discover and discourage the loitering workers. The spies in the overhead catwalks were supposed to be making patrols each quarter hour instead of once every shift. It was said that there were a number of secret inspectors disguised as employees; they were on the trail of a paper-clip and rubber-band boosting operation that was costing the department sums in the neighborhood of twelve to fourteen dollars a month.

Kenneth felt angry about the idea that he was now supposed to be frightened of what the bosses and the various cops were doing, that he was supposed to be working faster, that he was wasting his time thinking about any of this nonsensical swarm of bogus news and fake reportage. He knew that he would have to be caught doing something really quite seriously illegal before the authorities would trouble themselves about him; they had too many other people to watch. Nevertheless, here was this continuous threat of being fired for breaking some minor regulation. It would take a great deal of time and effort and worry if he had, at this point in his life, to go out looking for another job. He had scarcely any savings, he had absolutely committed himself to paying his legal bill. It disgusted him to think that he was, after all, afraid of being caught misbehaving, afraid of losing his temper if any of the bosses were to question or reprove him. All these fantasies and interior rages tired him. He felt trapped. He wanted to quit the office, never again to have anything to do with this world they claimed was real and serious, a world which (to his way of thinking) barely existed, which, if he tried to examine it calmly or seriously, faded away. The swarms of authorities, the childish rules, the tensions created by the strict time scheduling, hurry noise and music, the fakes of terror and discipline and guilt and punishment were a continuous bad movie written by a third-rate disciple of Franz Kafka. But the moment Ken's attention was diverted by a trip to the toilet or a break for lunch, it would lose its hold over his imagination.

Ken didn't see many women. He met agreeable ones at the few parties he attended. He didn't form any long-term attachments to any of them.

Marilynn's cousin, Kate, appeared in town several times a year. They had a pleasant kind of bantering relationship. They had made love a few times, but they weren't seriously interested in each other. Kate wanted as much as he did to stay loose. She had been married before, felt she'd seen what it was all about and had decided it wasn't the best arrangement for her.

It made Kenneth cranky and sad not having a woman in his house. At the same time, he hated spending the hours it required to court and lure some young person into sharing it with him. Consequently, he was often alone.

He tried bullying Marilynn into bed with him, but she said that she was really too busy with her book. He threatened and stormed, but she didn't choose to be frightened. She told him to drop it and go home. He considered hitting her but he didn't do it.

Marilynn said, "I like you very much, Kenneth, but I just have too much to do right now."

Ken could see that she was quite serious and at the same time not trying to put him down. She looked at him when she spoke to him, and she replied quite clearly, but Ken could see that she wasn't really seeing him, not in rapport with anybody, she was writing.

During the war Ken experienced long periods of living without woman's company. He swore then that he would have, after the war, a thousand wives, paramours, concubines, and trained nurses who would wait on his pleasure. In college he had found himself surrounded, it seemed to him, by acres of nubile feminine flesh and he was very happy and confused for three years. Later, he met Helen, they had a long and exciting courtship, and then they married. He began a new kind of education, or reciprocal education. He couldn't say precisely what he had learned, but he saw and felt a number of things in his own private world in quite different lights. These feelings, these areas of his mind, seemed to recede, to begin dimming out, after Helen left him. He gradually forgot them until a meeting with Joan or Kate or Marilynn made him conscious again of these parts of his world, his being. He realized, he became absolutely certain, then, that there was more to his mind, more to the world around him than he could easily keep track of by himself. He realized that living alone made him profoundly insecure, quite as if there were great gaps in the floor of his apartment or in the earth itself through which, if he weren't very careful, he might fall into total withdrawal, total insanity.

He thought about fucking Marilynn. It was exciting and rather uncomfortable, like playing doctor with the neighborhood girls when he was a boy. But Marilynn could never repel him, turn him off, sexually, render him impotent by uttering a few words. Helen could do that if she was in an evil mood. He wondered whether the possession of our desires, their fulfillment, simply makes us nervous. He had for years wanted to see further into, make his way inside of a piece of agate, a crystal ball, a gem. Yesterday, he dropped into a cafeteria for coffee, one of the many in San Francisco which have, as a main feature of their decor, mirrors and tile. He sat halfway towards the back of the long, narrow room...although its true length and width were unguessable because of the mirrors...looking out the window that faced the sidewalk. The window was much longer than it was high, and his view was interrupted and dislocated by a long vertical mirror fixed to a pillar that stood just ahead of him and to the left. He was, he realized, right where he had always wished to be, and without wanting, right then, to be there, in this cafeteria, this absurd twelve-cent coffee and bad beef palace. A woman in a red coat passed by the narrow window. A woman in yellow, a woman wearing grey, they passed by together. Outside.

He was frightened. The fulfillment of an imaginary desire turned out to be like an erotic dream from which he did not wake in the midst of or immediately after an orgasm. The dream story is completed and rolls away to disclose a false void, the popular, even official definition of emptiness. This false emptiness annoyed him as much as the fake movie which preceded it; he was aware of being in what was only an empty theater where he had fallen asleep during the performance. Now everyone had gone away and there he sat in a more or less spooky building, confused, somewhat frightened, but knowing that he would presently get up and find his way out of it.

How far inside! Dimly. He might move, but the gesture would branch out from his fingertips into thousands of hairlines and fractures filled with crystal. He sat still, thinking of the song,

> *Far away places*
> *With strange-sounding names*
>
> *...book that I took from the shelf...*

the mirrors around him shone. Blank eyes, Joan's eyes, Marilynn's eyes with writing or other voices behind them. Helen reflected in the blank, bright chrome-plated toaster. Flare, bright. "Past ruin'd Ilion." Fare thee well.


Ken found Bruce sitting in the swing room. He was leaning back in a chair, a cup of coffee before him. He was looking long, thin, and more wrinkled than usual. A slow card game was happening at another table which was surrounded by a ring of spectators. Ken put a quarter into a green machine which hiccoughed and clanked as it paid him three nickels and a small paper cupful of weak, lukewarm coffee. He carried it to the table where Chadwick sat.

Bruce said he had a headache and wanted Ken to give him some aspirin. Ken said he had none, but that he should drink lots of coffee. The coffee would get his stomach messed up to a point where he wouldn't feel any head pains any more.

"What are you, a smart guy? Give me four bits. I'll slide out the side door and get some pills at the drugstore. I'll sure be glad when I can cut out of this place for good."

Ken said, "I ought to be able to leave in a couple of months."

"Oh yeah?"

"I want to get out of town. I want to make a trip into the mountains. I want fresh air."

"Well, you can take some annual leave and sick leave I guess."

"When I leave, I want to leave here for good. I don't ever want to see this building again, even from the outside."

Chadwick rubbed his head. He'd recently had most of his hair cut off. This made him look older or younger, Kenneth couldn't say which, but it made him look continuously surprised.

"Good," he said.

"I'll have the last of the court costs paid off by that time, and maybe a few bucks for the trip," Ken told him. "I got a letter from Helen yesterday. She thinks she may be pregnant."

"That's nice. What do you think you'll do when you come back from the hills? Get another job?"

"Not if I can help it, not for a while. I have a lot of things I want to start or finish . . . whatever I should call it, I don't really know . . . after a while I'll probably go to work again."

Chadwick stood up and stretched his arms. The joints of his shoulders popped. "I've got to get back to work," he said. "I been in here almost forty minutes. Old Hammerhead is on a rampage tonight. I'm surprised he hasn't come in here to throw everybody out."

"He knows this card game is going and he doesn't want to be bothered with seeing it and telling the guys to break it up. They're a lot of his old timers, the only ones who know all the operations around here, all the systems. They do all his work for him when the schedule gets fouled up or there's a sudden overload of incoming stuff. He doesn't want to pester them."

"Sure," Bruce said. "I guess you've got it all figured out. I'll be seeing you later." He walked slowly out the door back to his job. A small group of men came bustling in the door, bought themselves coffee, and sat down nearby to have an earnest discussion about baseball. Ken finished his coffee and went back to work.

He told the man with the green eyeshade that he had returned. The man looked up, recognized him, nodded once. The two ladies on his left were analyzing U.S. foreign policy as it was conducted between the years of 1946 and 1956. They agreed that they could not give their approval to the policies of the State Department as it was then constituted. The loudspeaker overhead squealed and whistled. It commanded the attendance of Bruce Chadwick in the front office. Ken wondered if somebody had seen Bruce popping out the side door. Then the music resumed, a kind of Sibelius treatment of "Red Sails in the Sunset." The music flowed on high above the ladies' encomiums of President Eisenhower, the late Senator McCarthy, and Stringfellow Barr.

Marilynn had said that it would be a simple dinner, but she took some trouble to provide a very good one. She had lunch at her favorite fish store, then ordered a supply of fresh oysters and salmon to be delivered to her house later in the afternoon. She bought a few choice vegetables and fruits from a shop in Japanese Town. The roast came from a celebrated butcher in North Beach. French bread and soft Teleme cheese came from the same neighborhood. She thought for a moment about pastry, but decided to serve fruit and cheese for dessert. "Why should the *Ladies Home Journal* ladies have all the fun?" she asked herself.

Marilynn seldom enjoyed shopping unless she could see that it made something happen immediately afterwards, as for example this dinner for her cousin. The stuff was carefully selected, it would look good on the table, taste good, it would please her guests and her family, and that would be that—a complete experience, a total composition. On any ordinary day she might make a casserole or a souffle and a salad for herself and children. Travis was seldom at home to dinner any more; the government was rushing him again. Several different agencies wanted to hire him, and the representatives of these agencies had, it would appear, unlimited funds at their disposal. They wined and dined Travis in the best restaurants in town; sometimes Marilynn was invited to go along. Knowing how much Travis enjoyed good food, she had to admire his strength of character in being able to hold out against such blandishments as an especially catered dinner, in a suite at the Fairmount Hotel, which included Beluga caviar, fresh Chinook salmon, haunch of venison, and other delicacies that had been flown in for the occasion.

As Marilynn gave the impression of solidity, calm, and wisdom, so her cousin Kate appeared vivacious, witty, swift-moving. Kate taught French literature in a large state university in one of the northwestern states. She had been to an expensive women's college in the East, and she had spent a number of years in France, studying and traveling. She had been married, for a large part of that period, to an American student whom she had met in Paris, but they had divorced after they returned to the United States. Kate had not remarried. She claimed that it was easier for her to live alone.

Kate was thin without being bony. She was a true redhead, with pale skin, freckles, and bright green eyes.

Kate and Kenneth spent the day together, Kenneth having telephoned his office to say that he was too sick to work. They wandered up and down the city together. They ate crab louis at Fisherman's Wharf. They bought a large frowsy bunch of tough-looking celery and fed it, a few stalks at a time, to the elephants in the zoo, who bowed, curtsied and trumpeted with delight. They drove back to the city and sat in a bar in

North Beach, drinking *espresso* and munching on *cialde*.

"How I love San Francisco!" Kate exclaimed, setting her glass back on the bar. Ken waved at the barman for another round. "I've been finagling by mail for a job in these purlieus. If it comes through, I'll be able to bid farewell to the foggy north forever."

"Then you can come down here and join the search for a habitable apartment," Kenneth said. "And set up a social calendar so that you'll always know what you're going to be doing two weeks in advance, like all the other ladies in town."

"I love social complications! I shall choose a day for holding my own salon. It must include all the most intelligent, rich and handsome men in the city. You must bring them all to me, and Travis must help, too."

"I don't know any such folks," Ken said.

"Painters, writers, musicians, *philosophes*...?"

"Most of them live in Berkeley or Stanford."

"Not San Francisco?"

"Everybody loves San Francisco but nobody lives here. The few who really live here and get some good out of it are New Yorkers who react to the place violently. They want to go home to New York, but they must live here, and that stimulates them to becoming great."

"I like New York," Kate said. "I like Paris, Rome, Florence, and I like it here better. Shouldn't we be getting back to Marilynn's?"

"There's quite a lot of time yet. I'll take you to my place for a drink, an aperitif. I want to change my shirt."

"I don't think that's a very inviting proposition. Don't you have a collection of handmade butterfly wings or anything?"

"I have a new number of the *National Geographic* that you can look at while I change."

"I think you might drop me off at Marilynn's first and then come back. I want to take a bath before supper."

"Take one of mine."

"Could I have one of those fizzy white drinks before we go? What's in them? I always forget the name."

"Liqueur of some kind. I don't remember either...booze, milk, and steam." He asked the bartender to bring him a straight brandy and a White Nun for the lady.


Marilynn and her guests sat at the table drinking coffee and liqueurs. They were worrying about the world.

Kenneth said, "I used to worry because the country, the whole world, seemed to be controlled by a few old men with a few antiquated ideas. Now it appears that all the young people have come around to believing these same old notions. They'll soon be out crusading against anything they think of as being new or different, any kind of change."

"Which old notions are these?" Marilynn inquired.

"That the government, law, society in general, are more valuable than the people, the individuals who created them. That money is the only thing anybody wants and so every person has his price. That the government is so far away and has got the world into such a mess that a man can't do anything except obey the authorities and finally allow himself to be suffocated in an air raid shelter under the direction and guidance of the Civil Defense people."

"Nobody really believes any of that," Travis said. "They may talk that way, they may appear to be acting that way, but I still believe that the old kind of ornery, individualistic American hasn't been taken in. He still persists and I think he'll prevent the really irresponsible ones among our statesmen from blowing us up."

Kate said, "I don't know. I think he disappeared around about 1940—or was killed in the war, that individualist. I see my students, reasonably intelligent kids, they seem to be going the way Ken was saying. They want money, or at least credit cards, and they want to start living like those people who have their pictures in Holiday magazine or Vogue. They all expect, in only a year or so after they get out of school, to be beautifully sun-tanned and fantastically rich."

"Nobody told them that the folks in the pictures have already got all the money and there isn't any more," Travis suggested.

"Exactly," Ken said. "A lot of them are smart enough to know that the system is working, but they expect to join it. They think that it's possible to get some of that moola, that there's enough of it to go around. Everybody can live part of the year in the Waldorf Towers and part of the year in Majorca and make side trips in between to Rio and Singapore and San Francisco just for kicks."

"But there is money enough," Travis said. "The sums that the government turns loose every day in order to fight the war or discover the moon or whatever it is they want—that money isn't just melting or disappearing—it's floating around where you really can grab fair-sized handfuls of it if you want to."

Marilynn said, "That isn't exactly so, Travis. You keep forgetting that not everybody has a college degree in one of the natural sciences. Not all of us can work in places where that government money piles itself up in big drifts. Even people who do will never have the kind of money Ken means, the stuff that grandpa started salting away and which has been sitting there in the bank or in the trusts where it has been multiplying and proliferating for the past thirty or fifty years—more money than even I could spend in a month—and that's the kind of money it takes to live that beautiful gin-soaked, sun-tanned life. Either that or an unlimited expense account."

"So what are you trying to prove?" Travis asked. "That the rich gets all the pleasure and the poor takes all the blime?"

"I don't really believe that," Ken said. "I think everybody is too busy with all this baloney of the gilded existence to care about the fact that their freedom is disappearing. The government has been going hog wild, busting into our personal lives with their anti-communist investigations, they've clamped down on passports, they've declared that most of the continent of Asia doesn't exist or if it does, no American is allowed to go look at it. They have laws against reading books the postmaster general chooses to consider unfit to read. People who don't look like they might be voting a straight Republican or Democratic ticket are thrown out of their jobs as teachers, whether they work in college, grade school, or kindergarten. In the meantime the government ignores the fact that a quarter of the population isn't allowed to vote, isn't allowed to live a decent life..."

Marilynn said, "Well, of course, I hope that they'll all buy eigtheen million copies of my new book. I want a villa on the Bosporus. I want a harpsichord in every other room. I want to send the kiddies to school in England or France, we haven't decided which—anyway, I want them out of here. Did I tell you that I'm really going to New York next week? I'm going to scare the pee out of my dear old publisher. I can't get anything more out of him by telephone."

"Find me a copy of Plotinus when you go," Kenneth said. "I haven't found it in Berkeley or anyplace in town. It takes months to order things—you know how our bookstores are."

"I got a letter from Helen," Marilynn said. "She's on some new kind of pill. She says her husband is now in charge of one of the departments at Boeing."

"Isn't that nice," Kenneth said.

"You're not really of a jealous nature, are you?" Kate asked.

"Of course not," Kenneth said. "I'd only like to wring his neck."

"Have some more brandy," Marilynn said. "Travis, pass the coffee."

"My life is ruined," Kenneth remarked, in a fake theatrical tone.

"I don't see how anyone who lives in San Francisco can be thought of as ruined," Kate said.

"I think it's a case of you Nordic types coming down here and being ruined by the tropical climate," Marilynn said. "Would you rather have gin than brandy?"

"Sewweet Opium and Tea, yo-ho!" Travis sang.

"That particular life was ruined or at least, like they say now, terminated, I know that much," Kenneth said. "Let us now go on to more edifying things."

"I have a new Gerry Mulligan record," Travis said. "Let me play it for you."

"Let us retire to the drawing room, Cousin Kate, and leave the gentlemen to their rum and segars." Marilynn and Kate rose from the table and curtsied simultaneously.

"I declare I forgot to bring my *Em*broidery frame, Cousin Marilynn. I do hope that you have a spare one that you can lend me while I'm here?"

"Why, Sugar, here at Belle Reve we got everything. We'll just ring for Butterfly."

"We better ring right soon. If I have to curtsy again, I'll need help getting up off the floor."

"Gentlemen," Marilynn said, and left the room with Kate, both of them whooping and laughing.


The pay-day came, at last, when Kenneth was able to put the final check into an envelope addressed to Helen's lawyer. He celebrated a large weekend; there was a party at Chadwick's house; he had a hangover all day Sunday. On Monday he went to work. He had been working for nearly two hours before the thought struck him that he was at last working for himself. The next paycheck he could bank or spend on ice cream cones, whatever he wanted to use it for. He paused, in his working, long enough to light a cigaret. He figured that if he wanted to, he could leave the office right now and never come back. They owed him a week's pay, vacation pay, sick leave, and the money he had been forced to contribute to the retirement fund. He smiled to himself. He kept working. He decided to quit at the end of the week. He went into the swing room and bought himself a cup of coffee.

He worked through Friday, but he was tired on Friday night, his nose hurt, he left the building without remembering to write out a resignation form. He returned to work on Monday. He intended to work this one more day and then resign formally at the end of the shift. Then he remembered that if he quit at the beginning of a work week there'd be an endless delay, because the finance office would need weeks in which to prepare a final check. He must reconcile himself to working until the end of the present week, the next regular payday. That way he'd have a fair sum of cash on hand when he resigned. He was afraid that it would be hard to wait that long, but the days went by very fast, there was a great deal of work, many hours of overtime.

On Friday night, he received his paycheck, and in return, he passed his resignation papers to the man at the window.

"You leaving the service, hah? You sign these all okay? You give me the badge. You give me the locker key after you get your coat and clean out your locker. They'll mail your checks in a couple of weeks."

As he went towards the guarded exit, Ken felt naked without his official badge. He walked nervously past the guards, one of them said, "Good night." Kenneth smiled nervously and replied, in a somewhat shaky voice, "Goodbye."


Long before he was awake, Kenneth had been looking into the bright sunlight and leaves beyond the window. That was where he lay. That is I, he told himself. He felt cramped in bed but the air in the room was damp and chilly enough to make him put off the moment of actually arising. At last he managed to get up and get dressed.

He went out to the back porch. The sun was warm, the air very still and fresh. Huge leaves of hollyhock shape, dark furry green and fat, had begun to spread and cover the ground between the back porch and the pepper tree, which dangled thin strands of paired light green leaves down past its gnarly trunk and branches. The porch floor boards, the tall posts that supported the floor above, the stairway which descended across the center of the scene, all were grey as the trunk of the pepper tree. The bay in the distance was yellowy blue.

He went back into the kitchen and put the teakettle on the stove to boil. He turned on the little radio. A recording of *The Well Tempered Clavier* was playing. He put a pair of eggs in a pan and covered them with cold water and put the pan on the fire. Then he sat down to listen to the music.

When the eggs came to a boil, he took the pan off the fire, and put a couple of pieces of bread into the toaster. When the toast was done, he removed the eggs from the pan, ran cold water over them for a few seconds, then opened the eggs into a cup. He buttered the toast, poured himself a cupful of instant coffee, and then sat down to eat his breakfast.

He didn't read the morning newspaper, although it lay where he had placed it on the kitchen table. He listened to the music instead. After he had eaten, he washed the dishes, cleaned the kitchen, and turned the radio off.

He brushed his teeth and shaved very carefully. He made faces at himself in the mirror. Then he turned off the lights, put on his jacket, and left the house.

He walked the whole length of Golden Gate Park to Ocean Beach. He went into one of the restaurants facing the ocean and had a piece of pie and a cup of coffee while he looked out the window upon the sunny ocean.


It struck him that he had reached the feeling or condition which was the exact opposite of the feeling of collapse, or of disintegration. Today he knew that he was free to choose . . . anything; he was also aware that if he didn't want to choose or want to think about anything, he was free to sit, stand, walk, or he might lie in the bathtub doing nothing. The air was calm. The sun shone. The old hallucination of scornful crowds looking briefly back at him as the world glided off with them into bright pleasure and music had gone. He was alone, relatively speaking, but there were a great many other people in San Francisco. They were busy driving bread trucks and selling nonskid garters. Let them. Who needs them will call them. If he wanted to talk to anyone, Ken knew that he could telephone one of his friends and pay a visit.

He wanted to be walking. He didn't want to be visiting anyone. The people in the street he was free to ignore or examine, just as he chose.

They were free to look at him. There he was.

He didn't feel very strongly about anything, just this moment. He was relieved from worrying about his debt, from having to think about going to work. He enjoyed the sunlight which seemed to have enlarged the city, magnified the day.

From time to time he idly wondered, "What next?" What would the encore be, what would the next trip be like? For he imagined that one way or another he was bound to step, all unconsciously, onto the large round balanced metal plate, which, under his weight, would swing downwards, setting into motion a giant Rube Goldberg machine that would manufacture more trouble, more bother, and reduce him again to a condition of desolation wherein he could do nothing but count plaster apples and flowers.


Kate asked Marilynn, "Why did Kenneth get so upset when you mentioned having heard from Helen? I thought he must be used to the idea of being divorced from her, after all this time."

Marilynn said, "He's a monogamist—a masochist—something—I must go look at the children. I imagine that Dottie is reading her eyes out."

Together they went upstairs where Marilynn found her sons asleep and in the other room, Dottie still awake and reading.

"Go to sleep, now, Dottie. It's late."

"Oh, Mother!"

"What're you reading, Dot?" Kate inquired.

"*Lady Susan with a Memoyer.*" Dottie held up a small leather-bound volume by Jane Austen.

"Honey, Kate is going to think you're illiterate if you don't come on with a better French accent than that."

"What, Mother?"

"Never mind. You go to sleep, now. Tell Kate goodnight."

"Goodnight, Cousin Kate."

"Goodnight, Dottie."

The child sighed and turned out her lamp. The women left the room and crossed the hall, into the upstairs sitting room.

Marilynn muttered to Kate, "I always linger around for a while in the hope that she'll really go to sleep if she knows I can see if she turns her light on again. Usually I can wait longer than she can."

"I used to read in bed with a flashlight under the covers," Kate said.

Marilynn looked into a mirror and patted her hair.

Kate asked, "You say he's still in love with her?"

Marilynn said, "Who?"

Kate replied, "Kenneth and Helen."

"I have good reason to think so," Marilynn replied. She turned to look at Kate. "He told me—well, *he* said so."

Kate said, "That's certainly awkward."

"Kate, what are you doing, going gaga at this late period of history?"

"That's just it. It *is* a late period of history, I'm growing more historical every minute. I'm losing my looks. I'm tired of living half in and half out of that false cloister. I want to have a private life."

Marilynn looked at her again, and then she remarked: "If you want something, you better go get it, like Bernard Shaw says. Personally, I don't think Kenneth—"

"I don't know," Kate said. "I think he might be admirable. I wonder more about myself, whether I've become too old and dried up."

"Kate, you know I've always been quite fond of Kenneth. In a lot of ways, he's wonderfully perceptive, a very understanding person. He really does have, in a way, what people used to call a sweet nature. But you see how he can be. . .jealous; and at the same time, he's really awfully self-indulgent when it comes to sexual matters. Helen left him because she was tired of his constant demands as well as his tom-catting around."

Kate said, rather sharply, "What?"

"Helen told me that she tried and tried to get him to see a psychiatrist. She felt that it was more than just promiscuity."

"Listen, Marilynn, Helen has always been a great friend of yours, and that's between you two. All I know is, that in Seattle, everyone has always believed that Helen ran away from Kenneth because he wouldn't support her properly, that he wouldn't work. He was supposed to be a surly drunken brute. When she had a chance to run away with Ronald, she left him."

"Nonsense," Marilynn said. "You know Kenneth better than that."

"Any of our friends in Seattle will tell you—but of course they all say that you're too snooty to write to them any more."

"Is that so?"

"Of course some people made the usual cute remarks when Helen's first child was born, all about how premature babies are a superstition and so on, but Helen is still received into polite society and her husband seems contented, the boys named after Ronnie's father. Fortunately Kenneth lives here and has no plans to take up residence in Seattle."

"Them Yankees," Marilynn said. "They all the time talking about votes for women but they got no respect for a lady."

"I've seen them myself. He's a darling little boy who is the absolute image of Kenneth, round blond head and all. If Kenneth is still interested in Helen, it's quite natural: she's the mother of his son. It isn't a matter of great unrequited love at all."

Marilynn laughed. She lit a fresh cigaret and then she told Kate, "I'll tell you something. Kenneth doesn't know anything about that baby except that Helen had it after she went away with Ronnie. Helen hasn't told him and neither has anyone else. I've known Helen for quite a long time; I believe I know what to expect from her. . .from any of the people I'm interested in. I expect to be surprised. I thought, for example, that we

80

might find Dottie reading some slimy comic book, or something even more unsuitable."

Kate laughed. She stood up and began to pace slowly up and down before the fireplace. "What must you think of me—something like an old movie of Bette Davis?"

"Not exactly, no. I told you that if you want something go and get it.

"Are you saying, like Diaghilev, '*Etonne-moi*'?"

"I'm saying that I'm about to go to New York. I'm actually too interested in my own affairs right now to care terribly much about what anybody else does. I'd like it if you made a happy marriage, if you could get along with Kenneth. You know I like him myself, he takes spells from time to time of imagining that I'm still an interesting woman—suit yourself."

"Why not," Kate said.

"Why indeed not. Let us rejoin the gentlemen."

Kate looked at her. "Who's being Bette Davis now?"

"I thought that Miriam Hopkins was more my line. Come along."

Kate didn't move. She said, "Marilynn, I think you're going to end up becoming a pious fraud."

"If you say so," Marilynn replied, smiling brightly.

"You mean you're willing to accept the consequences of being whatever you are, and so it's all right."

"If you put it that way, yes. Precisely. The consequences of being myself are educational and also enormously entertaining. Even if they aren't particularly attractive to other people. I do what I must. I'm too lazy to do more."

"I think that I'm as strong as you, in that case," Kate said.

"It isn't a case of power, but of clearly seeing and knowing what you want and what you're doing and how you enjoy it (or not)—and how, finally, you disengage yourself from it. It's really very simple," Marilynn told her.

"It doesn't seem simple to me. I never heard of anything so tangled in my life. That's why I say you're likely to become a fraud. How can I act in the middle of all that kind of casuistry? How can I know, now, what I want to do, what it is I think?"

"I'll tell you more plainly. Eating chocolate cake may or may not give you indigestion...assuming that you do like chocolate cake, I just mean it for an example. It may be that you know it'll disagree with you every time, in which case you're supposed to be smart enough never to eat it again. It may be that it only makes you sick if you eat it before breakfast, in which case you make sure to have it only at dinner or supper. But it may be that you don't know that much about your relationship to the stuff. If you like it, find out about it. Really decide to have it, enjoy it as completely as possible. It may be that you'll be able to take it or leave it alone, after a while. It may be that you'll have to build yourself a universe that will absolutely preclude the existence of chocolate cake if you want to go on living a satisfactory human life. That's what I have to say."

"It may be clear to you, but it's over my head. I'll have to think about it," Kate said. "Thanks anyway."

"That's the whole thing as I see it," Marilynn said. "Feel free to try it. Feel free to make what you can of it. Have a ball."

"Thanks piles," Kate said. "Let's go."


Ken finished his pie and coffee, then he got another cupful and sat down to drink it. He didn't much enjoy the taste of it but he wanted it while he smoked a cigaret. He smoked and looked out the window. On weekends, all the poor of San Francisco, Northern California, and Missouri were used to walking up and down the great promenade outside. This being a weekday, there were very few walkers—old men from the neighborhoods nearby, high school students playing hookey, a couple of sailors looking at the ocean.

Ken went out of the restaurant and began walking north towards the Cliff House. The sea lions had come back; there they were stacked up on the islets just offshore, barking and diving into the sea. He looked to the north again and saw the clear profile of Mt. Tamalpais against the sky. He thought to himself, "Of course. If it doesn't rain, I'll go walking there tomorrow."

He remembered his little car with a pang of regret. It had been sold to a collector in order to extract from it Helen's portion of it, in its character as "community property." He had done without it for more than two years.

Ken telephoned Bruce Chadwick and asked him for a ride to the trail's end on Mt. Tamalpais. Bruce agreed to meet him early in the morning. Ken spent hours inspecting his walking shoes, his pack, his trail map, quite as if he were planning a summer in the Himalayas instead of a few hours in a state park. In the morning he found himself in a state of indecision as to what book he wanted to carry with him.

Bruce arrived, complaining about the early hour, about how Kenneth had browbeaten him into performing huge favors in the darkest and gloomiest part of the day. He demanded coffee, grapefruit, eggs, waffles, little pig sausages, Kenneth must feed him instantly. And why hadn't he been invited to go along on this hike. Was his company no longer suitable for such an occasion?

Kenneth poured a cup of coffee and brought it to Bruce. "I want a nice quiet day outside, that's why I want to go alone. We can make a trip into the Sierra later—Travis wants to go too."

"I refuse to spend any more time in the Sierra with Travis," Bruce said. "He stays in bed, once you make camp. I end up having to find all the wood and carry all the water while Travis lies in the sack complaining about his feet and about having a headache and how he's cold and hungry. Then when dinner's ready he scrooches over to the fire and holds out his dish for chow."

Ken said, "I know, that's your story. I've always kicked him and made him get up. If he refuses, I shove his head down inside the sack and tie it shut. Then I won't let him out until he promises to behave."

"You're some kind of disciplinarian, all right," Bruce said. "Are you ready to go? We better get started. It looks rainy."

They got into Bruce's car and set out. The fog and clouds loured close above the city's hills. The sky was grey and dim until they drove just beyond the center of the Golden Gate Bridge. The sun came out brightly and the sky was a brilliant blue over the hills.

Bruce said, "I got a card from Marilynn in New York. Wystan took her to lunch at Rockefeller Center. Carson is still mad at her and Bunny says hello. The book club people are buying her novel."

"No kidding." Ken looked out the windows at the Bay and the sky. He said, "I wonder what she'll do next. Maybe she really will have a marble palace overlooking the Bosporus."

When they arrived on the shoulder of the mountain, they could see that the fog had cleared away enough so that the northeastern edge of the city and Coit Tower were visible. To the west, the Pacific lay blue and limitless. A dark blue fogbank far at sea obliterated the boundary between sky and water. The sun was hot on the mountain. The trees in Muir Woods, below the ridge where they stood, were sharply outlined in the bright air, as were the meadows and groves on the mountain above them. There were only a few cars parked at the trail end. A couple of walkers were visible on the steep hogback trail almost directly overhead.

Ken got his pack out of the car and put it on. Bruce helped him adjust the straps.

"There you go," Bruce said. "Can you get back all right?"

"I'll hike down into Mill Valley and take the bus back to town. I won't get lost."

"I wish I didn't have to work today."

"There's a phone at the inn right here; call up and tell them you're sick."

"Nah...I can't. I was off one day last week, and now Old Hammerhead screams every time he sees me. I got to go. I'll see you later."

Bruce got into his car and drove off down the hill. Already sweating in the sun, Ken began to walk up the dirt road behind the fire station. A young buck sprang out of the bushes and dashed across the road in front of him and plunged into the brush on the other side of the road and then down towards the trees in the gully below.

Some of the brush was blooming—wild lilac, several kinds of broom, and thorn trees with bright red and yellow or intense magenta-colored flowers. There were wild irises, star lilies and Indian paintbrush all in bloom. Bluejays and doves flew clumsily among the short pines and manzanitas. Miniscule wrens and tits rushed about through the leaves like insects. Lizards jumped out of the way as Ken walked along. He stopped for a drink of water near the tanks at the trail junction, the point where the ridge connects with the main bulk of the mountain. He looked eastward and saw the white stone campanile on the Cal Campus, in Berkeley far across the Bay. The sharp top of Mt. Diablo rose above the hills behind Oakland. In the pebbly clay at his feet he saw prints of many walking boots with lug soles, stamped into the clay when it was wet, and now baked by the sun into hard castings. There were fresh deer tracks in the moist dirt near the drinking fountain.

Ken set off slowly along the level fire road towards the start of the Matt Davis Trail. The West Peak rose before him, looking, today, very classical and civilized, with all its shades of green, its isolated groves of laurel and alder, of redwood and pine, appearing at various levels across the south face. It reminded him of pictures he'd seen of Italy, and he thought of Shelley sitting lost in thought beside that pool in the piney woods while Trelawny wandered around hunting for him, calling his name. (Did he holler "Shelley!" or "Percy!"?) Shelley sat there high out of his mind with antique poetical vision, knowledge of death, beauty, love and all delight, himself angelically beautiful and utterly mad...partly by inheritance, partly by choice, but mostly by his gorgeous blind drive to free himself and the world...

A small rock turned beneath Kenneth's boot-sole and he nearly fell on his head. He swore. Then he felt angry with himself for letting such a small thing upset him. He walked on, distracted from himself in the next minute by the rushing whirr of hawks' wings directly overhead, a pair of them hunting the road for bunnies. Ken recovered his feeling of delight with the scene and the day by the time he reached Fern Creek. He stood on the foot bridge and looked down the small steep ravine. Small as it was, great redwoods grew there, as well as huge old laurel, alder, and madrone trees. The creek fell down over short rocky cascades into pools and elbows of smooth water. The stone of the creek bed was partly old shale, partly the crumbly, scaly green serpentine stone which cropped out at different locations all over the mountain. The water roared as it dashed along. Kenneth watched it, feeling temporarily free of ideas or wishes; there was only the sound of water. He felt that he ought, perhaps, to move on. The sound was meaningless, hypnotic, mildly dangerous, but he loved to watch the water. He listened, he looked; the water flashed or was dark in sun and shade. He broke away from it, suddenly, and continued his walk.

The path changed under his feet; first there were pebbles and clay, then fallen leaves of bay and oak, then rock, then redwood needles and twigs. The sun was almost too hot in the open; the deepest shade was almost too cool. Blue flowering hound's tongue sprang up beside the trail. Creamy lily-of-the-valley-shaped madrone blossoms opened overhead. Above a tiny rivulet that crossed the trail there flew a pair of startling blue dragon flies.

Ken rested a short time at Bootjack Camp. Although it was still early

84

in the spring, there were voices on the hillside and a couple of cars in the parking lot downhill from the camp; a white canvas tent stood among the trees on the opposite side of the creek. He could see none of the inhabitants; they were nearby, speaking and calling to each other, but he never caught sight of them. He walked through the campground and onto the trail again. Presently he was beginning the steep climb up the Easy Grade Trail to the Mountain Theater. It seemed, by the time he reached the top of the hill behind the theater, that he had worked hard almost thoughtlessly, almost without effort. Pleased with himself, he sat down and smoked a cigaret.

The city shone brilliantly in the distance; the fog had entirely dispersed. From where he sat, it appeared that the level of the ocean was higher than the Bay. There seemed no reason why the city should not be engulfed, but the enormous blue mound of the sea—a cabochon sapphire—lay against the endless shore, irrationally and completely beautiful.

Here he was where he'd feared that he might arrive, having seen what there is to see, having had several kinds of lives, recognizing his present state as one of neutrality, disengagement. It seemed that the whole concept of futurity—the notion of next year, tomorrow, the coming night or the next hour—had fallen away, had lost any meaning or existence. There was nothing more to be done. He wouldn't burn his fingers on the now very short cigaret; he stripped it and smeared the tobacco into the dirt, wadded the paper into a minute ball and threw it away. He got tired of sitting; he stood up, adjusted his pack, and set off towards the top of the mountain.

At last he sat among the rocks looking out over the steep hills and valleys north towards Mt. St. Helena and the bigger Coast Range mountains. The Pacific lay immense and silent to the west.

The earth was plainly a garden, a park, a being having its own life. There were minor lumps and blisters here and there about the surface, outcroppings of artificial rock and garbage that men are pleased to call cities, nations, empires. But even these weren't really alien to or different from the rest of what there was, what appeared to the eye. The men and tin cans were a phase of a larger expression, a bigger composition that was working itself out regardless of the notions or wishes or theories of the men who thought of themselves as being in complete control of the entire show. Here it all was in the sun, or, as Ken was fond of thinking, temporarily bright, actually it all existed in endless darkness and silence, a being that was acting out its own curious desires and their consequences. It had been born, it was of a certain age, and it would—if men didn't annihilate it—one fine day, die and decompose. The process had all happened before and would probably continue. There was a local, a parochial concern today about whether men and women and children shall be permitted to live in this world. It appeared to Kenneth that they were nearly all convinced that they wanted to stop, that they were tired of the show, that they wanted to leave the world before it left them. Kenneth sighed. He felt his muscles beginning to stiffen. The wind was blowing rather annoyingly, now, in his ears. Why can't they let it alone? Why do they want to die? Why must they blow up the world at the same time? Why should I, Ken wondered, go on worrying about it? I've had my lives and times, they have been both great and miserable, I can let it go. I hate to think of the annoyance and chagrin of all these people who are going to wake up dead some morning and complain that they've been cheated.

"Some other guy, out of ignorance, jealousy, fear, greed or despair, pushed the GONE button and here we—innocent, beautiful, brilliantly intelligent, all-virtuous we—are suddenly and most unwillingly translated into Beulah Land before we even had a chance to drive the new 1975 Dragonmobile Special XR 508 with radium transmission and automatic pleasure control switches. What an injustice! What a crime! Bring us back! Bring us back!"

Kenneth looked out at his world: blue, rocky, green and sunshine, plenty of fresh air from the sea—then he set off, down the trail to the village below. He knew what he had to do. Start over.

# III

While Marilynn was in New York, her cousin Kate made a more or less unexpected appearance in San Francisco. At least Travis was surprised when Kate telephoned him to ask if she might come to stay at his house for a very short visit. He assured her that he'd be delighted. He'd take her to the opera. (The government people had pressed the tickets upon him as a gift—rather pointlessly or carelessly, he thought. He knew that they possessed a complete dossier on his entire history and character; apparently these particular agents hadn't read it all or had forgotten that he was a regular annual subscriber to the opera. They had wasted their money. And Travis had declined, once more, to work for the AEC or the CIA or whichever bureau of the government these people claimed to represent.)

Kate told him that she was to have an interview with the French

Department at the University; she would be in the city Friday and fly back home on Sunday. She could have made it down and back in one day but she absolutely refused, she told Travis, to knock herself out. She'd be delighted to see the opera.

"If you tell me what time your plane comes in, maybe I could arrange to pick you up and bring you to the city—or ask Ken if he would—"

"No, thanks," Kate told him. "There'll be a rented car waiting for me—I arranged it from here. I don't want to make a lot of bother. I know all you people are busy all the time. I shall be at your house between five and six p.m. Friday, if it's all right with you."

Travis laughed. He said, "You've got it all figured out, have you?"

"I've never been slow when it came to making up my mind. I'll see you when I get there. How's Marilynn?"

"She'll be phoning again tonight, I expect.I'll tell her you're coming down."

"Give her my love."

Travis could guess what it was that Kate had decided. He telephoned Kenneth's house, but no one answered.

By the time he arrived home on that Friday—somewhat belatedly—he found that Kate had already been shown to the guest room and was, according to Mrs. Fynch (the temporary housekeeper-governess-maid-cook and butler) occupied with bathing and bedizening herself against the evening's jollifications. Travis went to his own quarters to refresh and array himself. When he had finished, he came downstairs to find Kate in the kitchen, chatting with Mrs. Fynch and the children, who were eating their dinner.

Dottie reproved him. "Poppa, you should wear tails for the opera, especially since Cousin Kate has a formal."

Kate laughed. She said, "Honey, this is only a cocktail dress. I wouldn't get really gussied up unless we were going to the opening night."

"That's where she got the idea," Travis said. "Marilynn wanted to go on the first night last year in order to see what it was like. It reminded me of something out of *Humphrey Clinker*."

"Momma looked like Catherine the Great," Dottie said.

Her younger brother, Henry, asserted that his mother had sparkled considerably on that occasion. Dottie told him to shut up and eat his supper. Clancy maintained a dignified silence.

"I think you're stupid," Henry replied. "Momma didn't look like a grape. I wish I were going with you tonight, Cousin Kate. I know all the songs." Henry began to sing the sheepherder's song from the last part of *Tosca*.

Kate laughed. Travis reproved Henry for singing at the table and promised to take both children to the next matinee.

Mrs. Fynch brought a salad and some sandwiches to Kate and Travis in the living room.

87

"I thought we'd have a snack before we go," Travis said. "We can eat a proper supper after the show."

"Oh, thanks, Travis, that was very thoughtful of you—I'm starved, actually. Thanks, Mrs. Fynch, I'm sorry to make so much extra work."

"How was your day?" Travis asked her.

"Splendid. They're giving me a contract. I must say it's a good one. I'm to begin next fall."

"Congratulations. We'll be glad to have you for a fellow citizen."

"I've decided to stop complaining about the weather and start doing something about it."

"Excellent. I took the liberty of telling Ken that you were coming down this week-end."

Kate laughed. She asked, "How is he?"

"I haven't seen much of him lately—not since Bruce Chadwick's wedding. But he was in fine shape then—of course, all of us were."

"No doubt. What did Marilynn say—or have you telephoned her since I talked with you the other night?"

"She said that she hoped you'd get things fixed up the way that you want them to be. She thought it was high time. If you're around when she calls again—and I expect that she'll call tomorrow, because she didn't today (and if she doesn't call tomorrow, I'm going to call her)—I'll let you know and you can talk to her yourself. I'm sure she'd like to hear your news directly."

"Why thank you, Travis. If I'm in the house at the time, I'd appreciate it. Only don't grin so owlishly. I'm not expecting the world to become totally subject to my whims right away."

"You foresee a long campaign?"

"Damn it, Travis, I can't afford any long campaigns. I'm too old and ugly. If it were a *matter* of a campaign, which it isn't."

"Propinquity and sunshine should work wonders. I think you're looking very well."

"Thank you very much. Now please do me the favor of changing the subject."

"I was only joking, Kate. Marilynn always says that I kid around too heavy-handedly."

"That's all right, Travis. Being alone for all these years makes me a little over-defensive. Shall we go? I think it's nearly time."

"As soon as I see that the children are put away. I'll only be a minute," Travis said. He went upstairs.

Kate looked into her glass, poured herself a small slug of white wine and drank it. She stood up and walked across the room to look at herself in a mirror. Her hair was in place and so was each freckle. She sighed, thinking of her face as a kind of ruined landscape. She didn't realize that her sharply defined Greek profile and her splendid heavy hair were quite unchanged, nor was she able to catch that look which others saw in her great eyes, a gaze which at once met and fiercely demanded of the world that it conform with her intense and exalted vision of it. She could never truly know that she was a magnificent looking woman.

She turned as Travis came running down the stairs, and she wondered at his momentary appearance of surprise and great interest as he caught sight of her. Travis smiled and said, "Come on. Everybody's fine."

Travis wondered if it would be incest or something else uncanonical if he seduced his wife's cousin. He thought she was looking extraordinarily beautiful this evening. Marilynn was gone, and he knew that Kenneth had gone, for the weekend, to Joan Chadwick's lodge at Lake Tahoe.


Marilynn wanted to go home. She was tired of walking about New York looking for buildings and other places she had known, only to find that they'd been turned into parking lots, large square glass buildings, or half-demolished ruins. The same thing seemed to have happened to such of her New York friends and acquaintances who still lived in the city. A great many had migrated to the West Coast, some were living in Europe or the Orient, and the rest had hidden themselves in upstate or New England villages a few hours away from town.

Looking at the city from the Park or from Morningside Heights it seemed to Marilynn that the pace was more than half deserted. She was surprised that when she took a ride on the subway—she wanted to see if it might have been changed—she saw nothing of the huge crowds of people in the stations or in the cars, the crowds that had so frightened her when, during her student years, she used to visit the city in order to hear an opera or to visit the museums. She could imagine the subways being at last forgotten, but operating forever, mindlessly, empty except for their cargos of yellow light.

New York looked like a great idea that had interested a lot of people thirty years before her present visit. Almost all of these people had since walked away from it and had occupied themselves with something else. The island itself, undeniably real and beautiful, sparkled quietly in the sun; it was a rock in the River.

Her editor asked her, "Aren't you having a good time in town or what?"

"Sure," Marilynn replied. "I haven't been here more than ten days, everybody's still glad to see me, still giving me dinners and parties and planning excursions to entertain me. But by this time next week I'm not going to be new or interesting any longer. People are going to be casting about for something more exciting, something more entertaining."

"You mean we're all consumers here...but you know lots of people who turn out work that even you must admit is important, has validity, who have lived here for years."

"Oh yes. All the giants: Auden, Barzun, Cowley, the Trillings, Edmund Wilson. We read nothing but The New Yorker back home—can't wait for the latest issue."

"What are you, salty or what?"

"What do you expect? I live in the sticks."

"Why don't you move back to town? Nobody said you had to live out on the coast. I personally happen to know that orange juice is cheaper here."

Marilynn winced inwardly at the sound, his 'arrraange jus," the slurred or misplaced "r's." She said, "Listen, I've only been back here a little over a week and I'm sick of it already. Nobody lives here any more, I don't even see many people on the street. You tell me Martin is in Ceylon, Tom is up the Hudson playing quoits, Keesler's in Europe—nothing's happening here in your own office."

"You got the check didn't you? You got the contract right there didn't you? What more do you want?"

"Why isn't Martin here to take me to lunch in the Palace of the Fourteen Caesars and give me the check himself?"

"He's in Bombay, I told you. I can get him on the phone if you want to talk to him, although it's probably yesterday there or next week or whatever. What should you care? You now own an undivided one-eighth interest in the U.S. book trade, a piece of a movie that will bring in royalties for the next ten years, fan mail from all the Sitwell family—what more you want?"

"I want you to get me a ticket on the next jet to San Francisco. I want you to get me a cab to take me to my hotel. I'm going there to get my things packed so that by the time the limousine comes to take me to the airport, I'll be ready to go. I'll be ready and waiting from three o'clock on. It's now one-thirty."

"Why not stick around, Marilynn? Everybody still loves you, everybody still wants to see you—you getting paranoid or something? Let me take you out to West Babylon for a nice dinner, Bessie wants to see you. We can have a quiet evening at home, or you can stay the weekend, whatever you want. It's quiet there and very private."

"I wouldn't be caught dead in any Babylon or Ur-or-the-Chaldees-on-Hudson—I don't mean to hurt your feelings or Bessie's, I really appreciate your invitation—but I want to go home. You understand. You and Bessie come to my place for dinner. Fly out and put it on the company tab. Tell them you're scouting a hot new property in Fresno. They can take it out of their income tax. Right now, I want out of this town fast. If Martin gets back from Bombay, tell him to come by my place for cocktails. Tell him to phone first, though. Make sure I'm there."

"You are salty, but then you're tired. You're the best writer we got; I can put up with your nerves, it's all right. No offense. Just write me another one next year, okay?"

Marilynn explained what she was going to do to him that would render him incapable of reading another word or performing much else if he didn't instantly call a cab to come and take her away.

"I'll take you down to the front door and pay the taxi in advance, just to show you there's no hard feelings."

Marilynn thanked him. They went out.

Marilynn returned to her hotel, ordered a pitcher of martinis sent to her room, then went up and began packing. She thought of how Travis and the children were looking, and about her house—the big brown shingled place with a tiny garden in front and tall trees behind, its view of the Bay from the east side of Potrero Hill. It was large and comfortable enough, certainly, but the ocean wasn't visible from there. Marilynn hoped that she'd be able to persuade her husband that the house she planned to buy would be just as comfortable. It was a huge old Victorian family home near the Buena Vista park. Its front windows overlooked part of the Golden Gate park and the ocean; the side and back windows faced the city and the Bay. The main rooms and passageways were paneled with dark redwood. The main staircase—whether mahogany or walnut—ascended in a gorgeous half-spiral to the floor above. Marilynn thought, I'll buy it anyway, even if I have to take the bus there and back every day. I want to sit in that tower and look at the ocean. If Travis doesn't want to move, we won't. I'm going to just sit there three hours a day and mess around. Maybe I'll write another book. Maybe I'll study Sanskrit. Maybe I'll become a junky. I'm going to have that place. I'll do it there, whatever it is."

Joan Chadwick's house at Lake Tahoe was built for use as a ski lodge. It had a steep roof and a knotty pine or wormy cedar—some kind of modern wood—paneled interior. One end of the house was a glass wall that went from the sundeck straight up to the roof ridge, under the gable. It faced on the lake. The view was interrupted—or improved, Ken thought—by the trunks of some very large conifers that stood a few yards down the hill from the house.

The sun was warm. Joan and Kenneth lay together on mats on the sundeck, slowly baking. At frequent intervals, one or the other of them—after a short debate—would get up, blunder into the kitchen, and make up another pitcher of sloe gin highball.

Joan asked him, "Do you ever think of marrying again? I couldn't."

Kenneth opened one eye and looked at her. She was lying flat on her stomach on the mat, and he lay beside her in the same position except that his head was turned to look at her. With her suntan, her black hair and huge eyes, she reminded him of the girl in the Gauguin painting, *The Spirit of the Dead Watches.*

"Sure," he said. "I'm going to marry a sailor, nineteen years old, six-foot-two, sunburnt and tatooed. He'll be at sea most of the time and I'll have all those government allotment checks to spend."

"What'll you do when he comes home on leave?" Joan inquired.

He seized her, wordlessly, and she laughed. "Are you really as bad off for money as all that?" she asked.

"Not really. I can always get a job. What I want to do is sit around for a while and do some philosophy. A couple days ago, I was able to get a few notes down on paper—after about three weeks of figuring."

"Are you going to do a book?"

"Nah. Maybe just a little paper with a few questions. I don't know enough. Maybe I could write something later, but it's discouraging. I've been away from it for so long. It all takes such a lot of time reading or simply sitting still doing nothing, or taking long walks in no particular direction."

She opened her eyes and looked at him. "Is that all you really want? Just wander around thinking lovely thoughts and sometimes writing them down? You used to fuss about wanting a family."

"Oh, yes—I want a family, a home, I want to walk around, eat steak every day, I want more gin—I want everything. Quite naturally."

"And I already have everything—pretty much the way I want it," Joan said. "It takes up a lot of my time, though. I see what you mean. What if I were to marry you?"

"What?" Kenneth inquired, quite flatly.

"I was thinking that I'm probably too old to have children with any ease or grace—and I have no idea who'd watch the store—but yes: What would you do? Would you write your notes and take your walks—or would you just sit around and drink gin and talk about it?"

"I'd get drunk every night and beat you, of course."

"I wouldn't put it past you. The way you say that you and Helen used to carry on, maybe you ought to have a sailor for a sparring partner."

"Come on."

"I withdraw my proposal."

"Don't withdraw any farther than the kitchen. The ice ought to be frozen by now."

"Don't be flip," Joan said. "I really want you to listen to me."

He reached over and patted her. "I'm listening," he said.

"We could have a very quiet, very pleasant kind of life. If I really can't have any children, we can adopt some. You can have all the family life you want."

"You're always busy," Kenneth complained. "Always having to travel. I'd never see you."

"There'd be the children for you to look at. You could be teaching them Greek or something."

Kenneth laughed. He said, "You are a wicked woman. Trying to seduce me out of my pickle tub into the delights of international society." He seized her again and they rolled about on the deck, laughing and struggling. The pitcher spilled and they were presently daubed with luke-warm pink gin and gingerale.

Joan said, "I've got to go wash—I can't stand being sticky a second longer. Let me up."

"You're so sweet," Kenneth said, giving her a lick. Joan squealed and broke away. She ran into the house, laughing.

Later in the day, they wandered slowly through the woods and up the hill behind the house. There was a view of the valley, its meadows and forests. The big granite Sierra peaks rose above them all around.

Joan said, "You're right, as usual—I wasn't thinking seriously. We want different things. I'm as selfish as you are."

Ken held her. "Who knows what he wants?" he said. "I know—you know, yourself, you've been married before—that our living in the same house would make a new place, a strange kind of color or feeling that neither of us knows anything about right now. It could be sloppy and ugly or it could be a ball, depending on how we went at it. The question is, do you have the time, do you want to do this—would *I* rather do this than write my papers and study."

Joan sighed. She turned away from him, to look at the view of water and trees. "I don't know, after all," she said. "You make it sound so mechanical or like a psychology experiment or something..."

"I'm too old and set in my ways to take a romantic vine-covered cottage love-nest Blue Room attitude, or to experiment with that kind of feeling any more. We get along fine right now...but think how it would be, having me around all the time, seeing me every day. I plan to be doing nothing in the way of working outside at a job; I'll be home a great deal of the time."

"Slothful beast. Do you mean that you couldn't stand to have me reproach you for not being a big successful businessman who spends all day in an office?"

"That's it. I've heard too much about the dignity of toil, about a little hard work never hurt anybody. It's hurt me as much as it ever will. I'm out of it until my shoes wear out. Then maybe I'll steal a pair."

"You're serious, aren't you? I don't know if I could enjoy it now—I've been living as I please for so long. If it could be like today, I'd lock you into the house and drive like mad to kidnap a Justice of the Peace and have him marry us. But then, my nerves are good today. A week from now, two days from now..." Her voice trailed away. She sighed. "I do love you," she said.

Ken gently squeezed the back of her neck. He looked out on the barren granite domes and whalebacks. He wondered to himself, "Why not?" Quite simply choose Joan and begin, life and pleasure both being speedy, ephemeral propositions—make a new and interesting confection: Joan and Kenneth. KennethandJoan. "Pick yourself up / Dust yourself off / and start all over again" (he could "hear" the song, as it might be an echo in his mind). There were a great many reasons why not, but he felt that it might have been a satisfactory kind of arrangement. Why did he think, just then, "might have been"? Had he made up his mind before he realized it?

The sun disappeared behind the Sierra. The sky remained bright and blue, but the air seemed to cool immediately.

Ken said, "Let's go in. I have a strong hankering for food."

Joan laughed. She said, "I guess I know what you really think about me."

"I'm serious all the time," Ken said. "Especially about women and food."

"Food and women—don't think you can flatter me. We shall have beer and coldcuts for supper. A bottle of warm dill pickles."

"I think I shall go home," Kenneth replied. "At least there I could fry myself a hamburger."

"You didn't imagine that I was going to cook tonight?"

"If you don't, I will. I'm starving. Maybe there won't be enough for you."

"I'll get there first," Joan shouted, and she began to run back down the hill towards the house. Kenneth stood and looked at the light changing on the great stony peaks. When he calculated that supper was nearly ready, he began walking slowly down the hill. He had nearly reached the house when Joan came out to call him.


Helen and her mother sat in what had once been thought of as the sewing room—Helen's father still called it that—discussing Helen's many problems. Mrs. Beckwith had fitted the place up with an enormous rolltop desk, a couple of filing cabinets, typewriter, adding machine, telephone. Each year she gained a hundred dollars or so by preparing income tax returns for such widowed friends as had not the time or patience to either compute their own taxes or make a journey down the hill to turn the job over to a lawyer.

There was one other chair in addition to the bucket-shaped wooden swivel chair in front of the desk. The room was too small to contain more than it already had. The desk was very untidy and overcrowded. Although it possessed every kind of cubby-hole, pigeon hole, tray, drawer, and secret receptacle, the desk was piled high with a confusion of household bills, personal letters, advertisements, premium coupons, and gardening columns clipped from newspapers and magazines. Several books about flowers, investment banking, and the federal income tax were stacked neatly among the clutter of papers.

The room's tall casement window looked out past a big cherry tree and many evergreens beyond it. . .the hill dropped sharply away, not far beyond the back of the house. . .the view was of Elliot Bay and the Olympic Peninsula far to the west. When the weather was clear, the snow peaks of Mt. Olympus and its neighbors came into sight, rising vast and distant between the Sound and the Pacific.

The telephone rang, interrupting the conversation. Helen's father was calling to inquire whether he should take Amos, his grandson, to the zoo before lunch. Mrs. Beckwith consulted with Helen, who gave her approval, provided that her father made sure that Amos wore his sweater

94

all the time they were out of doors, also his red wool knit cap.

Mrs. Beckwith said, "That Amos is the best natured child I ever saw. He's so funny looking, but he's a dear. I mean just naturally: I'm not complimenting you on your skill in civilizing him."

"I suppose you're implying that he takes after Kenneth, your favorite ex-son-in-law in the whole entire world."

"*I* never had anything against Kenneth—all I ever said was, that he was the wrong man for *you*...or that you were wrong, as I see now, for him...but why rake all that up? That's done and that's that. Amos is very likely my favorite grandchild."

Helen fumed inwardly, but she tried to conceal her impatience. She could hear herself saying, "Amos was your idea," but she actually said something else: "Ronnieboo, your other favorite son-in-law forsaking all others is stepping out on me. Here I am swollen up like a poison pup—the doctor says it's twins, beyond a doubt—and he's running all over town with some red-headed hussie—it's really terribly embarrassing. What have I done to deserve all this bad luck? Where did I go wrong, to end up with such a sloppy life?"

"Helen, you've been luckier than most women because you've been able to be more independent. I don't believe that Ron has time or energy enough to run anyplace. I always think of him as a hunk of limp celery...even if his mother is my best friend and his father was foolish enough to get wiped out in 1929. Yale seems to enervate people. I told Minnie years ago, "Send him to Oxford or Harvard. New Haven is a swamp and Stanford has lost what little pretension to gentility it ever had."

"But what am I going to DO?"

"Helen, why do you suppose there's anything more to be done? Take care of yourself, take your pills, exercise a little, and stop smoking so much."

"What have you got against the Sorbonne or Padua?"

"The Sorbonne hasn't had a professor worth speaking of since Abelard, and you know what happened to him. But seriously, Helen, you have nothing to worry about. You're healthy, you seem to have no trouble delivering babies. As a married woman and a mother, you have the entire support of the law and the blessings of all the mores and morals and what-not of Western Civilization. Stop complaining and enjoy yourself. Even if Ron were to elope to Guatemala with some chorine, Minnie would see to it that he supported you properly, or she'd cut him off and do it herself...after all, those twins are relatives of hers, as well as ours. Why don't you get interested in something...what happened to your thing about Cimabue?"

"Mama, I don't want to dabble in all that right now. Maybe never, it's taking me such a time to raise Amos and Ronnie, and now this has to happen to me. I don't really know anything about painting; I'd have to start studying all over again. I'd make myself ridiculous unless I really concentrated on it, and even if I did finally publish something, people would just think of me as another fat American lady culture hound."

"Speaking of culture," Mrs. Beckwith murmured, and began searching through the papers on her desk until she turned up a magazine. "This arrived in the mail today—have you seen it?" She held up a new copy of *Time* magazine. Its cover bore a very recognizable (if quite unflattering) portrait of Marilynn Fellows, with the caption, SAN FRANCISCO MAMA LAYS THE NOVEL DOWN.

Helen screeched with jealousy and outrage. Then she laughed at the ugliness of the picture.

"I can't believe..." she ruffled through the pages, hunting for the text. "So wonderfully ugly...look at *these* pictures! How FAT she is!" Suddenly, Helen closed the magazine and replaced it on the desk. "But Marilynn has oceans of talent and so much time..."

"I haven't heard about your having to work as a waitress in any greasy-spoon restaurant lately. You seem pretty adroit when it comes to parking Amos with us or with Minnie while you go to the movies or whatever...not that I begrudge the time I've spent with Amos, I love him most dearly and so does Pa. But you don't have half the trouble that you might; I'm getting tired of hearing you fuss about nothing. And I think you'd feel happy that a close friend such as Marilynn has always been to you..."

"Close friend," Helen interjected. "She betrayed me! She seduced Kenneth practically two seconds after she met him."

"Helen, how can you go on dwelling on all that old sad business so much of the time? No wonder you're unhappy, or feeling unlucky. I feel totally out of patience with you. Marilynn Marjoribanks hasn't an ounce more of talent or brains than you. If you'd just move out of the past and try to take hold of something now, get interested in your own affairs, your own life, start moving outwards instead of drooping around in all that imaginary sadness, imaginary trouble with Ron."

"Mama, I just can't stand it. Everybody in the *world* is allowed to do everything and I just have to sit here having babies!" Helen began to weep.

Mrs. Beckwith sighed. She told Helen, "Well, I didn't mean to speak harshly to you, I don't want you to become any more upset, I know it's hard for you when you're so nearly due. I'll make us a nice little lunch and we'll make a pleasant day of it together. Your father will be delighted to entertain Amos the rest of the day."

"Oh, Mama, I'm so miserable. I don't know what I'd do, if I couldn't come and talk to you."

"I don't either, child. It's a mystery to me, too. I wonder where I went wrong." Mrs. Beckwith paused for a moment, looking at Helen, then she said: "I did what I could. I did what I thought I should. Now here you are, going on thirty years old. I believe that you're intelligent enough to realize that you must learn for yourself what you want, who you are. We've tried to provide you with every opportunity to find out—but that's a dim reproach—I mean, I don't really feel sorry for you any more, and I'm tired of reproaching myself, I just realized, for the person that you've become."

"Mama, what do you mean? You're so strange!"

Mrs. Beckwith reached out and took Helen's hand; she held it gently between her own. "I know that I'm partly to blame for your predicament, but surely you've had plenty of time to learn better. You have nothing, really, to worry about. You have a life of your own. I only see part of it, but I suspect that there's more to it than all the little things you complain about to me. If you've got one lick of sense, and I know that you have, you must have something outside yourself that gets your attention, that requires your personal involvement, your imagination..."

"Mama, look at me—what can I do in this shape? Mama..."

"You're secretly doing soap sculpture. You're cutting intricate paper dolls out of cellophane and gold paper. You're counting the incidence of Old Icelandic words in the earlier works of John Gower. You spend the days that I don't see you manufacturing beautiful cookies that you deliver late at night to friendless elderly people. You collect old clothes for the orphans of Korea. You do volunteer work one day a week for the NAACP, for the University Women, for the League of Women Voters, for the Communist Party USA, for the St. Bennet's Altar Guild. Don't you. Don't you?" Mrs. Beckwith was now standing at her desk, leaning above Helen, almost shouting. "I don't believe that you're just a silly suburban housewife. You're too intelligent, you've seen too much of the world. You're just too ornery for me to believe you when you come here and fall apart weeping 'Mama, Mama' all the time. I just can't believe it. You know that if you need help of any kind, we'll help you. We love you, I love you...I know that I'm supposed to love your brothers better, but you're my baby, I expect so much of you...perhaps that's what's wrong, it is my fault." She sat down, suddenly; the padded back of the swivel chair whacked her softly on the back.

Helen wasn't sure what to do or say. Her mother was sitting very still, her hands grasping the arms of the chair, she was looking at nothing, apparently, while great tears slowly ran down her face. It was frightening but at the same time a liberating experience for Helen to see her mother weep; she hadn't seen her cry before, that she could remember. Helen had always thought of her mother as perfectly calm, perfectly sane, perfectly in control of her own life...in some odd way, perhaps she felt that her mother had quite a lot of secret control over the whole visible world.

Helen slowly hoisted herself out of her own chair and pried one of her mother's hands loose from the chair arm. "Mother," she said.

Mrs. Beckwith looked first at her own hand in Helen's, then her gaze moved slowly to Helen's face. Tears continued to stream from her eyes.

"Mother, don't cry. Don't worry," Helen spoke softly to her. "Don't worry, don't cry. Papa and Amos are coming. I'll fix the lunch, I'll bring you some if you don't want to go down, tell me what you like. Don't cry any more. Papa will worry."

At last Mrs. Beckwith spoke. She said, "Just let me alone for a while. You can find a few things in the refrigerator for Pa and Amos, fix something for them. I don't want anything."

"Can't I do anything for you?"

"Just take care of your father. I'm too tired to see anyone for a while. Please close the door when you go out."

"Will you be all right? Do you feel all right?"

"Of course I'm all right, Helen, I just want to be alone."

"Call me if you want anything. I'll see you for a minute after lunch, then I must go home."

"Thank you, I'll be fine."

Helen went out. Mrs. Beckwith looked out the window towards the Bay. A bank of clouds obscured the Olympics. A flock of robins was having a noisy party in the cherry tree. She felt better. She liked the way Helen had said, "I must go home." She couldn't recall having heard Helen use quite the same tone before.

Travis sat in his office, alone, looking out at the lawns and trees. Three grackles appeared among the grass, hopping and scolding; their open beaks and blank yellow eyes flashed in the sun. They wandered about, Travis noted, in a certain order while they were on the ground. Then something frightened them; two birds flew away. The shiny black bird hopped about alone for a few seconds longer, then it flew away. The grass returned to being a uniform, undifferentiated surface that stretched from the office windows to the oak trees that were growing a couple hundred yards away.

Travis tried thinking of what he had seen in terms of four different lawns, then in terms of four different states of his own consciousness. He wondered whether Wallace Stevens might not have been *Monsieur Teste*. He remembered his own refrigerator, and the curious results he had obtained by slowly freezing certain operating components of a simple electronic circuit, how the increasing cold and pressure registered on a meter and also, for the fun of it...simply for aesthetic effect...as blinking lights of different colors. Why had it stopped after exactly 1958 hours? Why was the oscillator off frequency in exactly the same way daily from 4 to 7 a.m.?

He tried writing the problem of the grackles in the simplest of equations. Then he tried expressing it in the most elaborate and complicated set of formulae. He wrote very neatly on a blackboard. He looked at it all, sighed, and shrugged. On another blackboard he drew a picture of a man looking at three grackles and five oak trees. Beside this picture, he tried to draw the mazy pattern of walk the birds had in the grass. He said aloud, "Blackbirds!" None appeared. He said, "Black birds." The trees looked the same, the lawn was quiet. He understood that they were personages, and the grass kept shaping itself, slowly, into beautiful brocade patterns, something like carved velvet. Looking at the trees, he could feel the damp yellow stringy solidity encasing him, he saw the building from outside and several hundred yards away. Then he was flat on his back, looking at the sky and at the same time feeling the grit of dark soil among his fibres; he stirred himself and noted that he was looking down from some height, there was gravel on the roof, he could see a rabbit sharp tooth blackberry bite. The tin hooded vents of the heat pumping system poked upwards, breathed him into themselves; he was dark moving metal for a time, then he moved again. He walked in a cloud of music, a very complicated piece of Vivaldi; he had gone quite a distance beyond the solar system, he disappeared from his own conception; temporarily, the stars or a fish engulfed him. He sighed. Then he sat in brilliant silence beside the window—not the window of his office—emeralds and sapphires were falling through his right hand and forearm. He waited. He could see himself again, he had been waiting for some time and he would be there until somebody arrived or he arose to go meet them.

Four grackles appeared on the lawn; they were actually flames and living platelets of colored glass. He turned his head a little to the right, without thinking about it, and discovered that he was reading over Alice Chadwick's shoulder. Alice occupied an office several doors away from his own in the same building. She was reading about Eskimo cat's-cradle designs. She wanted lunch, a dish of french-fried potatoes, a large cherry coke, and she had run out of cigarets. She wanted to finish reading a chapter or a section before she reached. . .Alice reached into a drawer of her desk and groped about for a packet of cigarets but there was none. In the process of shuffling things about in the drawer, she broke a fingernail and said, "Damn!" She bit at it, then found an emery board in the same drawer with which to file down the nail. It was sore, so she searched in another drawer until she found an adhesive bandage to wrap around the end of her finger. Travis saw her swear, but didn't hear, nor, he realized presently, did he hear the rasping of the emery board. He said,

"Blackbirds," and thought about his picture on the blackboard. He picked up a piece of chalk and added some blades of grass under the feet of the birds. He could hear the chalk scraping on the slate blackboard. He looked at his hand. He shook his head. He had looked all over the place for an expression of the grackle problem: what broke the continuity of the lawn, turned it into separate blades of grass and then allowed it to become lawn again, smooth greensward? Was there a break in the existence of that grass or of anything else? It seemed that there were pauses that resembled rests in a piece of music, but he remembered that when he didn't see anything, he *was* something being, there was no break, the idea of nonexistence must be a paradox; contrariwise, the birds and the grass could not occur simultaneously, somebody had reminded him.

He opened a drawer of his own desk and took out a pair of small bar magnets. He played with them, trying not to see or think of anything else but these two chunks of magnetized metal alloy. He stopped for a minute and relaxed. As he looked out the window he could see himself floating in green water, with the faces of Clancy, Dottie, and Henry and Marilynn bobbing wet and smiling beside him. He wanted to go swimming, that was the answer.

Travis turned back to his desk and telephoned Marilynn.

"We must go to the beach this afternoon," he said, "I want to go swimming. Do you and the kids want to come along?"

"When do you plan to be here?"

"Hour and five minutes. Is there any ice cream or shall I bring some?"

"I'll get it," Marilynn told him. "And a couple of chickens to barbecue...I'll be all set by the time you get here. Just come home."

After he hung up the phone, Travis went down the hall and knocked at Alice Chadwick's door. When she asked him to come in, he told her that he was in a hurry, he had no time for a visit.

"What's the name of that anthropologist who collected all the string games. I can't remember, I only saw it once. I want a copy to take home so that I can learn to astound the children."

Alice said, "I've got a copy right here, I was just looking at it yesterday. Do you want to borrow it?"

"No, thanks, I just needed the author and title so I can get my own copy."

Alice said, "Wait a second, I'll write it for you." She scribbled on a memo pad. Travis noticed that she had a bandaid on her forefinger. She handed him the slip and smiled. "There you are," she said. "Have a nice time at the beach."

Travis was surprised. "I only just decided to go a few minutes ago," he said.

"Isn't that odd," Alice said. "You looked so happy when you came in, I thought 'He's on his way out for the rest of the day; I bet he's going swimming.' Tell Marilynn and the kids hello for me."

"Thanks, Alice, I will. I'll see you tomorrow morning if you have time, I'd like to talk to you about blackbirds."

"I'm not an ornithologist," Alice replied, looking surprised in her turn, "I only know about...oh, animal totems, for example, or stories about them the Indians tell."

"That'll do it. Please think up or look up some of the local ones about grackles or blackbirds and tell me."

"I can tell you where to look so you can read them yourself," Alice said.

"I'll explain tomorrow. You have to tell me the story or stories, otherwise it won't work."

"Oh...you're working...oh, certainly. I'll be here at ten...or anyway I'll be free by then. I'll be ready."

Travis thanked her and ran down the hall and out of the building. He picked up his car from the parking lot and drove home.

Marilynn told him, "Thank God you decided to have a day off. I've been driving myself crazy trying to read Whitehead all morning. I didn't

100

have sense enough to simply walk out the door and take the kids to the beach."

Travis held her and gave her a kiss. "I guess you know who's the real genius aroung here. But it may be foggy at the beach."

"If it is, we can drive out towards Sonoma where it's bound to be sunny...or if you're set on the beach, we can take our great pavilion and set it up on the sand. I've got the food all packed and the children indoctrinated. They think now that they want to be marine biologists. They want to hunt for pretty creatures among the rockpools. I've put a couple bottles of champagne and a couple of Rhine wine in the portable cooler. As far as I know, we're on our way."

Travis kissed her again. "You are my precious treasure babe: little mother of all the Russias."

"Ain't it the truth," Marilynn replied, and kissed him in return.


Joan Chadwick invited her ex-husband to supper. She had thought of calling Travis and talking with him, but she decided at last to call Bruce because he had known Kenneth longer.

"Can I bring Alice?" he asked her.

"No, I want to talk to you alone. I'll ask you and Alice together some other time—any time you say, for that matter, if you'll just come to me Thursday."

"What do you want to see me for? Can't I just come by this evening?"

"If you would, yes—although I couldn't give you quite such an elegant dinner if you did. I'll give you lots of booze. I want you to talk to me."

"What about?"

"About Kenneth."

"Oh, no. What about him?"

"Don't be obtuse. That's why I'm asking you. I want you to sit down and calmly tell me all about him."

"What's he done to you?"

"Bruce, will you please either say yes and come over and talk, or tell me that you won't? I don't want to argue with you about it over the phone."

"All right. I'll come. What time will suit you?"

"Six o'clock Thursday."

"Okay, I'll drown Alice, or something, and come for dinner—but it better be elegant."

From what Kenneth had told him, Bruce had no trouble guessing Joan's probable line of questioning. He was fond of both of them and he wanted to see them happy. At the same time he didn't feel free to enter into any indiscriminate exchange of confidences which would lead to his getting into trouble with both Joan and Kenneth at the same time.

He asked Alice, "What should I do? Answer all her questions or just call up about Wednesday morning and say I can't come and then avoid both of them for a while?"

Alice said, "Some people would say that it was scarcely proper for your former wife to seek your opinion in such a matter. I think it's nice that she feels you're still her friend, and that she wants to stay friendly with you. She's asked for your advice: advise her. I think you can do it without either misleading her or hurting Kenneth, if you pay attention to what you say . . . but don't ask me. All you people have known each other for years. Certainly Joan should be able to read you without any trouble."

"Oh, yeah? You notice that Joan and I aren't married any more, too, don't you?"

"Well, you do what you please. And tell Joan that I'd be delighted to come to dinner at her place any time. I think she's the best cook in the world. In fact, you ought to ask her to come to us for dinner in a week or so. Tell her that I'll give her a phone call and we'll arrange a good day."

When Bruce arrived at her door, Joan greeted him with a short sudden kiss. He said, "Hello, there. I brought you some candy kumquats. I remember you used to like them." Joan was delighted. She took his coat and hung it up, then she led him into the kitchen.

"We're having our cocktails in here where I can keep an eye on the cookery," Joan told him. "You're used to eating in the kitchen anyway, I expect. I don't imagine Alice has time to do much cooking."

"No," Bruce replied. "She never had to learn until now. She's doing a good job, though. Kate gave her a copy of the *Cuisine Bourgeoise* for a wedding present."

"Then all you must be getting is soufflés, soups, salads, and eggs Christine. You'll get thinner than ever. But then, I'm just being catty. How is she?"

"She's doing just fine. She told me to ask you over for dinner next week. She says she'll call you herself and make a date that's good for you—or for you and Kenneth, if you like."

"Let me get you the booze. Are you drinking as usual or are you on something else?"

"If you please," he told her.

She brought out a great platter of hors d'oeuvres from the refrigerator, then the cold bottles of gin, vermouth, a pail of ice, a bowl of olives, the mixing pitcher, and two chilled glasses.

"Great God," Bruce declared. "This is overwhelming."

"I want to talk to you for some little time. I don't want you to fade away."

"I don't know but what I'll have to be carried out, after all that. You must have started getting this dinner on Tuesday."

"Oh, no. Just since last night. I'm too busy and too impatient to do very much cooking right now; I just do this once in a while to stay in practice. Do you want to mix them or shall I? Have a goody to eat."

"You go ahead," Bruce told her. "I'll sample just a little of this guacamole while I wait."

In addition to guacamole, there were cornucopias of prosciutto stuffed with good things. There were Chinese barbecued spare ribs. There were slices of many kinds of raw vegetables. There were deviled eggs decorated with truffles, profiterolles stuffed with paté, small crackly things to dip into the guacamole, or into the heavenly sauce that inhabited a hollow artichoke which rose up in the middle of the platter.

"You said elegant, I guess that was it," Bruce remarked.

"Please help yourself. There will be no other guests. Have a nice martini."

Joan's martinis were made according to a recipe which no one else ever discovered. Even Bruce had never found out how she built them; they were better than any other drink that has ever been tasted by sea or by land. They were freezing cold, they were strong, they were subtly scented, yet they did not, like so many special martinis, produce instantaneous paralysis or coma after one had imbibed the third glassful in succession. Instead, they produced euphoria, which in turn led into *hilaritas*: joyful contemplation and delight...they sprung each individual brain cell into something very like that "undifferentiated aesthetic continuum" of which Professor Northrop has written. Simply holding a glass which contained this fluid had an immediate effect upon the person holding it: he would smile, quite unconsciously, as if in anticipation of his coming translation.

Bruce drank and sighed. "Maybe I really will drown Alice and then run away with you to Peoria."

"You and I have already been to Peoria, not to speak of South Bend, Shaniko, Topeka, and La Jolla. I want to marry Kenneth and settle down. I've been everywhere I want to go except home."

"Joan, you've done lots of people and seen lots of places, like you say—how come you picked Kenneth?"

"I like him. I just remembered, myself, a little while ago, it's as simple as that. I like him, you like him, he's a very dear person. How could I not pick him, after all?"

"Because you picked me once—for *my* sweet nature—and found out I was a lemon."

"After eight years—of course I wasn't home a good part of that time. But now..." Joan took a bite of stuffed prosciutto. She looked at it and said, "That is good, even if I do say so as I shouldn't." She got up from the table. "I must look at the roast—do you want to see?"

Bruce watched as Joan opened the oven and peered inside. He whistled involuntarily. Within, there was the biggest standing rib roast he ever saw. The color and aroma were heavenly. Joan closed the door.

"The fish will be steamed," she told him, "in that Chinese way, with a crust, and served with a fruit sauce. Artichokes with melted butter. Pommes à la batard...that was the dish in the other oven. Eggplants Bottacinni. Green salad with little homey touches. The soup is real turtle, prepared with great trouble and expense; I found them live in

103

Chinatown."

"We going to live high. What would you do for Sunday dinner?"

"You know what I have Sundays...beer and coldcuts and potato salad. Don't be silly. I want you to do me a favor."

"Maybe," Bruce said. "Maybe not. It depends on the favor."

"Have more martinis. I must cook for a few minutes, now."

"I haven't seen so much food since our wedding supper," Bruce said. He dipped into the hors d'oeuvres. It occurred to him that he'd already eaten an appalling quantity of them. He sipped his fresh drink and immediately felt better. "It's all such fantastic grub it can't hurt me much," he thought to himself.

Joan busied herself with the fish. Bruce got up in order to check his own reflexes. He felt splendid. He discovered that he could walk to the bathroom, and later, into the living room without the least difficulty.

The living room was tall and square, a huge but beautifully proportioned space. The walls and ceiling had been painted a dark, warm ochre. A great Moroccan lantern of pierced brass-work swung from the center of the ceiling. A Tibetan tanka was hung above the fireplace. Tiger skins and zebra hides were draped over the big sofas and chairs. There were carved and inlaid chests of Indian manufacture that faced each other across the room. In the bay of the windows, which were curtained with a heavy, dark yellow velvet material, there stood a bodhisattva figure of marble carved in the Gandhara style. A great bouquet of summer flowers was arranged in a big brass basin that stood on a long, low teak table before the image.

The room next to it was fitted up as a music room and library. A radio-phonograph machine and a long cabinet for records stretched across one wall. Bookshelves reached to the high ceiling; there was a small stepladder of polished wood. Here was one of Joan's chief treasures, her 18th century French writing table. The wall above the phonograph displayed a collection of exotic musical instruments made of rare woods, inlaid with ivory and pearl. There was another brass bowl of flowers.

Bruce looked at it all, sighed, and shook his head. He went back to the kitchen. Joan helped him to another drink. He helped himself to a profiterolle.

"This layout is too much," Bruce told her, "a seraglio out of *Better Homes and Gardens.*"

"It is a little gaga, isn't it? The bedroom's a mess. But the nervous little men I do business with get all sorts of ideas in that living room. You'd be surprised how most of them live—little California outdoor ranch-style places down the Peninsula with Renoir reproductions on the wall—their wives wear pedal-pusher pants all the time, and keep their hair wound up in those aluminum things."

"And you get to play the Dragon Lady in an atmosphere of Oriental Splendor."

"I'm just a poor woiking goil tryna get along in a wicked world," Joan replied. "Let me tell you, it grows more wicked and less delightful every month."

"Fighting off these little men and their big ideas?"

"Fighting them, fighting the Government, fighting to get really good things out of the Orient, out of Africa which is all torn up now, out of South America which is going to be torn up again pretty quick. It's a mess."

"Say not the struggle naught availeth," Bruce quoted to her.

"It availeth very well indeed—every fag decorator in town spends plenty of money at my place. There's more money rolling around right now than there was just before the war—and more people doing without any, right here in town, in California, and you can imagine how the rest of the world is—we've got it all."

"You seem to come out of it looking awfully well."

"Thank you very much. Let me pour you a little more."

Joan's clear white skin was smooth and yet looked warm. Her great eyes were clear, very dark brown. Her long black hair was wound up in a complicated but appropriate fashion. Her flesh was firm, although she was a large woman. She looked like an odalisque but wasn't as fat as the models for those pictures. Her face was very quiet—some people said, "sort of blank-looking, or like a mask"—but Bruce never thought of her in that way. He always thought of her as a very positive person, able to arrange the world to suit herself; and the arrangement usually amused her, kept her interested in things, in people. If any of her plans came unstuck or went haywire, she was able to take a loss with quite a lot of detachment. It was quite uncharacteristic of Joan to openly ply anyone for information or anything else; Bruce remembered her as being used to operating more independently, letting information find its way to her, rather than going out and asking the world point blank, "What about such-and-such?"

"Have you seen Marilynn's new place, now that she's got it all rebuilt and fixed up?" Bruce inquired.

"No. She called me the other day but I haven't been there yet. She says she'll send me a special invitation to her house-warming party."

"Be sure to come. The house is a great place, a real old San Francisco family house. It's worth it just for the view of the ocean and the city from there. She asked me over to talk to her about the colors for it. She's got it done up beautifully."

"Have just another bit of guacamole—it won't be any good later."

"Thanks. It's delicious." Bruce noted that the whole platter was almost empty. He felt quiet and happy. Joan refilled his glass.

"We'll be eating in just a few minutes," she said. "I'm just about to put the sherry into the soup. I'm surprised that Marilynn didn't take a long trip or something, after all the hoo-rah over her book. But she's always a surprise. I always get a kick out of talking with her. I've never talked much with Travis, although I like him very much. I trust him, I feel very warmly towards him, but we never talk. He just grins and gives me another drink.

105

I thought of talking to him, before I called you."

"Maybe you should have. Travis is really quite a great man—one of the few people who are really alive, really functioning in this town...or in this country, for that matter."

"He's certainly rich enough," Joan said. "Successful enough."

"Listen, he's not half as rich as the government could make him if he'd work for them instead of hiding out down in Stanford or the Institute for Advanced Studies and all those special goofy projects he gets into. He refuses to have anything to do with the government, or with the war industries. He could be a millionaire seven times over."

Joan wasn't impressed. "He has an independent income, in addition to what the project gives him. He can afford to be virtuous. Anyway, I thought Kenneth was your greatest friend...how come you build up Travis so high? Here—open up this bottle for us, and we'll see whether the soup is edible. I'm starved."

"Kenneth is another problem," Bruce replied. He eased the cork out of the bottle and sniffed at the wine. He poured some into his glass and examined it, tasted it, and then he swore.

"What's the matter—is it a bad bottle? I'll get another."

"No...it smells perfect, but I can't tell now whether it's Liebfraumilch or 7-Up, I've had to much gin." He looked at the label. He said, "It must be good; it's a good year."

"When you and Alice come over, I'll serve nothing but the finest Rainwater Sherry before dinner—with those lovely tasteless kind of sweet crummy English biscuits. You'll be able to taste everything including my thumb-print on the plate...although I doubt that you can taste much of anything really, at the rate you always smoke."

The conversation quieted down quite a lot as the soup gave place to the fish, which was followed by the roast, the salad, and a sudden blazing of blue fire as the dessert came, rum baba topped with ice cream smothered with a sauce of cherries flavored with sugar, kirschwasser, and a slug of warmed akavit flaming over the top.

Joan asked if he was ready for coffee.

"Yes, and I hope that you've telephoned for a priest. I may not live through the next course."

"Oh, you'll be fine. I'm going to perform the whole opera for you." She stood up and began clearing the table. "You go into the other room and put some nice music on the machine and relax. I'll be right there."

Bruce wandered into the music room, hunted up a record of some Hindu ragas, and then seated himself in the middle of the floor to listen. Joan came in, carrying a big Moorish table which she set beside Bruce. She went away, and returned presently with an enormous brass tray which she set on the low table. On the tray was a complete set of equipment for making coffee in the Arabian manner—an alcohol stove, brass water pot, the hour-glass shaped pot in which the coffee is actually boiled, the coffee mill, a canister of coffee beans, sugar, cups, spoons, a small dish of the candied kumquats that Bruce had brought her, and a dish of sticky-looking real hashish candy from North Africa.

"Joan, I never saw such a production. You've really knocked yourself out. I give up. I'll tell you anything. I'll do whatever you say."

"I promised to do everything elegant. I had to spend a whole week extra in Marakech, trying to get hold of this set of equipment and then hiring people who'd teach me how to use it. Don't laugh."

"I'm not laughing, I told you, I give up. I'm only surprised you didn't come in on a dromedary."

"Go ahead and laugh, if you want to. It tastes good, and maybe you don't think some of the visiting merchants don't lap it up. I had to go to endless trouble getting the majoun for you...I expect the narcotics agents are waiting in the kitchen for a propitious moment to leap upon us."

Joan silently ground the coffee and boiled it carefully. She poured the mixture into cups. She went out for a moment to put another record onto the machine, then she returned. She raised her cup to Bruce. "*Slain leat*," she said. He said, "Cheers." They drank. They listened to the music of Mr. Shankar's sitar. Bruce nibbled some majoun. Joan ate a kumquat.

"Now tell me about Kenneth," she said.

"I'm too full or too drunk or something to talk. This coffee is superb."

"Have some candy rose petal. Have another taste of majoun. I'll boil up a little more coffee."

"I've told you about Kenneth for years. What haven't I told you while we were married? You've known him almost as long as I. Anyway, what has knowing him got to do with your decision to marry him? You've decided already, you say."

"It has a lot to do with it. Do you think, for example, that he's stable?"

"Certainly. He's almost as bright as Travis. He's sane enough but he's aimless, undisciplined, careless. I think that if he concentrated even a part of his potential on a single project, he might break through to a realization of his really unusual faculty for seeing connections between apparently disparate objects, for getting new turns out of old notions everybody else thinks of as being useless. He could generate a new understanding, I think, of what we all see; he'd be sure to discover qualities in life, qualities in things that had been overlooked. I think he has all this going on in his head most of the time, but he hasn't yet put it all together, hasn't yet been able to project it, to realize it outside himself, outside his own head. He must figure out a way to build it with his own hands or tell it to some other person, to live it out among other people."

"You make him sound like an archangel or something. Is he really that bright? That good?"

"Sure. But I think it's going to be difficult for you or any other woman to live with him until he does find out how to DO what he knows, how to produce his ideas concretely. And of course he may never find out how to do this. He may just go on being an amiable dreamy guy who reads most of the time. . .and who is, it seems to me, irresistible to all women. I sure wish that I had the faculty of capturing the imagination of as many beautiful women as he has—you included."

"Helen never did much with him," Joan remarked. "He says that he wants a family. He thinks that children are the greatest thing in the world. Children love him, I know. . .I've seen him around Dottie and Henry, for instance. I don't think that I'm so old and dried up but that we might not have one, at least, of our own. . .if that isn't enough for him, we can adopt more."

"But you've been married to this business for so many years," Bruce said, with a trace of bitterness. "How is it going to do without you to travel for it, to watch it, while you're bringing up babies?"

"That's what I really want to talk to you about," Joan said. She smiled at him. "How would you like a job. . .travel abroad, see the world, visit romantic Samarkand. . .you do the buying and the hassling, I'll keep an eye on whatever manager I can find for the local works. I'm tired of being the Dragging Lady. I want to live quietly with Kenneth, if we have to live in a tree-house. I want out of this apartment. I want to be a woman again, for a few years, instead of a store. I want you to help me. What can I do to land him? What is he really like? What does he really want?"

Bruce heard her out, astounded by the quiet intensity with which she spoke. She seldom let herself sound so deeply moved.

He asked her, "Why must it be Kenneth?"

"I just feel that he's the right man. He's good to me. He's gentle. He understands me. I think I can be good for him. I don't know—that's why I asked you about him, asked you to help me."

"Joan, I can't think of anything more to tell you. As for helping you—I haven't any idea how to begin."

"Tell him. Tell him I'm attached to him—that I depend—no. I don't know. I see what you mean. But do you think it's too late for me—for him—for us to make some kind of sensible life together?"

"Of course not," Bruce tried to reassure her. "But you know as well as I do that anything we choose to do is chancy. It may be a terrible mistake; it may go haywire in a thousand ways. But the only way you can find out is to go ahead and try. If just 'finding out' is what you really want. I don't think age or lateness has anything to do with it if you really try to make a full-sized, full-time life out of your relationship. . .I sound like some love-lorn columnist or something. . .But you know what I'm like, you know my limitations as well as anyone. I can't tell you what you ought to do. I'll be glad to help you if I can figure out a way to do it. Certainly I wouldn't try to dissuade either of you from getting together. I just don't *know* anything more to tell you, except that if this is what you want to do, go to it. Try the best you can."

Joan smiled. She looked at Bruce's long, earnest face a moment. Then she said, "I have to. I must."

"Please don't think about me being in the business, though. Or at least not right away. I'm going to have to be here in town for the next few years, at least. Alice is pregnant; I'd like to stay here a while."

Joan was surprised and pleased. "That's wonderful," she said. "I'm so glad you told me. When will the baby come?"

"We just found out a few days ago. It won't be until early next year. I appreciate your thinking of me though, about the job."

"I don't know—everything is so complicated—you must tell me if you can think of anyone suitable."

Bruce went away in a roseate haze, some hours later, wondering at Joan, at himself, at the whole evening. It was very warm outside. The moon hung low above the western part of the city. How different Joan was, how remote he felt from her now—yet he could feel her deep concern. He actually did want to help her, but he'd been completely honest when he'd said he couldn't think how. He wondered what Kenneth really thought of it all, what he might do in the future. Bruce decided that he had better wait until he was asked before he said or did anything more about the matter. He warned himself, "Let them both alone."

On the afternoon of Marilynn's house-warming party, who should arrive on the newly varnished doorstep but Helen? She had to come, she had decided to accept Marilynn's invitation; she had flown down from Seattle in order to see Marilynn in all her new glory. She had to bring Amos to see and be seen, and must announce to the world that she and Ron were divorced. Now here she was, scouting San Francisco for a place to live. She planned to move her household within a month.

Marilynn embraced her and patted Amos's head. Amos was a shock to her, although Kate had told her about him, but there he actually was, quite as if she were looking at Kenneth aged six years old. She thought to herself, "Holy Toledo."

"You must stay with me, of course—we've got all the room in the world. I can't wait to show you the place."

"Just a couple of days right now," Helen told her. "It's certainly large, but I don't want to make a lot of unnecessary bother, putting both of us up. Besides, Mama's watching the twins; I should go back in a day or two. My God, you look so much better than those pictures—what'd you do, insult Clare personally?"

Marilynn laughed. "Wait till I tell you about New York," she said. "You'll never believe it. It's even worse than those pictures."

"They made you look like a decaying madame. You ought to have sued them."

Marilynn led Helen into the house and soon they were having a drink together in one of the tower rooms. Amos had been turned loose in the back yard to play with Dottie and Henry.

Marilynn thought that Helen was looking more beautiful than ever before.

"It was really very hard to take," Helen was telling her, "There I was, great with child, and that pinhead running around to motels in Everett with this lady draftsman. That was only the beginning. Shortly after the babies were born and I was coming apart at the seams, having one of those huge post-delivery depressions—Ron began coming home late from the office again. The joint checking account began going gaga. That was a little over a year ago. I tried to reason with him. I felt that I really should try to straighten everything out; I couldn't see myself failing in this marriage thing twice in a row. Nothing seemed to do any good. He was just completely self-indulgent, totally irresponsible wherever it was a question of his own pleasures. It was hopeless. I felt awful about it at first, but something sort of happened to me when the twins were born. I'm more interested now in what I can do for the kids and myself than I am in all the past hassle."

Marilyn felt rather skeptical about Helen's claim to have detached herself from the past, but she didn't say so. Instead, she told Helen, "I'm glad that you decided to come down. Things have been very quiet around here. I thought that when Kate moved down here last fall, the world would be somewhat livelier—not that I feed on excitement—well, anyway, nothing's happening."

"I'm sort of shy about seeing Kenneth," Helen said. "I want to see him, but I feel strange about it."

"Well, you won't have a chance at him for a while. Kenneth and Bruce and Travis have all withdrawn to the inner fastnesses of the High Sierra. They've gone hiking and camping down around Mt. Whitney someplace."

"Right in the middle of your party? The rats!"

"Right in the middle of everything. Bruce had the chance to get away from his job for a couple weeks, Kenneth isn't working anyplace right now, and of course Travis gets out of his office and out of town whenever he gets the notion. . .and he's so crazy about the Sierra; he's been going up there since he was a little kid. They're probably trudging up some dusty old trail right this minute."

"Why do you allow Travis to do this kind of thing to you? And he may break a leg, besides—Bruce and Kenneth are so helpless, and they sort of cancel out each other's capabilities when they're together. Good heavens!"

"I imagine that they'll be all right. There was only a quart of brandy among them, and no cigarets. They've all taken solemn vows to stop smoking."

"That Bruce Chadwick, he's just bad news for everybody. He used to encourage Kenneth into perpetrating—oh, outrages."

"His wife had a beautiful daughter this spring. You ought to meet Alice—she's a beauty, too. Travis found her working in the project at Stanford. How he ever sold her on Bruce I'll never know. She's a remarkably bright girl."

"But what does Joan do now? Is she in town or in Zanzibar?"

"She's in town. . .she told me that she'd come to the party tonight."

"And Kate? How's she doing?"

Marilynn asked herself at this point, "How indeed?" She'd recently had two conversations that interested her in an abstract kind of way; now the reasons for her original interest were becoming clear. Bruce Chadwick had told her that his ex-wife, Joan, was—after all these years—determined to remarry. "I never can think of Joan as the marrying sort," Marilynn had told him. "She's too much the Circassian slave maiden or like a movie star: she's complete as she is. I can't envision a husband in her life."

"She thinks that marrying Kenneth will solve all her problems," Bruce said. "She wants me to sort of talk Kenneth into the idea. I don't know what to do."

"Don't do anything," Marilynn said. "Just let nature take its course."

"I don't know. Kenneth is practically the only friend I've got. I feel like I ought to kind of cue him in...at the same time, I don't want to mess up Joan's plans, I'd like to see her enjoy herself for a while. She's always so hung up in that importing business she never does anything much that she likes."

"Well, I'm sure they'll make a lovely couple," Marilynn remarked, somewhat distantly. She could remember Kenneth's telling her of his long-term fascination with Joan, but she thought to herself, that fascination and being married are two different things.

"Marilynn, you've got some sort of inside scoop that you're not letting me in on. I can tell by the way you're looking. Your eyeballs are commencing to roll upwards and I can hear the little gears turning in your head. Tell Brucie."

"No, sir. Everybody knows that you're the biggest gossip in seven states. You don't hear anything except the arteries popping inside your own busy brain."

"How is beautiful Kate these days? I thought we'd be seeing more of her than we do. I told Ken a long time ago that there was a woman that he ought to get serious about."

"Very well, Bruce, if that's the case, I'll tell you. Kate is absolutely batty about Kenneth. I'd like her to have him. I think they'd really do well together. They like the same kinds of things, they're both very bright, and they're both, essentially, very simple, very loving people. There you are."

"Well, okay. Now we know where we stand. I've promised Joan to do whatever I could for her, but I'm actually on your side. Shake, partner." He extended his hand to Marilynn.

"If you start telling any of this around town, I'll know exactly whose scalp to lift," Marilynn warned him.

"Don't worry. I'd only be exposing my own wickedness—still, I feel obliged to deliver Joan's message. I really owe her that much. And like I say, she ought to be happy for a while."

"I expect we all get about as much happiness as we deserve. How's Alice? How's young Barbara? And your show at the DeYoung? I'm sorry I couldn't make it to the opening. I fell asleep right after dinner that night."

"The show's still there. It's embarrassing...everybody likes it...the reviewers, the people who come to see it...I've sold four or five pieces. Barby now weighs at least forty pounds and her mother's worrying about developing enormous biceps from hoisting the baby all the time. But we're evading the issue. What about Kenneth? I've already told him that he ought to change his name and move to another town. He said that he likes the climate here. I told him that he wasn't going to be in much shape to like anything after he gets torn up and scattered across the landscape by the Thracian women hereabouts."

"If I were you, I wouldn't worry too much about Kenneth. He has a strange kind of innocence that saves him."

"Come on, now. Level with me."

"I'm quite serious, Bruce. Kenneth does have, after all, something essentially funny about him that lets him survive all kinds of mess and bother that I couldn't stand."

"Kenneth is my oldest friend. I know he's not a booby, but I think he's going to need a little bit of help."

"Well, I don't envy you your job," Marilynn said. "And at least we know who's where. Suppose we talk about something else. I like my friends just fine, but I get bored with them when they dominate my private conversations."


Marilynn blandly told Helen, "Kate is just fine. She's always loved this town, she has a very good job at the University. My publisher is about to print a collection of her translations from the Dada poets and theoreticians. She's done a beautiful job on it, I think. What about you? Have another dab of gin."

Helen said, "Thanks." She picked up her refilled glass and gazed through it—green of the park, lighter bluey-green of the ocean, blue of the sky; she drank a large mouthful. Then she said, "Marilynn, I'm going to tell you something, strictly a secret. I want to try getting Ken back."

Marilynn replied, "Hm. What for?"

"I know that it sounds idiotic—I still hate him—I expect we'll be miserable—maybe I won't succeed in getting him back—but he's the only person, outside of the children and my folks, that I really love."

"Well, Helen, I think it's more or less logical, of course. Certainly Kenneth has clamored for years to have a family. Why not. Here you are."

"And I must ask you," Helen hurried on with it, "It's probably none of my affair—don't answer unless you want to—is Kate terribly attached to him?"

Marilynn was caught off balance. She replied very simply and directly, "Everybody's suddenly mad for him: Joan Chadwick is resolved to marry him, Kate's been crying on my shoulder for months about it all, and now here you are. . . I don't mean I'm not glad to see you. I've always liked Kenneth, and you know that he was attracted to me for a moment, but I really can't imagine why all the world is suddenly pursuing him, and he's funny looking into the bargain. Poor Amos! Will he have to go through all this too?"

"That Kenneth! The minute my back is turned, he blossoms out into a Don Juan. I never heard of such a thing! He always used to scream around about all he wanted to do was read and have a quiet family life."

"Well, Helen, things have changed. He's been on the loose for six years or so. What do you expect? But of course, you've got all the artillery—if you really want him, I expect that you'll get him, once he sees Amos."

"I didn't intend for Ken to meet Amos until after I'd had quite a long talk with him—with Ken. I don't want to club him into submission if I don't have to. After I've talked to him. . ." Helen broke off. She rubbed her forehead with one hand. "I'm not at all certain what I'll say actually. It all seemed much simpler when I was up in Seattle. I don't even know whether Ken will talk to me at all, but I must try. When did you say they'd all come back?"

"Not for about a week and a half from now."

"Then I'll have to see him later. I'll have time to think about what to say."

Marilynn could think of no reply. She looked out the window, saw no one below, then emptied the ice and dead waters from the bottom of the martini pitcher. The spray sparkled in the sun as it scattered across the calla lilies and geraniums. Marilynn slowly and carefully mixed a fresh batch of martinis. Helen sat quite silently, looking at the view. They could hear the children bellowing and squealing in the back yard.

"I ought to go down and see if Amos is causing any mischief," Helen said. She rose from her chair. "They've been out there for some time."

"Don't worry," Marilynn told her. "They're just civilizing one another. Mrs. Fynch will be keeping an eye on them from the kitchen windows. Have some gin."

When they finished their drinks, Marilynn showed Helen over the rest of the house. They joined Mrs. Fynch for a few minutes, to have a look at the preparations for the party, and also to peer down at the children— Dottie, Amos, and Henry were racing around a palmetto tree, screeching at the top of their lungs. At last they ascended once more into the tower. Marilynn sighed as she sat down.

"I do love this room," she said. "It's why I bought the house in the first place. I like to write here, or just sit and look out. Nobody else is allowed in here except by my most express invitation. There are nooks and crannies of every kind elsewhere in the house, plenty for Travis and the children to hide themselves and all their treasures. Clancy's away at school, but when he's here, he uses the room above this one."

"The house feels so comfortable," Helen said. "It's really a home."

"I'd no more live in one of those Bauhaus glass boxes than I'd live in a store window," Marilynn said. "This house has closets, an attic, a cellar. There are all kinds of rare and fascinating things about it, or anyway I find them endlessly amusing...the speaking-tube system, the wood-lift that comes up from the cellar to the bottom of the window seat beside the fireplace. The sideboard between the kitchen and the dining room revolves like a secret panel in an old Karloff movie. There's a wonderful dumb-waiter from the kitchen to the hallway on the second floor so that breakfast can be sent up in the morning...all kinds of oddities like that."

"I like the colored glass window in the closet," Helen said. "I've always been excited by closet windows anyway."

"Well, it was almost ruinously expensive to buy this place and fix it up, but I don't care. I've got it now and I expect to stay in it. Like I told you, New York has disappeared or is disappearing. The French are having a new revolution, I won't go to Spain because Franco's still there, and I don't like England. I might just as well stay here and tend to my own knitting."

"Marilynn, you've always seemed to me to be at home wherever you're living. You always managed to be comfortable, even when we were living in those awful dorms at college."

"I can't do anything unless I've got someplace that I can sit down comfortably," Marilynn told her. "Give me a decent chair and a rug on the floor and a window to look out of...just a little gin...and there I am."

"You certainly have done a wonderful job of organizing everything, training Travis and the children."

"Piffle. Travis trained me. I wouldn't be anywhere if it weren't for him."

"You always used to do everything yourself," Helen cried. "You always decided what you wanted—you wrote three books before you even met Travis. He didn't have anything to do with the way you were, the way you are...you're you, you're unique. You haven't really changed."

Marilynn said, "I feel that I have. Whether it's immediately visible or not. Without him I should have been...oh, you know, how women get, successful and emancipated and sort of like fake newspaper reporters. I only congratulate myself that I had sense enough to marry him, to stay with him, and to learn from him. I know a great many people think that he's mentally deficient. It pleases him to be thought so."

"Oh, *I* always liked Travis," Helen said. Then she laughed. "I can't say that I ever had any long illuminating discourses with him, but I never thought of him as being a dullard."

"Maybe Kenneth isn't the one who could do the same for you."

"What?"

"Maybe you're wrong about needing Kenneth."

"Why does everyone keep telling me that Kenneth is bad for me? You know my mother kept telling me that from the time she first saw him."

"I don't know, Helen, maybe I'm wrong. It was just a feeling that

I had."

"I'm going to try, anyway," Helen said. "I don't care if he does get cranky with me. It won't hurt him to suffer a *little* bit."

"Why do you feel privileged to have him? And is just 'having' him enough to suit you?"

"I love him. I always have and I always will. He'll always be mine, forever, no matter what anyone ever says or does or thinks. He's mine. My husband."

Marilynn looked at Helen. Helen's face had the strange rapt gaze of a sybil—or a fury. It gave Marilynn a sudden chill, the shock produced by her contact with a truly alien, archaic sensibility. Helen seemed possessed. Marilynn shrugged her shoulders and trembled a little. She was confused. She felt that Helen needed her help, and at the same time she felt a strong urge to protect Kenneth. She refilled her glass and Helen's; she drank most of her own at once. She looked at Helen again, who now sat strangely silent, her beautiful face composed and serene as the prospect before her.


Because their camp was set near a lake in a small canyon, Kenneth couldn't see far enough to suit him; he had to climb a goat-trail through a random scattering of granite talus blocks and the scree slopes above them in order to reach, at last, a knife-edge ridge at the top of one of the canyon walls. From there he could look out over the little valley and its lake, and back into the group of giant, dead monuments, most of them over thirteen thousand feet high, which form the crest of the Kings-Kern Divide. To the northeast were the peaks above the Evolution Valley; southeast lay the Whitney massif, which appeared to be an almost smooth low series of granite whalebacks. The fingers and pinnacles and hanging slabs of the Divide looked vastly higher, grander, more ferocious than the rest of the range.

The floor of the canyon where their camp stood was a green meadow. It was just at or a little above the timber line. Clumps of cypress and red pine grew above the rocks and grass in natural groupings which suggested that they'd been carefully set out according to the plans of a very expensive landscape gardener. Not only the trees and the plantations of flowers and shrubs, but the white granite stones themselves appeared to have been placed where they lay, after a great deal of deliberation.

There were flowers beside him even where he stood, on the windy little ridge—a piece of the Sierra 12,000 feet in the air—they were intensely blue, the size of large clover blooms, with fat furry stems and thick fuzzy leaves. He caught sight of something moving at the lake's edge, beyond the camp site. Ken watched, and presently he was able to make out that it was Travis, fishing his way around the lake. Travis was wearing his red hunting hat.

The sun was very bright and the sky was completely clear, as it had been all week; nevertheless, it was chilly on the ridge; the wind was sharp. Kenneth climbed down slowly, watched by fat ambling golden marmots. He could hear them whistling among the rocks farther down the slope. He felt a little dizzy and his head hurt slightly, but he was enjoying himself immensely. He knew that after another few days he'd become accustomed to living at altitude.

Ken found Bruce seated on a rock some distance above the camp. Bruce was sketching the general scene, drawing it on a page of his journal.

Bruce asked him, "How are you doing?"

Ken said, "Fine. I've got to go down and get some more aspirin, though. How do you feel?"

"Alternately excited and sleepy. I feel like walking, but after a little bit I feel like sitting down again to look at everything and sleeping at the same time. . .something like being high on marijuana."

"This would be a great place to blow up a couple of joints, but we haven't even got tobacco. We've got to make it on landscape and anoxia."

Bruce continued to draw. He included a very tiny bug-like scratching of tines and dots which represented Travis and his fish pole, far on the opposite shore of the lake. Kenneth watched him draw and enjoyed the warm sunshine. He could hear some woodpeckers shouting and racketing in a nearby clump of red pines.

Bruce said, "I had a long seance with Joan a week or so ago. She made me the most enormous dinner I've ever seen in years. She says you're driving her to distraction or something. You understand I'm not concerned or anything—Joan's no longer my problem. I told her I couldn't think of any way to help out her case. She's cuckoo about you—that's about it. You've known her a long time; I know you've always liked her. She says she hopes you might get together with her."

"Is that so? That's very flattering. My word." Ken felt rather confused. He supposed that he knew how Joan felt about him, but he was surprised by the way Bruce spoke of it. Not only that—he was also struck by the idea of Joan's choosing to discuss the matter with Bruce.

"She says that she wants to get disentangled from the import business, or most of it—she even offered me the job of being a traveling buyer for the outfit (I said no)—and become a homebody. She figures that you're an essential part in all these plans."

"Oh, yeah?" Kenneth retorted. He was incredulous.

"No, really—I'm not kidding. She's got it all figured out that nothing less than marrying you will make her happy."

"She told me something like that a while back, but I thought she was just being sociable. I like Joan, I've always thought of her as a very exciting, very beautiful person. I feel very close to her. But as for getting married again, to anybody—no, thanks. No more. I've got too much to do right now and I'm going to be even busier later. I've made as much of a domestic scene—as much of one as I ever will—with Helen, and that was it. No more."

Bruce was silent. He glanced from his sketch to the mountains that reared up, apparently straight ahead of them, and then he looked at his sketch again. "She's quite a woman," he said. "And she sure creates a wonderful martini. I expect that what she wants, now that she's older, is a quiet comfortable life."

"I don't believe it," Ken said. "She likes a considerably larger social life than I do. It involves too many people, too much booze, too much sitting around yakking about the latest shows and movies. She's used to a more expensive life than I want to get involved with."

"Yeah, I know," Bruce said. He sighed. "I wish that I had just one cigaret. What time do you figure it is? My watch stopped."

Ken looked at his own. "Ten-thirty a.m., Pacific Daylight Saving Time. It is the 14th or so of July, Nineteen Hundred and froze to death."

"The days are so big up here. There's so much time that there isn't any to speak of." Bruce stood up and stretched himself. "Let's go eat eight or nine aspirins. Maybe we'll think of something else besides smoking."

In camp again, Bruce decided to take a nap. Kenneth seated himself on a great stone in the sunlight. He thought he might read from the pocket copy of Dante that he'd brought in his knapsack. The few pages that he looked at seemed to fade out of his consciousness. The flowery Tuscan hills, flames, the farting devils, the Paradise Garden of the *Purgatorio*— none of it seemed to mean anything in the present surroundings. The Garden of Eden seemed like a William Morris tapestry in a suburban room. He closed the book. He imagined that Shelley's great operatic pieces might be more like it—*Prometheus Unbound*, for example. But the rocks and the blue sky had their own meaning. The trees and flowers, the lake—all of them were leading individual lives, and yet they were connected to each other, related into a world existing. The books misrepresented them as badly as the books misrepresented human beings—or at least described them only partially, drew unskilful pictures of the world, distorted by the author in order to prove some abstract point or other.

Ken raked about in his knapsack until he came up with a plastic sack of raisins. He put a handful of them into his pocket and carried another handful away to eat while he walked along the shore of the lake. He felt restless but very happy to be where he was. The mountains changed color as the sun moved across the sky. The lake and the sky itself began to change, also. A few soft high cumulus clouds floated past the sun's face; the colors and shapes of the landscape flowed and changed, revealing new relationships between rock and water and open space. Watching these changes moved him deeply; he experienced new pitches of sensuous delight.

Ken walked around the lake to the point where the flat little stream that was its outlet flowed between great boulders and then suddenly broke over the edge of the canyon floor and fell in cascades into the wider canyon beyond. Further still, that canyon dropped in its turn into the great stone valley of the Kern River. He sat down nearby, listening to the water, and watched the young trout moving in patterns like branched lightning in the flat water towards the lake. Thick sedgy grass lined the banks of the outlet creek, and also covered the lumpy hummocks of earth which divided the water-course into a number of channels. The fish played in these small canals between the banks and the grassy islets. At some places the water was so shallow that the fish were half exposed to the air, splashing mightily, but soon they'd recover the deeper parts of the stream and venture slowly out into the lake. They'd turn again, swiftly, as if frightened, to re-enter the creek, after only a few minutes in open water. Pentstemon and heather bloomed among the rocks along the bank. Small birds bathed in the shallows along the lake shore.

Ken ate raisins. He wasn't especially hungry but he was aware that it would soon be time for lunch. He began walking back toward the camp.

They enjoyed a leisurely and elaborate meal, for Travis had caught several large trout. Everyone drank several cups of coffee afterwards, but this didn't prevent them from sleeping for an hour or so after lunch.

Kenneth woke first, feeling chilly. The wind made ripples in the fabric of Travis's jacket, flapped Bruce's pants legs. They lay very still, sound asleep. Ken suddenly turned away to look at other things, the lake, the flowers. For quite a few years after the war he had not been able to enjoy a hiking trip because living out of doors and sleeping upon the ground brought back old war-time feelings of continuous danger and worry. The landscape would become more than just landscape; he'd see it as "terrain" which must be crossed in a certain manner. It would provide certain covered places of comparative safety and wide tracts of possibly fatally open country. He gradually lost this feeling, after a few seasons of hiking by himself. The mountains and trees regained their own significnce, their own value. But when he traveled in the company of other men, he was soon aware that his old recollections of terror and misery hadn't completely left him; they might appear at any moment, quite fleetingly, for no more than a second's duration, but as strong as ever. He had learned to accept them for what they were. He was able to say to himself, the next second, "Yes. Very well. But that was then, that's over, here and now everything is what I see it is, neutral rock and water, sun and tree. The other is far away in space and time. I brought it back to scare myself, now that's over, it's back in place."

He sat under a tree, much later in the day, writing in his diary. Travis came along slowly in his direction; he had been fishing the near side of the lake.

"I got half a dozen for supper," Travis said. "What's Bruce doing? Is he still asleep?"

"No. He went up the trail to take a look at the pass and see if there's any snow on the north side of it. He'll be back before supper time."

Travis set down his rod and took off his creel. He opened it to show Kenneth the big golden trout he had caught. They were fat, insolent looking creatures, seeming much too wise to have been lured into Travis's basket.

"Before we go out, I've got to catch a mess for Kate. I promised to bring her some. She's never had golden trout before."

"They're awfully good, considering that they come out of the lake. Up home, lake fish tend to be soft. The good trout are in the mountain streams where the water's fast and cold."

"Kate's a great girl," Travis said. "She's got quite a fix on you."

"Is that so?" Ken replied. "I think she's an awfully intelligent woman, considering how pretty she is."

"She thinks you have an interesting mind or something—I don't know where she got that idea—but you like her, don't you?"

"Sure I do. Kate and I have a lot of fun together."

"She figures that she'd like to marry you, she says."

"I must be going out of my mind!" Kenneth shouted. He threw his book down and stood up.

Travis looked surprised. "What's wrong with you? What are you hollering about?"

"Every lady on the West Coast has decided to marry me. Why don't they let me alone?"

"What's wrong with that? You don't have to get paranoid about it. Relax and enjoy it."

"Helen wrote me a letter just before we came up here—she was planning to come down to your housewarming party. She's divorced from Ron. She wants to talk to me. She seems to think I'm the only friend she's got or whatever. Then Bruce just told me a while ago that Joan has some sort of plan to hogtie me, and now you spring this on me."

By this time Travis was shouting with laughter. "Why fight it?" he managed to gasp out. He presently recovered his breath. "All you have to do is move into a very large house. If the neighbors complain, say that one's your sister, one's your cousin, and one's your wife. Why worry?"

Kenneth complained, "Why me? Why's all this suddenly got to happen to me? What'd I do to deserve all this? All I want to do is read and study and get some philosophy done—why do all these ladies show up ten years too late? If I was interested in a career as a great cocksman or something, it'd be great. But right now...hellfire and damnation!"

"You'd better not come back to town with us, then," Travis said. "You'd better just get out in Fresno or Bishop, even...it may be safer on this side of the Sierra...and stay there under a new name. Or maybe try a sudden trip to New York. Your days are going to be few and your nights busy if you try to stick around San Francisco."

"Damn it, I don't want to live anyplace else. Joan has a giant industry to manage, Kate has the University to run, Helen has all those babies—what more does any of them want?"

"You'd better think up some sort of answer before long or be prepared to move, that's all."

"All I want to know is, 'Why me?' "

"You brought it all on yourself," Travis said, beginning to laugh again. "It's a moral universe. I go now to wash myself. Goodbye. Think hard." He patted Kenneth's round blond head and walked off towards the camp, singing a bawdy ditty.

Kenneth sat still, looking at the water. Then he picked up a handful of small rocks and began pitching them out over the lake. He felt cold, now that the sun was below the west ridge; soon the alpenglow would begin to show on the eastern peaks. He wondered what kind of party Marilynn's housewarming was likely to be, what with all the ladies in question getting together to compare notes. He thought, "I don't really have to decide anything—let the best girl win." He laughed to himself. "Or if I'm lucky, I'll meet somebody new when I get back to town—that's all I need is just one more."

He supposed that all the women would be angry with him, no matter what happened. He told himself that they'd get over it. If his luck held. He must remain at home for a few weeks and stick closely to his own work. The mountain scene before him was pleasing. The actual intimate presence of a woman could occupy his consciousness, evoke his love in the same way, but no single woman he could think of could bear the whole weight of his love; he must build a work of his own which would bear the rest of that weight, that pressure, distribute it to the rest of the world.

He sighed. He was thinking, "For a short, tow-head Swede I must be the biggest megalomaniac now at large. Nevertheless, I believe I've got it. The problem is—logistics, the transport of materiel? Communication—drama? But always the main question: how to tell my love, how to act it out."

He threw a whole handful of pebbles into the water. They made a splash and many ripples. The lake was smooth for a few minutes, but then he began to perceive other ripple circles widening away from the dimple made in the surface by fish rising to take mosquitoes and other flying bugs. As Ken walked along, he could hear the sounds that they made, a little "CLIP!" and the bright washing of tiny waves upon the gravelly shore. He began to gather sticks for the supper fire.

*Mill Valley*, 4:II:63

*San Francisco*, 4:VI:63

# Imaginary Speeches for a Brazen Head

*Burden.* I tell thee, Bacon, Oxford makes report
        Nay, England, and the court of Henry says,
        Thou'rt making of a brazen head by art,
        Which shall unfold strange doubts and aphorisms,
        And read a lecture in philosophy...

                  —Robert Greene, M.A., *The Honourable*
                  *History of Friar Bacon and Friar Bungay.*

...these two with great study and paines so framed a head of brasse, that in the inward parts thereof there was all things like as in a naturall man's head. This being done, they were as farre from perfection of the worke as they were before, for they knew not how to give those parts that they had made motion, without which it was impossible that it should speake...

                  —*The Famous Historie of Fryer Bacon*

*The Brazen Head.* Time is.

*The Brazen Head.* Time was.

*The Brazen Head.* Time is past.

        (A *lightning flashes forth, and a hand appears*
        *that breaks down the Head with a hammer.*)

*Miles.* Master, master, up! hell's broken loose; your head speaks; and there's such a thunder and lightning, that I warrant all Oxford is up in arms. Out of your bed, and take a brown-bill in your hand; the latter day is come.

                  —Robert Greene, M.A., *The Honourable*
                  *History of Friar Bacon and Friar Bungay.*

Tom was carefully building a cigaret while he listened to Dorothy read the latest letter. When she stopped, he asked, "Is that it?"

Dorothy looked at him as if he had just entered the room. She said, "Yes."

"I don't know," Tom said. "I was just thinking about how fifteen or twenty years from now, he'll still be writing to you, whenever he's out of town or whenever we're traveling."

"He'll stop, after awhile," she said. She turned to face the window, walked into the tall embrasure and looked out. The flat white light of London hit her and she backed up a little. At that moment, Tom saw her lose all coloration. She appeared to be a flat, black and white picture. "But I like his letters," Dorothy continued. "He always answers my questions and tells me what's happening and where everybody else is. And they're partly to you, too."

"I guess I could live without his creepy messages," Tom said.

"He's always liked you," Dorothy replied.

"That's what I'm talking about. He's got some kind of morbid, masochistic kind of kick going. He doesn't care anything about me."

"Oh, Tom, who's a masochist now? Come on—let's go out."

"What time is it?" Tom asked. He was standing in front of the mirror that hung above the fireplace, rubbing his chin. "Maybe I ought to shave."

"How should I know? I guess there must be some pubs or bars open by this time. Move just a little." Dorothy had joined him in front of the glass. She began re-securing the pins in her hair, which was a peculiarly metallic blond color and quite wavy. She wore it in a complicated arrangement of rolls and soft braids; it was very long.

Tom looked at her, expressionlessly, and said, "Hello."

Dorothy grinned at him in the glass. "Hello," she said. She kept on fiddling with her hair. He watched her. Suddenly she was hugging him; she kissed him across the mouth. He kissed her in return.

"I like you best, after all," she said. "I love your big round old head." She kissed him again.

"I guess your old man is pretty good," Tom said.

"I'll say," Dorothy told him. "Let's go."

■ ■ ■

At the Nepalese Young Gentlemen's Elegancy Academy, Clifford Barlow stood before a class of adolescent boys. "This," he said. "This." And he inscribed a large ♉ on the black board. Facing the class again, he repeated, very clearly and distinctly, "THIS."

Forty-five rich, dark, and handsome Nepalese young gentlemen looked Clifford right in the eye and replied, clearly and distinctly:

"DISS!"

■ ■ ■

The Grand Mahatma says: "SHE comes along and lights up each of our senses, then SHE selects a different partner and moves away. The numbers on the watch dial glow for a while after they've been exposed to the sunshine, then their light finally dies away. They remember for a while, then they rest. The circulation of the blood, the flow of the breath, what did I have for breakfast—each of these trips a different brain electric relay network chain, brain clouds of light, the great Andromeda nebula, other universes outside this one which we usually think of as true and real, which we in fact keep insisting is the only one...bright billowing clouds that mix together into "I," "I want," "I see," "I remember,"...and more of the same sparkling fog produces this earth we're sitting on, produced Queen Victoria, Ashurbanipal, the cobalt bomb, all kinds of gods, buddhas, unicorns, the fried egg sandwiches we shall eat for lunch."

■ ■ ■

Dorothy was trying to answer Roy's last letter. Clifford was raving and shouting in the kitchen. At last, Dorothy got up from her desk and went to find out what was the trouble.

"Wild beasts of the forest are invading my kitchen!" Clifford pointed to a very small slug on the floor near the sink. Clifford seemed to be in a fit of some kind, a thousand miles off.

"Well, just don't keep shrieking about it," Dorothy calmly replied. "Take it outside."

"My fingers are too big," Clifford said. "I can't get hold of it without hurting it!"

Dorothy found a table knife with which she carefully scooped up the slug. She handed the knife to Clifford, who regarded the slug with a worried gaze. "There," Dorothy said. "Now take your little friend outside."

Clifford turned to regard his wife with his great brown eyes. He tugged at one side of his mustache. "Is he all right?" he asked.

"Of course, ninny. He can walk over the edge of a razorblade without hurting himself. See his little horns peeking out?"

"I'll put him on a leaf," Clifford said.

"He'll eat your entire garden," Dorothy called after him.

Clifford made some sort of unintelligible answer from outside the house.

■　■　■

At a bar in Sausalito, Roy Aherne kept drawing great circles on the oil-cloth before him. It was already inscribed with various hieroglyphs, gargoyles, mathematical equations, graphs, astrological signs, Chinese ideograms, chemical formulae, and bars of music signed "Johann Sebastian Bach."

Roy had a great felt pen full of Magic Ink. Wreathed in fumes of banana oil, booze, and tobacco, Roy wept with the beauty of his visions. "Down through the flames of Hell and Torment, all that screaming and torture, all our dismal evasions and failures and mistakes—but he says 'RISE!'—and up we come, translated out of that earth, breaking out of that garbage, mortician's wax, and pickling sauce into STARS! You must see, at last, that the circle is only a circle if you keep looking at it from one direction. If you turn it only a little, you discover that it is a helix: the circle's bounded in one dimension, but there's really another one to it—the CYLINDER! The Worm Ourobouros! The Angels *have* to fall, we all *have* to be here, but we don't have to stay..."

One of the young men who had been reverently listening to Roy set a fresh drink in front of him. Roy took a sip of it and sighed. He rested his heavy hawk face against his hands for a second, then slowly passed them backwards across his kinky red hair and clasped them behind his imperial head.

"It's so beautiful," Roy said. He smiled and his big green eyes appeared to be dark and warm for a moment. "You realize that Blake actually showed it in his pictures of Jacob's dream...a SPIRAL stairway from Earth to Heaven, with men and angels ascending and descending in the midst of starry clouds; the Bible says 'ladder'... now it's all owned by some English earl. Of course, Blake had read about the Gnostic idea about the Zodiac being a giant water-wheel that carries the Soul through the great circle of all the worlds and heavens and hells. Naturally the church put the Gnostics down very early—first or second century A.D.— the Church said the Soul can go only two ways, down or up—and must eventually stay up with God or down with the Devil, absolutely, for eternity. You certainly have beautiful breasts, my dear," Roy told the girl who was sitting directly across the table from him. (It was a small table.) "They are so yummy-looking that I'd like to spend several weeks kind of studying them. You wouldn't mind if I licked on them a little bit, would you?"

The girl, who had long black hair, very white skin and big blue eyes, laughed and told Roy, "People usually say nice things about my eyes. Don't you like them?"

"They *are* unusual, aren't they?" Roy said. "Why don't you come over to my place and let me look at them, too?"

"I came with Neely and Terry," the girl said. "I have to go back to the city with them."

"Are you part of their act?" Roy inquired.

"What?"

"Do you have to do it all together in order to get your kicks or can Neely and Terry do it by themselves?"

"You're getting kind of nasty, aren't you," the girl said.

"Honey, being a nasty old man is my trade." Roy gave her a dazzling smile. "But seriously, why don't you take me with you when you go? I have to get back to the city some time tonight. I have to go to the unemployment office in the morning and pick up my check."

"I don't know," the girl said. "I never been in an orgy." She rolled her eyes and squirmed a little bit in her chair.

"I wasn't thinking of anything quite so ambitious, myself," Roy said. "Besides, I haven't met Neely and Terry. Maybe we ought to be introduced?"

"They're sitting right across from you, at the bar," the girl said.

■ ■ ■

"One of the least delightful things about Europe OR Asia," Dorothy's letter continued, "is the people from home that you keep meeting and having to talk to—people that I used to see sometimes at home and who I didn't want to know *then*—not to mention several thousands of others I have to look at. I don't think that it's really a money thing, and it isn't really that they are Americans. They're just not interesting. I wish they were all dead or would all go away or something."

■ ■ ■

Tom and Dorothy drank ale in the family section of a neighborhood pub.

Tom said, "I can do without his creepy interest."

"I thought you admire his writings so much," Dorothy remarked.

"You told me yourself that he's as queer as a nine-dollar bill and I can see the kind of icky look in his eye. I don't have any use for him. Let him run around with all the other queers and leave us alone. It's embarrassing to see him, to have him around—"

"All right, Tom," Dorothy said.

"I mean it," Tom said.

"All right, Tom, you've been very positive and masculine."

"Ah, cut out all that psychological bullshit!"

"All right, Tom. Have you thought where we might have dinner?"

128

"I'm not ready to eat yet. Let's have a little more of this ale."

"I've got to pee," Dorothy said. "I'm sure you'll excuse me. Order one for me. A small one."

■ ■ ■

Clifford was playing through the *Art of Fugue*. The organ was a small electronic American one. He hated all electric organs, but this one had a pedal keyboard and it was the only thing that resembled a pipe organ in the city of Katmandu. He had had to spend considerable time searching it out. It stood in the chapel of a French Catholic mission hospital. Clifford had enough high-school French at his command to beg the priests to let him practice on this machine.

He kept his eye directed upon the page of Bach before him. He knew that the mountains were there outside the window. They were the real reason for his own presence in Nepal. But he had to keep his fingers in training, had to spend a certain amount of time every day in Bach's company in order to improve his own character, as he told the priest. The good father approved of the idea of character building, but it was to be hoped that Clifford might play music by Catholic composers from time to time: the continuous association with a Lutheran mind could not be entirely salutary. Clifford obliged him by playing a piece of Rameau or César Franck at each one of his practice sessions.

■ ■ ■

Dorothy wasn't attending to what Tom was saying, nor to the vision of the London street before her. She was thinking, "Well, here's London. It certainly isn't like Delhi. That's the point of its being London, isn't it. Just as 'now' is this year and not last; Cimabue isn't Massaccio. Isn't that right? Yes, it certainly is, Dorothy; I'll tell the world."

She remembered, just then, that Clifford had once apostrophized a large cockroach:

"Fatuous, extravagant insect!"

and that was in Delhi or outside Kandy or in Saigon? "How clever of you to remember, Dorothy," she told herself. "Only you don't really remember—not specifically, not accurately. That was certainly Clifford's voice that I just now heard in my inner ear, and I could see his fist and bent arm raised above his head like somebody in a Victorian steel engraving."

She must, after all, stay with Tom. She might, when she got older, be able, at last, to live by herself and not worry about any man anymore—but maybe not. Why not have what there is now. Considering that Clifford and the rest had been, finally, impossible. *That* life had been great, she had needed it, she wouldn't have been able to recognize Tom if she hadn't known Clifford and Roy. But there was too much *of* them: they were too complicated, too specialized—and at the same time, too various, too competitive, too ambitious, too egoistic—whatever it was, Dorothy had Tom now, and must stick to him. There were only a few strong colors and textures about him: fine bronze and cedar wood and ivory all joined and polished; she thought of him as if he were an artifact that had been produced by craftsmen of some remote island tribe. She liked him, she loved him, there was a great deal of *him*, she thought, "My copious husband." Tom was massive but he moved well. Dorothy hated to think about how he could eat almost continuously all day long without getting fat. He remained solid, massive. He had played football when he was younger— not many years ago. He never complained about growing old, like Clifford did, and he was ten years or so younger than Roy. Dorothy sighed. Had she remembered to take her pills? She thought of her mother's elephantine shape. She was determined not to go like that. Clifford was perhaps the most beautiful of all, though—heavy, dark hair, big eyes and perfect, olive-colored skin.

■ ■ ■

Roy was one of the guests at a cocktail party being given by Max and Alice Lammergeier. Alice had been cross with Max for having invited Roy. "He talks so loud," she said. "He dominates the room. It's like having a sound truck in the house."

Max told her, "There's going to be lots of people. He won't attract or bulldoze all of them. I like having Roy at a party; he loosens the other people up. Otherwise, they all try to be stuffy and normal. They're shy of me being a shrinker. Anyway, he probably needs a dinner."

"Why don't you just give him a dollar and let him get something for himself to eat in Chinatown or someplace. It'd certainly be easier on my nerves."

"He'd only put it on his bar tab or buy a magazine with it. Mrs. Gorman's cooking tonight, anyway, isn't she? You're not having to make the dinner."

Alice tried to explain, patiently, but she was growing more annoyed with Max. "You forget that it's as much work for me to supervise the old battle axe and keep her from drinking too much Bordeaux and keep an eye on the catering people—caterers! Hah. All those beatniks they so foolishly hire as waiters, all hair and fingernails..."

"Just like Paris," Max said.

"It wasn't *my* expensive handmade wristwatch that disappeared from the kitchen windowsill where you were silly enough to leave it the last time we had a party. I might just as well prepare everything myself, for all the help these idiots are."

"Come on, Alice, you've been crazy about Roy for years."

Alice was immediately piqued. "Max, that gag isn't the least bit amusing and it never has been!"

Max was laughing and trying to tickle Alice's ribs.

"I mean it!" she yelled, trying to break away from him. "You carry everything beyond any reasonable limit, now STOP IT!"

"Aren't you my angel baby?" Max inquired, hugging her close to him.

"No, you idiot, stop it."

"Will you be nice to Roy?" Max said, tickling her.

Alice shrieked and chortled, "NO! STOP!"

"He'll tease you if you aren't."

"Why does he have to come at all STOP IT, I SAID. Oh, all right. All right. But not again for a long time, huh?"

"Mmmmm," Max said, and tenderly tweaked her.

Later in the evening, Alice set her jaw and gave Max a hard look from across the living room where Roy was gassing on and on to a small circle of the other guests.

"The whole 'Matter of Europe,'" Roy was saying, "has been that of Classical logic—the conventionally accepted...that is, we always think of it in such terms as 'inescapable common sense' and so on—that order of progression from A to B to C: A, you're on the main floor; B, you're moving with the escalator, and C, you're at the second floor. There are perhaps three or four more stories to the building, not to mention a couple of basements, but the escalator isn't concerned, isn't connected to them—those other places don't exist in terms of the universe represented by that escalator."

A bright young broker, late from the Stanford business school inquired, "Don't you think that Camus was trying to show us that there was a question of riding or not riding the escalator—and that really adult, mature, responsible people must choose to ride it?"

"No, I don't, and I think Camus was a booby when it came to philosophizing."

The young broker and the rest of the people who were listening to Roy were shocked and offended by this statement. All of them were Americans, all of them believed what they read in *Life* magazine (namely that the newly dead M. Camus was the smartest man the West had to offer in its ideological battle with the International Communist Conspiracy), and all of them were shocked to hear someone speak so carelessly of the noble dead.

Roy sensed their disapproval and immediately began to try outraging them further. "Where'd you ever get such a lunatic notion? But I suppose that I let myself in for it, as usual, by introducing this brilliant analog or Parable of the Moving Stair...all I'm trying to tell you is that Europe was a dead issue long before these very good novelists like M. Camus came along and tried to glue it all back together...I suppose if I had to choose between Karl Barth and Karl Marx, I'd kill myself, too..."

Alice gave Max a hard look. Max fixed his gaze upon her and slowly crossed his eyes. Alice turned away swiftly to attend to the guests who were standing about in the other rooms. She greeted several new arrivals, then passed into the kitchen to remove the Bordeaux out of Mrs. Gorman's reach.

Roy's ex-wife, Margaret, was talking to Beth Sanderson in the library.

"Max is gorgeous," she was saying, "but he's an utter lunatic. Imagine being hooked up with that weensie little Alice and her glasses and her sinus and her genius children."

Beth said, "Max is really very gentle and sweet. We went together for a long time when we were in school, but we kept quarreling about politics and everything, so I started going with Mark. Alice was in nurse's training when Max was at Langley Porter; that's why she's kind of bossy and hypochondriac now...but Max is such a tease and such a clown that he really gets her going sometimes. Aren't these hot canapés good!" A nasty looking young man with a beard and a stiff red jacket had come up to them with a big tray full of Swedish kickshaws.

■ ■ ■

The Grand Mahatma says, "We must practice doing everything right. We must practice being perfect. The Saints, the Bodhisattvas, the Confucian Sages—all of them practiced at it until they could do everything perfectly, and they were perfect themselves, of course. Any one of us can do the same thing. What else is there to be done, after all?"

■ ■ ■

Dorothy washed her hands very carefully. She messed with her hair a little bit, and even though she kept turning her head slightly, in various directions, she kept her gaze fixed on the eyes in the mirror. She would write to Roy about the hotel, and the fake crown jewels and the Tate Gallery and how everything smelled of wet wool and coal smoke and all the good food. She thought of how much younger Roy looked when he was undressed and how much he used to worry about the size of his cock. When it stood up, he could certainly do a lot with it. Other times he stayed away too long. "Well," she told herself, "I fixed all that once and for all, didn't you, Dorothy, and he's still wondering what's happened. I don't care. What else shall I tell him, in my letter: Dear Roy, Tom's jealous of your little thing even though I've told him and everybody else that you're not only a faggot but impotent as well and even though they may have heard that we went to bed together, nothing ever happened, did it. Aside from which, Tom thinks you want to do it to him, whatever it is or however they do it and the idea makes him vomit and he hates you. I don't care. Please write to me soon about Max and Alice. Does Alice have any new glasses? Love beyond measure, Dorothy. That would be an answer, all right. And a PS: If you see Clifford or write to him, please tell him that my mother must have that piano back again *right now*. (I really do have to tell him that. Mama is such a pest, yelling about that piano in every letter.)"

■ ■ ■

Alice Lammergeier began wearing spectacles when she was a little girl. Her mother made a great fuss about how it would spoil her looks and what a shame it was. She hoped that the spectacles would be only temporarily necessary. But Alice liked to read and her eyes were bad, and she had to go on wearing glasses and she was sensitive about it and hated to wear them.

She was fussing about all this one morning while Max was reading the Sunday papers in bed beside her.

"Try mine," he said, removing his heavy plastic-rimmed specs. "See how they suit you."

Alice took the big glasses and went to her dressing table. She put them on and peered at herself in the mirror. "They're only window glass, compared with mine," she said, and then she laughed. The huge glasses on her small face made her look like a young girl.

Max said, "If you've got to have glasses, really *have* them. Have lots. Get a lorgnette. Get prescription sunglasses. Get seven sets of contact lenses and have purple eyes on Thursdays. Go see that new kid oculist across the hall from my office. He can fix you up."

■ ■ ■

"But this way, every day is the same," Dorothy complained. She hated the idea. She hated Ceylon. Elephants are actually cranky and unreliable. Dr. Bitteschoen was being difficult. Orchids in profusion are not amusing. Monkeys and bugs and flies and primitive toilets..."Clifford, I just can't repeat the same routine, I want to have something happen next."

Clifford sat quite still, watching her. "You want a big operatic climax of some kind?" he inquired.

"I want *something* to happen," Dorothy wailed.

"Everything is happening, right now," Clifford said, gently. "You're happening. What more do you want?"

"It's not the same thing," she said. "Maybe I want surprises. Maybe I don't want to know what's going to happen and I already do. I know I want more than that..."

"Then make something else happen. But after you've cooked it, you're going to have to eat it or wear it or sell it or bury it. And after that, what will you do for an encore?"

Dorothy collapsed upon a screechy rattan chair. "I don't know," she said, "I just hate it, that's all. I know I'll get up in the morning and the house will look a certain way and I'll be washing and dressing and taking pills and drinking coffee. At a certain time I'll be going into town to work for Dr. Bitteschoen or not, depending on which day it is. You'll be here or not, and you are a certain way in the morning, you'll be doing all your morning things, answering letters, and I'll be writing in my journal and

133

then sorting over my Singhalese-Dravidian file cards and you'll. . ."

Clifford felt himself growing a little impatient with Dorothy's recitation. He interrupted her.

"You could run away and join the circus, I guess. You'd see a new town every week and have different problems every day and spend the winter in Florida," he said.

"Well, I'm trying to be honest with you, Clifford, seriously trying to tell you how I feel."

"I'm being serious. If you don't want to stay here, go away. If you're tired of trying to be a linguist, quit your job with Bitteschoen. You could stay home and we could have babies. I'd like that."

■ ■ ■

The Grand Mahatma says, "Plenty of people will tell you that it's the Fate of Man to be eternally a day late and a dollar short. Don't you believe it."

■ ■ ■

Dorothy and Tom met Dr. Bitteschoen quite accidentally in a Dutch museum where they had gone to look at Van Gogh paintings. Dorothy squeezed Tom's neck in the bend of her elbow.

"This is my new husband, Louie. I took him away from a movie star. He used to be a faggot but now he's reformed. His name is Tom Prescott."

"How do you do, Mr. Prescott," Dr. Bitteschoen said, shaking Tom's hand. "I very seldom attend the cinema," he added, rather apologetically.

Tom said, "I don't either."

"Dorothy has mentioned you quite often in her letters to me," the Doctor continued. "Please allow me to congratulate you. You must know that Dorothy has always been like another one of my daughters."

"All sticky and incestuous," Dorothy said, seizing Dr. Bitteschoen in a great embrace. "Oh, Louie, I'm so glad to see you. We must go and have a drink right now and talk. Come on, Tom."

Later on, Tom asked her, "Say—what's all this business about faggots? You know what you're talking about? Do you know what it means?"

"Of course I do, Old Meany. Don't be so gloomy and grouchy."

"I don't think you do," Tom said. "You keep saying it to everybody. You say Roy is a faggot and then fix him up to marry your best friend. Now you call me that to some guy I never met before. I don't like that. I don't think you know what you're saying."

"Tom, I'm not totally stupid," Dorothy indignantly replied. "Gigi Fiske's brother, Luke, used to borrow her false eyelashes when we were all at Harvard."

■ ■ ■

134

The Grand Mahatma says: "It is absolutely imaginary—the world of other people's wishes and feelings and our notions of them and our mistakes about them. We imagined that they loved or hated us; they were engaged in remembering an old movie, occupied with inventing the Binomial Theorem or rehearsing to themselves what they were going to tell us next because they imagined that we were thinking about them in a certain way...and about all the rest of the world...And they supposed that we were on the point of saying or doing something that they had imagined we ought, 'characteristically' (or 'morally' or 'naturally' or 'insanely') to be doing in the present circumstances."

■ ■ ■

Roy was out rock hunting with Max Lammergeier. It was a warm day, early in the spring. The sunshine was hot, where they were sitting on top of a greater boulder. A freighter was slowly making its way towards the Golden Gate and the Pacific. Roy said, "I don't know—fuck it. All I really like is fucking and food and poetry and landscape and music. But I get tired of people too easily—and they get tired of me: I talk too much and too loud. I want too much from them, I want to consume them, get so close that we both disappear. They don't like that, they get scared, bored...I belong in a monastery...an asylum...jail."

■ ■ ■

Clifford yelled for Dorothy. "Please come and set the table now, I'm ready."

Dorothy obediently cleared away all the papers and flowers from the dining table. She went into the kitchen. Clifford was industriously stirring a pot full of curry. It smelled exactly right. "Can I taste it?" she asked.

"No," Clifford said. "We have to have drinks, first. I've put them with the nuts and other good things on the big brass tray. Take them in, now, if you please."

Dorothy looked at him. He was seeing something else, he was somewhere else. She might have yelled at him or pinched him but he wouldn't really attend, would only ask, patiently, attentively, "Well, what is it?", and she would be unable to stand that, right at this particular moment. She took the tray with its little dishes and its two bright thin glasses into the living room and set it on a low table. She put a record on the phonograph and started it playing; it was music from a popular Broadway show. Dorothy said, "Hello, Shitface," to the lizard who lived upside down on the ceiling. An elephant honked in the distance. The room was filled with yellow light. Bugs clattered and pestered at the screens which surrounded the living room.

Clifford joined her. "Let's have our drinks, now," he said. "I hope they're all right."

Dorothy tasted the cold bright fluid. It reminded her about how she used to imagine drinking perfume, how nice it would be to drink something which was liquid and which smelled so good. The martini was cold, aromatic, and heavy... not heavy the same way syrup or oil is, but massive as liquid metal: mercury...

■ ■ ■

The Grand Mahatma says, "All American children are fond of saying (even when it's both untrue and unprofitable), 'I can if I want to.' The children say, 'When I grow up, I'll do exactly as I please. I'll be my own boss.'

"The reason why Americans look the way they do when they're forty years old (mean, whipped, half crazy) is that they've done everything that they wanted to do and have had everything they've always wanted and now (at age forty) they've found out that there's a great deal more of the universe to see, to own, to control, and all of it is quite indifferent to the powers and accomplishments and fading charms of these successful maniacs. These people figure that if they really wanted to, they could have all this extra territory and experience for their own... but they also know, now, that they'd ask (after the having, the owning), 'What shall we do now?'—the same question they've been asking their wrinkles and their fading hair and bright plastic teeth every morning in the bathroom mirror:

" 'What in hell am I going to do now? I ought to study Sanskrit but it's too hard, my memory doesn't function any more. I used to love playing chess but I never learned to do it right so I stopped playing years ago. I wish I'd learned to play the piano, but I never had time to practice. Now my fingers are old and stiff and my reflexes are too slow and I can't concentrate on anything any more like I could when I was a kid.'

"When they were children, these people used to pester their mothers, always asking 'What shall we do now?'

"Their mothers told them, 'Go wash your hands and practice your music lesson. Go out in the garden and pick a big bouquet of flowers and take it to old Mrs. Prendergast—poor lonesome old thing, I've been meaning to call on her myself and take her some flowers, but I've been so busy I don't know where the time goes. But I do know that I want you out of the house for a while, right this minute—I have work to do.' "

■ ■ ■

Dorothy came into the hotel room. Tom looked around at her and said hello. He was lying on his belly on the bed, reading a book. He was all naked and pink and clean.

"You look like some awful baby picture," Dorothy said. She sat down beside him on the edge of the bed. She peered over his shoulder at the book, and then she began to tickle the back of his neck. Tom shrugged and wagged his head. "Don't do that," he said, trying to continue his reading.

"Do you know who I just saw in Trafalgar Square?" she asked him.

"Yes I do. You saw the Beatles and Lord Snowdon all walking arm-in-arm and singing the sextet from *Lucia*."

"Aren't you smart. How did you know?"

"OW! Quit it, will you?" Tom rolled about on the bed; Dorothy had yanked a single hair from his left buttock.

"I met my old teacher, Dr. Bitteschoen that I've told you all about. He bought me tea and he wants to meet you but he's leaving London tonight for Tübingen. We'll see him when we get to Germany."

Tom asked, "What's the old geezer got to say?"

"Oh, we talked about Ceylon and Clifford Barlow and all our friends and linguistics people."

Tom said, "Uh-huh." He was reading again.

"Poor baby," Dorothy said. She stroked his scarred legs. Tom kicked his feet and shouted, "HEY! I told you all that scar tissue is still real sensitive!"

"I'm sorry, Tom. I forgot. I won't do it again."

"Well, we got some good out of it all, anyway," Tom said. "They got us a trip to Europe."

"That insurance man was awfully snotty, though," Dorothy said. "You'd think it was all his own personal money."

■ ■ ■

Roy and Clifford were driving to Seattle. Clifford had been engaged to give an organ recital at the University. Roy went along to help drive the car, to keep track of the scores and turn the pages and cheer Clifford up.

Roy said, "You know how she'll finally be—she'll have a little apartment in New York, or San Francisco—possibly she'll go back to Cambridge, but I doubt it—she'll have a big whiskey voice, weight about 175, all her hair piled up on top of her head like Amy Lowell (no cigars, though). She'll have learned how to cook, at last, and with luck, she'll know how to mix martinis. She'll give little dinners for old friends when they come to town. Young people will make pilgrimages to her door. She'll go to one or two of the best parties and openings every year, and write about seven volumes of reminiscences..."

"You've got quite a scenario going there, haven't you," Clifford remarked. "I hope she'll get pregnant right away and have lots of babies."

"It isn't in the cards," Roy said.

"You sure sound positive," Clifford said, rather sharply.

"She doesn't like the idea of having children except as an idea; Dorothy will always be too young or too busy or too old for actually doing it. Anyway, she has her work," Roy told him.

"So she says," Clifford glumly replied. Then he sighed. "I want to have a family," he said. "I'm going to find me a nice healthy country girl and marry her. She doesn't have to be smart. She doesn't have to do anything except keep house and take care of the babies."

"It's a little hard to imagine you living with some squaw," Roy said.

"I've had all the wiggy intellectual chicks I need," Clifford told him. "Enough is enough."

"I expect she and Margaret are having a great time in Reno," Roy said, and immediately wished that he hadn't, for Clifford was looking very sad. "Remember the time we hitchhiked to Portland and it snowed all the way from Ukiah to the north?" Roy asked.

Clifford said, "If I had a nickel for every time I've hitched on this road, I'd be a rich mother today. Let's stop and get a beer at this place up here. Are you hungry?"

■ ■ ■

"Let me have some before we go out," Dorothy said. She had her coat and boots on. Tom passed her the cigaret. She held it carefully in her gloved fingers, then inhaled some acrid, aromatic smoke along with deep sniffs of fresh air. She held her breath and crossed her eyes as she handed the cigaret back to Tom, who smoked again.

Dorothy exhaled and then she said, "Give me just a little more. This isn't quite as wild as that other stuff we had in Tangiers. Then we'll go. I don't want to get too blasted."

■ ■ ■

Roy hiked very slowly up the dusty trail towards Forester Pass in the California Sierra. He carried the same Army surplus A-frame pack which he had sworn, the year before, never to carry any place again. He sweated a lot, but he was determined not to drink very often from his canteen.

Simply by walking, he had transformed the world into granite rock and blue sky and dust. His shoulders hurt but he knew better than to shift the rucksack into a "new" position. He set his left foot one pace ahead, rested his weight on it, then his right foot swung itself one step up, solid and square on a block of granite. He tried to speed up a little bit. It was mid-morning and he felt nervous about getting over the pass and down to a good camping place on the other side before it was night. It seemed to him that he was going so slowly that it might take him until late afternoon to reach the top of the pass.

He kept remembering different fragments of the Brahms Double Concerto. Thinking of the music and trying to remember what passage came next beyond the one he was hearing in his inner ear made him forget the straps cutting into his shoulders. But sometimes the same few bars of music kept recurring, obsessively, and simply added to his misery. Then he'd suddenly be remembering another part of the music and yet another and he'd forget about his feet and about the difficulties of breathing.

Roy stopped to rest at the big bronze memorial tablet which marks the place where a trail crewman was killed while working on that section of the path. Roy poured out a small libation of water to his ghost. He didn't remove his pack; he simply leaned against the boulders and looked back down the vast rocky basin towards the small dark pines that mark the highest camp on Tyndall Creek, miles below. It all looked like pictures of Tibet, which he'd seen in books. Roy wished he could go to the Himalayas. He told himself, "I'd be great in the Himalayas; I can just barely go along this trail without fading away, and I'm so old now, that I'd probably have a heart attack if I tried wandering around in country even higher than this."

He began walking again, slowly gaining altitude. Soon he began to smell the dead burro. It lay where it had lain two years before, no further changed, as much as Roy could see; it hung across the jagged rocks, an old moth-eaten steamer rug. Someone had scattered powdered lime across the carcass and the surrounding stones. The animal had been half-mummified by the dry air, and probably it was also still partly frozen. When the frozen parts thawed in the summer sunshine they rotted enough to stink. The stench was very loud in that place where there was nothing else to be smelled—"Not even my own sweat," Roy thought. There was a faint roaring of distant flies.

He followed the switchbacks of the trail through the odor of carrion and at last he was beyond it. He climbed higher. The trail to the pass seemed even longer than he had remembered it. Here was a whole section of it that seemed unfamiliar, a steep winding through scree and gravel. Soon, however, the trail became a narrow ledge carved into the face of the mountain and he began to see flowers growing out of the cracks and joints in the dark, fine-grained rock. Roy knew that he must be approaching the crest. There were very short-stemmed sunflowers, heather, and purple penstemons. Higher still, he began to find the brilliant blue flowers of polemonium which local climbers call "skypilot." He picked one; the stem was thick and furry. He looked back to the south but he could no longer decide which one of the long brown whalebacks was Mt. Whitney. He had trouble squeezing his diary shut upon the thick blossoms of polemonium that he wanted to keep.

He was surprised when he got to the top of the pass and looked at his watch; it wasn't yet half past twelve. He took off the pack and put on his sweater and a windbreaker. The breeze was light but very cold. He sat on the rocks near the trail sign that says "Forester Pass 13,200" and ate his lunch while he looked out towards the great blue and tawny peaks to the north—Mt. Brewer and the tops of the Palisade group beyond. The distant peaks all stood out with clear, sharp edges against the blue sky. Roy looked into the miles of wilderness, exulting in the idea of its emptiness, its comparative uselessness to anyone and its fantastic beauty. Nobody wanted to live there, nobody could make much money out of it, not many people had the energy to visit much of it. It was all a marvel and a delight to him. He loved every rock, every pond, every twig.

One year he had been hiking with his friend, Mark Sanderson. At the top of a 12,000 foot pass they had met a minister and his ten sons. The minister invited Roy and Mark to join him in meditation and prayer; it was, after all, a Sunday. Since there was nowhere else to go, and they wanted to stay and enjoy the view for a while, Roy and Mark resigned themselves to prayer. The minister shut his eyes and raised his face to the Heavens. He addressed the Deity at great length. His boys knelt about him on the rocks. The youngest of them was perhaps eight or nine years old, and the oldest was a serious personage of eighteen or twenty who wore a splendid blond beard. Each boy covered his eyes with one hand as he knelt. Roy noted how much all the boys resembled their father: they were long thin people with beaky noses and lantern jaws. Each of them wore gold rimmed spectacles. All of them were blond.

After the departure of the holy family, Mark Sanderson raved for ten minutes about the baleful effects of the Christian religion, its apparently endless powers of proliferation, its stultifying effect upon the political, educational and cultural life of America. It was responsible for dishonesty in government, hypocrisy in education and censorship of the arts. Mark inveighed against the growing power of the Black International, both at home and abroad, and about the possible dangers involved in having a Papist for president of the United States. Very soon, superstition, censorship and fascism would envelop and destroy America.

Roy said, "I expect."

He preferred to travel alone in the mountains. Going with a party was like going to a museum with other people: you must wait for them or they must wait for you and nobody can see anything and you have to go back alone, later, to find out what was really there. If you want to see mountains, why bring people with you?

Roy lit a cigaret and began writing in his journal about the pass and the weather and the flowers. He wondered when he'd get around to quitting cigarets. "Why should I quit anything I like," he wondered. "Because then I'd be able to breathe. But why go on breathing—all it does is keep you alive and while you're alive you have trouble breathing and your shoulders hurt and you can't see straight and you're tired of the whole proposition anyway. Dorothy is gone, you're a flop as a great poet, you're too crazy to hold an ordinary job for very long, you bother people, other people bother you—and so on, around and around in a puddle of mush and slobber."

Roy stood up. He felt as if he kept right on going up, since he wasn't wearing the rucksack. He laughed and jumped around on the rocks. Little birds flew about, cheeping querulously. There were mountains all around. Below him to the north were lakes and tarns and little piney meadows where he would sleep this night. He sang and whistled; the wind flapped his hair. "No wonder I was tired," he told himself. "Carrying all *that* up 13,000 feet of mountain."

A moment later an Air Force jet fighter came crashing and screeching miles above him in the sky overhead. It hustled off to the west while Roy jumped and waved and yelled: "Hollow wooden head son of a bitch! Get out of here! Get out of these mountains!"

■ ■ ■

Dorothy said, "I'm going to the store. Do you want anything?"

Tom looked up from his book. He looked at her as if she were a total stranger who had wandered into the room by mistake.

"What?" he asked.

"Do you want anything from the store?"

"I don't know. Which store are you going to?"

"To the little one."

Tom thought for a minute, then he said, "Get some of those hand-made doughnuts. And get me some ice cream. Ah. . ." He paused, looked blankly at Dorothy. "Chocolate," he concluded. Then he looked back at his book.

"Is that all?" Dorothy inquired. She was suddenly wildly angry with him. "We're supposed to go to Mark and Beth's for dinner tonight. You always stuff yourself whenever we go over there. Must you eat a great mountain of goodies just before dinner?"

Tom said, "Look, you asked me if I wanted anything. I was quietly minding my own business. I'd like to have some doughnuts and ice cream and coffee. It isn't anywhere near dinner time, it's only a little bit after two, and they never have dinner before eight o'clock."

"You'll die, that's all," Dorothy exclaimed. "You'll eat all these pounds of ick and have a heart attack and die. You're greedy and self-indulgent and disgusting. I hate you! I hope you choke!"

"You haven't even started for the store yet," Tom said. He was trying to remain calm and to be patient. "I don't have anything to choke on. But you've been taking those god-damned pills again and they're going to drive you so goofy I'm going to have to have you committed—if your liver doesn't quit first. I asked you not to do that."

"Do you want me to be a big fat sow like Mother? I *have* to take them. I don't have that hummingbird kind of metabolism you've got. It just isn't fair!"

Tom looked at her and quietly asked, "Are you going to the store or not?"

Dorothy was still excited. "Yes!" she said, almost shouting. "I've got to buy soap and pepper and things. . ."

"Well, go do it," Tom said. "I've got to read."

■ ■ ■

141

"I always thought it would be lovely to play the harp—so lovely and grace-ful." Such were the sentiments of Margaret Gridley's mother. Often as Margaret walked beside the glassy Willamette near her California ranch-style home outside Eugene, she would recall that wistful thought of her mother's. Usually, however, Margaret was thinking of the voice of her friend, Herbert Wackernagel, singing the baritone solo in Bach's Cantata 517, O Heilige Stern Gefallen, and about Mr. Steadman, the organist, who used to faint in the middle of the passage about the crown of thorns. Whenever the choir had to practice that part of the cantata, a pair of boys had to sit at either end of the organ bench beside Mr. Steadman in order to prevent him from collapsing forward onto the keyboards. The choir would continue singing *a cappella* until Mr. Steadman, who had been vigorously fanned and patted and restored by a jolt of amyl nitrate, was able to continue playing.

Margaret Gridley could sympathize with Mr. Steadman. She no longer sang in his choir nor attended the First Methodist-Episcopal Church. Gazing at the stained-glass windows in that building regularly sent her off into semi-cataleptic trances during which she was incapable of any other knowledge save that imparted to her by the splendid baritone voice of Herbert Wackernagel and heavenly vistas of red green yellow blue light. Her mother told her that nice girls don't have those kinds of feelings. Margaret became a Unitarian; there were no stained-glass windows in that church. Her parents insisted that she must attend some kind of Divine Services every Sunday; they said they didn't care which church it took place in, so long as it was a Protestant one.

Everyone in Eugene was horribly shocked when the fact was learned that Mr. Steadman, Herbert Wackernagel and the two choirboys who used to keep Mr. Steadman from collapsing, had been observed on several occasions while they were playing snooker together at Glad Charley's Old Time Pool Hall Tavern in the old bad part of Eugene down by the Southern Pacific tracks. All four of them were formally excommuni-cated from the First Methodist-Episcopal Church with bell, book and extinguished candles—the Reverend Mr. Soames was very High Church; some of his parishioners suspected that Mr. Soames's heart inclined towards Rome and Popery. There were certain citizens who told it for a fact that four surplices were hung upside down on the back wall of the vestry of the church; however, this was considered by the more charitable members of the community to have been a slander that had been origi-nated by certain regrettably censorious members of the United Brethren Church which stood on the opposite side of the street from the First Methodist-Episcopal.

To the surprise of everyone, Mr. Steadman didn't leave Eugene under a cloud. He was invited to become the organist for the Unitarian Church and also to give lessons in organ playing and composition at the Univer-sity. The president of the University received a few letters and anony-mous phone calls about Mr. Steadman's Moral Character, but the president of the University was a notoriously liberal churchman and probably a Radical. Mr. Steadman kept his job.

"Now that all the fuss is over, Margaret, you can start coming to church with me again," Mrs. Gridley said.

"I like it at the Unitarian," Margaret replied. "It's so much quieter and simpler."

Margaret's father bulged his great blue eyes and hollered, "You just want to go down there and look at that damned Wackernagel kid!"

"I've already told her about that," Mrs. Gridley said. "There's no sense of running it into the ground. This is a small town, they grew up together, they're bound to see each other now and then, but she's not to talk to him or have anything to do with him."

"God-damn little heifer wants to get bred," Mr. Gridley shouted.

"Orval!" Mrs. Gridley shouted back at him. She couldn't bear his coarse language.

"I don't know why he don't get to hell out of here," Mr. Gridley continued. "After all the scandal and shouting down to the church. That's what anybody else would have done—and that goes for old Steadman, too—but Herb's a stubborn Dutchman, just like his old man. That old Calvin set right there and died rather than use that phone to call himself the doctor. Mad at the phone company. Didn't want one in the house, but old Sister Wackernagel says her and the kids got to have it and got one put in and paid for it, too. Old Calvin he wouldn't have no more to do with it."

■ ■ ■

Dorothy was undressing. Roy was already in bed, as usual.

"I wish you wouldn't look at me, dressing and undressing, I'm so awkward, my body's so ugly," she said.

"No you aren't. I love to see you," Roy said. He lay propped up on one elbow, admiring her pink and white skin, her golden hair.

Dorothy got into bed and turned out the light. They embraced each other.

Sometime later, she asked him, "Did you ever really make it with other men?"

"Sure," Roy said. "Lots."

"Then why do you like making it with me so much?"

"Because you're beautiful and you feel good and I love you and we fit together in more interesting ways and it makes me feel, somehow, more righteous or justified or something. . . ."

Dorothy said, "You really like doing it don't you. You ought to get married."

"I'm too crazy, too queer to marry anybody," Roy said. "Besides, you have to marry Clifford and I have to be alone to read and write."

Later in the night, Dorothy awoke and found him sitting up on the edge of the bed, smoking a cigaret. "What's wrong?" she asked. "What time is it?" She hugged him gently around the belly.

"Nothing," he said. "I got too hot and woke up and wanted a cigaret. Go to sleep."

Dorothy said, "Ummmm." She clung softly to him. Then she woke up again and was aware of Roy wandering about the room. "What's wrong?" she said.

"I'm looking for my socks," Roy said, kneeling down on the floor and groping about.

"Come back to bed and go to sleep. Don't go away."

"I have to go home and work, now," Roy said.

"Why do you always leave me?" Dorothy asked. She was still wrapped up in the bed clothes. Her eyes were closed but she spoke very softly and clearly.

"I always come back, don't I? Don't be afraid. I'll see you after work tomorrow and we'll have dinner," Roy told her.

"Don't leave me."

"I told you, it gets too hot and sweaty and uncomfortable in bed and I can't sleep so I start writing in my head and I want to look things up and it drives me cuckoo to have to stay in bed if I have to be up. I have to go home," Roy said.

Dorothy clung to him softly. She gently squeezed him. "All right," she said. She didn't let go.

Roy felt impatient, he had to get out of doors, he wanted some fresh air, he wanted to check a phrase in Yeats's *Per Amica Silentia Lunae.* He kept quoting it to himself inexactly; he wanted to use it in a paragraph, a long strophe that he kept hearing, now, inside his head.

"Let me go, now," Roy said, quite softly, and kissed her.

She squeezed him again and said, "All right." Dorothy tried to let go of him and stay asleep, let him out of her dreams, she was dreaming this story about Roy and he was temporarily fading out of the script and he'd fade back in again but the dreaming was only true dreaming as long as she was warm in bed with her eyes shut and it was night. Was it still night? "What time is it?" she asked.

Roy said, "Quarter to three," and he kissed her again and went away.

Dorothy had had her orders from Clifford, which was a part of the scenario as well, "Be nice to Roy, take him to bed and make it with him, he is lonely and sad and thinks that he's an old queer that nobody can ever love, and he has never known what it's like to be happy with a girl. Help him out. He's really a beautiful old guy but he doesn't know it and he likes you."

■ ■ ■

Dr. Ludwig Bitteschoen was a short, neat, very handsome old man with soulful brown eyes and beautiful wavy white hair. He looked distin-

144

guished, he looked like somebody famous.

He told Dorothy, "When I was young, I was often taken for a popular actor from the Berlin Staatstheater. I'm still mistaken for somebody else. When I go stay with friends in Pacific Palisades, young persons with autograph albums approach me and ask where do they remember me from. Of course," he continued, smiling, "I *am* famous, among precisely a dozen people who are concerned with linguistics and philology. Nobody reads what I write, however—not even my book on world language which is so politely designated a 'quality paperback.'"

Dr. Bitteschoen had, at an early age, been a very junior member of the Weimar Government. No one had ever forgiven him for that. He became a refugee in 1932, but he returned to Germany for a few years after the war. They gave him the Goethe Prize and honorary degrees from half a dozen ancient universities. He had formed enough American connections during his exile to provide him with the scholarships and foundation grants which made it possible for him to travel about the world and to carry on his linguistic researches. He was often invited back to America as a visiting professor or as a special lecturer in the more expensive universities.

At Berkeley, for example, he held a lectureship which required no teaching. He had only to address the public and the academic community once a month in Wheeler Hall. Not many people attended these occasions, but Dr. Bitteschoen was always there on time, on what he called his one "working" day, happily discoursing upon the development of the morphemes in ancient Peruvian Indian languages.

Dr. Bitteschoen loved California and he was particularly fond of Dorothy, who was about the same age as his own daughters. He had long ago accepted her as a member of his family. He had first known her when she was an exceedingly bright undergraduate. She was one of the few Americans whom he had chosen to train as one of his own disciples. (All his European protégés were long since installed as full professors in the largest and most prestigious European and American universities.)

Dr. Bitteschoen had been a guest at Dorothy's wedding, when she married Clifford Barlow. He loved to play violin duets with Clifford, who could make jokes with him in German. Dr. Bitteschoen could never understand why Dorothy and Clifford should be getting a divorce. He told Dorothy, upon that occasion, "It seems to me very middle class, very American; I am surprised. Clifford is a very fine man. Why can't you stay with him?"

Dorothy was confused, then. In a way, she was angry with Dr. Bitteschoen for offering a defense of Clifford (that Monster!) and at the same time, she was profoundly touched by what she recognized as the Doctor's real interest in her happiness and welfare. She also knew that he was right, that it was middle class and American and careless, like people in Hollywood gossip columns who kept marrying and divorcing and having "great friends." But there was no help for it. She was American, she

145

was middle class: that was the way her world was organized; she must adjust to it. She had to be married in order to have any kind of real world—she had lived alone, but living alone, her life became too disorganized, too chaotic. She drank too much, wasted too much time, became careless, afraid she was going insane. She needed some person and some place where she could remain connected, a person and a place with whom and in which she could remain certain and settled. Being married to Clifford had been good for her; he had taught her something about how to discipline herself, how to organize her work and her time. She had become more certain of her own identity and surer about the value of her research. At the same time, she felt herself and her work gradually being crowded out and smothered by the large and complicated life of studying, practicing, teaching and socializing, of which Clifford was the center. He wanted her to participate in all of it, to keep his house running and to do her own work as well; it became too difficult. She had fled, she had found Tom Prescott, who promised to provide her with a quieter, simpler home life.

Dr. Bitteschoen had a hard time understanding about Tom. How could Dorothy have any intellectual relationship, any discussion of her thoughts or of her work, with Tom? Tom was a presentable enough young man, but he wasn't an intellectual, he had never been to the university—how could he and Dorothy have any really satisfactory kind of life together? Tom was a good pinochle player and a fine photographer and Dorothy loved him. Dr. Bitteschoen accepted the fact of the relationship, at last, as another example of Dorothy's American eccentricity.

Dr. Bitteschoen's wife, Berthe, was a perfect companion and a perfect mother to his children as well. She was warm, smiling, gentle, and silent, a wonderful cook and housekeeper. She could read and speak almost all of the modern European languages. She could play the little harp that she had inherited from her Austrian grandmother. She typed all of Dr. Bitteschoen's notes and papers for him, brought up four beautiful daughters, and she devoted her efforts to soothe and comfort and protect Ludwig Bitteschoen.

■ ■ ■

The Grand Mahatma says, ''We never think of ourselves as having motives for what we do. We ascribe motives to other people. What is the engine that makes the wheels go round.

''Now the engine is called psychology. It used to be the Four Humours, combined with those ambitions and propensities which were labeled the Virtues and The Seven Deadly Sins, abstractions which were personified in poetry and represented by Giotto on the walls of Italian churches.

''Before that, it was 'emulation'—life was a contest, an Olympic Game: who can give the more persuasive speech in court, who can write a better tragedy, who can succeed at being wise and sane?

"And before that, it was simply a question of who's going to be master: who shall command, who shall obey, who's going to get all the women and all the food?

"We returned to this last point of view (i.e., to our earliest human point of view) in the 1860's. Alfred Jarry makes King Ubu tell it to us: 'Kill all the people, take all the money and go away.' Here's where we actually are (we don't believe in 'psychology') after two and three-quarters world wars, wondering why we feel frustrated and unhappy and half mad, asking each other, 'How could so-and-so *do* such a thing?' and 'What ever possessed you to do a thing like that?' "

■ ■ ■

Roy took a great bag full of dirty clothes to the coin laundry nearest his apartment. He seldom patronized that one, it was more expensive than the place two blocks away, but it was raining, his head hurt, he felt that he should probably go to bed and go to sleep until the rain and the headache went away. But he was tired of listening to himself worrying about "when shall I ever do the laundry?," so out he came, in spite of headache and weather, and he carried a little volume of Walpole's letters in his coat pocket.

The moment he entered the laundromat he began to lose his temper. He had imagined that on a rainy day in the middle of the week there'd be only a few or possibly no other customers in the place. He found it occupied by a mob of harried young people with many children. There were also several dogs milling about underfoot.

Roy located a washing machine that had just been emptied a moment before by a nervous mother. The tub held a fine warm stink of pee. He jammed his own smelly shirts and sheets into the machine and then he discovered that he'd forgotten to bring the laundry soap with him, and that he hadn't the right kind and number of coins that the washing-machine demanded.

The money-changing machine was empty. He had heard people working it while he had been searching for a washing machine, and while he was putting his clothes into it. Several children had been entertaining themselves by making the machine turn dimes into nickels. At last they went away to put the nickels into the Coca Cola machine, then a lady bought what sounded like two dollars worth of change, after which the machine died. Although the lady hammered industriously on the front of its cover for some time, no more money came out.

Roy walked out of the laundromat fuming and muttering curses. He tried getting some small change from the corner grocer, who informed him that there was a shortage of coins because people were always coming in and taking them away to put into the laundry machines. The grocer had scarcely enough coins in his cash register to make change for his customers.

Roy stormed away to the little branch bank on the next corner. There was a slow-moving line in front of every window. His anxiety and rage mounted higher. Someone in the laundromat was bound to begin flinging Roy's clothes out of the machine and Roy would have to wait for an hour before he had the chance to use another one.

The man ahead of Roy at the teller's window gave the bank clerk a big bundle of checks, a mass of bills and a small sack full of silver coins. All this had to be counted twice over, one item at a time, and each item recorded on several kinds of forms and in several ledgers and a number of rubber stamps had to be applied to all the papers and ledgers. Then the man produced a bill from the gas company—there was some argument with the clerk about that, but at last, the man slowly wrote out a check for the correct amount and the teller read it, and went away to make sure that the man really had enough money in his account to cover the amount of the check, and then the teller stamped the bill paid and stamped the check OK and the man ahead of Roy went away.

Roy moved up to the teller's window. The clerk presented him with a small prism of black plastic which was elegantly engraved in gold. In case Roy might have been illiterate or blind, the teller very kindly read the golden words aloud: "Next window, please," then he shut the brass wicket and went away.

■ ■ ■

Beefy Johnson's father was a successful lawyer and a member of the Urban League, the NAACP, the ACLU, the University Club and the Democratic Party. He had once been invited to join the Most Worshipful Sons of Light Masonic Lodge, but he had declined. He thought of it as being a slightly comic organization, one of the kind which, he supposed, white people thought of as a "nigger lodge"—like the Mystic Knights of the Sea in Amos 'n' Andy. Edwin Johnson and his wife belonged to the Episcopal Church, where he was a vestryman.

He used to tell Beefy, "Basil, I wish to god you'd quit hanging with that Fillmore element. I'm not saying they're bad. I know they're mostly just poor and phenomenally unlucky. But you've got to be careful. Bad luck rubs off easy onto you."

"The color don't," Beefy said.

"I'll disregard the ad hominem remarks, Basil. I know these boys don't do half the things that the cops say they do, but most of the guys who're sitting over there in Q right now only did half or less of what they got sentenced for. They're serving time for getting caught. Now listen. Try not to be lingering around that corner innocently minding your own business on the day when the narcotics people come around to select their candidate for the boy they're going to run in the newspapers as the key man in their annual multi-million dollar bust. Understand?"

"All right, Papa, I'll be careful," Beefy said.

"I know you think I'm a square and all that. The more people in this town that think so, the easier it is for me to get along. But damn it, I want you to have as many chances as you can and all the dice are double-loaded..."

"I think you're my Papa," Beefy said. "Dr. Lammergeier says he thinks you've made a remarkable adaptation."

"What else does that damned quack have to say about me?" Edwin asked. Then he sighed. "Well, I got enough to worry about besides him. That reminds me, I've got to mail him a check for you and your Mama. Anyway, you keep your money in your wallet and your pecker in your pants, OK?"

"All right, Papa. I've got to go rehearse now, uptown."

"What are they playing this week?"

"The First Brandenburg Concerto," Beefy said. "They've got me a real baroque trumpet, one that goes so high it almost sounds like a whistle."

"Then I suppose you'll be down on Sutter Street later. I wish you'd just bring your friends to the house. That's why we've got a house with a play-room in the basement—a place I paid too much for in a nice neighbor-hood and then kept on living in until the expensive neighbors got tired of breaking the front windows and making creepola phone calls at three in the morning and they got used to seeing our bizarre-looking coun-tenances every day. Your mother won't care as long as you don't burn up a lot of pot. I'll talk to her if she fusses."

"Where are they going to park?" Beefy asked him.

"Park in the driveway, park in front of..." Then Edwin stopped him-self and sighed. "Yah, yah, yah," he said quietly. "I remember the cops tag everything in the neighborhood that isn't an $8500 Merce or something. OK, I'm sorry. Go blow. But be careful, Basil. Remember I'm here if you need me."

■ ■ ■

Dorothy said, "It's really all your fault, Roy. You introduced me to Tom. I suppose I could kill myself or something."

"Why?" Roy asked her. "If you can't live with Clifford any more, quit."

"It's a lot more complicated than that. Clifford is very upset. I don't care. He's so impossible. But it's so—"

Roy interrupted her. "Yeah, I know, I know."

"Well, all my things are still in Delhi," Dorothy said. "And you know Clifford. But he's so quiet and so kind of cold that I feel awful. Anyway, I'm going to live with Tom; we're getting an apartment, soon." Dorothy paused and stood up. "It's all totally irrational." She began to pace the little hotel room.

"You don't have to explain anything," Roy told her. She looked very unhappy, walking back and forth, with her arms crossed before her and her shoulders hunched up as if she were cold. Watching her, Roy experienced a peculiar mixture of impressions and feelings. Dorothy's voice, her manner of expression, her usual phrases—none of these seemed to have changed. But he had never, in the past, heard her acknowledge the reality of her own unhappiness, or that other persons might experience unhappiness on her account. She had been used to joke, half-seriously, about the unreality of other people and the imaginary character of their feelings; other people were either too stupid to feel anything or they were only pretending to have emotions they didn't really feel.

It seemed to Roy now, that Dorothy was at last trying to understand her own choices, her own feelings, and that she was finally aware that feelings and actions have consequences. Here she was, consciously willing to risk her own feelings, her own resources, in return for her freedom of action...and to accept the responsibility for injuring Clifford's feelings, as well.

"There'll be all the thing of going to court and talking about it," Dorothy said. "So awful—I don't know how I can stand that. And I don't know what I'll wear."

■ ■ ■

The Grand Mahatma says, "Nothing exists, really, except the Absolute Brute Necessity which is our Heart's Desire, our in-most private dream—the dream that shocks us most when we remember it. Its appearances are very fleeting, very swift, but it really hits us, really makes us tremble."

■ ■ ■

Margaret Gridley and Herbert Wackernagel used to play doctor under the front porch of Herbert's house in the country outside Eugene. No one ever caught them at it. They had heard about other children being found out and punished; they were, consequently, very discreet.

When they graduated from high school, Herbert got a football scholarship to the University, but as he put it, "I don't care about studying all that stuff that don't mean anything. I'm tired of school." He went into the Army and Margaret went to Radcliffe.

Herbert came home to Eugene after he got out of the Army. He got a job in an electrical repair shop. He lived with his mother. In the evenings he drank beer and shot pool at Glad Charley's. On weekends he'd go with his friends to one of the little towns on the Oregon coast where they'd rent a couple of motel rooms, find some girls and have a good time with them, far away beyond the purview of the Godly city of Eugene.

Margaret Gridley came home from Radcliffe one Christmas holiday and brought a dead portable phonograph with her. She took the machine into the repair shop and there was Herbert.

"How's tricks, Maggie?" he asked. He always looked her straight in the eye and grinned. One of his front teeth had been broken in a football game, and the tooth had been repaired with a bright yellow gold inlay. Seeing that gold tooth reminded Margaret that she'd never liked any other man but Herbert Wackernagel.

Margaret knew that he must be slightly insane. Certainly his father had been eccentric and his mother was a sweet, timid little lady who seemed to be always on the verge of schizophrenic withdrawal. Herbert's older brother, Cleveland, came home all strange from World War II. They had to send him to the State Hospital in Salem.

■ ■ ■

Roy wondered why he was so easily led to believe that his friends—indeed, that everyone else in the world—knew, better than he did, how he should conduct his own life. He imagined that he had a clear sense of his own necessities, his own feelings. He thought that he had learned a little bit or at least was able to remember fairly clearly what had been his own experience of the world around him.

Why did it seem so completely reasonable, so compellingly true when a friend told him, "You don't want any potato chips, do you. They're no good."

Roy would find himself automatically agreeing with what his friend said, and would decline the opportunity of eating the potato chips, although he was all too aware, a second later, that he loved potato chips, and that he was capable of eating a pound of the things with the greatest possible relish and pleasure. Why didn't he trust his own senses? Why did he allow his friends to make him ashamed of what he liked?

"And what demands do these senses make upon the world, anyway?" Roy asked himself. "All I want is some potato chips—preferably fresh ones. I don't want to be Atilla, I don't want mankind to obey my every whim, I'm not Hitler. I'm an idiot! I've allowed myself to be taken in again! Contrariwise, even if I was Atilla or Hitler, the world would simply watch and suffer: it has stood still for all they could do and worse besides. But I suppose there's an attitude, a point of view, a system in which the desire for potato chips is equivalent to the desire for the sadistic destruction of whole worlds and peoples...but I also remember Blake's line, 'O God, protect me from my friends.' "

■ ■ ■

Dorothy drank coffee with Dr. Crowley in the Faculty Room. The sun shone through tall Gothic windows. The warm yellow light felt wonderful on her tired legs. She stretched them out and felt one of her stockings give. "There goes another $2," she thought. "Oh, well..."

"You've got new specs," Dr. Crowley remarked.

"Oh, this is a pair I've had for a long time. I couldn't find one of my contact lenses this morning," Dorothy told him. She liked talking with Dr. Crowley. He was a tall, courtly, quiet man. Although he'd been on the faculty for many years, the experience hadn't marked him, hadn't dyed him with the pedantic tint. He seemed as much a visitor as Dorothy herself.

"How are your classes going now?" he asked.

"Fine, thanks. But I'm afraid I don't really like teaching. I always hated schools and colleges when I was young, and I was never interested in being a school teacher—but somehow I've ended up doing a lot of teaching, anyway. If you free-lance at all, like I do, it isn't so bad—in between jobs I can travel and buy a few things."

This last struck Dr. Crowley as a mild understatement. He and his wife had been dinner guests at Dorothy and Tom's house. He'd seen the collection of primitive carvings and metal castings from seven or eight different cultural areas. (Tom's photographs he considered a waste of time; they weren't interesting, no matter how many of them had appeared in national magazines.)

Dr. Crowley said, "Therese and I were wondering if you people would like to drop over on Friday night. We're having just a little gathering for cocktails and dinner."

Dorothy told him she was very sorry they wouldn't be able to attend; some of their friends were arriving from Chicago on Friday. "We'll be entertaining them all weekend," she said.

She disliked turning down any invitation but she couldn't allow herself to ruin another weekend with aimless delightful socializing and lush. But now she'd have to remember, the next time she saw Dr. Crowley, that she'd told him this mild fib. It had taken her a number of years to learn how to decline a social invitation and how to keep track of which scenario she was acting out with what other person or persons. "I'm getting old and cynical," Dorothy thought.

■ ■ ■

Roy could see that he had come to the slaughterhouse. He was preceded by beef cattle of different ages and sizes, then it was his turn. They had him hold his hands together above his head and they tied them together with a piece of cord—not too tight, but tight enough, just as they shoved the two sharp steel hooks through the meat between his Achilles tendons and the ankle bones and he was heaved up by the hooks and hung spraddle-legged upside down. They sliced open his throat with a knife in order to start him bleeding (that's why his hands had been tied—so he couldn't grab at his throat and get his arms in the way). The skinners were simultaneously cutting and stripping his skin off, and the dresser was cutting carefully around his anus and scrotum on either side of his penis to meet in a single line at the belly to divide the skinned writhing muscles and yellow fat and tumble balls guts belly lungs heart liver pancreas more guts all sliding falling down past his eyes onto some fast-moving conveyor belt into the dark and they inspected the carcass with a ten-cell flashlight and stamped the purple ink government inspection stamp onto the meat.

The accompanying medical record reported the presence of gold teeth. The head was now chopped from the carcass and the gold teeth extracted from it. (Had the medical record showed the presence of a platinum skull plate, surgical pins in the bones or other metal parts, all this metal would have been carefully salvaged.) After they got the gold, the brain was removed.

And after Roy there came some geese and chickens, several lambs and sheep, and then there was Margaret, looking strangely innocent, childish—she didn't know what was going to happen to her and Roy couldn't tell her, he was already dead, he didn't really know, himself, and that was the end of that.

All this intelligence had reached him in the shape of pictures and phrases, after he had awakened out of a sound, undreaming sleep at four o'clock one winter morning. It all began with the line, "...several sheep and lambs and then there was Margaret." It had felt like having a nightmare, but he was wide awake, and he had to follow the whole thing through completely, experience every detail. Then he was appalled by the knowledge of his total horrors: suicidal, masochistic wishes, of course—these were things that he really wanted to have done to himself and to do to other people.

At six o'clock he got up and turned on the big overhead light in the bedroom. Then he got back into bed and went to sleep. He awoke an hour or so later, somewhat refreshed, then fell asleep again, dreaming what seemed to be part of some story by Ernest Hemingway, all about World War I. Roy was a young officer who must go on a dangerous mission with another couple of officers, under the leadership of an older English army man. Roy was frightened, but he would go and do whatever was expected of him. The old Englishman was Ford Madox Ford.

■ ■ ■

When she was a girl, Margaret Gridley kept finding and making odd and beautiful things. She kept them in her room. Her mother would ask her,

"Margaret, where did you get this...thing?"

"I made it. I found that metal jigger in the street and I got the wire out of the basement and those big beads are some that Aunt Maude gave me to play with when I was little."

"How did you get it all together like that?"

"I borrowed some glue and pliers from Papa's workshop," Margaret said.

"It *is* kind of pretty...but what do you call it? What's it for?"

"I don't know, Mama, it's just a thing."

153

When she got to Radcliffe, Margaret found out about Art. She went to museums and galleries in Boston and New York. Other girls and boys asked her, "Isn't Picasso sublime? Isn't Rauschenberg too much?" and Margaret said, "I guess so," and shrugged. She couldn't see why they were so extravagant in their praise for things that they saw in museums; she had been making works of art for years. The only difference was that none of her things were in museums.

Margaret's room in Cambridge was different from anyplace else in the world. She decorated and furnished it herself, after having spent many days investigating and shopping in the remnant stores and junk shops of Boston and its suburbs. Her fellow students were scandalized and delighted. The Dean of Women wrote a letter about it to her friend, Frank O'Hara, at the Museum of Modern Art. Nobody had ever seen a room done up in velvet, fur, panels of solid black or yellow oilcloth and softly gleaming surfaces of metal and glass.

Margaret's clothes were very simple and nicely fitted, but the colors and textures of the materials that she liked to use for making them caused lots of discussion around the campus. Some days she wore a one-piece gabardine coverall with a zipper from crotch to neck, the kind which Air Force pilots wear. She had a big fur and leather jacket and strange suede boots to go with it.

■ ■ ■

Clifford went to the market to buy a bucket of yogurt and whatever good-ies the day might afford. He wandered slowly with the noisy Nepalese crowd. The sun shone; there was a fine stink of burning dung, spice, and incense in the air. He felt a cold flash of terror when he glimpsed a tall red-haired woman just as she was turning a corner out of the main market into a side alley. Clifford was afraid that it was Flora McGreevey, Dorothy's mother, who had come directly to Katmandu in order to find him and compel him to give her piano back to her.

The piano had resided, for several years, in the living room of his friend, Mark Sanderson. Mark was a composer and teacher who lived with his wife and many children in a big brown-shingled house in Ber-keley. The piano was in daily use. Mark had a few private students; his wife, Beth, practiced daily and taught their own children.

A large assortment of other instruments inhabited the same room. In addition to books and musical scores, the ceiling-high bookshelves housed an assortment of horns, flutes and fiddles. A shiny baritone horn stood underneath the piano. There was a cello in one corner of the room, and shiny metal music stands were waiting in unexpected places to be knocked over with a great crash by unwary guests.

Clifford got letters from Mark on very rare occasions, but when he wrote, Mark always mentioned the piano, it was in fine condition, and he still hadn't been able to manage to get another one which he liked as well, and it was sort of embarrassing to keep this one of Clifford's—or Dorothy's—or Flora McGreevey's. Maybe he ought to try buying it instead of continuing to worry Clifford about it; it would take him a couple of years to pay for it, if Clifford wouldn't mind—or Flora?

Flora McGreevey had originally bought the piano for her children. She had unexpectedly inherited a little money from a distant relative. Flora thought that Dorothy and her brother ought to have a really good piano when they started taking lessons—a better instrument than the baby grand which she got when she was first married. (Baby grands had been fashionable in that era. They were used to support elegant, deep-fringed "Spanish" shawls of silk velvet dyed orange and red. People had begun to make living in penthouses a chic thing to do, and a baby grand piano was a regular fixture in penthouse apartments which overlooked the East River. These pianos were very seldom played because it was so much bother to remove the big shawl and find a place to put that. When the shawl was, at last, removed, however, a couple of white circles and a cigaret burn were displayed on the mahogany case, emblems of a couple of large parties which Percy McGreevey had given for some old Yalie friends.)

Flora spent a little of her inheritance on the big Steinway parlor grand which now stood in Mark Sanderson's house. She gave the baby grand to a cousin who had asked her for it. He had a wonderful time refinishing it in "antique white" and gold trim. His talented roommate painted an extremely bawdy picture on the inside of the piano lid. From a distance of five or six feet, the picture seemed to be an innocent 18th century style pastoral scene of shepherds, nymphs and flocks and trees, but when it was more nearly examined, it becamse very clear what all these assorted people, sheep and mythological beings were actually doing.

■ ■ ■

Dorothy and Roy were lunching together in a Russian place on Clement Street.

"I don't think we should have any of those," Dorothy said, nodding in the direction of a refrigerated showcase. Behind the glass was an assortment of bizarre looking pastries of the most counter-Revolutionary order, all swollen with whipped cream, and shamelessly bedizened with colored icings. Each one was an insult to the suffering masses of the world and to the memory of Nikolai Lenin.

"We have to," Roy said. "It's expected of us. They won't let me come in here again if we don't have some, and I like the soup here. Anyway, we owe it to the memory of his Late Imperial Majesty, Nicholas II, Tsar of All the Russias." Roy toasted the memory of that Monarch in coffee and pretended to throw the empty cup over his shoulder.

"Well, all right," Dorothy said, doubtfully, "But we really *do* know better, don't we."

155

Roy said, "Sure we do." Then he held a short conversation with the waitress, in Russian.

Dorothy said, "I forgot you could do that. It really is impressive. I can tell which are the verbs, though."

"I expect so," Roy said, and he laughed.

"Anyway, I'll tell you all about Vienna," Dorothy said. "They really have whipped cream on everything. There are crystal chandeliers made out of real rocks—quartz and amethyst and topaz chunks like eggs—and polished mahogany everywhere that there isn't brocade or crystal or whipped cream. It's funny the difference there is between the ways they use wood and stone in Europe and Asia. In Europe it all smells different, it all means something else. In India the stone is all alive. In Europe it's part of a graveyard. I don't see how elephants can stand to live there—but I suppose it's their job."

■ ■ ■

The Grand Mahatma says, "Nobody loves you when you're old and gay. Everyone forgets that while fairies aren't exactly mortal, they have to live through several millennia before they finally fade away; their old age is very long."

■ ■ ■

Tom Prescott woke up in the dark. Something was the matter; he couldn't move one of his legs, and something was holding his left arm and hurting it every time he tried to move it. With his right hand he groped about for the lamp which ought to be on the bedside table. His hand struck metal and glass which crashed on the floor and broke. Where was the telephone...

"Hey," Tom said. The crash of glass and metal and the sound of his own voice made a strange echoing noise. There was no echo in his bedroom; he must be in jail or something.

"Hey," he said. "Darlene." He heard footsteps, there was somebody running. It was Darlene; Tom could hear her dress rustling as she came towards the bed. "Darlene," he said.

A strange woman's voice said very clearly and quietly, "It's all right, Mr. Prescott. Don't shout; you'll disturb the other patients. I'm going to give you another hypo and then I'll fix that IV in your arm, you've got it all pulled around..."

Tom said, "Where are you? I'm in a hospital? Why don't they put the lights on?"

"Now, then, Mr. Prescott, just lie back again. The sun's right on your face. I'll fix the blinds."

"Hey," Tom said.

"Please don't yell, Mr. Prescott. You're in the hospital. You'll disturb the other patients."

"What time is it?"

"Two forty-five," the woman said. She sounded like Tom's teacher in the second grade.

"Miss Telfer," Tom said. Someone was tugging at his left arm, hurting him. "Hey," he said. "Cut it out! Why don't you turn on the god-damned lights?"

"We don't need the lights right now," the woman said, calmly. "There's a bandage over your eyes. Please don't pick at it. Your eyes will be all right, Doctor says. The lids will be a little scarred, that's all, and they'll be painful for a while. That's why I gave you another hypo. You mustn't thrash around quite so much. Your left leg is in a cast. It was broken in two places, but it will be all right, soon. Don't worry about all that. Try to rest."

"Miss Telfer," Tom said.

Another woman's voice said, "I'm your night nurse, Mrs. Gustavson. Don't try to wave that left arm too much. We're feeding you intravenously until tomorrow morning. We'll take out the IV when Doctor makes his rounds."

Tom heard her go out of the room. She wasn't Darlene. He was in a hospital, all banged up. He hadn't seen Darlene for a couple of years. Now she and Ted lived in Santa Monica. He was driving to San Francisco, going up the Waldo Grade and here came this truck out of its own lane and down the hill a thousand miles an hour.

"Hey! Hey! Hey!" Tom shouted.

"Well, Tom, how are you feeling?" a man asked him.

Tom said, "Augh?"

"You've been getting lots of rest. That's good. Don't bother about making small talk."

"Augh," Tom said. "I can't think of your name."

"That's all right," the man said. "Ed Bancroft, your doctor. You're doing fine, Tom."

The nurse's voice said, "Do you want him to have this now, Dr. Bancroft?"

Tom heard them leave the room, still talking. Then he thought he could hear Dorothy talking, but he was too tired to figure out what she was saying.

■ ■ ■

Clifford cut fresh bananas and cucumbers and mangoes into a bowl. He ladled curds of fresh yogurt over the fruit, then he poured a couple spoonsful of dark, Nepalese honey over the yogurt. The honey fell in vagrant golden loops, garlands, and jolly swags of gold. While he ate, he read a chapter of Mansfield Park. He could hear someone blowing a conch horn in the distance. The neighbors were singing a mournful native ditty while they cooked up a curry which smelled like a Chinese herb drugstore.

Clifford wondered what Jane Austen's handwriting looked like. Do any of her manuscripts still exist? He had seen Beethoven's notebooks the first time he went to Europe. It had taken lots of time and patience to get letters from several very important professors in order to get him permission to examine the notebooks. If he was going traveling and was planning to stay in some place for any length of time, he carried a reproduction of Blake's *Jerusalem* with him.

■ ■ ■

Dorothy said, "It could be sort of fun, sometimes, though. So many people came to Delhi and it was easy to get from the city out to where we were living. Of course, everybody had to come and see Clifford Barlow, but a few of my friends came, too—Margaret Gridley and Gigi Fiske and Max and Alice Lammergeier from San Francisco. We had some great parties when Alice and Max were there. And of course there were all the other Americans and people from Europe. . . we all went out a lot to hear music together. We'd smoke a whole lot of bhang and get out of our heads listening to Ravi Shankar and Ustad Ali Akbar Khan and everybody. They used to play all night. And of course the linguistics people came by—Dr. Bitteschoen, and Dr. Chadwick from London and Dr. Saru from Japan and Professor Ptichki from Moscow—people I knew when I was at Radcliffe or when I was teaching in Michigan."

Tom asked her, "Can Clifford really play a sitar? Or does he just fake it?"

"He had a teacher and everything," Dorothy said, "And you have to be really good in order to get an Indian teacher. It isn't like Japan, where all you have to do is pay and you can get a teacher to teach you anything you want to know. Clifford's teacher was quite certain that Clifford was the reincarnation of some prominent Bengali musician, otherwise Clifford wouldn't have been able to learn anything, much less play music. Clifford used to practice for hours on end. Then he started learning the tabla. That's really hard. Even I can get some kind of noise out of a sitar or a sarod, but I'm nowhere nearly coordinated enough to even start with the tabla. Of course Clifford's left hand is in training from the organ and the harpsichord and all the other lovely instruments that he's been playing since infancy. He has fantastically quick reflexes—the big bore!"

"Margaret Gridley's the one who married that jazz player, what's-his-name, isn't she?"

"Oh, yes. She married Beefy Johnson. He was a junky. They didn't stay married long; he already had a wife in Pascagoula, Mississippi or someplace. She wrote Margaret a nasty letter. Then Beefy Johnson got killed. Everybody knows all about that, it was in *Time* and everything. Margaret was only about eleven years old at the time and *very* skinny, but she was bright for her age. She's lots different now."

Tom laughed. "I can imagine," he said.

"Every time they print a picture of Françoise Sagan, I say to myself, 'There's Margaret.' Of course, Margaret's much better looking than that in real life."

"Was she really in the movies?"

"She certainly was. She was in a couple of B movies and then she had a small but very good part in a big movie. She can upstage anybody any time. She made thousands of dollars for a while. She knew James Dean. But she had to stop; all the makeup was ruining her skin like some terrible disease and she met Beefy Johnson and they got married in New York. But all that happened years ago. We'll probably be seeing one of her movies on TV almost any time now. Won't that be something!"

"Come on," Tom said. "How long ago?"

"*Years* ago—at least six—"

"That isn't very long ago. You always talk like a year lasts forever," Tom said.

"Well, we all move around so much and everything happens so fast, it all seems like ages ago," Dorothy told him.

■  ■  ■

Roy had a hard time sleeping in the airplane. He'd had a lot to drink before he got aboard, and he'd taken a pill to prevent airsickness. He stayed awake a long time, talking to the college girl who had the seat beside his. Now she had curled up in her chair and covered herself with a big blanket and gone to sleep. Roy felt half asleep and half sick.

He thought that he'd been awake all the time, but he had fallen asleep for a little while. The plane was flying out of the mountains and the very earliest dim light of pre-dawn showed the leaden shine of the River Platte lying in great meanders and loops across the flat grey prairie below. It reminded Roy of pictures that he'd seen of Mesopotamia. He was excited by the thought that he had known without the effort of trying to remember that this was the Platte and that now he was out of the West, heading into a strange land without mountains.

■  ■  ■

Flora McGreevey was looking very smart. Dorothy no longer hated her but she was jealous of her mother's clothes and expensive hair.

Flora was saying, "I like society. I *am* society. Society is all my friends. Some people imagine that society is rich people, but there haven't been any rich people since 1929. Your Uncle Terry got a Hispano Suiza when he graduated from Yale, but he had to go over and pick it up from the factory himself. I remember he went tourist class. It was very funny, we brought all this champagne and a couple of enormous *bon voyage* baskets down into the absolute guts of the *Ile de France*. I was only a little girl at the time, of course. Terry was years older than me, he was born in the year before the Fire."

Flora McGreevey, being a native of the city, never mentioned the great earthquake of 1906; it was the Fire which had destroyed San Francisco. Dorothy was as distressed as ever to watch her mother extinguish cigarets in the sauce which remained on her luncheon plate.

Flora McGreevey loved to eat and she was a very good cook. When Percy McGreevey left her, all her friends told her, "You ought to open a little tea room, Flo—you could make a mint of money just serving tea and coffee and those delicious biscuits and rolls you know how to make."

Flora told them that she was too busy to operate a restuarant. She wasn't having any trouble finding enough to eat. She had all her committee work to do, for her favorite charities and for the Democratic Party. She was a great success with all of it.

Dorothy's father had run away with a young person who had not quite had a career in the movies. During the Second World War, Percy McGreevey made lots of money in some not quite illegal way. Dorothy had been able to study at Radcliffe, instead of at Cal or Stanford.

Flora McGreevey was enormous, but she wasn't the noisy, jolly type of fat lady. She had perfect teeth, beautiful red hair, and a very sweet looking face. She had sometimes been described by her husband's friends as "pretty in the face, but Big."

A rich broker, eating luncheon with a rich lawyer, observed Flora and her daughter in the restaurant. The broker said, "You let Flo McGreevey into your office and she talks you out of your back teeth for the Children's Hospital or whatever it is she's collecting for or organizing. But I always tell my secretary to send her right on in. Flo's a real lady and a very genuine person. There ain't many like her left in the world. I know people had a lot to say about her and that symphony guy—that Russian fellow with all the long hair—"

"There's nothing to all that," the lawyer said. "Anyway, everybody knows all them guys is queer. Flo's always been interested in getting money together to back the opera and the symphony, that's all—she's a very refined and highly cultivated person. That damned Perce McGreevey ought to have been shot, walking out on her and those kids like that. I fixed him, though. We tied up his business hand and foot until he signed a support agreement and made over the house to Flo. He paid, too."

The broker lighted a big cigar and leaned back in his chair. "Well, old Percy was kind of a bastard," he said, "But you can't help liking the guy. I saw him down in Nassau last winter, still the same old big-talking Percy, always laughing and clowning around, always on the lookout for a piece of ass. He's pretty well fixed, you know, even after you guys were done trimming on him."

"That little piece that took off with him," the lawyer said, stirring his coffee, "did she stick with him?"

"I guess so, but she's dead, now, you know—took pills."

Flora was telling Dorothy, "I went to see your friend Dr. Lammergeier this morning about the Opera Fund. He's absolutely the most enchanting person in San Francisco. He could charm the buttons right off your coat!"

■ ■ ■

Roy flipped the little paper book onto a pile of other ones that lay in a corner of the cupboard, saying, "Well, Mrs. Woolf, thank you very much." Instantly, he knew a flash of terror and delight. He had said exactly what he meant, exactly what he felt at that moment. He had been telling himself, earlier, that it wasn't one of her best novels, but when he actually came to the end of it, he felt pleased and satisfied and he had thoughtlessly addressed himself to the woman whose "voice" was still in his head: "Well, Mrs. Woolf, thank you very much," and there was this terrific sensation and it was followed immediately by the knowledge that Mrs. Woolf had received and acknowledged his gratitude.

■ ■ ■

Clifford asked Dorothy, "How's your mother?"

"Awful, as usual," Dorothy replied. "We went to the Palace Hotel, of course. Everybody kept looking at us."

"The two of you in one restaurant is quite a production. Your mother is a great looking woman."

"You should have married her instead of me," Dorothy cried. "You're both so awful!"

Clifford was becoming impatient with her. "Come on, now," he said. "Stop flittering around and tell me what you're trying to say."

"She's talking about marrying that awful Alex," Dorothy said. "She gave me a hundred dollars to fix my hair at Elizabeth Arden's. She's going to buy a house in Phoenix from that awful friend of yours I don't like from Bull Run College, what's his name, the fake architect fairy—"

"Hawthorne?"

"Yes—only how she ever happened to even meet him is beyond me."

"It was at our wedding party," Clifford said, gloomily.

"One of his icky five-sided triangles that keys in with the Sacral Universe once every twenty-five years for ten seconds on her birthday. Roy would love to have a house like that, he's so crazy about magic and birthdays and stars, but he's penniless, of course."

"He came to lunch with me today," Clifford said. "He has a part-time job now, and he brought some whiskey."

"Roy's such a bore. Why do you waste your time?"

"I told you to stop flittering around," Clifford shouted at her. "You're babbling again. Go take a hot bath or clean up the kitchen or feed the cats. Calm *down*!"

Dorothy came and sat on his lap and kissed him. He tried to jerk his head away from her.

"You're so smart," she said. "You're always so calm and good."

"Come on, quit it!"

"I don't care," Dorothy said. "Let's go to bed and fuck."

■ ■ ■

For no reason at all, Roy was trying to remember the name of a mongoloid idiot that he'd seen in a freak show, years ago, when he was a boy. The mongoloid, billed as The Marvelous Pinheaded Lady, was of uncertain age. Her thin hair had been arranged to stand up in a little braid at the summit of her almost bald, pointed head. She wore a big shapeless dress of red and white checkered gingham. Great circular spots of rouge had been applied to her cheeks and brilliant red lipstick painted on to her mouth.

Roy could remember being frightened, repelled, and fascinated with looking upon this wonder. The side-show barker had addressed her by a lewd-sounding name with a diminutive ending. Roy couldn't remember that name, when he tried to think of it more than twenty years later. He could remember the face and the dress and the way she moved—bearishly soft and clumsy—but the name seemed lost to him forever.

■ ■ ■

"You must *work*," Clifford told her.

"I'm doing something else, right now," Dorothy calmly replied, looking up from her book. "Anyway, I'm not interested in gardening. I like to see the flowers in the morning, but if there wasn't a garden, I wouldn't miss it."

"You must work in it, or you can't enjoy it," Clifford said, quite pointedly.

"I might work on it tomorrow—I work on it a little bit sometimes, if I don't have anything else to do—right now, I'm doing something else."

"You're sitting on your ass in front of a mirror," Clifford said.

"You go dig in your garden all you want to and enjoy yourself, but don't shout and yell at me about it," Dorothy replied.

"I'm right!" Clifford told her. "It'll take you fifty years to find it out, but you will. You'll find out I'm right."

"Of course you're right, Clifford. Look at yourself—nobody could be more correct—nobody could be more perfect. There you are in a raving screaming fit. Very rightly so."

Clifford lectured her for a little longer, but at last he disappeared among the flowers. Dorothy sighed and put on her glasses. She returned to the book that she'd been working with all morning. It was difficult at first for her to concentrate on it again. She was annoyed with Clifford's self-righteous roarings. "Why must he have a uniform world where everyone feels like doing the same things at the same times?" she asked herself. "Not only feel like it but be doing it enthusiastically..." She felt that the world was quite uniform enough: one place reminded her of another, one person had eyes or voice or nose or some other feature or combination of features which resembled those which belonged to another person. And people keep doing the same things over and over again—want the same things. Why must Clifford have it even more organized, more controlled?

Dorothy got up and went into the kitchen. She set the tea-kettle on the stove to boil. Out the window she could see bamboo and orchids growing. She could hear the intermittent scrape and rattle of Clifford's gardening procedures: pick, pick, pick, pick, pick, snip, rattle, silence. Click, shaky rattle snip. That garden was going to straighten up and do right, or Clifford would know the reason why not. It must be as correct as he himself was.

Dorothy suddenly laughed, listening to Clifford's indignant thrashing and snipping. She brought the tea tray into her study and sat down to her book again. Soon she was absorbed in reading and occasionally writing extracts or queries or cross-references on three-by-five file cards. When she came to the end of a chapter, she put all her things away and began preparing lunch for Clifford and herself.

■ ■ ■

Margaret Gridley had felt a little bit lonely and out of place at Radcliffe, when she first arrived. She found out right away that the western part of the United States and its inhabitants were great subjects for humor and comedy to her fellow students who had lived all their lives in New York and New England. Most of Margaret's classmates had only a vague notion as to the geographical location of her ancestral home. "And who are the Gridleys?" the more snobbishly inclined asked each other. A Miss Peabody remarked that they were, perhaps, still Navy people.

Margaret only smiled. Her mother had taught her the old-fashioned White House Cookbook etiquette; her stiff, rather dusty formality amused the Deans and professors. Margaret's manner, combined with her distinctive sense of style in dress and living, soon established her as a remarkable individual. A few of the girls were afraid of her sarcastic style of speech. However, her roommate, Miss Gigi Fiske, spoke very highly of her, and Margaret began going about in the company of Gigi's brother, Luke. She was no longer so much of a figure of fun as she had been at first. The Fiskes were a very old and proper family down in Maine. They had Back Bay connections and they owned some islands off the coast. (The U.S. Navy leased most of its ships from Gigi's father.)

Gigi's brother, Luke—Mr. Lexington Fiske III—was at Harvard, then, a very handsome boy with long blond hair in a slanted bang across his forehead. Margaret thought he had a rather interesting mind. She enjoyed hearing him talk about psychology and literature faster and faster while he very shyly touched her breasts and legs. When she asked him whether he had a contraceptive, he was abashed and a little angry.

"Don't you have anything?" he demanded.

"You didn't expect that I'd be carrying a supply of such appliances with me, did you?" Margaret inquired, in her turn.

On another occasion, she armed herself in advance, and they had a pleasant afternoon together.

"It's awfully nice of you to be interested in Luke," Gigi Fiske told her. "He was all mixed up with this awful creature from Bennington who was a bondage queen and it sort of got him disillusioned with women for almost a year. I'd certainly appreciate it if you'd go out with him, now and then. You don't have to get emotionally involved or anything..."

■ ■ ■

"Damn it, I'm right," Clifford told Roy.

"Abolutely," Roy said. "You're right in exactly the same way that Mr. Kant said that *he* was: 'apodeictically.'"

"You go ahead and laugh. Dorothy used to say the same thing. She left me, and you'll drop me, but I know I'm right."

"Sure, you're right," Roy told him. "I expect that I can forgive you, after all."

Clifford was angry. "You're afraid to have a serious discussion! You're afraid to believe in anything, to face up to reality! You won't take any responsibility for your own feelings!"

Roy tried to calm him down by apologizing. "OK, Clifford," he said, "I was teasing again. I'm sorry; I won't do it any more."

"Your teasing and laughing are only hostility! You laugh because you're embarrassed—you don't want to think about what you're saying or what I'm saying. You're afraid of any sincere feelings, any direct communication."

Roy felt terrible. "All right," he said. "I'm very sorry."

They walked on down the street. Roy felt bad; Clifford appeared to be miserable.

■ ■ ■

Herbert Wackernagel said, "I got a new Lancia outside, Maggie—you want to see it?"

"I saw it outside the shop," Margaret said. "I wondered whose it was."

"You got to let me take you for a ride in it."

Margaret smiled and thought a moment. "You pick me up at Marjory Grimshaw's place tonight. My folks still don't want me to see you, but I'd like to talk to you, OK?"

Marjory Grimshaw was Margaret's closest friend in Eugene. She was a student at the University. She had wanted to go to Radcliffe with Margaret, but she hadn't been able to pass the entrance examinations and she had been too late in applying for admission to Stanford, so there she was, still in Eugene. She planned to go to Stanford or Europe, next year. It was for thinking of lines like these—"Stanford or Europe"—that Margaret sincerely admired Marjory Grimshaw. Marjory had a natural sense of style; Margaret had to work at it.

The social columns of the Eugene *Register-Guard* quite accurately recorded the fact that Miss Marjory Grimshaw gave a dinner party at the lovely home of her parents, the fashionable and popular Forest Grimshaws, for the young lady students who were home for the holidays. Margaret Gridley's name appeared at the head of the guest list. The name of Mr. Herbert Wackernagel didn't appear in the social columns or anywhere else in the paper.

Mr. Wackernagel and Miss Gridley strapped themselves into the black leather bucket-seats of the Lancia and in a remarkably short time they were miles from Eugene, speeding through dark rain forests. They went to a little hunting lodge in the woods, a place Herbert owned in common with the two whilom choirboys who had been the companions of his youth. (On this particular weekend, they had gone to Coos Bay to get laid.)

There was lots of beer and sandwiches and pretzels and crackers and cheese and salami. A wood fire roared in the little iron stove and a kerosene lamp shed a warm yellow glow across the knotty pine boards of the walls. It was raining very hard outside.

The pale steady light made Margaret's fair skin look warm and mellow. She had very perfect breasts; she appeared never to need a brassiere. Herbert watched her lips and throat and belly moving while she talked about the past, about her parents, about Cambridge and Mr. Lexington Fiske III. "What do you want to mess around with a dope like that for?" he asked.

"Oh, I get lonesome sometimes—you aren't there," Margaret said. Then she laughed, because she thought Herbert was looking very solemn and jealous. "He's only a little boy," she said. "He's nothing like you. Nobody is." She laid her open hand against the end of his nose. He regarded her steadily between her outspread fingers. He didn't move.

"He has green eyes and a kind of pointed chin," Margaret said, and laid a finger on the dimple in Herbert's chin. "His neck is kind of skinny and his chest is kind of bony. He doesn't have nice solid titties like you, nor a pretty bellybutton." She kissed Herbert's belly and her long hair fell silkily across his genitals, and Margaret softly seized his rising penis in one hand, kissed its throbbing head and licked on it a little bit. "I haven't seen you for so long," she told it, and caressed it a little more. "There," she said. "Now, hold me once again and then we have to go."

■ ■ ■

While Tom was locked up in his darkroom, Dorothy was trying to give the living room a quick run-over with the vacuum cleaner. The rug was filthy, and Mrs. Hurst, the cleaning lady, wasn't due to come until Saturday, and this was only a Wednesday. Dorothy tried very hard to run the machine slowly and carefully; she tried very hard to keep her temper. She hated to do housework.

Tom didn't like Mrs. Hurst. He was convinced that she was drinking up the household brandy supply. He told Dorothy that he didn't like to have strange types wandering around his house. Dorothy told him that she was too busy, herself, to keep the place properly in order. She was thinking about having Mrs. Hurst work on the house a couple more days a week. The place always looked grubby to her. And Tom had never learned to pick up after himself.

The vacuum cleaner wasn't working very well. Dorothy guessed that Mrs. Hurst hadn't emptied the dustbag. She detached the metal pipe from the rubber hose of the cleaner and applied the roaring tube directly to the carpet. She found that it cleaned very well this way, and she had done several square feet of carpet before she realized that it would take a number of hours to complete the job at the rate she was then going. It had already taken up more time than she felt that she could afford to spend on the job—she ought to be reading, there were letters to be answered, she was supposed to be thinking up something nice to do for Professor Crowley and his wife, she ought to be giving herself a shampoo...

Dorothy applied the hose to a full ashtray. All the matches and wrappings and butts made a cheery rattling sound on their lazy journey towards the machine's tank. Dorothy cursed, thinking that now she'd have to empty the dustbag herself, because the carpet must be finished and there were six more big ashtrays full of garbage.

"Try to remain calm," she told herself. She turned off the machine and stood still in the center of the living room. Sunlight shone through the dirty metal slats of the Venetian blinds, and in the beams of yellow light there danced eighteen trillion, three hundred million, nine hundred thousand, four hundred sixty-seven motes of brand new (or old) super-adhesive, ultra-grimy dust (the wind was blowing outside) which someone, some vacuum cleaner, some Mrs. Hurst, somebody, was going to have to move out of the house again tomorrow.

Dorothy went into the kitchen and poured herself a slug of brandy. She sat down in the living room and lit a cigaret. She drank a little of the brandy.

"The main thing to remember," she told herself, "is that there's plenty of time for everything, isn't there. I'll have to wash out this ashtray I'm using. I'll have to wash out this glass. Calmly. How do I get into these fits, anyway?"

Dorothy finished her brandy and extinguished her cigaret. Neither alcohol nor nicotine seemed to have been of any use. She took her glass

166

and a stack of ashtrays into the kitchen. She wondered whether she might be pregnant. "That's just what we need, isn't it, Dorothy. Right now. Something else to wash and put away and take care of."

Roy used to yell at her, "Why don't you just stop? That's all you really have to do is stop. Why let yourself get drug off on these trips that drive you cuckoo? Refuse to go. You know what it feels like when you're starting to go over the edge. Stop falling."

"You're a great one to talk," Dorothy told him. "Who's the one who has a complete and utter nervous breakdown if one of his shoestrings breaks?"

She washed her glass and all the ashtrays, and then finished cleaning the rug in the living room. "No more," she told herself. "No *more*. That's all. I refuse to monkey with any more of it."

There was a small cobweb on a bronze head from Benin. She picked it off and it smeared itself across her fingers. She gritted her teeth when she noticed—again—the grimy Venetian blinds. "Enough," she said, wiping her fingers on her apron. "Screw it all. Did I take that pill or not?"

■ ■ ■

At a large new university in New England, Roy was being treated to a dinner in the company of seven hundred young ladies. (The young gentlemen, he guessed, must have their own dining halls or maybe one big common mess hall like the Army.) The elderly genteel housemother led the girls in a short prayer. They all recited it in the Spanish language, each young lady standing with her hands on the back of her chair. The housemother explained, after they were seated, that the Spanish prayer and the practice of holding conversation in Spanish while at table one night in each week were traditions of the place.

Roy was charmed by the idea. The room, the building, the whole school—could not have been more than six or seven years old, but it had a tradition. It seemed very strange to hear people speaking Spanish in New England; the sound of the language made him homesick for California.

The young girl who was seated on his left asked him how long he had been writing poetry. Roy told her, "Twenty years or so." She seemed to find the information incomprehensible. She was silent during the remainder of the dinner. Roy was obliged to chat, rather formally, with the housemother.

Seven hundred New England young ladies watched Roy talking with her. Mrs. Buckleigh was a great admirer of San Francisco. She and her late husband had visited that city in the year of the world's fair, just before the war.

Mrs. Buckleigh was very dignified, very self-assured. She had only the dimmest notion of who Roy was and how he happened to be seated next to her, eating chicken à la king and making polite conversation...he had come to lecture on something or other. He seemed to be a rather dull young man in a ready-made suit. He reminded her of one of the graduate students.

Dr. Kratzke from the English Department had approached her and asked if she wouldn't like to entertain a visiting lecturer at dinner. Mrs. Buckleigh pulled in her soft little chin and cocked her head to one side like a bird listening for a worm. She peered at Dr. Kratzke through her spectacles and gave him a tentative, wavering "Yes..."

Dr. Kratzke said, "Perhaps I should warn you—he's a Westerner—he may be somewhat informally dressed."

"Indeed?" said Mrs. Buckleigh, as a mental image of the late Mr. Will Rogers, wearing a ten-gallon hat, bandanna handkerchief around his neck, baggy shirt, blue jeans, cowboy chaps, and high-heeled boots with spurs arose before her mind's eye.

"I understand that our younger men have rather given up the use of the necktie. I hope that you'll understand that any sign of unconventional attire is not intended to be a personal affront to you."

"Perhaps the Faculty Club might...," Mrs. Buckleigh began.

"Ah, yes, but Mr. Sidgwick and some other gentlemen from the Regents will be there. I believe that our poet will find himself much more comfortable with you and your so delightful young ladies."

"That's very kind of you to say so, Dr. Kratzke, but if it should happen to be our Spanish Night..."

"Splendid, my dear Mrs. Buckleigh, thank you so much. I'll have him brought to Godkin House by whoever meets him at the bus." And Dr. Kratzke sped away before Mrs. Buckleigh had a chance to think of any more objections.

Now here was Mr. Roy whoever-he-was, wearing a quite unexceptionable necktie. But she observed, with consternation, that he was beginning to eat the peel of the baked potato which ought to have been left on his plate. Mrs. Buckleigh turned away to address a few remarks to her assistant, Mrs. Grimes. Mrs. Buckleigh couldn't bring herself to watch someone devouring garbage.

A very young girl scurried into the dining hall and whispered something to Mrs. Buckleigh, who in turn informed Roy, "There's a—Mr.—ah—telephone call for you, if you please?"

Roy thanked her and excused himself from the table. He followed the round-eyed blonde child to the lobby of the building, where she directed him to a telephone booth. He shut the door and picked up the phone. He supposed that it must be his agent, calling to find out whether he had arrived at the right time and to remind him of his next day's engagement.

Roy said, "Hello," into the phone.

A very quiet male voice said, "Mr. Aherne?"

"Yes."

"We are going to kill you," the man said; then the phone went dead.

Roy stood and read the numbers and the instructions on the coin box.

Then he replaced the phone on its hook and walked out into the lobby. Who did he know—a man with an Italian or Spanish accent—who might want to kill him? The Cuban Revolution was upsetting lots of people, and Roy's writings and lectures were replete with comments on many political matters. Well, he told himself, that's that. What can you do with an anonymous phone call?

He rejoined Mrs. Buckleigh. The process of walking through the dining hall made him feel a little bit like having to perform Aida all by himself on the opening night of the Metropolitan Opera before a large and brilliant audience who had come out expressly to watch Miss Maria Callas do Salome. Roy ate his dessert and drank his coffee and continued making polite converstion with Mrs. Buckleigh, but he felt removed, remote from the scene, he had been killed by the telephone.

In the lecture hall, Roy recited none but his most violently political verses—ones he had not planned to read at all, ones he had not read for years, and he added a great deal of political and anti-clerical commentary before and after each poem. At the end of his lectures, he told the story of the anonymous phone call. Someone had tried to silence him, had threatened to kill him. Let them go ahead and do their worst; he had had his say.

The audience was embarrassed. They didn't understand what he had been saying all evening, and this final statement . . . was it another poem? The ones who understood that it was a statement of something which had happened didn't believe him. One or two people in the audience asked questions about the future of poetry and what ever happened to Stephen Vincent Benét and the tradition of The Beautiful, and then the audience was gently but firmly dismissed by Dr. Kratzke.

Dr. Kratzke told Roy that it was rushing season for the fraternities on campus. The phone call was obviously a student prank—in regrettable taste of course, but only a joke.

Roy told him, "You pays your money and you takes your choice."

"I beg your pardon?" Dr. Kratzke said. He sounded quite offended.

"You're quite right," Roy said, giving him a large shit-eating grin. "Kids are always full of hell. I've been traveling around a great deal this week and my nerves are a little frayed. I always get stage fright. It doesn't matter how often I appear before an audience; I get scared every time I have to do it again. And lots of people don't like what I say. I know that."

"Well, it was a most enjoyable evening," Dr. Kratzke said. "Very stimulating." (His statements, Roy thought, are worthy of the smile he received.) "I'm only sorry that more of the English staff wasn't here," Dr. Kratzke concluded.

A white-haired gentleman in the group which had formed about Dr. Kratzke and Roy now shook Roy by the hand and assured him that he, for one, had been surprised and delighted with Roy's poetry.

"I thought that I wouldn't understand, but I did! Now I see that I must go back and look at those moderns. For years I've had great doubts about Hopkins and Bridges and their radical experiments—let alone such extremists as Mr. Eliot! I've been avoiding *his* work for years!"

■ ■ ■

Clifford told her, "You haven't got any ideas, you've only got opinions."

"What've you got, Mr. Fulbright Fellowship Declined (isn't *that* great—it sounds like the name of a move in chess)? What did you ever know that was so marvelous?" Dorothy inquired.

"I know all the scholarship in my field and I've kept track of the current journal articles and if I get an idea about any of it, I write an article myself and it gets printed, too. Dr. Gedeckt was my teacher. He's still recognized by everyone as the only man who knows anything about what's happening in geography. What do you know?"

"You know perfectly well what my qualifications are," Dorothy said. "I had comparative and structural linguistics from Sapir's best students. When I was only a sophomore, I was in correspondence with Dr. Chadwick in London. I know three and a half classical languages and seven living ones, including Navaho. I can also play the flute."

"You can't count the beats in a bar of music to save your ass," Clifford calmly remarked.

"Well, I can fake it pretty well," Dorothy said. "I played with the All American Youth Orchestra under Leopold Stokowski."

"Don't yell," Clifford said.

"Don't talk like I was a dumbbell, then. But I'll yell if I feel like it. I paid the rent this month."

"That's what I mean," Clifford said. He retained a calm and reasonable attitude which infuriated Dorothy. "That's a matter of fact, not of opinion."

"That isn't really what you mean!" Dorothy shouted. "You really hate women is what you mean! You're just a big faggot, like all the men I've ever known!"

"Whatever in the big wide world could lead you into making a lunatic switch in subject like that? Why are you so upset?"

"Oh, I don't know," Dorothy said, suddenly sitting down and lighting a cigaret. "Why do I *always* let you get me so excited? I have too many other things to worry about. I've got to take a bath and wash my hair and write a thousand letters."

"Did you answer Roy's letter, yet?"

Dorothy said, "I have one page written, almost."

"Don't seal it up, I have to put in a note to him," Clifford told her.

■ ■ ■

Dorothy dreamed that she had been placed in the Women's Ward of the State Mental Hospital. She was supposed to have been taken to Dr.

170

Springald's private sanatorium, down the Peninsula. Someone at the courthouse had put her papers into the wrong file basket, by mistake, after the lunacy hearing that had been brought by her brother, Ted McGreevey.

Dorothy herself, totally withdrawn, had no idea what was happening. They had put her into a large warm concrete room. She lay down on the floor and curled up small. She could, at the same time, see her brother's freckled face and crew-cut red hair, he was leaning forward, talking very fast to the judge, who was Dr. Bitteschoen, benign and white-haired in a billowing black robe.

Dorothy was all curled up small. Several hours later an attendant raised her out of a filthy puddle, hurled a bucket of tepid water over her, then mopped the floor with a dirty rag mop. "You go lay over there, now," the attendant said, and she led Dorothy to a dry place on the floor where Dorothy lay down and curled up small.

Flora McGreevey telephoned Dr. Springald's Sanitarium, down the Peninsula, to inquire about Dorothy. Dorothy wasn't there! Where can she be! What have you done with my daughter? "Now, Mrs. McGreevey, please be calm, very likely there has been a clerical error of some kind—it quite often happens in these cases. I'll telephone the State Mental Hospital at once."

Dorothy woke up, feeling frightened and miserable. The names were all so real. Dr. Springald. The State Mental Hospital. "A clerical error of some kind." She had made a mistake in her dream; Dr. Springald was really Clifford being efficient and high-handed and correct, and it was all somebody else's fault, really. And her brother, Ted, had been killed in the Korean War: why did she still hate him, in her dreams?

■ ■ ■

Tom said, "I was never exactly sure about this geography thing that Clifford does. When I went to school, it was all about maps and the principal exports of Borneo and what's the capital of Bogotà?"

Dorothy laughed. "It's all fake," she told him. "He's really doing a kind of environmental anthropology. It's concerned with how people live in a particular place, how do they fit in with the ecology."

"Anyway, he gets lots of big grants all the time to do it," Tom said.

"Oh, yes—he'll only teach if they come and get him and pay him lots of money, and even then it's never for more than nine months at the most; he never likes to stay home more than a year. But he likes to talk to the students, he says that's the only way he can find out what's really happening. He's so sententious—so awful—what do you want to talk about *him* for?"

"Oh, I don't know," Tom said. "I just wondered. Get me some more bananas when you go to the store. And some of those black chocolate cookies with all the nasty inside."

■ ■ ■

Margaret found her mother waiting up for her.

"Who drove you home, dear?" Mrs. Gridley asked.

"I took a taxi. Marge and I had a long talk—she wanted to bring me but I told her that there was no point in her barging around on a night like this. It's absolutely pouring. You shouldn't have stayed up; it's very late."

"The rain made me nervous," Mrs. Gridley said. "I couldn't sleep, so I got some darning and came down here where I wouldn't disturb your Dad. Can I fix you some coffee or tea or something? There's ice cream and cake that you didn't have the chance to eat for supper . . ."

"No thanks, Mama, I want to take a bath and fix my hair and go to bed. I have to stay home and study all day tomorrow. We have examinations when I go back to school."

"Well, you mustn't work too hard. You're supposed to be on vacation, aren't you?"

"I have to be really good in order to keep my scholarship," Margaret said. "You and Daddy have sacrificed so much for my education, I've got to make it pay off."

"You make it all worth while to us, as long as you feel that way," her mother told her. Margaret noticed that tears were beginning to appear in her mother's eyes.

"Use the downstairs bathroom so as not to disturb Daddy," Mrs. Gridley said. "I think I'll go up now. Don't forget your prayers." She approached Margaret and gave her a tiny kiss on the cheek.

"Honey, have you been D R I N K I N G tonight?" she demanded and gave Margaret a piercing stare.

"Marjory and I had just one beer—a half a can apiece. We were talking in the kitchen—"

"Your D A D D Y better not find out! You know how he feels about Women Who Smoke And Drink. And you know how I feel. I realize that we're old fashioned and that you're a big girl now, going to college way back East and everything, but it really hurts me to think you'd. . ."

"Oh, Mama—a glass of beer—"

Mrs. Gridley was growing more indignant as she went on. "It doesn't matter how much it was. The Grimshaws are different—they belong to that country club and have all those big drinking parties, that's their way of living and it's their business, but it's not Our Way. We've never lived like that and we're not about to start. And a girl, a Woman in particular, can't let herself—"

"All right, Mama, I'm sorry. I won't do it again."

"Don't lie to me," Mrs. Gridley snapped. "You've been on your own, back at that fancy school, back there where you think nobody knows you and notices what you do. I don't know what kind of people you know there or their folks or how they live. I don't see why you couldn't have stayed with us right here in Eugene and gone to the University, it's a perfectly good school."

"Now, Mama, don't get all upset. I have to bathe and go to bed. You should go to bed, too. I know that Daddy still has to have his breakfast at five-thirty."

"No, I suppose so," Mrs. Gridley blew her nose on a dainty pocket handkerchief and wiped away her tears, impatiently. "I just hope that nobody else *saw* you and Marjory drinking beer. Marjory's mother isn't above telling it all over town."

"Don't fuss so, Mama. I'll go up with you and get my nightshirt and haircurlers."

"Don't stay up much later," Mrs. Gridley said.

"No, Mama, I won't," Margaret told her. They went upstairs together, and Mrs. Gridley clung tightly to Margaret's arm all the way. Margaret wondered, "How often have I said that?"

■ ■ ■

Roy ate a species of breakfast pastry which he had always known by the name of "butterhorn." It was served hot and it had a pat of butter melting all greasy and yellow on top. He slowly drank poisonous chemical-tasting coffee while he ate. He was sitting in a big cafeteria in Harvard Square. The place was almost entirely occupied by college students who looked to him like English movie stars. The ones who weren't really beautiful appeared to be very distinguished and aristocratic. Roy told himself that they probably all came here from Lincoln, Nebraska and Bellingham, Washington.

He ate the last of his pastry. There had been a little difficulty in obtaining it. The lady in back of the counter was a native of Hingham and understood no other dialect; Roy's West Coast drawl was hard for her to follow. Fortunately, Roy had known a number of New Englanders when he was in the Army. He had not much trouble understanding the lady from Hingham, and he luckily remembered the correct dialect word:

"I want a Danish, please. Set it on the stove, first, with a piece of butter on top of it. Leave it there until the butter starts to melt."

The lady said, "Ayuh? I can give yiz a hot Danish. I'll call you."

Roy sipped the coffee slowly. It had been served in the native style— with cream in it. Roy had forgotten that one must ask for black coffee.

He thought about breakfasts that he had known, all kinds and sizes and shapes and flavors. In his grandmother's hotel room a lot of electric cords dangled from a light socket in the ceiling: electric breakfast of eggs boiled on electric hotplate, coffee (which he wasn't allowed to drink when he was at home) from an electric percolator, and toast from an electric toaster which Roy was supposed to be watching, but which he kept forgetting...the toast burned while he was gazing dreamily out the window at the towering slash-burners and big yellow trolley cars and fir trees in the rain, thinking of his mother.

173

Limp tepid hospital breakfast arrived in many tiny dishes under aluminum covers. It looked like a child's pretend-teaparty, all wheeled in on a metal table. A very small portion of some nasty food substance lay in the center of each dish and slowly melted down into a puddle of clear fluid and a faintly brownish sediment. It smelled of eggs and iodoform.

It was embarrassing for him to eat in a dining car while he was traveling any place, any year. The heavy starched linens and the lead-weighted silver-ware were impressive, and the eggs were always nicely cooked, but it all seemed so difficult and unpleasant for the stewards and waiters, they were all unhappy and hung over and bad-tempered, no matter how large or how small a tip anyone left for them. The coffee always tasted good, but who had the nerve to sit at a dining-car table long enough to enjoy drinking it? It was too harrowing on his nerves to watch all the waiters suffering.

Army breakfast in a clattering mess hall was a constant reminder that one must eat to live, not live to eat. The American Puritan's disgust for the body and its requirements, and his total indifference to the taste of food and its proper cooking was given full rein in the great kitchens. A carton of cornflakes opens cleverly down the center, two flaps pop up to admit the application of sugar and milk to the insipid contents—curled shavings of Dead Sea fruits. On a tin tray moulded into divided compartments was placed a small mountain of dehydrated eggs all rainbow-hued, accompanied by two small strings of bacon that had been cleverly constructed of cardboard, and a couple slices of toast rescued from the burning wreckage of some ancient bakery, and huge soggy pancakes hand-knitted from pure Australian flannel with brown sweet water soaking through the threads, and fresh oranges and cold milk and black, Lysol-flavored coffee with lots of canned milk and sugar. Roy remembered that everyone drank lots of the cold milk and devoured pounds of ice-cream—which wasn't surprising, he told himself, considering that in those days all of us were 19 years old and away from home for the first time.

Clifford had taken him on a visit to the ancestral home of the Barlows in the mountains of Idaho. Breakfast in that household was a very large event. There was hot mush in two kinds—farina, and a marvelous oatmeal which had had to be soaked in water over night and then slowly steamed in the morning. There were eggs—boiled, fried, and scrambled. There were bacon, ham, and pork chops. There were fried potatoes and gravy and hot baking-powder biscuits and hot rolls and home made bread, all served up with real honey, hand-made jams and jellies and preserves and relishes and pickles. There was home-made butter; there were fresh milk and cream and lots of coffee. There were fruit pies and two kinds of cake for dessert and everybody ate a lot of everything. Once there was a fresh pheasant for breakfast, in addition to all the usual goodies. The pheasant had tried, injudiciously, to cross the road in front of the farm pickup which Clifford's father was driving. There was *faisan sauté en beurre* the next day.

There was a period in his life during which Roy used to tell everybody that he hated breakfast, and in that time, he seldom ate breakfast. Then there was a long period during which there was no breakfast to be eaten, even if he had liked breakfast. Later, he went on a soup kick, and in the morning would open a can of tomato soup and mix it up with lots of milk and butter, or he would have clam chowder or oyster stew. Another season he became addicted to graveyard stew: rich hot milk and melted butter seasoned with salt, black pepper and cayenne pepper with a touch of garlic, into which was broken a pair of big fresh eggs, the whole mixture gently kept hot until the whites of the eggs were solid. When he was temporarily prosperous—had a job or was living on unemployment insurance, he liked to eat cheap steak or liver for breakfast. The meat had to be fried very fast and very lightly, in butter.

Dorothy introduced him to the pleasures of hot *café au lait* with hot French rolls and an assortment of cheeses and fresh fruit. Tom showed him where to go in Chinatown to get small elegant steamed dumplings and pastries made in the Cantonese style, and what kinds of tea there were to drink with them: Dragon's Well, Silver Needle, Lichi, Lapsang Souchong.

In the mountains, it was mandatory to eat Clifford Barlow's Non-Skid Swiss Morning Preparation. That was a combination of quick-cooking oatmeal, powdered milk, assorted nuts, raisins and other dried fruits, all pre-mixed and carried in a big waterproof plastic sack. A measure of this compound would be placed in a big John Muir tin cup and then hot water would be mixed with it, sufficient in quantity to make a thick gruel. It was to be eaten along with hot coffee. It tasted somewhat like stale pastry. It was believed to provide the hiker with every protein, carbohydrate, mineral and vitamin that is known to nutritional chemistry. Clifford loved the taste of it; to everyone else it was only a horrible necessity.

Roy left the cafeteria and walked across the Square among the beautiful children and on across the Yard to the Fogg Museum, where he spent the rest of the morning writing enthusiastic notes and commentaries and descriptions in his notebook, about all the Japanese and Chinese antiquities. He later lost the notebook during the course of a big house-party in New London, Connecticut.

■ ■ ■

Clifford walked all afternoon in the hills outside Katmandu. He stopped in the market on his way home to buy some gin and a few vegetables. By the time Sarah arrived, Clifford had created a small but elegant supper. He was delighted to see her again.

"I got out again as soon as I could," Sarah told him. "It's getting really vile in New York. Washington can't get any worse. I brought you a new record."

"You're looking great," Clifford said, and kissed her.

"I feel a lot better, now I'm home."

"I wonder myself, which one of my homes I really depend on," Clifford said. "I suppose I'll always go back to Ideeho. I like your hair that way."

"Thanks—do you really? I got tired of having it long; it's too much bother while I'm traveling."

They ate the elegant dinner. They watched the moon rise and listened to the new record. Clifford accompanied Sarah back to her own place and stayed with her for a long time. At last, he kissed her goodnight and returned to his house, singing in the moonlight. He was feeling very satisfied and happy. He could imagine himself living with Sarah and lots of babies and cows and chickens on a big ranch in the country around Lake Coeur d'Alene. Or maybe back East where the land was cheaper and there were exciting winters: he could buy five hundred acres of New Hampshire for practically nothing, he thought. "But I don't really want New Hampshire, either." Anyway, he was happy that Sarah was back; she was a great companion, a great pleasure, bright and honest. She had no pretentions to learning or the arts. He would marry her: she was the plain, healthy woman he'd been hunting for. They could live right here in Nepal for a while, then move to England, later, to stay clear of the American paranoia vibrations. ("But the English," Clifford thought, "have never truly believed in the pedal organ. I'm probably kidding myself again— Sweden is more like it, there are mountains and trees and lakes more like Idaho...")

Of more immediate concern to him was the question of what was to become of Laura, the lovely French botanist he'd been dining with, while Sarah was in America. Laura had a beautiful body and very fixed ideas about politics, her career in botany, and about the proper relationship between men and women. Although Laura was a few years younger than Sarah, she seemed to be more mature, better organized, more complete. Clifford thought she was just a little bit lacking in spontaneity; on the other hand, she was steady and solid in a way that none of the American girls he had known ("—and married," he regretfully added) had ever been. He loved her broad forehead, her heavy-lidded black eyes.

Sarah had a kind of stability, but it was discontinuous. She laughed at things, she doubted things which Laura tended to take for granted. There were many things, many questions of life and conduct which were, for Laura, settled things, and a few such notions which were beneath the notice of educated people. Clifford was fascinated by what he took to be Laura's Continental outlook on the world. Laura, in spite of all her theories, was able to enjoy herself with Clifford; she was perhaps becoming attached to him; she always seemed to have a fairly clear idea, however, that their relationship was temporary in nature. Laura appeared to have few extravagant illusions about herself or other people.

Sarah was no longer a young girl, but she was still rather uncertain about what there was for her to do in the world. Laura had a job that interested her; she would go on collecting plants, and having a pleasureable personal life. She would teach, write, travel and have love affairs; all

176

this was clearly understood. Eventually she would marry someone of her own social class and raise a proper French family (with the help of at least one servant) all on a carefully arranged schedule. If Sarah got married, she'd do everything herself with the help of Dr. Spock's book and a few electrical appliances. . .

Clifford sighed happily. He crawled into his bed and went to sleep. He dreamed that he and Dorothy were trying to be on time to catch a train in some very large oriental city where there was too much traffic and they were going to miss the train and it was all Dorothy's fault, she had deliberately made them late, and when he complained, she told him, "Go fuck yourself." And he hit her and then it was morning.

■ ■ ■

Roy told Dorothy, "It's funny to be old enough to remember knowing people who knew words and customs which had gone out of use before I was born, all kinds of things that people of your generation never hear about at all, or maybe see them mentioned in a book and you have to consult a dictionary or an encyclopedia to find out what they mean. Of course my folks were country people, from a different region than California; your folks wre all rich."

"Some of them were, up until the Crash," Dorothy said, "but that was years before my time. I don't think you're so old, you have hardly any grey hair yet. And I like your belly, smooth and pink, it's not old, and neither is this," she said, giving his penis a gentle squeeze.

■ ■ ■

Margaret wound long strands of her hair onto pink plastic bobbins while she sat in front of the mirror. She berated herself for arguing pointlessly with her mother. She realized that she had no longer any immediate feeling of respect or liking for either of her parents. They were a little bit too human, if anything—ignorant, superstitious and totally self-centered. They had tried very hard to keep her brother, Elvin, from marrying Jane Swanson because Jane's parents were "Old Country" Swedes with "funny ways." The Swansons were very clean and they went to the Lutheran Church and they were honest, good farmers, but they couldn't talk English plain, and they were foreigners. Let Elvin marry among his own people; there were plenty of nice American girls.

Margaret had tried to talk to her mother about it. "Janey is an American girl. She was born right here in Eugene and went to school here just like everybody else."

"She was brought up to *their* ways," Mrs. Gridley said. "How could I have them here on a visit? What would people think?"

"God-damned Squareheads! They's too many of them in the world as it is," Orval Gridley put in, bugging his blue eyes. "The *government* ought to round up all these foreigners and send them all back where they come from, every last one of them! Why Elvin ain't got brains enough to marry that Dickerson girl I'll never know. He used to run around with her all the time. That Betty Dickerson is smart as a whip!"

"Cute as a bug's ear," Mrs. Gridley added. "Why, she got a scholarship to the University when she graduated from high school last year. And her sister, Normajean—that child is the best natured little thing in the world! Always looking out to do something for other people. She worked like a trooper when we had the big church bazaar in January. Elvin is just ungrateful—I hate to say it about my own child, but he's ungrateful and that's the end to it."

"Well, you was the one that spoiled him," Orval Gridley shouted. "I tried to take the damn kid and knock some sense into him but you'd never let me. I never could get a lick of work out of him."

The Gridleys refused to attend the wedding, which was to be held at the Swanson farm. They forbade Margaret to go, but she defied them. She said, "Elvin's my only brother and Janey was always good to me when I was little and she was the leader of the Campfire Girls. I've bought them a present with my own money that Grandma sent me and I'm going to the wedding. I wish you'd come with me, but I know you won't."

Her mother and father both said quite a number of intolerable things upon this occasion, but Margaret went to the wedding anyway. It was a very large affair, with a smorgasbord, gallons of beer and wine and other drinks that Margaret had only read about in books. Jane's brothers and sisters and other relatives played music for the dancing—polkas and schottisches and hambos and waltzes. There was a stupendous wedding supper. Margaret was welcomed into the family, along with her brother.

She had a wonderful day, but when she thought of her parents sitting obstinately at home alone, she felt ashamed and angry and sad. Margaret told herself that she was finished with them. They were some other kind of creature, different from all the rest of the world. She must continue to live with them, and she must continue to defer to them, but the meaning of their relationship would be changed. She would always feel a sort of subliminal, unconscious love for them, an automatic response, a learned, memory-bound thing, but it would be that— something in her past life, like her love for dolls when she was a girl, or for a horse she once had owned, or for the landscape around Eugene. It would be absolutely different in quality from the feeling she had for Elvin and Jane and her grandmother, or for Herbert Wackernagel.

Margaret's parents withdrew all their objections to Jane Swanson when their first grandchild appeared. Jane's mother was dead, by that time, and Mrs. Gridley decided that she must go to her son's home and take charge of the household while Jane was in childbed. Mrs. Gridley's praises of Jane became as loud and extravagant as her condemnations had been. And the grandchild was the Eleventh Wonder of the World. Since Jane had managed to reproduce such a wonder twice more, she

178

became a great favorite with the Gridleys, who introduced her to all their friends and neighbors as "Our Daughter, Jane."

Elvin and his family removed to Salem, to the tune of tears and heartbreak in the Gridley household. Elvin had got a good civil service job with the state government, and although he was (his parents told him) far too young, he bought a fine old house in West Salem where he and his family were now happily living, away from Eugene at last.

■ ■ ■

Roy decided to fly home by jet liner. He had lots of money; he'd go first class. The plane seemed about ready to do a nose-over into Long Island Sound, right at the end of the runway, before Roy was aware that he was leaning far back in his seat and the Sound was falling away at a sharply increasing angle below him. Very soon the plane was high above the clouds; he imagined that they must be passing over Cleveland by this time.

Roy thought of the first airplane ride he had, with a staff sergeant in a Piper Cub recon plane. They flew only a few hundred feet above the flat South Dakota wheat fields. The first several minutes of the flight were pleasant and interesting, but soon the plane had gained a lot of altitude and the pilot began to practice "lazy-eights" on his way down to lower altitudes. The plane turned and swooped like a figure skater above the green and brown revolving earth. Roy felt desperately ill, far too ill even to be able to vomit. He had never before experienced feelings of such total wretchedness and despair.

Much later, when he became used to airplanes, Roy was able to eat peanuts, candybars and sandwiches while he was flying. It used to upset new crewmen to watch him; they would be feeling queasy to be flying anyway, and then to discover Roy in the act of devouring a big greasy ham sandwich with mayonnaise and lettuce was enough to make them wish they'd never heard of airplanes, let alone subjected themselves to the horrors of riding in one.

Roy loved to lie in the transparent nose of a B-17, alternately reading and watching the landscape below, until he fell asleep, hypnotized by the drone of the engines. The land and the light would change slowly— mountains of purple stone, tan and chocolate desert, river with its green squares of palm orchards and little fields on either side of it, all in the midst of sand, heat, stone: then a surprising stretch of ocean where the Gulf intruded itself into the desert. He nearly got killed a couple of times, and he had been badly scared, but that was a feeling he could never exactly recall; he didn't want to feel it ever again.

■ ■ ■

Margaret spent a long time in the bath, messing with the pumice stone, fiddling with her toenails. She thought about her parents and their life together, something out of Theodore Dreiser, only worse: her mother's long-suffering, slowly souring endurance of Orval Gridley's half-hillbilly, half-old maid sensibilities, their continual mutual browbeating campaigns to establish spiritual superiority, the self-righteousness of both, their concerted judgment and condemnation of all the rest of the world with the exception of those happy two or three members of the First Methodist-Episcopal Church who were a little richer than the Gridleys. Those were the people the Gridleys tried to be nice to, entertained in their own exclusive home, and whom they regularly hoped they'd be invited to visit.

Margaret thought, "If I had any sense, I'd make Herb marry me now and we'd go live in New York or Berlin or someplace. Then I could be Margaret Gridley Wackernagel. But I suppose I'd have to live here in Eugene and be disowned because Herb would want to go on living here, so he can go on shooting pool down at Glad Charley's. He's absolutely worthless except for that one trick thing he can do better than anybody. I should make him come to Cambridge—that would be a bringdown for Mr. Lexington Fiske III, known to his friends as Lukey Boy, and whom I owe it to all my friends and my lovely parents to marry in order to show that Education Pays Off. Then everybody would leave me alone and I could maybe get going on my own work at last, my own little trick thing."

In her room, the picture of her brother, Elvin, grinned at her. Their mother thought it would be nice to put it on Margaret's dressing table, particularly since Elvin and Jane wouldn't be coming down for Christmas this year. The picture was an enlarged, smeary color snapshot in a blue and gold gesso frame. It usually stood on a lace doily on top of the TV set in the living room, enshrined among Walt Disney animals made of porcelain and a lamp which contained a turning smoke-jack so that the forest-fire scene painted on the glass chimney flickered and blazed and sparkled very realistically indeed.

There was Elvin, holding one of his sons on his shoulders while the younger one stood clutching his father's left trouserleg. Janey stood beside him, holding the baby and smiling. The baby was called Eleanore, "named after one of Her folks, this time," as Mrs. Gridley said. Elvin was a big raw-boned man with big blue eyes, like their father; Jane was small and gentle. There they all were. "And that," Margaret told herself, "is what life is all about. After all the Beethoven and the Sappho and Matisse and moonlight, this is what really happens. Lots of fun at first, then it's all limp and soft. That's all there is to that."

She went to her bureau and took out a photograph album. It was crammed with formal photographs and snapshots, and there were also a number of envelopes full of negatives and loose pictures. She would need several more albums, eventually, in order to mount all the pictures. Between two pages of the bulging book was a thick white envelope addressed to Maggy Gridley. It contained a letter from Herbert

Wackernagel—one of the few that he had ever written in his life. It was little more than a note, badly spelled, about his life in the army. He was having a fine time in California, he wrote. The army was OK and he was learning lots about electricity. Swimming was great in the ocean, wish you was here, ha ha. Enclosed with the letter was a very clear full length snapshot of the writer. He was standing with his feet wide apart, his hands clutching the ends of a white towel slung around his neck. He was grinning and the gold tooth gleamed. He was wearing nothing else. The Pacific Ocean showed in the background.

Margaret smiled at the picture, and then put it away again. She felt tired and happy. She put on her reading glasses, took up her copy of R. W. Hutchinson's *Prehistoric Crete*, and got into bed. She read only a few pages before she fell asleep.

She awoke a few hours later; the glasses were jammed against her eyebrows; the book was on the floor. The lamp was very bright. She wondered where she was. She said, experimentally, "Luke?" and then she laughed, softly. She put the book and her glasses on the night table and turned out the light. She giggled to herself. Grey dawn was showing behind the blinds. She could hear her father coughing and swearing in the bathroom. She told herself, "You're such a fraud. It sticks out all over you. Probably God will strike you with lightning, one of these days and haul you away to Hell. Darling Lukey. Darling Herbert. Darling little Nell, a retreating curious egg. . . ."

Margaret was surprised when she awoke again, to see a dark, wet morning—more nearly, noon. Rain had continued all through the night. She was warm, she thought it was quite bright outside, and she had been quite certain that Herbert was with her, weighing down the other side of the bed.

■ ■ ■

The Grand Mahatma says, "For lots of people, nothing that happens to them is real unless they end up in jail—or at least vomiting and weeping as they writhe on the bathroom floor screeching 'Never again!' Most of these people happen to be Americans."

■ ■ ■

Roy felt compelled to visit the library regularly—had to, with something of the same feeling of urgency which other people have experienced only in connection with their toilet training. Before he had gone to bed the night before, he had been reading some poems by Ezra Pound. He had read a word which his own small dictionaries didn't gloss. Perhaps the word had been misspelled or mis-printed in the edition which he had been reading. It might have been a foreign word. He'd have to make a trip to the library, in the morning, in order to find out the answers to all these questions. He'd consult the big Oxford Dictionary, several different print-ings of the poems of Ezra Pound, and probably a Spanish and a big French dictionary.

In the morning, Roy happened to sleep a little later than usual. He felt that he could stay in bed all day, if he wanted to. He got up long enough to go to the bathroom, then he crept back into his warm, comfortable bed. He began thinking about writing. It would be a fine day. He had no engagements, had made no promises. The apartment ought to be com-pletely swept and garnished, but not today. He would leave the house as soon as he possibly could, after he got out of bed. Then he would go to the Ocean Beach and have coffee and pie for breakfast. It was then he remembered that he must go to the library.

He arose and dressed himself. He shaved, although he hadn't planned on doing so. Yesterday's wool socks lay under the sink; they had to be washed by hand, since they were home-made ones which would be ruined by a washing machine. He got the soap powder out of the kitchen and very carefully washed the socks and set them out on old newspapers on the back porch to dry. The sun was brilliant on the Park, the spires and domes of St. Ignatius Church, the complicated Victorian facades of the Sunset district; the Bay was dark blue. . .he must get out of the house and in and out of the library right away.

Roy made the bed and did a hurry-up job of sweeping the floor. The trash box was almost too full to receive the contents of the dustpan. He had to carry the box and the dustpan down the backstairs and empty both of them into the incinerator, which was also nearly full. He set fire to the mess and stood (for endless minutes) watching it, in case any of the neighbors should see the conflagration all untended and dangerous and so, incontinently, send for the fire brigade. It took no longer than he had planned, but Roy waited until it had all burnt out. He went back to the stairs and washed his hands, then it was suddenly time to go to the bathroom.

In the kitchen, he noticed that the garbage pail was full. He carted it down the backstairs and emptied it and washed it out and carefully made a new lining for it, using an old paper shopping bag. He carried it back up the stairs and replaced it in the kitchen, where he paused for a drink of water. The teapot was standing on the drainboard; it was full of last night's tea leaves. He emptied the pot and rinsed it out, hurriedly, and put it away. He wanted out of the house.

He found his notebook, he was almost ready, and what book would he carry with him to read while he wasn't looking at the ocean or writing? Or he may need it to look at on the bus, or while he waited for the bus, if he decided not to walk home. "Out, out, out!" he told himself. He rocked from one foot to the other while he stood in front of the bookshelves. A small book such as would fit into the pocket of his jacket; he must always have one book to write in and one book to read, just as everyone must carry money, identification, matches, jewels, handkerchiefs, rosaries and lipsticks. Out, out out out! *Silver Poets of the Sixteenth Century.* Sir Thomas Wyatt / Henry Howard: Earl of Surrey / Sir Philip Sidney / Sir Walter Raleigh / Sir John Davies / Edited with an introduction / By Gerald Bullett / London: J. M. Dent and Sons Ltd. / New York: E. P. Dutton & Co. Inc. (n.d.)...OUT! He put on a jacket, picked up the book and a notebook, went halfway down the front stairs, went back to his room for his sunglasses, came out the front door of the house and down the front steps, cursed and turned away and went back inside to get his wallet (which contained his library card) and he congratulated himself upon seeing a half pack of cigarets lying on his desk, he put those in his pocket, and even remembered to pick up a book of matches, as well (out, damn it, OUT). He slammed the door, went down the stairs, closed the heavy front door carefully, down the front steps, down the walk, down the hill towards the library...He had taken the wrong jacket; the letters which he had written the night before and which he had felt it was essential to get into the mail today, were in the pocket of the other jacket, the one which he'd decided was too heavy to wear on a sunny day, and he would not go back right now to get them, he was too far towards the library, and he stomped on down the hill in the sun, raging, damn, damn, damn, no, no, no, no, TO THE LIBRARY!

■ ■ ■

Dorothy looked at herself in the mirror. Her hair was all wrong. It was too much trouble when it was long, it didn't look really right when it was short. If it was really short, she was afraid that it looked too dykey. And it was the wrong color anyway, no matter how long or how short. The next time she was in Paris, she would absolutely have to buy a couple of wigs and a fall.

"You old harridan," she told the mirror, "you're so close to thirty-five, now, why should you care what you look like?"

She stood up too suddenly; she felt one of her stockings give and the other one twisted itself around her legs. She swore and adjusted all her clothing. Clifford was shouting, he was waiting, they were late.

■ ■ ■

Tom Prescott made a lot of money one month by selling many photographs and a short text to a local magazine which was devoted to domestic interests. The pictures showed rich San Francisco bachelors in their kitchens, creating solid, down-to-earth he-man food: breasts of Arctic ptarmigan surprise, roast goat shanks Peloponnese, and Sea Urchins Salvador Dali. The idea had been Dorothy's. They had been having dinner at Max Lammergeier's place. Alice was out of town and Max had taken this opportunity to invite Dorothy and Tom to taste his version of gazpacho, magnified hearts of young spring lamb, a complicated salad

made from wild grasses, anise roots and mandarin oranges, a vast casserole of riz à la Valenciennes, three kinds of wine, and a flaming dessert,
followed by cheeses, fresh fruits, brandy, and coffee. Max was a good
cook, and since he'd been married to Alice, he had learned a great deal
more about food; however, Alice hated to cook. She could do it very well
indeed, but she didn't like to bother with it, she said; it was too time-
consuming, she was too busy with the house, the children, golf, the garden. Max seldom had time, himself, to do anything more than work with
his many patients. He loved the practice of psychiatry, but he loved, even
more, "every pleasure of the belly and the groin." Whenever he could
manage to find or steal the time for it, he would prepare a small delicious
dinner for a few friends. This time, Dorothy and Tom had been the lucky
guests.

"Naturally he's a good cook," Tom said. "Anybody who has all that
cream and butter and nice French wine to do with is bound to be a good
cook."

"Come on," Dorothy said, "He might have burned it all, or had lumps
in the gravy, but he didn't."

Max came back into the dining room with a pot of fresh coffee.

"I wish you'd show Tom your kitchen, Max. I want one like it, some
day," Dorothy said.

Max said, "Oh, yeah?" and Tom went to look. It was a vast room with
one wall of bare brick, the rest of knotty pine. A great number of copper
pots and pans hung over an overhead rack. There was a pair of cooking
ranges such as might have been used in a hotel.

"In the old days, when my Mama had help and gave dinner parties,
they needed stoves," Max said.

Tom was outraged. "My folks thought they were coming up in the
world when they rented a house that had an electric stove in it. How do
those things work—do you have a stoker to take care of them?"

"They're gas, now. I guess in Grandpa's time they were wood or coal
burners. I don't know. They work good, now."

"All this for just one family," Tom exclaimed. He sounded aggrieved.

"Well, the family was big then," Max explained. "When my father was
a boy, a lot of people lived here—all my uncles and aunts, my grandparents and various unmarried or widowed cousins and in-laws and out-
laws—they all had to eat. There were a couple of hired girls and some
spare cousins that did the cooking and baking, under Granny's supervision. But after all, Tom, this was only an ordinary middle-class establish-
ment, for San Francisco. People with money had a lot more complicated
kind of layout with roasting ovens and baking ovens and barbecue pits
and the whole works. Our outfit was good enough to bake the bread
twice a week and rolls and roasts and pies for Sunday—nothing extravagant. You ought to see some of the big ones—and some of the new
places, too—they're interesting."

By this time, Dorothy had joined them. She'd grown tired of sitting alone at the table. "*You* take him to see Barney's new place—*I* can't, since he's married to that awful Beverly person, now. Tom, you have to do a story on San Francisco kitchens so that little old ladies will come here and demand to see Max's."

"Sure I do," Tom said. All his radical sensibilities were aroused. "Show them how the other half lives. It always sells."

"Come on, Tom, let's go have some coffee and brandy," Max said.

"Okay, okay, I'm ready," Tom said.

While they were driving home, Dorothy remarked, "I always forget that you've got so many marvelous liberal sensibilities."

"Hell, Dotty, I'm just not used to rich people."

"Max isn't rich people, he's one of my oldest friends. He wasn't snotty to you, was he?"

"No—it isn't that—but it makes me mad to think that kind of life goes on and on as a matter of course while the rest of the world's in a mess—that it was going on right through the Depression while there were bread-lines and all my folks were on Relief."

"My mother still does lots of social work," Dorothy said. "She doesn't have anything to give away, any more, but she puts in lots of time organizing and getting really *rich* people to give the money."

"And the house at Lake Tahoe needs a new roof," Tom added, mockingly. "And I've simply *got* to get away to Italy for a few months this year, Doctor says I must rest more, and the taxes take everything—I know, I know," Tom said. "My old man used to say the same thing, after he started making a little money in the shipyards, early in the war. It's all the same. I just hate poor-mouthing; I hate to listen to it."

Dorothy said, "All right, Tom."

They drove on in silence.

"You and your great ideas," Tom began again.

"Why not?" Dorothy quickly replied. She was tired of what she considered his fake politics. "*Sunset Magazine* will be crazy about it. You can give the money they pay you to Women for Peace or the Viet Cong or some other worthy cause."

Tom said, "You're getting pretty smart, aren't you."

"Well, if you keep dividing the world up into sides, all the time—"

"Yah, yah, yah," Tom said, more gently. "You're right; you're right. I keep forgetting I own a piece of it. But it still makes me mad."

"I'm sorry that I teased you," Dorothy said. "It really is all fucked up; we ought to change it, somehow—but our political ideas are all goofy, too. We just change the color of the paint on the outside—we need a new idea, a new factory—we're doing it all wrong now, that's for sure."

■  ■  ■

The Grand Mahatma says: "You see it, and seeing it makes you dodge, and that sudden reflex movement makes you hit your head on the door.

The Buddhists call this the Law of Karma. It is more or less the basis for the idea of reincarnation. Or it describes that principle which keeps reincarnating itself: that energy that keeps on going until it can be described at last by the mathematics of the Second Law of Thermodynamics as having reached the state of entropy."

■ ■ ■

Roy had a great three weeks at Monterey—parties and talks and booze and exciting arguments and feuds and fights. He spent lots of time talking with Dorothy, and he got to see Clifford for the first time in several years.

Several hundred students sat and looked at him whenever he came out of doors or sat down in the local coffee shop or in the campus cafeteria. They listened while he talked, they brought him their manuscripts, they shared their wine and tobacco and dope with him. As many as could manage it made their way into his bed.

Roy returned to San Francisco long enough to buy a passport and a steamship ticket and to store his belongings. Max Lammergeier produced a titanic farewell party for him, and the next morning, Roy left the city, bound for the Orient.

■ ■ ■

Tom's mother arrived for a short visit. She was on her way to see her sister in Hawaii. She went there every year and loved all the Islands, even though they were all well on their way to being utterly ruined by Henry Kaiser and hordes of tourists.

Nessa Prescott was handsome, thin and nervous. Every year, she had a new psychiatrist or a different kind of doctor or team of doctors who were treating her for a new and alarming set of symptoms. She joked about her illnesses, but she never complained. She could afford them; Tom and his brothers all helped to support her.

Dorothy found her appalling. Dorothy told all her friends, "Nessa drinks a great deal more than she ought to, considering all the things she claims are wrong with her. She keeps yakking away to me about clothes and hair and real estate and lawsuits and Hawaii and all her gentleman admirers until I want to hit her. Here I am, trying to write something, at last, about the morphemes in Pali and Sogdian, and just enough time left over to make it to my classes in Berkeley and find Tom a clean shirt before *he* goes crazy. (He's in the darkroom all the time, of course. If he has to spend any time alone with his mother, he starts breaking out in spots and blotches.) But the poor woman's got to see him some time, I suppose. And she's looking so gaunt and haggard, you wouldn't believe it. I imagine I'll be looking exactly the same way in about another two weeks."

"I guess we're all of us about as old as we can get," Roy said. "Nessa is only five or six years older than I am, after all. My only hope is for a serene and beautifully quiet antiquity. I may make it, too—I'm not as nervous as Nessa."

"You drink as much as she does," Dorothy said.

"Yeah, but I have a good time and then pass out, when I drink; I don't get all manic and sleepless and phobic."

"You and Nessa ought to get together and cheer each other's declining years," Dorothy suggested.

"She's too skinny and leathery," Roy told her. "You're more my type."

Dorothy said, "I was once, maybe, but that was a long time ago."

"All I know is, I'm a great failure as a poet," Roy said. "My present great age proclaims it. I should have been ruined twenty years ago by whiskey, dope, and beautiful women. Or the war should have killed me."

"*I* tried to ruin you, but you were too old and tough," Dorothy said. "Don't come crying to me now, with your tragic fate. Face. Anyway, you look years younger than you are. I could kill myself, I guess."

"That's the real cure, all right," Roy said. "But if you were dead, you wouldn't know what everybody was doing, and nobody would be able to see you."

"That's right. I certainly couldn't stand *that*. And what *are* they all doing," Dorothy inquired. '*I've* been too busy, lately, to find out. Tell me everything."

"I don't know. Clifford hasn't written lately and I haven't been to Berkeley for months to see Mark and Beth, and Max is always too busy to talk so I seldom see him or Alice. I'm busy reading all of Chaucer again. I don't care what's happening here—all I wonder about is Troilus: is he going to get at Criseyde or not?"

■ ■ ■

Roy woke up in the middle of the night. He needed only to reach out one hand in order to get his pen and notebook. By shifting his head a little, he could see the clock. Two thirty-five A.M.

He congratulated himself on having had sense enough to leave a light on in his room before he went to sleep. He began writing, setting down the lines of a poem which had come into his head the moment he was awakening. He lay on his stomach. He had shoved the pillow aside and dragged the notebook under his nose. The blankets were arranged in a great cape over his shoulders, their soft weight and evaporating warmth consoled him; he felt happy. Later, he thought about all the times he'd awakened and risen from a warm bed with great reluctance and suffering in order to find a light, a paper and a pen with which to record some fleeting idea. Now he was at last old enough and smart enough to leave a light on if he wanted it (he paid his own electric bill) and to keep writing materials near at hand at all times.

He had learned, in the past few years, that he was always working, asleep and awake, as long as he went on living alone and nobody was trying to put him on some schedule of business hours eight-to-five in some office, some job that nobody (much less Roy) ought to be doing in the first place. He wondered how much pain, anguish, and general confusion he might have been spared if his parents had simply allowed him to have a lamp in his room at night. He was afraid of the dark. He had nightmares and his screams drove his parents to panic and rage. One or both of them had to try to calm him, reason with him (their feet growing cold, their patience wearing away), persuade him that everything and everybody was asleep; that the world was in God's care. His parents themselves were in the house and would protect him from all harm. All was well, the stars were shining, that noise was only an electric wire tapping lightly, scraping the eaves of the roof. The wind was swinging it back and forth, and the same wind was playing a sleepy music in the poplar leaves. "All is well, God is good, it is a beautiful night."

Roy could never believe that the darkness was benign; for him, it was filled with brain movies—frightening abstractions of contracting space mixed with memories of Hollywood horror films about Dracula and Frankenstein and homicidal maniacs and torture and murder and falling. He never truly came to believe that he had been mistaken about night and darkness. He had seen demons by daylight, too. He must either leave a light on or have someone to sleep with. Temporarily, he had a light.

■ ■ ■

Nessa told Dorothy and Tom, "You must let me take you out for dinner tonight. We'll go to some fun place. There's one I was reading about in a magazine on the plane. It looked marvelous."

Tom said, "Ah, Mama, most of them look all right, but all you get from any of them is the same old stuff. It costs more in some places, that's all. They look good in the magazines because I took the pictures. I got to eat in some of them while I was doing the job. It's all a big tourist con. The food's lousy."

"Well, you and Dorothy decide on a place, then, someplace *you* like."

"Mama, when we have money, we buy a big roast of beef and cook it ourselves. We don't eat downtown. The food in San Francisco is lousy, except in Chinatown and one or two little places that aren't 'fun places,' they just have food."

Dorothy said,"We could have something we never bother to fix at home—go to that fish and chips parlor."

"Come on, Dorothy," Tom said.

"Or we could go to that little place down by the docks where they have good chowder and fish. It's really good," Dorothy explained to Nessa. "Just clams and potatoes and celery. It's the only restaurant I've ever seen where they really put clams in the chowder."

"I know just what you mean," Nessa said. "They usually keep one little clam on a string and sort of wash it off in the soup once a day."

Tom laughed. He said, "It's a good place, but it isn't open at this time of night."

Dorothy made several other suggestions. She hated San Francisco restaurants as much as Tom did, but she didn't want to disappoint Nessa. And she really wanted to go out for dinner. She told Nessa all about the curries in India and maybe they ought to go to an Indian place for a change.

Tom finished his cigaret and walked to the window while Dorothy was talking. He was thinking of the scandal he had caused in a restaurant once when he was a little boy. The waiter on that occasion had a cold or a broken nose and he spoke in a muffled, snuffling adenoidal tone. Tom had announced, very loudly and distinctly, "That man talks like he had hemorrhoids!" Everyone in the restaurant turned to stare; Tom's parents were beside themselves with shame and anger and mirth all combined. They reminded Tom of this incident, later, whenever they wanted to tease him about using big words at the wrong time, and to correct him for "talking out of turn." He looked out the window and chuckled to himself.

Dorothy said to him, "Well, *you* decide, if you think that *my* suggestions are so ludicrous!" She imagined that he was laughing at her, making fun of her.

"OK," Tom said. "We'll go down to that place in the Marina and eat pizza and eggplants and salad—that's good enough. Mama, you still like Italian food?"

"Well, if there aren't too many strong spices..."

Dorothy said, "If we have lots of wine with it, that will take care of the spices. Don't worry. Tom and I will buy the wine, that will be our part of the dinner."

They drove to a place where a rich editor had once taken Dorothy and Tom to dinner. It was called Filthy Florian's. Plastic grape leaves and real oak branches and plaster fruit hung from a false arbor ceiling of redwood lumber. On the walls, pictures of Venice painted on black velvet alternated with photographs of opera stars and movie people. Quaint copper lanterns hung above tables decorated with red and white checkered cloths. Each table bore a sugar caster full of grated cheese and small flasks of red wine vinegar and of peanut oil, in addition to the usual salt and pepper shakers. There was a delicious smell of hot olive oil, burning pizza-crust, and melting cheese. These odors were mixed with less inviting aromas of cigaret smoke, stale beer, and the hair oils with which the waiters had anointed their hyacinthine locks. And a goodly crowd was there, and the jukebox played selections from highclass operas, and there was also a very popular recording of Mr. Jan Peerce singing "The Bluebird of Happiness."

Tom and his mother had a short argument about the propriety of drinking martinis before dinner. Nessa simply said, "I require a couple of martinis, my dear. It's time. You and Dorothy please order whatever you'd like to drink."

"But Mama," Tom said, quoting Max Lammergeier, "gin kills all the tastebuds."

"My tastebuds are going to have to look out for themselves," Nessa replied. "I want a drink."

Dorothy said, "Actually, I think martinis will be fine. I want a couple myself. You go ahead and order sherry, Angel." She gave Tom a brilliant toothy smile.

Tom ordered three double martinis on the rocks from the gleaming waiter. Then he made a serious effort towards making agreeable conversation.

Nessa cheered up when the gin arrived. Soon, she was telling about Prohibition and the Great Depression and the time she got loaded with Clark Gable. She became more relaxed and more amiable when it became apparent that there'd be time for at least one more large drink before their dinner would arrive. But it was just as well, Dorothy thought; the dinner would probably be inedible if they were sane and sober.

■ ■ ■

Clifford tried playing all the way through Franck's *Grande pièce symphonique* without looking at the score. The windowpanes of the chapel rattled. He heard the door open and close, as it often did when he was practicing; he was used to hearing it and he didn't mind. In a Catholic place, he remembered, everybody drops in and out all the time, not like a Protestant meeting house, locked up tight every day except Sunday.

He could see the music in his head all unrolled like a map: ochre and rose and pale green, sky blue—there was a mountain range (dark brown wrinkles) here was a winding blue river. The organ clattered and laboured as Clifford massaged its keys and tromped up and down the pedal boards with his bare feet. Sometimes he shouted and sang a stave or so in a large passage of the music which particularly delighted him, one of those curious polychromatic knots which Franck had tied into the music that turned part of Clifford's head inside out whenever he played it or heard it—the musical equivalent of a trip through a Klein bottle. One such knot stopped him. He forgot, suddenly, where it was the separate strands were leading. Why did he forget.

He'd been thinking of Dorothy, of Idaho, of a stone wall outside the house where he'd lived when he was a boy and of the nasturtiums, a swaying green and orange yellow curtain in front of black crystal rock; of Mrs. Elliott, his piano teacher, telling him to keep his wrists level; of dancing with Betsy Jean Kramer at a high school party and trying to persuade her to make love with him and she wouldn't quite; of the small round graham-colored pup which had arrived in the house by the stone wall, he was afraid of it, it was too fragile to play with, his father called it Spike, and after a week, it suddenly died and his father and mother were heartbroken, so Clifford couldn't keep any more pets, even though he wasn't interested in having any in the first place. He could remember everything quite well, nothing was wrong with his memory, the ice man came to the house in a horse-drawn wagon and he wore a complicated kind of leather apron that buckled around the legs like a cowboy's chaps, and a leather shield on his right shoulder where he carried the big blocks of shining ice caught in massive steel tongs, and the sound of those tongs clanking when they were empty, and he could remember the name of the older man with the same kind of leather apron who brought boxes of groceries up the back stairs to the kitchen while his horse and wagon waited in the alley, the man Clifford's father always referred to as "Old Sour Balls," that man's name was Mr. Dahlstrom.

Clifford sat still on the organ bench, his hands pressed together between his knees, trying to think his way back to César Franck again. There was Frescobaldi and Pachelbel and Sweelinck and Rameau and Francis Poulenc and Olivier Messiaen and Leo Sowerby and Charles Ives and Marcel: Marcel Dupré, Marcel Duchamp, and Marcel Proust and Clifford's mother talking with the high school girl who was going to stay with Clifford Wednesday night while his parents went to the movies, all about water-waves being softer and more natural-looking than marcelled hair, and he could remember the smell of the magazine, and the faces in the ads for Palmolive soap, the magazine lay on a bright colored "Indian blanket" on the grass in the yard where his mother had been sitting in the shade, reading.

Clifford sighed and looked at the red pilot-light which showed that the organ was ready to operate. César Franck wrote something else, very like what it was that Clifford was trying to remember. Which place? Clifford reached out and played a few notes, a phrase from the Violin Sonata. That didn't work. He tried a bit of the string Quintet, a line from Le Chasseur maudit...he thought of Psyché, and the name handed him the chord progression he had been unable to remember a few minutes before. There was a near relation to it in Psyché, a long, otiose composition for chorus and orchestra.

He almost reached the end of the Grande pièce symphonique when his memory quit again.This time, he opened the score and played from it; he wanted to finish the piece, he wanted out of that universe. He came to the end at last, and turned off the organ and closed and locked its lid. He gathered up his music, put on his sandals and started walking out of the chapel. He saw Laura sitting alone in a pew at the back of the room. She was wearing a bright colored scarf over her hair. She looked very unhappy.

■ ■ ■

One fine day, Roy very slowly and completely realized that all his knowledge and learning were only worthless clumsy decorations that were quite insecurely glued onto an essentially trivial, nearly moronic mind.

191

For many years he had persuaded himself that learning things was a value in itself. He had believed his parents and his teachers when they had told him that learning would raise him out of the nameless lower social class into which he had been born. He had believed that his accomplishments in learning, coupled with his ability to study and learn more, made him qualitatively different, made him quite a lot better than all but that happy few people that were as bright as or brighter than he was.

But now Roy discovered that he was able to stand aside and see that all his learning amounted to no more than a large catalog of information; it would make a book rather larger than an encyclopedia, for there was more detail—there were more diagrams and color plates and musical examples. (These last were also simultaneously accessible to the inner ear as sound in various timbres and colors and combinations.) Trees and mountains and flowers, the windowsill, the pen in his hand, all these became greater and stronger and clearer than he (there were birds outside, now—they and the leaves were becoming great presences, one of the birds was eating a red flower). Did he feel afraid. In this world of Thrones, Dominations, and Powers, its motions and colors a roaring flame and thundering music, each organ of his own body was a multitude of spirits in a whirlwind of singing and color, at once fearless and conscious of the reality and the powers of other beings...a multitude of universes he knew nothing about, but in which he was immediately participating: or which were, perhaps, nothing more than projections of his own metabolism, as the local gurus had always said. It was all this and more. All simultaneous, the birds a rapid succession of nerve explosions in his head or liver, and the notes of the song were different letters of the Devanagri alphabet and the Twelve Church Modes and the seven notes of Guido's Scale, the divisions of Pythagoras his Monochordion mirror of planetary singing.

"Unless I see that the world really is this way," Roy told himself, "a dancing, singing, raving collection of brilliant interpenetrating universes of horror and delight and knowledge and brainlessness, I'm *really* a failure. If I only see the windowsill, and not that it is also a street of dusty mud-brick houses in Baghdad blazing sun heat crowd of men women camels babies horses mules Chryslers and unset rubies and Coca Cola machines emeralds pearls brocades furs silver plate and filligree, great melons grapes marigolds lilies dates oranges pineapples mangoes and pomegranates, I'll have to turn in my suit and run for office in Wall Street Washington, D.C."

■ ■ ■

Sarah told Clifford, "There's something wrong with the idea that *everybody* in the world is cold and sick and wounded—but I see, sometimes, that it's really true and I hate it. I try to change it, I try to tell it 'NO!' but it continues, just the same. I think sometimes I'd like to have an expensive little apartment in Manhattan and a chinchilla coat and a thousand evening dresses. All I'd do is sleep all day and go out every night with a different rich boy from Yale or Princeton to do the Watusi in expensive nightclubs and go to the opera all the time and to fancy restaurants and drink too much and get fat and noisy and die."

■ ■ ■

Tom Prescott found a job in Hollywood when he got out of the army. He had been drafted early in 1945 and he was discharged at Jefferson Barracks late in 1946. Six months before that, he had met Darlene Hawkins in Colorado Springs, where she had come to visit relatives. Darlene had a job as page girl in the CBS studios on Vine Street in Hollywood, and she was going to return there at the end of the week. After she left, she and Tom exchanged a great many letters.

When Tom was discharged, he spent a month visiting his mother and his friends in a small town in Iowa. Then he took off for Hollywood. He found Darlene as soon as he got into town. She looked like a movie star, in her smart page's costume. She had an elaborate upswept hair-do; she told him later that it cost most of her week's wages to keep her hair looking good, but it had to look right, she was meeting the public all the time—and who knows, this is Hollywood—Anybody Might See you.

Tom hung around the lobby, waiting for Darlene to get off duty.

She told him, "Go walk around and look at the village, why don't you? I still have two hours to go."

"I'll wait for you. I want you to take me around and show me everything. I want to see it all with you. They won't throw me out, will they?"

Darlene laughed and said, "Gosh, no. This is a public place. A million people will be going through here between now and midnight. Nobody will bother you. But I'll be busy guiding people around. You'll get tired of waiting. Go out and have a drink or some coffee or something."

"I've got my new camera along," Tom said. "I can try it out while I wait—there's all kinds of faces and lights."

Tom was hired by a small independent studio as a cameraman. The studio made short educational movies, film strips and television ads. Tom had received a fair amount of photographic training and practice in the army. He had a good eye and he used the camera intelligently. Soon he had a reputation for being a good worker.

Tom and Darlene married. Tom got a GI loan and bought a brand new glass and plywood house in a tract of new homes in the San Fernando Valley, just north of Hollywood Hills. Their son, Ted, was born the following year.

Darlene wasn't very pleased with her new life. She had to watch the baby, most of the time. She didn't see anyone except Tom and the young housewives who were her immediate neighbors. (She thought of them as dull, unambitious girls without any talent.) Darlene could sing, she could act; in high school and college she had been in many plays and operettas. She dreamed of finding an agent in Hollywood whom she could trust, somebody who could arrange a break for her—an audition, a screen test.

She could play the piano well enough to accompany herself. In the afternoons when Ted was supposed to be asleep, he was usually awake and yelling. Darlene would tell him, "Wail, Sweetie. You and Momma are going to sing duets." Then she'd spend hours rehearsing songs from the latest Broadway shows. She would play the recording of a song fifteen or twenty times in order to learn the words and the singer's interpretation and intonation. Then she'd stand in the middle of the room and sing along with the record, smiling, gesturing, and working out simple dance routines. Later, she'd begin to work at the piano, picking out chords to fit the melody, plinking and planking and singing over and over again until she could play the song.

Darlene was young and healthy but not much of a beauty. She had a powerful voice and could sing on-key. Her singing effectively drowned out Ted's yelling. She kept asking Tom to find out who was really a good agent. She was convinced that there were lots of people in show business who had less than half her talent.

"MCA is a good agency, I told you before," Tom said. "They got a house full of them there."

"Yeah, but the trouble is they're an office—I need a real agent who gets around and people know him."

"Well, Honey, why don't you ask them if they've got one? I don't know any other way to do it. We get people from the Actor's Guild. We phone up the casting office and tell them what we want and they send us people. You could sign up with the Guild. Go ahead and try."

Darlene felt very sad. "What *you* do isn't really showbiz, though. You just don't believe that I've got any talent. I'm just a mouldy old housewife."

Tom gave her a big hug. "I think you're wonderful," he said. "No matter what you're doing. But for a while, anyway, Ted is going to need you pretty close by."

"He's going to be weaned pretty quick. Sylvia Morris has this high school girl take care of their baby twice a week so she can work part of the time. I could get somebody like that."

"But Sugar, Ted is so little. And these baby-sitter kids aren't any too smart—suppose something happened?"

"They could always yell for Sylvia, right next door, or for Trini, just across the street or telephone the studio."

Tom and Darlene had a great many arguments about when would be the right time for her to really start pushing her career in show business. She kept saying that she must have an agent; she must get an agent soon, no matter what else they decided. Tom tried to calm her, but Darlene seemed to be about one quarter cuckoo on the subject.

One day, Tom told her, "Wednesday and Thursday of next week I don't have to work. I'll stay home with Ted and you go to town and find an agent."

"Oh, Tom," Darlene said, "you know better than that—they have to find you."

"Listen: on Wednesday, or Thursday, you're going to go up to town. One of the guys told me that everybody's going over to NBC those two days to audition for a new TV show. The place is going to be full of actors and producers and agents. You go down there and do your stuff. You'll get a job or an agent or both. You're not going to get anyplace sitting home and fussing about it all the time."

Darlene went to the studio on the following Wednesday; they gave her a job singing in a chorus. She got a bit part in a TV drama. The TV director liked her work and began giving her longer parts in original TV plays. An agent approached her and offered to represent her; Darlene felt that she had arrived at last.

Ted Prescott was now being brought up by a team of high school girls who lived in the neighborhood of his house. They were all fans of Darlene. They worked without pay in order to be able to tell their friends at school that they knew Darlene Del Mar and husband and all about them and their house and how the Prescotts were drifting towards a Tragic Divorce for sure. A cleaning lady was supposed to come and do the heavier housework on Saturdays, but she didn't have too much to do; Ted's foster mothers kept the house in fairly good order.

It made Tom nervous to come home and find the house full of kids every day. The baby-sitters all had boyfriends and girlfriends who brought *their* boyfriends. They would slowly clear out when Tom would appear, after they had greeted him politely, compassionately ("the Husband is always the Last to Know"). Tom seldom saw Darlene except when she was exhausted after a day's rehearsing or when she was in a mad rush to get out of the house in the morning in order to get back to work. She spoke urgently of having to move into Bel Air or someplace closer to town . . . maybe it would be easier if they got an apartment right in Hollywood.

Tom was unhappy. He wasn't doing anything exciting with photography and his home life was less than satisfactory. He wondered what he ought to do. He worried about it for six months, then one morning he packed up his suitcases and cameras and Ted's clothes and toys, loaded everything into his big station wagon, set Ted into the baby seat beside him and began driving north.

He returned to the house late that same night. He realized that he couldn't handle Ted all by himself and there was no place that he felt it would be good to leave him. Nessa was too goofy and too busy; Darlene's people in Colorado were too old to start raising a three-year-old boy.

Darlene was very upset when she saw him come in, but she was glad to see that Ted was all right. She and Tom had a long, sad talk. She would get a divorce. Darlene would keep Ted, would hire a trained nurse or an experienced governess of some kind for him. Darlene agreed that it would be better for the baby to have a more settled kind of life. She might re-marry sometime. Tom would always be welcome to visit Ted, whatever happened. Tom kissed her and drove away.

■ ■ ■

Roy made himself drunk. He drank *sake* out of expensive Japanese folk pottery, ate octopus arms, chicken giblets, and shrimp teriyaki. While he ate and drank, he read a new little magazine from New York. All those young people who might have been his own children had sent him their poems and plays, news from home. He was very drunk and very happy.

He aimed the small powerful reading lamp into the garden, the stone wash-basin under shrub leaves—where was he?—would he step out onto (the fallen twiglets and needles of hemlock and fir trees mixed with moss and vine maple leaves and old fern fronds) Mt. Baker National Forest? Into a Japanese village, a northern suburb of the Capital, Heian Kyo, founded eleven hundred years ago by the Divine Emperor Kammu, for coffee (known to the West for two hundred years) under three kinds of light fixtures, *Bessa Me Mucho* by Muzak and blue gauze curtains blocking the neon trolley cars. "Why don't all the people employed by this outfit run stark raving gaga after a half hour on duty in this place? Which might as well be Canoga Park or Brentwood or Sherman Oaks, all desperately new and modern and nowhere fake crystal chandeliers and real chrysanthemums, true rubber trees, bromeliads and cycads of the Lower Carboniferous and a few doilies of machine-made lace all standing over what had been a handmade landscape garden of the earlier Muromachi period...as long as you are *inside* the building...outside are frogs in the rice paddies, the honey buckets' wild perfume. What a rhapsody of times and styles," Roy thought. "Not even Perez Prado, but a nameless rhumba band. And light from a Coleman lantern, wide band across the mountain top illuminates the eyes of a six-point buck, his forefoot on the second step of the stairs nosily searching for salt, for Perez, Mene and Tekel, for Paris mossy lichen granite under hoof, ten minutes after eight P.M. on Wednesday night—to the very day!"

Roy had finished his coffee; his head throbbed and sang. "Eleven years ago to the very day. It took three hours for the sun to go down; it quit, finally, twenty minutes ago, the glass in the windows on four sides of me totally black, the green paint of the woodwork gone grey, colorless under Coleman light anchored to rock top of mountain under thin boards under my feet under my sleeping ear tonight, floating on white rope net the lightnings of Heaven and Earth and Zodiacal Time: as I remember the place where I sit now was once the parking lot for the Mt. Hiei Taxi Company but if I walk a block and a half to more coffee in a place which also remembers the now non-existent parking lot, these blue plastic lights and gauze will (*o-shibori*! Boiled hot hand towel served up in limp plastic con-

dom pops MERRY CHRISTMAS wet sprinkle fireworks) D I S A P-
P E A R. Forever. Do I have any money in my pockets. Can I pay the bill."

Roy was still two-thirds drunk and uncomfortable; he wanted out of
that condition. He would have more coffee. He staggered along beside
the wide, nearly deserted street, to another coffee-ya, a small television
joint where six Japanese taxi drivers were watching American soldiers
"winning" what the local newspapers (Roy sourly noted) refer to nowadays as a remotely historical "Pacific War."

"At least one of these guys is old enough to have been there," Roy
thought. "And so am I. The rest look too young to have known more
about it than kids fifteen or sixteen years old may have heard on the
Imperial Radio. The curious thing about these men is that they seem to
believe what it is they're seeing right now as being immediately present,
this reconstruction of what was happening twenty years ago. Now here
we all are, drinking the same expensive coffee which gives us all the same
expensive cardiac heebie-jeebies. Only the lady behind the counter
doesn't care to look, she's busy making coffee. One boy turns the pages
of a magazine while he watches. Sweet potato steam whistle cart passes
by, beyond the black window and its machine lace curtain; station break
tooth paste ads, and then the war continues. We've learned nothing.
Sweet potato whistle. The only reality is mud swamp New Guinea death?
Tarawa Kwajalein, the boy with the magazine raptly picks his nose. I wonder where they all are, I watch their watching faces, what connection has
any of this fraudulent movie with any real experience, any life or hope or
recollection: echoing gunfire, machine gun rattle and rifle ricochet—the
film editor cuts back and forth from face to gun barrel to running squirm-
ing figures among vines, bamboos. The connection is the language. In this
movie, both sides are speaking Japanese. I understand the American
faces and gestures, but the voices are incomprehensible. The background music clues me in; we are winning: Whitey triumphs again (but
he's talking Japanese)."

Roy felt too embarrassed to stay any longer. He went to another larger
place further up the street where was the folk guitar Joan Baez Revolt of
the intellectual young; the clientele was all university people drinking coffee and tea and discussing Hegel and Marx. They liked Joan Baez because
her guitar sounded to them rather Japanese and like a koto; they hadn't
any idea what she was singing, except that *Time* magazine said she was
great and new and modern. Roy talked with some of the students in halt-
ing English and Japanese. They claimed that they were majoring in eco-
nomics. It turned out that they knew nothing about the subject, but they
were all communists. They knew nothing about communist theory, either,
but they all agreed that it was European and progressive and that all the
world, particularly China, was making great progress under the communist system.

This coffee shop also served everything out of folk pottery. There was
a beamed ceiling and a fireplace and furniture of a kind which the maker

imagined must inhabit Swiss chalets. There were lace curtains, an expensive stereophonic phonograph, potted rubber trees, cycads, a Cryptomeria tree masquerading as a Christmas tree with blinking lights, and Easter lilies blooming in a big jar. Small vases of chrysanthemums stood on each table. The Joan Baez Revolution disappeared, to be replaced by Miles Davis & Co. The stereo loudspeakers trademarked *Chrysler* vibrated and throbbed and chimed *Bags Groove*. (Major Hoople remembering the Crimean War—"kaff, kaff! Egad!")

Roy woke up in the middle of the night. What did he want. Why was he afraid of the Grand Mahatma. Why should he feel that he was in a false position vis à vis that Figure. He was hungover, his head hurt a little bit, his ears felt full of water, but actually his head was full of light and the light had awakened him.

Roy went to the bathroom. He took two aspirin tablets. He saw from the study windows that there had been a fall of snow while he'd been asleep.

"All that the Grand Mahatma requires—or anybody else wants—is my sincerity?" Roy asked himself. "Where's that at. I move from my own center which is a seated figure that doesn't move, needs not—but this is claptrap. Cold water with aspirin is more exactly what I 'did.' "

He wondered why he should feel afraid of the hour, then decided that he wasn't really afraid. He turned on the lights and sat down to accept the fact that he was awake in the middle of the night and that there was nothing wrong with being awake any time. He would keep the appointment that he had later that morning. He wouldn't oversleep, he wouldn't be late. The alarm clock was working just fine. He felt that it was quite important that he no longer felt unhappy or afraid. It wasn't a fit of insomnia, it wasn't a nightmare, it wasn't a "Dark Night of the Soul," he was just awake. The house was very cold; he might turn on the heat.

Later in the morning he was surprised to find no trace of snow or frost on the ground outside. He had made a mistake, seeing moonlight on the stones and moss.

■ ■ ■

The Grand Mahatma says: "You got to pick up the brocade and look at the wrong side of it: what makes the pattern—nerves, blood vessels, fluids—just as a child turns the mirror around, looking at the back of it, then into the glass again, a portable window: 'Who's that? Where did he go?' "

■ ■ ■

Sarah told Clifford all about her funny bohemian time when she was a teenager. She'd been a model for a famous artist who was a refugee from the war in Europe. He was fond of draping her nude flesh with white strings which he had first soaked in honey. The string divided her peachy skin into numerable, warped squares of reference. The man's pictures showed beautiful naked women performing curious tasks and ritual actions in a desert landscape. In the middle distance he would paint a fantasticated Byzantine ruin, while in the background rose the barren tan mountains of Spain. There was always a perfectly painted flat blue sky at the top of every painting, blue and exact as Piero Della Francesca might have made it. After each painting session, the painter enjoyed licking the long lines of honey off her skin and Sarah said she rather liked it, but the painter's wife felt that after all it was her own prerogative to be dipped in honey and licked, so Sarah was dismissed, with regret.

Sarah went to live in San Francisco, where she soon married a reasonably successful landscape painter called Max Gardner, a big white-haired old man with a beard. He had family connections with Old California but not much money. The family connections got him and Sarah invited, with fair regularity, to the more expensive houses in San Francisco. At their own place, they gave big wine and chili bean parties for all the starving young painters.

Max Gardner was acquainted with most of the American painters and writers of his own generation. He had studied in Paris in the late Twenties and early Thirties. He had met lots of famous people at least once. Whenever a gallery director from New York came to San Francisco, Max and Sarah gave a party and introduced him to the promising young painters they knew.

Quite unexpectedly, Max won a big painting prize. He and Sarah were able to make a trip to Europe, which Max hadn't seen since the Thirties. While they were in Italy, Max happened to meet his first wife, who was now a celebrated novelist. Soon it developed that Max and his ex-wife had a great many happy memories and a number of new interests in common. They decided that it would be a splendid thing to re-marry and spend their old age together in Europe. Max gave Sarah passage money; Sarah wanted to go back to New York. She would go to work again. There was a grand Roman farewell festival dinner and a tearful parting at the wrong railway station.

Sarah felt gloomy and hungover and a little upset, but when she got back to Paris, she met a woman whom she had known in school. They traveled back to New York together and set up an apartment on St. Mark's Square. Soon Sarah was giving wine and chili bean parties for the Abstract Expressionists and all the museum and gallery directors and movie stars and musicians. (Margaret Gridley met Beefy Johnson at one of Sarah's parties.)

Sarah kept her good looks and she dressed in a very distinguished manner. Her hair was blond with some grey in it, and she had green eyes. She had a long-legged figure, but she wasn't boney and hollow-chested like a fashion model. She had a big smile and a straightforward manner. She always seemed to be having a fine time, at least as long as other people were around. She only complained about her life during the course of long complicated telephone conversations with close women friends.

The friend who was sharing the apartment decided that she was going to marry and move away. Sarah would have to find a new friend to share the rent, or take over the whole place by herself. To the surprise and dismay of all her friends and acquaintances, Sarah decided to join the Peace Corps and go to India. "I've never seen that part of the world, and I might be able to do some good while I'm at it," she told them.

"Don't you realize you can't *do* that? It's nothing but a big counter-Revolutionary army," Sarah's roommate told her.

"Oh, I'm tired of political theories," Sarah replied. "I want out of New York. You can tell everybody that I am an unfulfilled middleclass intellectual with vast guilt feelings if you want to. I'm going to go, anyway."

Sarah was taught how to purify water, how to teach birth control, first aid, and kitchen gardening. The Government also made her take courses in Asian Psychology, The Development of the Underprivileged Child, Selling America Overseas, and Simple Home & Public Hygiene. The training period was three and a half weeks. She also had to learn conversational Urdu at the Berlitz School. Then the Government sent her to Katmandu.

"I was supposed to go to India," Sarah complained to the airplane driver. "This is Nepal!"

"It's all the same, lady," he told her. "They's just folks here like everywhere else, need lots of help from Uncle. You be all right."

Clifford liked Sarah immensely well. She was very wise and very solid, rather saner than most of the women he'd known. But what did she think of being a mother and keeping house? He told himself that she might be a little too old to be interested in all that. Laura was a lot younger, but even she was in her late twenties. Clifford said to himself, "I must decide; I've got to pick one or the other, I'm getting old myself. Sarah's a great woman—Laura is—Laura and I could probably have a whole different style of life. We could have lots of children, live in France or Italy if she wanted to. I suppose life with Sarah . . . but I have no business supposing: I have to decide what I want. I really want both of them, and more beside, that's what I really want, so what am I going to do?"

■ ■ ■

Dorothy felt sad. She had been working on her essay but it wasn't growing clearer or any longer. She had begun writing it because some recent articles in *The Review of Glottal Studies* had made her mad. The articles were written by professors and researchers of great learning and authority, but Dorothy felt that what they said was absurdly and outrageously wrong. Their statements must certainly start a lot of arguments and confusion among all the other workers in the same field, not to mention the untold numbers of imperfectly educated young people whom they were bound to mislead and to misinform. Dorothy felt that she must frame an immediate reply; she must enter a demurrer; she must try to correct the mischief which these articles were bound to cause.

She inspected her great treasury of filing cards. In a few minutes, she had extracted enough basic references to form the background for writing a paper. All she needed to do next was to check through a few of the current journals to find out who else had been worrying about the same problems, then she could begin to write her own article. She went to the university library for copies of some journals which were not regularly sent to her every month. There was one article in German; she wanted to consult with Max Lammergeier about it, to ascertain the correctness of her own readings. She telephoned him and he invited her to lunch.

They had a fine afternoon together, laughing and gossiping. Max was contemplating a rock-hunting trip to Nevada. "I've got to get out into the air for a few minutes," he told her. "I can feel myself eroding."

"Mother says that you're the most beautiful man in San Francisco," Dorothy said. "Maybe working a lot keeps you trim and polished."

"Yeah, all smooth and shiny and blank from the rubbing of so many faithful pilgrims, like the toes on St. Peter's image in Rome or whoever it is, all marble with a hole where they kissed the foot away.

> "O Doc, Doc, Doc, they all come in to the Doc
> The nervous into the nervous, the raging loony faces,
> The kinks and crackpots, prominent professors,"

Max intoned.

Dorothy laughed. "We do all depend on your being here, even when we don't come in. We're all your invisible patients; that's really what erodes you," she said.

"Look, why don't you and Tom come rock-hunting? We'll make a grand combined expedition. You can study the native tongues of the Pawnee or whoever is in the desert...that should give you a good start for your paper."

"Tom's been in the darkroom all week," Dorothy said. "He should be about ready to come out. If I start writing tonight, I can get myself organized, I suppose. When do you want to leave?"

Everyone had a fine time in the desert except for Tom, who suffered from hay fever and sinusitis. He complained bitterly and with much justification about being dragged through the dust which not only abraded his eyes and his brain but was also working its way into the mechanism of his pet camera. He and Dorothy had to leave the party rather sooner than they had planned. Tom had begun having attacks of asthma at night.

Dorothy, who loved outings of every kind, and who loved the desert in particular, was annoyed with Tom. She told him that he was self-indulgent and hopelessly neurasthenic and she called him a number of even less exact names.

Tom said, "Awright, awright. Just give me some air, some way, will you?

I can't *breathe.*''

At home again, they had a fight about politics. Then Dorothy made some unwisely critical remarks about Nessa. That fight took a long time to get settled.

Tom submitted some of his photographs to an award show at the De Young Museum. All the pictures were accepted for showing and one of them got a small prize. While the exhibition was on view, Tom and Dorothy went to have dinner with the Sandersons. Dorothy made a couple of joking references to "Our Show" during the course of the evening. When she and Tom got home they had a really serious quarrel. Tom was very angry; Dorothy tried to apologize but Tom wouldn't listen to her.

Tom told Dorothy that she didn't know what she was talking about when they were at Mark's place, and that she ought to shut up now, because she still didn't. And another thing, how often had he asked her to quit taking those god-damned speedballs. Dorothy said she needed to take them in order to keep herself going with her journal article. He told her to cut it out. Anyway, why should she take pills when she's got good old Maxie-boo to help her in his own person?

Dorothy felt angry and sad and hopeless and cold. She only said, "All right, Tom. Whatever you say. I'm going to eat some aspirins and go to bed, now. I have to work in the morning."

Tom shouted at her, she was a dirty Radcliffe slut and hurled his glass of brandy at her. He rushed out of the house.

Dorothy picked up the unbroken glass and took it out to the kitchen. She wondered where he was going. She couldn't really care, but she hoped that he wouldn't hurt himself. If the police found him, they'd bring him home again; he had a press card in his pocket.

She felt very tired and sad. And it made her sick to think that Tom should feel jealous of Max.

In the morning, she found Tom asleep, all rolled up inside the living room rug. Dorothy made a big pot of coffee, opened a couple of cans of tomato juice and dumped them into a big pitcher that she set in the refrigerator. She drank a glass of ginger ale, then filled a big mug with black coffee and carried it to her desk. She sat down and looked hopelessly at the neat stacks of three-by-five cards and the clutter of typed papers all scored and x'ed with black felt-pen markers.

She wondered when she was going to learn how to get along with her husbands instead of fighting with them all the time. Such questions lead right back to the psychiatrist, don't they, she told herself. The psychiatrist, even if it did happen to be Max, cost forty dollars an hour, and Max always said that the treatment wouldn't work unless the patient paid for it himself. She thought she might go to the group therapy sessions conducted by Max's friend, Dr. Givenchy—immutably young, with crew-cut hair, who so confidently believed that he was really hip, a kind of stale Tab Hunter—but she wasn't about to stand still for all that. She told herself that she was too old for all that kind of scene anyway.

202

"I could always go back into the Church and take the veil," Dorothy thought, "if all my lovely husbands would kindly drop dead first. . .but the Church is too bossy. I wonder what would happen if I were to write to Clifford—better yet, send him a cable—and say, "I'm coming back, I'm arriving at Katmandu Airport Thursday afternoon. Some Love."

■ ■ ■

Roy surprised himself. He turned out of his usual path directly down Imadegawa Street and began to walk, instead, along the bank of the Kamo River. Blue sky was beginning to appear through big breaks in the heavy clouds overhead. Low thick ropes and garlands of darkness passed northeast above Hieizan where the river made its turn into the Columbia Gorge.

He felt a great elation, a great freedom. He would stay in Kyoto and wander about, writing poems; he didn't have to do anything anywhere else and it was beautiful walking right here, although the wind was cold.

He walked along the sandy embankment. A man and a woman were exercising an elephantine collie, all orange and white, broad hips and needle nose; it regarded Roy, for a moment, quite severely. Then the man called it; the dog ran to him instantly.

Roy hurried along; he decided to walk all the way into the middle of town and eat lunch there. He looked across the Kamo and saw the Harvard Business School rising above the stone-faced revetment of the farther shore, just as he had seen it while walking along the Charles. He was very happy. It would be quite possible for him to think of living in Boston or Cambridge, sometime in the future; the idea of a New England winter no longer seemed so appalling, now that he had survived a Japanese one.

He walked across the Sanjo Bridge, with its wooden 17th century posts and rails rising above the concrete deck. The wooden parts appear in a Hokusai print, and the view of Mt. Hiei remains the same. Roy considered the idea of living in Kyoto "forever." He wondered why he had been bitching to himself so much about the difficulties and inconveniences of life in that city, and the impossibilities of trying to communicate in the Japanese language. What was wrong with him? Everything was going wonderfully well. Why did he want to go anywhere else? What would he be doing now if he were in Los Angeles, for example. His life there or in any other town must be much the same. But now he had lots to write, a place to live and food to eat. What difference did it make what the weather was doing or what was the name of this place.

"I been a lot of places, and there's still a lot of places I want to go," Roy thought, "but I bet that when I get there, the band or the Muzak or the jukebox will be playing those same records of *Adios Muchachos* and *La Comparcita* which I hear in every restaurant and coffee house in this town, just as I used to hear Xavier Cugat and his band playing them on the radio when I was a little boy in Washington, years ago."

■  ■  ■

Clifford told Roy, "My old man used to come home and tell my mother, 'I guess if I don't get a job pretty soon, I'll go down to the blacksmith shop and get myself fitted for a tin beak so I can go pick shit with the chickens on the manure pile.'"

Roy said, "My dad always had a job in the post office, a Civil Service deal. We lived in rented houses. I got a new pair of shoes when school started in the fall, and a pair of pants and a couple of shirts, all from J. C. Penney's. They had to last until the next spring. We always had a place to live and something to eat. I knew lots of guys in the army who had less than half of all that."

Clifford said, "I had a paper route. It took me months to save enough money to buy my own bicycle so I could handle a bigger territory, and then I got a magazine route in the afternoons after school. I was able to help buy my own clothes."

Roy said, "Well, anyway, it's funny to have been poor and still be poor, only here we are in Monterey and in International Society or something."

"You always had a lot of extravagant tastes," Clifford said. "No wonder you're poor. You can have my share of the society part, too—the middle class is just no fun, anywhere you happen to get mixed up with them."

"I expect that if getting mixed up with the middle class was like being married to Margaret, I was pretty well there," Roy said.

Clifford replied, "Dorothy had to train me or I never would have found out what socks to wear or when to drink the water in the finger bowls."

"How many shares of Coca Cola do you figure I own, anyway?" Roy inquired.

"I ain't saying you got any. All I say is, you've always been a lot better off than I ever was, but you're always broke and you complain more. I can't figure it out," Clifford said.

"I can," Roy said, equably. "I spend whatever money there is, then there isn't any more for a long time and I complain, and after a while, more of it comes. I complain because it doesn't last. But last night, I was reading some translations of Sanskrit poems, all about girls and jewels and palaces and rare silks and elephants—a really luxurious kind of life that nobody can afford nowadays, not even rich people. I understood, all of a sudden, that I'll never be rich, I'll never have lots of money—more than I could spend in a day—but *I* am something else, something developing along its own line, a kind of being or entity which has a quality of experience that hasn't existed before. It's a gas to be this whoever it is, whatever it is, and I try to write it all down. But it has nothing to do with money, it is free of the necessity, really, of money—it is happening to me, I am being this person, and this is what I really want. Maybe in another life I was or will be really rich, but that's a different career, a different

204

story line, one that's already been exactly known and described and understood."

Clifford said, "Tell it to John Maynard Keynes."

Roy said, "Tell it to John Kenneth Galbraith."

Clifford asked him, "Did you ever read A *Sentimental Education?*"

Roy said, "I sure did—along with your edifying Leninist marginalia—I read your copy while we were at school. Let's have a little more gin."

"The trouble with you is, you drink too much," Clifford said. "You ought to switch to grass. It's a better trip in every way."

"The stuff never affects me," Roy said. "It just makes me thirsty and my hearing goes all funny. Then I have to eat a big bunch of candy or a lot of food and the candy makes my teeth hurt. A little booze makes me feel good and I always know right where I am."

Roy and Clifford laughed and yelled and rolled on the ground.

■ ■ ■

The worst thing that ever happened to Roy was the loss of a friend. They didn't have a big argument and a fight. The friend didn't die; he withdrew.

Roy met Jim in the Army. They had many exciting conversations about art and literature and music. Jim was the brightest man Roy had ever met: he could write and draw and sing and play the violin.

Jim went home on a furlough and married the girl he'd been going steady with before he got into the Army. He wrote to Roy all about the wedding and Roy wrote a humorous reply and sent a present.

They wrote to each other when Roy went on furlough and later, after Roy transferred into other outfits. The letters were filled with sketches and poems and lists of books that had to be read immediately and of new recordings which must be heard and of new movies that must be seen. There was also a great deal of discussion about theories of creativity and of the intellectual bases of the arts in general and about the difficulties attendant upon making oneself into an artist.

Directly after the war, Jim invited Roy to come to his house for a visit. Roy and Jim's wife, Gloria, had a splendid time together, hiking and swimming and playing music and sitting up all night talking about art and philosophy and sex and politics and the lives and times of great historical figures. Roy thought Gloria was very bright and pretty. He told Jim that he was really lucky to find her.

The next year, Jim and Roy were attending different universities in different parts of the country; neither of them had been to college before the war. They wrote to each other occasionally. Roy was supposed to make another visit to see Jim and Gloria, but he ran out of money and couldn't go.

The correspondence dwindled. Roy received a card whenever Gloria had a new baby. There were several babies and Roy sent a long congratulatory letter in response to each card.

Several years later, Roy got a letter from Jim; he and his family had come to live near Seattle, the city where Roy was living then. Jim invited Roy to come out for a visit, and although they had a delightful time together, Jim felt that it was necessary to apologize to Roy, as they were driving together to the bus station; they hadn't had much of a chance for a real talk. Roy said that they could get together more often, now that they were living only thirty miles apart. Jim said that he and Gloria would probably be driving into Seattle soon to visit Roy.

They exchanged letters, shortly after this visit, but Roy realized that they were, in some way, strangers to each other now. They had lived different kinds of lives and had too many different kinds of problems and were involved in different kinds of societies. But Roy imagined that all these differences must gradually disappear, or at least become less important, once they began seeing each other more often.

Jim and Gloria never quite managed to visit Roy. Jim wrote a short note to say "hello" and to say they were sorry to have missed seeing him on this trip, but they'd be in again soon; watch out! That was the last Roy ever heard from Jim and Gloria.

When Roy's first book was published, he tried sending a copy to Jim. (Roy was in New York then; he sent the book to Jim's last address near a little town outside Seattle.) The book was returned, with a stamped notice, "Unknown at this address." Some time later, Roy wrote to Jim and addressed the letter in care of Jim's parents, in order to make sure that Jim would receive it, but there was no reply.

Roy wondered if Jim was mad at him; then it became plain to him, one day, that Jim was indifferent. Jim had received the letter and didn't care to reply. When he realized that, Roy felt himself turning into a chunk of slag, a clinker, and the Earth, all green and splendid as ever, turned swiftly away and beyond the Sun with great indifferent speed on its determined orbit, and there in black space hung Roy Asteroid, cold space metal ore freeze. And the Sun also receded, and its little, circling planets, then the great flat nebular disk of the "home universe"—the Milky Way—swung slowly up and away into the dark and there he was, watching it go.

■ ■ ■

Tom mixed up a new batch of solution and poured a slug of it into a film tank and sloshed it around for a certain number of seconds, then drained the tank and set it under a flowing cold water tap. While the film was being rinsed, Tom carefully rolled a cigaret. He hung up the new negative to drip over the sink.

He took a pack of negatives and dealt them out on his light-table, and selected one and prepared to print it. He put the negative into the enlarger and projected it onto a sheet of white paper. It was the picture of a boy of about twelve or thirteen, leaning against the twisted polished branch of a big driftwood tree on some beach. The boy was blond and skinny, with big front teeth; he was just entering adolescence but the thin, white droopy jock he was wearing emphasized the fact that he was already very heavily endowed; he would grow into a powerful man.

Tom made six eight-by-ten glossy prints of this picture. Then he began with another negative. He worked slowly and very carefully. Each print was done exactly right; every detail of each clear, sharply focussed picture was exactly reproduced. Several hours later, he carefully packed the finished pictures and wrapped them for mailing to Kalifornia Kidviews at a post office number in Van Nuys.

■ ■ ■

Dorothy received a letter from Roy. She could make very little sense out of it, only bright, brainless babbling that went on and on. It annoyed her; she was busy trying to write her article, and here was this aimless nonsense interrupting her. She threw the letter into the wastebasket. She remembered it, later in the day and recovered it from the bin—what was he trying to tell her? Then she realized that he had been high on something or other when he wrote it. "That's why it sounds so cuckoo; he was blasted out of his skull!"

■ ■ ■

Six or seven months after Dorothy mailed them her manuscript, the learned editors of *The Review of Glottal Studies* returned it to her. They said it was of the greatest interest and would she please cut it down to about 2500 words, so they could print it in their next issue? Although it was one of the best papers they had seen in years, considerations of space compelled them to make this irksome request. Perhaps Dr. Prescott was aware that they were also going to print a very important piece by Dr. Bitteschoen which would occupy most of the same issue of the *Review*. There would be only his essay and Dr. Prescott's, if she could return her manuscript before a certain date. The editors were of opinion that simultaneous publication of their articles would be a truly important event for everyone who was now working in linguistics and philology and allied fields of investigation.

Dorothy was discouraged and dejected, at first; she had worked very hard at perfecting her article; she felt it was already condensed and compressed as much as she could make it. However, on the same day she had received this editorial message, Dr. Bitteschoen telephoned her. She had a little difficulty understanding him. (When he spoke English, his enunciation was very good; his accent was Oxford. His diction and grammar sometimes tended towards the creative, but the thought was always very plain.) Dr. Bitteschoen was excited and shouting into the telephone which warped and buckled and buzzed under the weight of his voice and he had lapsed into a mixture of English and the Münchener dialect of his earliest youth. Dorothy could just grasp the drift of his meaning.

"We're taking over the *Glottal Studies Review* next month," Dr. Bitteschoen hollered. "They wrote to me. You must edit your essay—you never showed it to me! I'll help you. We are winning at last! My theories are justified! We shall have it all published in time for the great Monterey Conference. We shall both go there and deliver addresses of lightning and thunder intensity which will fall upon these academical spaghettis like the Uhlans fell upon Austerlitz. I come to your house at once by taxi over the bridge immediately to luncheon. I burst in upon your sanctum like Darius upon the Thracian mainland. Please find lots more of the good herrings of the kind you so graciously provided the last time. I find the beers. Tell Tom I expect him to be at home to play pinochle with after lunch. Then we edit your article in a good quarter hour and go to dinner in the Chinese City as my guests. O.K. I come now. Look out!"

Dorothy told him that she'd be ready. She hung up the phone and yelled for Tom.

A muffled "NO!" issued from the darkroom in reply. Dorothy went to the sealed door and shouted her orders. "You've got to go to the store; I've got to vacuum everything, Louis is coming to lunch instantly, I've got to fix the house and the lunch, you've got to go to the store!"

"NO," Tom shouted back. "I don't got to do anything except keep that door shut seven more minutes. Start vacuuming and quit screaming, you'll shatter my chemicals!"

Dorothy was hollering at Tom about going to the store again because there wasn't nearly enough sour cream when Dr. Bitteschoen arrived. He had dragooned an unwilling Berkeley taxi driver into lugging a case full of Lowenbrau bottles up the long stairway to Dorothy's front door. To her horror, Dr. Bitteschoen gave the man a twenty dollar bill and dismissed him. The cab man went grumping down the stairs.

"He's going away to spend the day in some low bar," Dorothy said. "Telling about crazy professors and his bad back. You're too extravagant. Kiss me."

"The university pays me such an extravagant honorarium," Dr. Bitteschoen said, and he obligingly gave Dorothy a hug and a kiss. "You look beautiful, my eggplant! I love to spend money on beautiful girls, especially on you. Nobody seems to enjoy getting what I spend; all Americans are so serious and sad."

Dr. Bitteschoen continued talking while he took off his coat, shook hands with Tom and followed Dorothy into the kitchen where she gave him a big glass of beer and a plate of crackers and cheese to work at while she finished preparing the lunch.

"We shall go all together to Monterey and devastate these yokels, these Backworldsmen. Tom shall expose them all with his camera by photographing them in interesting juxtapositions with motion picture stars from Hollywood. I shall read a paper which I commenced this morning in the bath to compose. I shall be ever so subtly suggesting that the

208

Dravidians are an expelled people from the borders of Egypt in Early Dynastic times, that they were thoroughly familiar with the major inventions and material culture of the Egypts, and they brought this learning to the Indus Valley with them. They were, of course, the people to whom the Egyptian record refers as inhabiting the Land of Punt. I shall introduce, in passing, a reference—only in a footnote—to a photograph of certain Pre-Dynastic Egyptian seals. The photograph itself will of course not appear in the article. And the Mohenjo Daro seals will by implication be inferred to be of African provenance. The effect of this hint upon the irritable (if regrettably undeveloped) sensoria of certain of your white Anglo-Saxon Protestant colleagues should prove to be of some slight interest to observe. Likewise, our esteemed British friend, Dr. Trabshaw with his puerile notions about the Sumerian genesis of the Indus Valley cultures will find himself being slowly unfrocked before the enraptured gaze of the international scholarly community. Comes then Dr. Prescott's corrections and destructions! Or perhaps you have lately received some other new and shocking revelations which you can announce to penetrate for however brief a moment that marvelously wicked (but profitable—consider, after all, how much money now cascades and gushes through the American university system!) Acheronian fog that surrounds the academy and which provides as well the comfortable and downy safety wherein are hidden these herds of unlettered buffoons, these parochial mountebanks who pretend to scholarship. Yes, a new statement, to make your printed remarks even more outrageous. Yes, yes! You will find something and tell me before we part this day; for the rest, we shall reserve a suite at the Hotel De Los Conquistadores y Cojones in Monterey. Berthe will enjoy the sunshine and the swimming and take care of our files and preside at the typewriter. We shall eat abalone steaks and drink Rhine wines. Tom shall photograph the wise and worldly faces of the intellectual leadership of the West (Russia is an Oriental country, of course). I shall telephone Mr. Luce and suggest that he publish Tom's pictures in *Life* magazine to illustrate whatever fatuous article about the conference—we shall find someone who can write up a popular journalistic account of the proceedings which will show you and me as being the only persons of any consequence. It must be a family triumph."

Dorothy said, "I got their letter of invitation months ago, but I didn't think much about it, I was so busy. I hate Monterey. Besides, Clifford Barlow is going to be there, giving a seminar and probably a recital, as well—he never passes up the chance to grab the spotlight and command the admiration of the entire civilized world. Blah!"

"It doesn't look like there's going to be much left for anybody to take over, after you and Doc move in with your demolition crew," Tom said.

"Ah, we only build up and break down abstractions and theories," Dr. Bitteschoen said. "Only words and patterns of an extremely limited use and effect. Clifford's music operates upon a completely other level of reality. It assaults the heart, it engages the mind, it is the motion of the

209

spirit upon the face of the waters."

"I thought Clifford would be talking about the geography thing or whatever it is," Tom said.

"Again, he deals there with living people, with persons and stones and plants and the weather," Dr. Bitteschoen said. "At best, we philologists are only making projections from philosophy, and as Whitehead told us, philosophy is no more than a footnote to Plato."

Dorothy said, "But language is people; it's what all of us really are. What do we think *with*, what do we handle, what do we see except words, after all? Even your darling old Plato is a *book*. The famous cave is a verbal image, is poetry—which is all that saves Plato from being a great big bore that nobody would be able to read, not even you, Louis, with all your patience. Those precious rocks and trees and mountains of Clifford's are words. Nobody has any real sense about it except dirty old Roy and what does he do besides run around drinking and fucking little boys and taking dope and starving and weeping in the mountains?"

Dr. Bitteschoen said, "Well, after all, Clifford truly has a genius..."

"Why do you always *defend* him, Louis?" Dorothy asked. She was getting very excited. "It's just because Clifford is a man! All of you stick together—all of you love each other—I hate you, all you dirty faggots! I have to go to the bathroom. Don't anybody say anything until I get back!" Dorothy precipitately left the room.

Tom and Dr. Bitteschoen laughed. "Let me get you another beer, Doc," Tom said. "There's still a lot left."

"Thanks very much, Tom. And when you come back you must tell me all about this Roy," Dr. Bitteschoen said. "And if there's another herring..."

"There's an immense quantity of herring," Dorothy replied, returning, "and it's all for you and Tom. I hate it. You met Roy the other night at that big party. He was babbling to you about Sanskrit poetry, of all things, and he knows nothing whatever about it, he's practically illiterate in four languages."

"The man who looks like Friedrich Schiller," Dr. Bitteschoen remarked.

"That's what you said at the time," Dorothy continued. "Roy can just barely write English, and then it's really sort of American..."

Tom objected. "Roy's a good poet," he said. "I get a kick out of what he writes. I can't read anybody else's poems and get anything out of them. Didn't you tell me he got some kind of award earlier this year?"

Dorothy said, "Oh, he got some kind of shitty little prize—$5 and a parchment certificate—I don't remember. Anyway, he's an idiot."

"How come you're so down on Roy today?" Tom inquired. "He's smarter than most of our famous friends. They ought to ask him to go to this conference thing."

"He can't go to places like that," Dorothy replied. "He needs the money. They have to give the money to all of *us* for being there because we're all reliable people who get big salaries from the university. You don't give money to poverty-stricken poets, don't be ridiculous. Anyway, he doesn't have a Ph.D. You can't get in the door without one. And besides, he's just another great big faggot, just like you."

"Miss Faggot to you, if you please," Roy said, entering the living room. "Is there any beer left? I'm rich, I've brought you presents—cheese and salami from the Beach—Clifford sent me ten dollars for my birthday."

Dorothy said, "Sit down, Roy, and I'll get you a glass. I was just explaining why you can't go to the Monterey Conference because you're a big faggot without a Ph.D. You met Dr. Bitteschoen the other night."

"How do you do?" Dr. Bitteschoen said. He shook hands with Roy.

Roy told him, "I'm afraid I was kind of drunk when I was talking to you, last time."

"Ah, you said some very interesting things about poetry...what was it you were telling me about Hölderlin? I was drinking a lot myself—"

"Roy loves Hölderlin," Dorothy said, pouring a glass of beer and handing it to him with a fond smile.

"I'm afraid I don't really like any German poetry," Roy said politely. "Dorothy's only trying to kid me."

"Roy loves Rilke," Dorothy said. "Rilke was a faggot."

"I don't enjoy the modern writers," Dr. Bitteschoen said. "I prefer Herder and the Minnesänger. Their language was more alive."

"I thought you were so crazy about Brecht—I remember you made me read him years ago," Dorothy said.

"Oh, yes, as an example of a metropolitan dialect—but that's not the true poetry, not the expression of a magnanimous soul, like Schiller."

■ ■ ■

The Grand Mahatma says, "In the depths of the great Depression, President Hoover used to say, 'The situation is fundamentally sound.' He is also reported to have advised his friends, 'Buy zinc.'"

■ ■ ■

Clifford walked out of town to visit an encampment of Tibetans. They were on their way to visit Bodh Gaya. They had set up their tents outside Katmandu in order to rest and to do a little trading—a few sheep for some salt and fresh vegetables and fruit, a few gauds and bangles of gold and turquoise jewelry for Indian rupees.

They seemed calm and cheerful. Tibetans always reminded Clifford of the American Indians who were his neighbors in Idaho when he was young. They had the same kind of reddish-tan skin and long black hair. Each individual was distinctly a separate person who knew his own powers and his own exact virtues. None doubted that he existed in a real world; none seemed worried; none seemed to experience feelings of

211

inferiority or found it necessary to assert his superiority over other persons. Each individual attended to his own business. The men and women laughed and joked with each other. The children ran about everywhere, looking at everybody and everything, laughing and crying.

Clifford squatted on the ground and visited with a man who had some bronze images to sell. They drank tea together and blew up some bhang. Clifford asked about the high passes which the Tibetans had just crossed. The trader said that there was still lots of snow in the high cols. Clifford asked him if he'd seen any Chinese people in his part of Tibet. The man certainly had; he was from Lhasa. He said the Chinese people yelled a lot and gave a great many orders. The Tibetans assured them that in time their wishes would undoubtedly be carried out. The Chinese soldiers were impatient and had killed some people. Mostly the Chinese wanted gold and jewels, and as long as they got them, they were reasonably easy to get along with. The man smiled. He wore a big fur hat, a thick sheepskin jacket and several layers of homespun woolen cloth coats and gowns. His face was very wrinkled but his teeth were good. Like most Asians, Clifford noted, the man had very finely shaped hands.

The tea was awful. Clifford had never been able to get used to the taste and texture of it, thick foamy rancid butter soap tea.

■ ■ ■

Roy hadn't intended to get drunk. He had gone to North Beach to buy a book, and he met Mark Sanderson in a bookstore. They hadn't seen each other for months. Mark was on his way to keep an appointment. Like all musicians, he had a very long daily schedule of lessons and rehearsals and work at his own compositions and the duties of a husband and father to be accomplished. His day needed 36 hours, but he managed to get everything done, more or less, in 18; however, he was always behind schedule, always more or less late. He had to spend a lot of time on the telephone while he was in one place, explaining to someone why he was going to be late in arriving someplace else.

Mark and Roy went to a little Italian bar. They had an energetic conversation about their work, about music, about the lives of all their friends. Roy was very happy to be having a friendly drink not too early in the afternoon. While Mark was making a phone call, Tom Prescott came into the bar and sat down next to Roy while Roy happened to be looking the other way, talking to the barman.

Tom said, "Tell him to give me a martini on the rocks."

"Hey, Tom!" Roy yelled.

"What are you celebrating?" Tom inquired.

"I got my Income Tax Refund!" Roy shouted orders at the barman.

Mark joined them. He told about his trip to the Venice Festival where he'd been invited to conduct some of his own compositions.

"At the end it was really scary," Mark said. "Everybody was yelling and

212

screaming. The manager said I was supposed to greet the audience and take a bow, then he shoved me out onto the stage. It was like the Reign of Terror or something; they were really wailing. I could see some of them winding up to throw things, so I began doing a quick fade—but it all turned out to be flowers and pieces of candy wrapped in tinfoil. They really liked the music, but I was scared; I thought they were going to attack the stage. Now I've really got to go—these people out at the auditorium are waiting for me to get there for a rehearsal. Call us up and come over sometime soon!"

Mark rushed away. Tom sat and drank with Roy for a while. He was very unsettled. He was worrying about whether he should marry Dorothy. Roy told him he should: she was a great woman and great women are few.

"How come you never married her yourself," Tom asked.

"She had signed up to marry Clifford when I met her," Roy said.

"She thinks a lot of you, you know," Tom said.

"I love Dorothy. She knows that," Roy told him. "We sorted all this out a long time ago."

"We've been fighting about everything again," Tom said.

"You mean you've been crazy enough to pay attention to what she *says*? Don't take all that stuff seriously. She says a lot of things, most of it is just talking."

"Well, there are lots of complications," Tom said. "She's as undecided as I am. She keeps fussing around about Clifford and what he said and what he's going to say and about her mother and about her hair and about her work and about getting older all the time—"

Roy said, "All that's bullshit. If you want to marry her, move in and get started. Start living together."

"I haven't found a place yet where I can fix up a darkroom," Tom said.

"For Christ's sake, get yourself a real estate agent, have him find you a place and make Dorothy move into it. Cut out all the nonsense!"

"Yeah, I guess you're right," Tom said. "I've got to get to work, whether I can get her to move in with me or not. I can't keep goofing around the way I'm going. It's driving me crazy."

Tom had one more drink with Roy, then he went away. The bar was fairly quiet during the dinner hour. Roy drank very slowly and talked with the barman; he played the jukebox and the pinball machine. He felt happy and relaxed. He didn't need to do anything except go to the toilet once in a while.

Roy wondered what had really happened between Dorothy and Clifford. He had thought they were very well suited. Now it had come all unstuck. O.K. Unstuck, uckstuck, fuckstick—why not.

Later, Roy was gradually surrounded by a group of his former students and current disciples and other solemn woolly types. He was well oiled and speeding along very happily, free to begin speaking out at last. For six hours he discoursed passionately and pointedly upon the works of

W. B. Yeats. He spouted enough ideas and cross references and learned asides to supply a university professor with material sufficient for teaching a four year course in the life and writings of Yeats. One of the six hours, for example, was devoted to a description of the works and character of A. P. Sinnet and the effect of his writings upon Yeats and the members of Yeats' circle of friends.

By closing time, Roy was gloriously weeping. He was pleading with a furry young man to eschew the false teachings of the nefarious P. D. Ouspensky. Roy's friends gently eased him out of the bar and into the back of an old truck parked in a nearby alley. In the laps and arms of several beautiful lady beatniks, Roy wept and sang and prophesied while the old truck roared through the foggy streets and across the great orange bridge above the Golden Gate to a shack among the eucalyptus hills of Marin County.

The rest of the night and most of the early morning, they all played music and made love and took dope and sang and danced while Roy continued to speak with the tongues of men and angels until exactly nine thirty A.M., when he fell off his chair onto the grassy floor where beautiful arms and legs and bodies received him and he slept.

Somebody with a beard came in later and said, "Say, who's he, anyway," pointing at Roy.

Someone answered, "I don't know man, but the old fart sure can talk."

Another said, "Don't you know who that is?. . .well, you can't see his face right this minute. . .that's Roy Aherne, the poet."

The one with the beard said, "Shit. Who are you trying to con?"

"I'm not putting you on; that's who it is."

"Listen," the bearded one said. "Roy Aherne is in Ceylon at some buddhist monastery."

"You're cuckoo," another bearded personage remarked; he had arrived in time to hear the other's closing remark. "Roy Aherne is in Italy at that big poetry conference they're having for Ezra Pound's birthday."

"Who's this guy, then?" somebody inquired.

"How do I know," asked the original beard. "Probably the C.I.A."

■ ■ ■

Dorothy told Beth Sanderson, "I never seem to get anywhere. I keep trying to work but it's probably all pointless—Clifford always said I didn't have any ideas. What do *you* do? I mean *how* do you do everything?"

Beth said, "I'm too busy to get anything done, what with the kids and the house and music—I just barely keep the entire scene from collapsing and falling down around my ankles so that I can't move at all. You're the only really successful woman that I know. You get to travel all the time and talk to all sorts of famous people, Tom is a famous photographer—he's happy, isn't he?"

"I don't know," Dorothy said. "We don't really seem to think in terms of happiness or unhappiness any more; we both go on sort of independently, but we spend our evenings together—we stay home a lot—I suppose if I could bring myself to think in those terms again, that funny psychological vocabulary, I'd soon be going to see Max again for treatment or take the veil or something—but I'm just babbling. Tell me what you did yesterday, for example."

Beth clutched her forehead. "My God! I don't know," she said. "What didn't I do? I can't remember, my schedule was all thrown out of whack, I had to take Sidney to the dentist, the cat threw up in the baby's crib and it had to be taken all apart and washed and rebuilt, Mother phoned to say she was going to Salem to take care of Aunt Myrtle again. In the afternoon I had to go over to the campus to rehearse the Schütz oratorio we're supposed to put on next month. I had to pick up the kids after school and then give a piano lesson because Mark was too busy right then, and I made five hundred cookies for the Bluebirds and wrote a letter about saving the Bay and sent it to Senator Engle—I was tired at the end of it, that's all I know about yesterday. But I always think of you doing all the things that you do very calmly and deliberately and *quietly* (there's so much sound here—the kids yelling, the telephone, music going on all the time) in your beautiful house where there's nobody to bother you or drag you away from what you're trying to do."

Dorothy sighed. "Maybe Louis Bitteschoen is right," she said. "He always says that the main thing is the style, the quality . . ."

Beth's daughter, Deedee, ran into the room; Sidney could be heard roaring in the distance.

"Mama, Sidney has taken the tumble-beans out of the play telephone and is feeding them to Terwilliger Panda and he won't give them back." Such was Deedee's breathless message.

"Deedee, I'm not the least bit sorry for you," Beth calmly replied. "You shouldn't come tattling to me about everything that Sidney does, he's always doing something, I know that already. He'll be doing something else pretty soon, and then you can play the tumble-beans. If Sidney is difficult, find something you can do by yourself. Practice your new piano piece or start knitting a sweater for Terwilliger or write—yes: that's what you must do right now; you must write a letter to your grandmother."

"Ah, I don't want to," Deedee said, pulling her hair down over her face.

"Put your hair back. You must write to her immediately. It can be a very short letter, but you must write it yourself and say thank you for the beautiful birthday present. And put on some clothes or you'll catch cold." (Deedee was wearing only a few yards of orange-dyed cheesecloth and spangles draped haphazardly about herself; she was barefoot.) "Now I'm going to talk to Aunt Dorothy. You run along, now."

Deedee said, "O.K.," quite happily, and ran out of the room, but she returned a few seconds later, much distressed. She couldn't find Sidney in order to whop him.

Dorothy said, "Oh dear. I should have kept my big mouth shut. I keep forgetting that everybody tends to take me literally."

Beth laughed at her. "Don't worry," she said. "Sidney is very tough. Excuse me a minute while I get this one fixed up with a piece of paper."

■ ■ ■

The first time that Roy met Margaret Gridley they had a big noisy argument. Dorothy was giving a small dinner party to welcome Margaret to San Francisco, and since Roy was in town, she invited him to meet Margaret, her old friend from happy Radcliffe days. There was a cocktail party to while away the hours between sunset and supper time, and since Roy hadn't had any lunch that day, the gin soon began to illuminate his active brain. He also found the presence of Margaret Gridley mildly intoxicating.

Roy saw a small, round-eyed woman with straight blond hair and a pouting mouth. She had a habit of rolling her great blue eyes upwards while delivering herself of some acidulous remark. She seemed to Roy to be very witty; she had an attractive figure as well. She made no effort to dominate the conversation—Dorothy and her other guests were all expert talkers—but Margaret's account of her early life in the rustic suburbs of Eugene, of the latest jazz and dope news from New York, and of the intrigues and excitements of life in the Carl Jung Institute at Zurich managed to keep the attention of the party focussed on herself.

Dorothy rushed about filling glasses, fetching ice and hors d'oeuvres from the kitchen, opening bottles. She was delighted to have something happening in her own little apartment. She complained to Roy, later, however. "Why did you have to be so snotty all evening? You and Margaret were both awful. What got you started, anyway?"

"I was drunk, that's all," Roy said.

Dorothy impatiently refused to accept this excuse. "You're always drunk," she said. "What got it all going?"

"It didn't amount to anything," Roy said, rather sheepishly. "It was all about *The New Yorker*. Margaret was trying to tell me how we all owe it to ourselves to read each page of every issue with devotion and fidelity, ads and all. I told her that the entire magazine is written weekly by two old aunties who had been roommates at Yale, except for the fiction, which is all done by a team of anonymous workers at the Walt Disney Studios in Hollywood. They use a number of pseudonyms—"

"Oh, stop it!" Dorothy said. "Really?"

"Sure I did. She got mad."

"Come on. Margaret was just needling you from the start. She never reads anything except my mystery stories and *Vogue*. She was just putting you on and you fell for it. Hah!"

"Anyway, she was mad," Roy said.

"Margaret? She told me you were the only attractive man in San Francisco and she's going to seduce you."

216

"Oh yeah?"

"There you are, Mr. Smarty-pants Roy."

Roy laughed. He said "Oh yeah?" again, but he felt very interested and excited by Dorothy's account of Margaret's impresssion of him. He wondered if Dorothy was putting him on, however, all unbeknownst to Margaret, simply in order to stir up a little mischief. Contrariwise, he thought, Dorothy was very busy with getting ready to join Clifford in Ceylon. It was rather late in the day for her to want or to need any more fuss and excitement than she already had to deal with.

At this period, Roy had been busy trying to simplify his own life. For years he had had the ambition of being able to pack everything that he needed into a large suitcase. He ought to be able to unpack the suitcase anywhere, set up his portable typewriter, and there would be home, a place to work and live. But he also needed hiking gear and a couple dozen books. The answer had come to his problem, in the shape of a little second-hand English car which one of his students sold to him for a very small sum. The hiking equipment had to be stored at Max Lammergeier's house, but the big suitcase, the portable typewriter, and the two dozen books almost fitted into the little car. (The single suitcase was, in actuality, a large old Air Corps B-4 bag almost as large as the car. Somebody told him he ought to put wheels under the suitcase and forget the automobile.) Roy believed that if it was necessary, he could sleep in the car, too. Quite often, lately, he was having to do just that. He was drinking a lot of the time, and he couldn't afford to keep up his drinking and pay rent as well. When Margaret Gridley appeared on the scene, Roy was living, rather crummily, in his little car.

Margaret Gridley wouldn't ride in it. She had her own car, a 1933 Packard sedan, black and square. The plush upholstery was beautifully kept and there was a pair of silver-mounted cutglass vases on the doorposts.

Margaret Gridley enjoyed drinking gin. Roy spent lots of time with her, drinking and talking. At last he had found someone who could drink as much (and more) than he could and who liked it, and who had style and brains that he could respect. Margaret made Roy laugh a great deal, but they sometimes had very serious arguments.

Margaret had begun trying to write. She hadn't written anything since she was in college, but now she wanted to make a clear and exact statement about the life and times of Beefy Johnson. She liked to wake up early in the morning and drink coffee in silence and solitude, trying to see again how Beefy looked and what he did and how he sounded when he talked, and then trying to make up exact sentences which would convey this knowledge to a reader.

Roy told her that he himself kept working all the time, morning, noon, and night, asleep or awake. He wrote down what he couldn't stop remembering. He wrote it only after he could see and hear the complete poem in his head. He'd look at it after it was written, to see what his eyes thought about it, how did it look as something to be read. He always remembered what he had written.

Roy hated schedules. He wanted to be free to go out and pick flowers all morning if he felt like it, or stay in bed. He was sure that the world would be better if more people stayed in bed most of the morning. As it was, everyone was up at seven, screaming down the freeways a hundred miles an hour between eight and nine A.M., in order to go sit in cold nasty drafty stores and offices all the rest of the day, composing duns, making out bills, threats of lawsuits, foreclosures, tax penalties, and summonses to traffic court.

Margaret contended that the pale wretched light of sunrise was the only medium by which one could possibly see the world or oneself as they actually are. Even then, it is necessary to look fast and look closely. All intelligent people, Margaret told him, take naps later in the day. The most intelligent sleep instead of eating large, fattening lunches. (Nice people seldom eat anytime.) In the evening was the time for cocktails and a little supper and a little fond affection and love. The evening ended promptly at 1 A.M.

Roy said she was anal-compulsive.

Margaret said he was enfantine. (She got the word from Henry James.)

The two of them drove (in Margaret's car) to Carson City. They shot up a lot of methadrine and stayed awake four days, gambling with some money Roy had received for a poetry prize. They drove down Highway 395 to look at the scarp of the Sierra. They visited the Mammoth Hot Springs. They got married in Reno. They ate lunch for the first time in days in a beerhall on Donner Summit. They bought new distributor points in Auburn, whilom capital of California. They quarreled about whether to visit Sacramento. They ate an expensive fish dinner in Berkeley. They went home to Margaret's apartment and went to bed.

For a couple of months, they attended the parties that their friends gave for them. Margaret and Roy were always the first to arrive and the last to leave. At one party they quarreled and broke things. At another party, they pursued each other from room to room, from conversation to conversation. One would be sitting or standing, talking to other guests, when the other would silently arrive and begin slowly giving gentle but persistent and intimate caresses.

One evening, Margaret went home before Roy realized that she had left the party. He arrived at her side, drunk, hours later, to wake her up.

"What's the big idea of leaving me all alone?"

Margaret wrapped the blankets over her head and said nothing.

"What's the matter, sweet baby?" Roy inquired.

"Nothingthmatter" issued from under the blankets.

"What?"

Margaret uncovered her mouth and said very distinctly, although it was a great effort for her to do so, "Nothing's the matter, dear heart, I took some nembies and now I'm asleep. Please come to bed and shut up."

Roy said, "Oh." He stood looking at the lump in the bed for a couple of minutes. He hadn't remembered yet who or where he was, what was happening. Then he turned off the light and left the bedroom. He found some gin in the kitchen, but somehow he couldn't begin to perform the operation of making himself a drink. For a long time he stood up, hanging onto the red formica counter in the kitchen, looking at the frosted glass bottle under the bright white lights.

Margaret seldom visited the center of the city, but one day she did happen to walk through Union Square and there was Herbert Wackernagel, gawking at the lady on top of the monument to Admiral Dewey. Margaret said, "Well, Herbert, if she only knew it was you—"

Herbert looked at Margaret and grinned. The gold tooth sparkled. He said, "Hello, Maggie," and gave her a large warm gentle hug and kiss.

Margaret tried to explain to Roy why it was that she must now go away and spend the rest of her life with Herbert Wackernagel. Roy said that he could understand perfectly well why, but that he still felt that he had a prior claim to her attention and services, being that he was her husband.

Margaret said, "Oh, come on, Roy."

"Childhood sweethearts are just keen if they're children," Roy said. "Later on, there's dirty old Roy. I need you. I love you. I deserve to keep you." He continued in this vein for some time. He was eloquent and persuasive, but in the end, Margaret told him, "We're too much alike, we both want the same parts of the same world, we agree too much. I think you're a great poet. I love you even now, in a way. Your only real defect is that you are not Herbert Wackernagel."

Roy said, "I've got three gold teeth."

"Roy, I mean it. Even if you contested the divorce, it wouldn't do any good. I'll be living with Herbert from now on, that's all. Except for the six weeks I'll *have* to be living in Reno being a legal citizen of Nevada."

Roy hit her several times. He cried. He broke things. He would kill himself. He would re-enlist in the army. He would have Margaret committed: she had obviously lost her mind. He would castrate Herbert Wackernagel. Margaret mustn't go away.

Margaret told him that he was only making it harder for himself to face reality. Roy screamed inarticulately and fell to the floor where he squirmed and rolled and wept.

Roy got drunk for three weeks in North Beach and then Max Lammergeier blotted him up out of the bar and took him for a hundred mile hiking trip in the Sierra.

■  ■  ■

The Grand Mahatma says, "The Christians tell us that the reason why all of us do the things we do is called Original Sin."

After Beefy Johnson graduated from the university, he organized his own group. They worked hard, traveled around the country playing in small clubs in big cities. In a few years, they started getting good notices in the newspapers and magazines. Beefy was a good musician; he wrote funny and interesting arrangements; his group worked together well. Other musicians who heard them told everyone that Beefy Johnson and his men were the best new sound going.

Beefy and the group cut a record for a San Francisco company and the record became a minor hit with the disc jockeys. Then Beefy made an entire album, and got money enough to go to Europe.

He traveled alone. He visited Leipzig and the Thomaskirche. He attended the big festivals at Bayreuth and Salzburg. He toured in Italy and got high with mark Sanderson in Venice. He married a young Italian movie actress who wanted to come to America.

Beefy enjoyed himself in Europe but he was homesick all the time. Other Americans told him, "I never knew what it was like to live without The Problem. You won't catch this baby running back there any too soon." Beefy laughed and said. "All you need at home is a good lawyer. I got one right in the family. It's nice here, but nothing's happening, there's no jazz. I've got to go back, I've got to be on the ground, I've got to hear what people are saying; otherwise, I can't work."

■ ■ ■

The Grand Mahatma says, "Art—real art—is really outrageous, actually beyond the Pale: extravagant, exorbitant. Craftsmanship may come into it, but there's a point beyond merely doing a thing expertly, completely, or correctly. There's a creation, which is the manifestation of a man's vision: his necessity to speak and explain himself—more than a response. There's a direct voluntary statement, which is a complete declaration of a man's feeling/knowledge/being. Form and craftsmanship (and the audience as well), the craft, the world—all are different, all are changed, after the occurrence of this creative action: changed from the dead things that they have been. There's another life."

■ ■ ■

Clifford received a letter of invitation from the First Interdisciplinary Forum for the Study of the Basic Humanities. This organization wanted him to participate in seminars, to lecture on whatever subject he chose, and to take part in panel discussions. There were to be brush-up courses and banquets, outings and junkets and balls. All this was to take place during the month of August in Monterey, California, U.S.A. The Forum proposed to pay Clifford's plane fare and all the expenses for a month plus what they apologetically called "a modest honorarium": the sum of $1500.

Clifford showed the letter to Laura. "You'll go, of course," she said. "I wish that such an organization existed in France and that they'd invite me to Deauville for the summer or some such fashionable watering-place. *Merveille!*"

"Why don't you come with me?" Clifford asked her, trying to keep his voice from trembling.

"If I had that kind of money, to fly about in airplanes, I should keep it in the bank and not go flitting off to California. When I get back to Paris, I'll buy clothes, if I have any money left. All my things are completely out of fashion. I have only a little time left on my present visa. I shall be required to leave Nepal very soon, and I must continue collecting specimens and preparing to have them all shipped back to France...no, not America today, thank you." She laughed, then.

"You know what I mean," Clifford said. "I want you to marry me."

"Oh. Oh, Clifford, what shall I say? I like you so much, I respect you, you have a maturity, a splendid mind—but marriage: that is a very serious notion. And your former wife..." Laura stopped. She seemed for once to be inarticulate.

"Are you really that good a Catholic?" Clifford gently inquired. "I thought the Church was a little more liberal, these days..."

"You supposed that I was more 'modern'? More 'scientific'? Oh, yes, I am a scientist, a rationalist, if you like; but after all, one feels certain things, one has been brought up in a certain way. I must make an effort to believe. This is very difficult to talk about in English...excuse me."

Clifford was quite shaken by her response. He had difficulty speaking, himself. He could only look at her.

"I'm very sorry, Cliff. I am very fond of you. I love to be with you. I will always remember your loving and that I love you also..."

Clifford suddenly kissed her on the cheek and ran away. It was impossible to talk with her about it any more.

■ ■ ■

Roy took Dorothy to lunch in a small Dalmatian restaurant on Sutter Street. They ate petrale fried in butter and drank Guinness stout.

Dorothy said, "I like this place. I've only been here with you; I never can find it if I look for it, and then it reappears when we go out to lunch together."

"Well, well," Roy said. "You'll soon be in Ceylon, eating barbecued alligator and roasted monkey stuffed with mangoes."

Dorothy looked vaguely sad. "I suppose so," she said. "I don't want to go to India, but Dr. Bitteschoen says I've got to in order to help him with his collection of Singhalese-Dravidian-Tamil phonemics. I told Clifford I'd come and we'd get married. I don't want to marry Clifford. Uk. I have to study and make a mess of more languages and read Pali inscriptions for Dr. Bitteschoen. Who did you make it with while you were in New York? I bet that Gigi Fiske had her hand down the front of your pants the minute you got to town."

"I told you in a letter that I saw her at a big party, but she brought her own man, some kind of giant Yaley—more precisely, he came to the party sort of wearing Gigi Fiske like some kind of weird costume. She stuck to him all the time, only her head would poke out now and then to make some cheery conversation."

"Did you see Margaret Gridley?"

"I still haven't met the celebrated Margaret Gridley," Roy said. "People told me that she was in the hospital with hepatitis. Everybody in New York is getting it, shooting meth with dirty needles."

Dorothy said, "Someone was telling me the other day—who was it?— that Margaret had written a letter from Switzerland. She was at Dr. Jung's place in Zurich. She was totally unhinged when Beefy Johnson got killed."

Roy said, "Everybody in New York had a different story about all that. One said Beefy was shot by a rejected faggot boyfriend, another said the Black Muslims got him for betraying the movement to the CIA— somebody else said that the Mafia did it because he pulled some kind of dope swindle on them—his grand piano, stuffed with heroin, was flown direct from Ankara to New York and Beefy was going to get half the proceeds, but he tried to get it all. Somebody said his ex-wife, that movie-actress, was in on it."

Dorothy said "Mmmm" into her glass of stout. Then she suddenly drank all that remained in the glass. "What would you do if you got a girl pregnant?" she asked.

Roy sighed. "Leave town, I suppose," he said. "Oh, I don't know—I like babies. I'd probably marry the girl. Why?"

"Oh, I just wondered. Margaret never was," Dorothy said.

Dorothy and Roy went to the San Francisco Museum and looked at the very latest new paintings from New York and at a show of Matisse's cutouts until they were tired.

Dorothy said, "I'm getting dizzy. Let's go to your place and have something good to drink."

They went to Roy's place and had a couple of drinks and played a few records and went to bed.

■ ■ ■

Clifford dreamed that he was lying in a big square bed on the floor of a big room with a very high ceiling. Margaret Gridley was beside him, talking, but Clifford was lying on his side or anyway had his head turned away from her. It was very light in the room and he felt wonderfully comfortable. The blanket over them was bright red and there were pink reflections from the red blanket on the bright yellow and white walls of the room.

Margaret said, "She wants to know why you keep seeing her, after all." (Margaret was talking about Dorothy.)

Clifford looked up at the ceiling where there was a painting: it was actually a number of different messages painted in large letters and different handwritings, each message was written by a different person. The words of the messages were mostly illegible, but the signatures were quite clear, they were the names of Clifford's friends who were painters. All the letters and scrawls and signatures together on the ceiling made a beautiful painting.

Clifford said, "Because I love her, of course."

"She wants to know why you keep coming to see me," Margaret said.

The light and space in the room, the high ceiling with its painting, the bright walls and the sense of there being other spacious rooms beyond the one where they were lying—all these things contributed to Clifford's feeling of ease and security. Above all, the calm, solid presence of Margaret Gridley herself was soothing and pleasurable.

"Because you're a woman, of course," Clifford answered. Then he turned his head and saw that Margaret was lying on her stomach and writing on a big legal-size sheet of paper whereon the questions she'd been asking him were beautifully handwritten in vermillion ink. She was busy recording Clifford's answers in black ink. The page of writing looked very beautiful, no matter what words said or meant or implied, no matter how damaging his answers might be when they were read by Dorothy.

Clifford understood that this paper was a letter that Margaret was writing to Dorothy. He suddenly felt a shudder of guilty fear and shame, the previous feeling of security went away; he was happily married to Dorothy, whom he loved, and he was two-timing her with Margaret and soon Dorothy and everybody else would know it. He felt scared. In the next couple of seconds, the feeling of security was restored: he had decided to ignore the shame fear guilt scare. If Dorothy read Margaret's letter and knew that Clifford was in bed with Margaret, Dorothy might be temporarily upset but she'd get over it and they'd all be friends and somehow Clifford would be able to sleep with both of them without there being any trouble.

Margaret's hair looked golden brilliant light, her flesh was a luminous chalky white and the red blanket humped up over her shoulders cast ruby highlights on her white skin. It worried Clifford to watch her writing down his words; she seemed to be feeling quite impersonal about it. At the same time, he understood that he and Margaret had a very clear and solid kind of realization of each other and of their relationship. They had been lovers for a long time and they were right now very quietly happy to be together and they would be staying for some time in that very comfortable bed with the red blanket in the big light room. And so the dream gently faded away and Clifford awoke.

Later he walked out of town and climbed a little mountain from which he could see the Himalayas. He didn't want to leave Nepal, but he wanted to talk with all his friends who would be in Monterey, and there would be people there whom he had not yet met in peson, but whose books he had read or whose friends he had already met. What were they like. What did they think about Mozart and Halford Mackinder?

Clifford was upset, still, about Laura's refusal to go with him. Few women had ever declined an invitation from him. He wondered if he was getting old and smelly. He had a couple of bad teeth which tasted funny.

The sky was a flat precise blue overhead. There was a low-lying cloudbank, indicating the location of the Gangetic Plain, to the south. The weather was beginning to work its way northwards out of India. The sky reminded him of the sky over Arizona and New Mexico.

He walked swiftly down the mountain. The light was beginning to pass. Rhododendrons blossomed high overhead among pines and deodars. A great deal of the time it seemed to him as if he might be walking in the high country somewhere north of Yosemite. Then he began meeting Nepalese lumberjacks and solitary Tibetans on the trail and he knew that he wasn't exactly in California.

■ ■ ■

Flora McGreevey telephoned Dorothy.

"Have you given any thought to my question about that piano?" Flora inquired. "I've promised it to the Middle Fillmore Neighborhood Improvement Association Center. I don't need it myself, I don't have time for it, but it's mine to give away if I want to, and I think it will do a world of good for those youngsters at the Center."

Dorothy obediently replied, "All right, Mama, I'll call Mark. But we really ought to think of a way of getting another one for Mark—he has to have one, and you know they don't have money enough for big things like pianos, with all the children and everything."

"I should think that by this time he could afford to have one of his own," Flora said. "Or at least be able to rent one. If he can afford to go flying all over Europe when I can't manage to get to Nassau for a couple of weeks, he can certainly afford his own piano. Really poor artists don't race around the world like that; they stay home and starve and work to make their art things. And anyway, I thought that he was *Clifford's* friend."

"Now, Mother, the school paid for his trip. He and Beth haven't a dime between them."

"Oh, Dorothy, I'm tired of hard-luck stories. I hear them all day, every day, and I tell a good number of them myself. Mark Sanderson gets a good salary from that university. He can afford to rent a piano or use the ones in the music department. I've been over there—I know they've got them. You can rent a little upright piano for nothing. The Goodwill Store and the Salvation Army practically give them away for the asking, they've got so many pianos."

Dorothy was annoyed with her mother's exaggerations. "Mother, why do you say those things when you know they aren't real? A piano costs hundreds of dollars wherever you buy it."

"Well, comparatively speaking," Flora said, as carelessly as ever. "Why don't you come downtown and have lunch with me? We can go to the Palace Hotel and try out my new credit card thing that gets you into all the nice restaurants without a reservation or waiting or anything, you just show it to them and the bank pays for it all, later."

Dorothy didn't feel like disillusioning her mother about her new magic. She simply said, "I'd love to, Mama, but I have to work all day on my article. And I'll call Mark for you. But if you see anybody rich today, who wants to get rid of a piano, tell them they must give it to a struggling young composer you know all about and how he deserves all kinds of help and encouragement."

"Just please get my piano back for me," Flora said. "I'll come to see you tomorrow for cocktails at five and you can tell me what progress you've made."

"But Mother—" Dorothy wailed. She tried to invent some fib to tell which would prevent her mother from descending upon her at a critical point in the day, but in this emergency, Dorothy's usually swift imagination failed her.

Flora sensed the collapse and her natural magnanimity took over. "A little after five," she said. "I'll bring you some of that good Plymouth gin. They've got it on sale right now at Goldberg Bowen's—you and Tom ought to have a case of it—it's practically a steal at only $59.95."

■ ■ ■

Roy felt himself beginning to run batty. While he'd been doing all the things that he demanded of himself every morning—getting up before ten, taking a bath, shaving, washing his teeth, combing his hair, getting dressed in reasonably clean clothes, making the bed and creating a small but hot breakfast—he kept remembering a line of poetry. He thought he knew whose poem it was, but where had he most recently seen it quoted? The line appeared in the midst of some prose book that he'd been reading.

*When in the world I liv'd, I was the world's commander.*

Roy left his hot breakfast before he'd eaten half of it, in order to begin looking for the source of that quote. He was sure that it was from some play-within-a-play in an Elizabethan comedy. Roy scouted about within a copy of Ben Johnson's plays, imagining that he'd find the line in the puppet-play section of *Bartholomew Fair*. He looked next into Beaumont & Fletcher's *The Knight of the Burning Pestle*, since there was an imitation of the *Spanish Tragedy* there. He found the line on his next try, right where it has always been (with, nevertheless, thanks to Thomas Kyd) in the Fifth Act of

225

*Love's Labour's Lost.*

Roy finished his breakfast, washed the dishes, took the garbage out, and burnt all the wastepaper. Where in God's name had he seen that Shakespearian tag used? He looked through *The Paris Review Interviews,* both volumes. He tried to reason with himself: "How much difference does it make where I saw it?" He decided that it wasn't important; nevertheless he would be unhappy and bothered until he knew. Then he recalled, for a split second, the look of that page of prose with a line of poetry in a wide space, down towards the bottom of a page of fairly large type—Caslon or Schoolbook face. He looked all through *The Road to Xanadu,* which he had been re-reading. He searched a book of essays by Ezra Pound, in which he had been looking up something else, a few days before. He realized that his memory, his brain, might actually have collapsed his time sense, and that he was perhaps remembering something that he'd seen months ago instead of only a day or so before. Contrariwise, the mental image of the page he was hunting for was so clear and fresh and certain, that it could only be a recent impression. He could remember that he'd been very busy reading when someone had interrupted him, just as he was on the point of trying to remember to look up something else. . .what had he been reading on that occasion?

Roy wanted to go outside. He had to get a haircut. He was going to be teaching that evening, and there were letters he had to answer before he had to go to work. He was getting more irritable and annoyed with himself. Why couldn't he remember? Why was he so hung up with the necessity for remembering? Why must he keep searching for this one out of the several millions of pages that he must have read in his life—reading that had done him not the slightest bit of good anyhow, except to unfit him for any kind of real human life. ("That's an operatic lie," Roy told himself, interrupting his previous train of thought.)

He brooded over an old *Life* magazine at the barber's shop. He was very cranky with the barber. In the street, he screamed curses at a Volkswagen that had nearly run over him as he was trying to cross the street against the light. Then he hurried home. He had remembered another book that he'd been looking at yesterday; he'd go search that.

He went to the school and lectured to his class about Coleridge and dope and the life of Hartley Coleridge and English Unitarianism and the Evangelical Movement in England and John Livingston Lowes in the United States. After he got home, he found himself opening one book after another, obsessively hunting and searching. He cursed himself. It was time to go to sleep. What book was it?

Just after he got into bed he remembered that he'd recently been reading one of the volumes of Leonard Woolf's memoirs, a book he'd borrowed from the library earlier that week, read, and returned almost immediately. He'd only spent a few hours with it; he'd go to the library tomorrow and look at it again.

In the morning, Roy wrote a letter, looked through half a dozen books which he'd already gone through twice before (including The Lowes book), then he hurried off to the library. He found the Leonard Woolf book that he wanted and examined it carefully, even though he was in a hurry—he was supposed to meet Clifford for lunch. The quote wasn't there.

That evening, Roy came home and put the teakettle on the stove to boil. He was wondering what book had that page he'd been looking for. He squatted before the bookcase and pulled out *The Allegory of Love*. The book fell open at the beginning of the chapter which carries Shakespeare's line for an epigraph:

*When in the world I liv'd, I was the world's commander.*

Roy felt such a sense of relief and ease that he nearly collapsed into a witless heap of joy on the carpet, never to rise again. Then he got up in a hurry to turn off the gas in the kitchen; the teakettle had ejaculated its water all over the stove and the floor and the bottom of the pot was nearly burnt away.

■ ■ ■

Clifford began to pack for his journey to Monterey. He had already lugged a number of small boxes of books and musical scores to the post office, where he had mailed them to Mark Sanderson in Berkeley. Mark stored all of Clifford's heavier gear in the attic of the garage behind his house. The garage had once been a carriage house and stable; it had a high dry loft where hay and feed used to be stored.

Long before he began the task of getting ready to leave, Clifford consulted a large map in order to determine the exact physical location of Monterey. He had gone to the town many times in the past, but it had been some length of time since his last visit. It now seemed like a distant magic land that he had never really seen. He had a set of US Geodetic Survey maps of California. He got out the 15-minute series chart for Monterey and spread it out on his table and spent an hour reading it carefully.

(Dorothy used to say that Clifford wouldn't go to the corner store for a pack of cigarets without first consulting a street map of the city in order to determine the positions of the house and the store with some accuracy.)

Clifford always checked the map in order to find out whether he might walk to the place that he wanted to go. If he were a prehistoric man or an Indian, he asked himself, what path would I follow? From Katmandu, for example, he could walk out through Siberia and cross the Aleutian Chain to North America. Or by island-hopping, with the help of a small coracle made of skins and wood, he might make it across the North Atlantic.

He thought fondly of Monterey. He could remember fairly well the big park where the Army Language School is, the big Spanish plaster hotels

227

from 1927 movie star days, the long dusty rooms in the white adobe house where Robert Louis Stevenson used to live, and the old Territorial capitol building. The air was soft there and the bougainvillaea bloomed and the sidewalks were warm and dusty under the pines and cypresses. Then there was the big open space along the shores of the Bay, and the messy part of it which Steinbeck wrote about, and then there was Pacific Grove, with its big houses that looked out across the blue water. Further south began the 19 Mile Drive, where giant pink Moorish villas lurked among the pines, and tourists in automobiles had to pay a dollar for the privilege of driving (no stopping) down the road and seeing the distant roofs and garden walls belonging to the happy few. The tourists, having spent their dollars, wouldn't have money enough left to stay in a Carmel hotel overnight; they must camp out in the redwoods of the state park several miles down the road towards Big Sur.

There was a little train which ran from San Francisco to Monterey called the Del Monte Special. Clifford rode on it once, to find out how it felt not to be hitchhiking, and also to figure out exactly what route the railway followed—was any part of the line an Indian route? He was shocked by the price of the ticket.

Once Clifford had gone with Roy to find Robinson Jeffers, but they got too drunk in a tavern between Monterey and Carmel to find anybody or anything. Roy said he needed a little juice in order to keep up his nerve. He was a great admirer of Jeffers' poetry and plays, and he wanted to visit the man and tell him so, but Roy was shy—he had the idea that Jeffers was a fierce and refractory creature who might turn them away from his door. Roy had a letter of introduction from a friend of Jeffers, everything was quite correct; the writer of the letter had assured Roy that Jeffers was a very kind, shy, and retiring man, gentle and wise. Nevertheless, Roy couldn't really get going, and Clifford berated him for his cowardliness and silliness in having come all this way to see somebody that he very much wanted to see and then finding that he was too embarrassed to do anything besides hide in a bar and get loaded. But no matter how much Clifford tried to encourage him or shame him or kid him, Roy wouldn't leave the bar, and soon he was clearly too drunk to be taken to meet shy poets whom he had not previously been introduced to. It seemed unlikely that Mr. Jeffers would appreciate a visit from a potted stranger.

Clifford checked out A. L. Kroeber's Handbook to make certain exactly which Indians had lived in Monterey and what language they spoke. He already had a reasonably clear recollection of the shape of the Bay and how the hills and the Coast Range lay behind the town, and how the great valley lay, in turn, behind the eastern mountains.

Because he was supposed to arrive there fairly soon, Clifford decided to fly to California. He thought he'd fly directly to San Francisco and then hitchhike to Monterey. After the expensive horrors of the airplane journey, it would be a relief for him to walk and stand on the shoulder of a highway in California. At this time of the year, the weather would be warm and quiet, and the air would feel soft and sexy, but fresh from the sea.

He packed his rucksack very carefully. It must carry all that he would truly need, except for the little Swedish portable typewriter. He had carefully planned what clothing he would wear; the suit he had on was of a wash and drip-dry plastic material, as were his shirts, underwear, and socks. One pair of each item of clothing went into the rucksack. He packed a pair of blue jeans and a wool shirt that he'd wear while walking in the mountains or at the beach on chilly evenings. (He'd pick up a pair of hiking boots at Mark's house.) Here was a sewing kit in case a button should fall off or the blue jeans should tear. Here was a first aid kit in case he hurt himself—a reasonable possibility. The first aid kit also contained a package of prophylactic appliances in case he should be required to treat a female patient. There was a tin cup of the kind made famous by John Muir. In the pocket of the top flap which closed the rucksack were a set of Geodetic Survey maps of the Sierra Nevada, a protractor made of thin plastic, a spare compass, a thin notebook with a small pencil attached to it by a thin cord, in case the notebook that he usually carried in the wool shirt pocket were to run out of paper or get lost. Into the rucksack went a lightweight waterproof poncho to keep out the rain and a very expensive lightweight down sleeping bag all squeezed and condensed into a little nylon sack the size of a peanut butter jar. There was a set of spare bootlaces and a hundred feet of parachute cord. There was a big hunting knife, useful for cutting salami and cheese and fruit and string. There was a tiny can opener and a harmonica and there was a plastic waterproof envelope containing a supply of toilet paper.

Clifford used to tell Dorothy, "I don't know how anybody can go anyplace without a rucksack." Dorothy, however, believed in steamer trunks, leather-over-aluminum alloy "airplane luggage," and hand-woven Peruvian baskets. She had an entirely different set of notions about why and how a person should travel. Her ideas were many and vague, Clifford said; just as his own (superior) ideas on the same subject were few and exact and soundly based upon historical principles.

"I am right," Clifford told Dorothy. "You'll find that out one of these days I'm right. You can't travel anyplace, the way you try to go about it. You get nervous and in a hurry and lose things, or lose track of them. You've got to sit down and think of a simpler way of doing it. You must not try to take so many things with you. Make lists."

Dorothy said, "Women are different. They need more and different kinds of things than men do. You'll never understand that, naturally. However many girls you know or have known, you'll never learn, will you?"

■ ■ ■

Tom went into his darkroom and smoked rather more hashish than he had intended—at any rate, he found that he was soon quite incapacitated. He had planned to do some enlarging and printing, and he always had supposed that he could see everything more sharply and exactly if he had pre-arranged a few of his brain cells. But on that particular day, his resistance was low or his volition was uncertain or the hashish was of a higher grade than usual—whatever the reason, he found himself translated into a swift succession of peculiar universes. His body was disconnected, as if he had been pithed like a frog in a biology class. In the red glow of the darkroom lamp Tom tripped out to the inside of his liver, kidneys, the backs of his eyes, then out into the brilliant dusty sunlight of Algiers and squalling music flabby drums and camel fur and suddenly back with a nerve shock tingle of his body which he realized again was quite numb then out to nighttime Maya temple colored feathers jade and marching jaguars in flat hook-nosed procession of warriors and priests with feather bead ankles and feather jade spears blowing conch horns and ringing golden bells

(TELEPHONE??/PARANOIA DOORBELL?
where's Dorothy? Flying horse ladies above a
ring of fire where she lies gold asleep.)

Tom suddenly left the darkroom and came into the living room, a totally new and glorified locale. There was the carpet butter wool, there was a Tibetan tanka, there was a faceted Chinese pewter flask set with gem stones, there was a tank world full of exotic raving monster fishes, there was a shimmering Siamese buddha corruscating and curly gold, there was the window and flashes of different color slices between Venetian blind slat mirrors. The telephone bell transformed both his ears into polychrome cauliflowers with flashing colored lights inside them changing and blinking. There was a heavily grained photograph of Dorothy standing before a gate of carved stone, somewhere in India; she was holding her hands loosely clasped in front of her breast; as in the Man Ray photograph of Gertrude Stein. Dorothy looked straight out over the head of the cameraman. The telephone rang. If he answered it what would he hear. And how could he answer it if he couldn't talk. As he watched it, the telephone turned into a kind of South American animal that is seldom seen in North American or European zoos. Tom couldn't move to pick it up—he didn't really want to touch...that...in any event. The Tibetan tanka (or big reproduction of Hieronymus Bosch's Garden of Earthly Delights?) flashed on and off in different colors when he looked at it. All the figures on it were sounding as well as wriggling and blinking— some kind of extremely fast Archie Shepp music. He watched and listened to all that for several weeks. Then he lay down in the middle of the yellow fur living room rug and watched the big-screen movies on the ceiling, a seven-second feature: The Life of Semiramis Queen of Assyria, Shewing also the Creation of the Celebrated Hanging Gardens of Babylon. There were many painted elephants and beautiful slave maidens who wore nothing but extravagant jewelry, flowers, and colored plumes. Semiramis was Margaret Gridley in a kinky black wig diadem all hung with golden

230

flowers and leaves of gold and plaques of lapis lazuli as discovered by Sir Leonard Wooley in the Royal Tombs of Ur. There were a lot of horns blowing and trumpets shouting, antique cymbals, fast work on the side-drums and tambours, lots of chimes and bells and tambourines while a great chorus of human voices, several thousands of people all sang.

O—A*hhhhhhh*!
A—O*hhhhhhh*!
O—A*hhhhhhh*!

while the camera panned about through scenes of revelry by night orgy and prancing. Dwarf slaves with huge golden trays of roast suckling pig passed among the throng; others bore trays of swans and peacocks and pheasants all served up in their own gorgeous feathers. Golden vessels of wine were carried about by beautiful Nubian ladies. Wine slopped over jeweled hands, naked bellies, gold, fruit, veils, brocades and velvets, asses, tits, bellies, hands, shoulders, eyes, fantastic head dresses, mouths, big eyes above transparent jewel veils, arms and legs glistening with sweat oil, mouth eyes—Tom could feel them all under his hands and belly and shoulders, he swam joyfully out among them, his penis visiting here a pretty momentary cunt, there a pretty mouth, a pretty ass, his mouth working over tit and tongue and clitoris and navel and cunt, tireless and insatiate, one sensation succeeding another, each one more beautiful and poignant than the last, a liberation of each impulse, every dream, a silent lake where he floated among lilies and lotuses, alone in silence of summer night, then Dorothy was floating with him, quiet and understanding, everything resolved, all peace.

Angela Lansbury stood looking down at him. "Why are you lying on the floor, Tom? Are you drunk or does your back hurt today?" For when Tom had smashed up his car on the Waldo Grade, something bad had happened to his back; it had never been the same since. Sometimes it hurt, and he could make it feel better if he lay flat on the floor, and, with his toes hooked under some very solid, unmoving piece of furniture (as for example, the combination radio-TV-phonograph cabinet) stretched his heels "downwards."

■ ■ ■

Clifford stood outside Halfmoon Bay for a long time before a car pulled up ahead of him and stopped and a young State Motor Patrolman stepped out of it. He was very large and he looked like a movie star. He towered over Clifford and the rucksack.

"No, you don't," the patrolman said. "Just a minute. OK." The officer had taken his gun out of its holster, but he aimed it at the ground. "OK. Now go ahead and open that rucksack. I know what you got in there. You beatniks think you can break the laws and laugh at officers and dodge the

Draft. You bring all that narcotics stuff over the Border in your socks. Come on. Dump it out."

"I've got letters here to show where I'm going," Clifford said. "I just got back from Nepal, and I've been visiting friends in San Francisco."

"I know where you've been. You got on that plane down in Mexico, didn't you. You should have stayed on it until you got to Frisco. You shouldn't have come out here on the highway with your little bundle of hay."

Another car pulled up and stopped behind the first one. A larger, fatter, older cop got out of it. He brought his riot gun with him.

"What you got, Charley?" the old cop asked. He gave Clifford a look out of one colorless, bloodshot eye that tried and condemned and executed the suspect all in a single glance.

"We got the messenger from Cloud Land here, Willie," the young one announced.

"OK," Willie said. "I got him covered."

They hauled Clifford to the county jail in San Mateo, where they searched his rucksack by ripping up all its seams and inspecting the various pieces of cloth and leather one by one. The metal frame was sliced open to see what was inside it.

Clifford had to take off all his clothes and be x-rayed, let a "doctor" peer into his ears and nose and mouth with a flashlight and run a long greasy finger into his anus, searching for a fingercot, a vial, a cap.

Afterwards, the policemen were all very polite and apologetic. They told him that there really was a law against hitchhiking in California, and against walking or standing on state highways, because hitchhiking is very dangerous. You never know what kind of people are going to pick you up, they might be all kinds of criminal types and sex fiends and like that. These laws are made for the protection of the public. Thousands of motorists every day are attacked and robbed and raped and murdered and have their cars stolen by monster hitchhikers. And if he really was going to Monterey he ought to have been standing on the other side of the road. (Clifford had been away for so long that he had forgotten temporarily that trafffic moves on the right in America.)

The policeman told him that he should always take a plane or a bus or a train wherever he was going, if he didn't feel like driving. All these forms of public transportation were, they assured him, fast and convenient and the fares remarkably economical.

Clifford had to leave all his belongings at the police station while he went out and bought himself a cheap canvas handbag from the J.C. Penney store and a Greyhound ticket to Monterey. He felt really bad about the rucksack; it was a good European one that he'd carried for years.

■ ■ ■

232

Dorothy got out of bed. When she stood up, all the nasty yellow green black marble internal organs groped and crawled slowly over each other and her brain slanted, a heavy mercury pool. She sat down again right away and poured herself a glass of water from the thermos jug which stood on the bedside table. Lots of light blared into the room because the blinds had not been closed the night before. She drank a sip of cold water and felt it spread thin and heavy across the slow moving lumps of marble inside. There was only one or a dozen things to do. She must take a shower at once. With luck, she wouldn't fall and break a leg.

At distressingly frequent intervals she found herself recalling with great vividness and clarity one or another of her speeches of the night before, to whom it was addressed, and who were the people that were standing nearby, listening, and what was their relationship to the person addressed, to each other, and to Dorothy herself. Furthermore, she could imagine exactly how each of them must have taken her disordered and outrageous remarks. Dorothy felt that it would be impossible for her ever to meet any of those people again, anywhere or any time; it would be overwhelmingly embarrassing to her. She had covered herself with obloquy. She had been worse than an idiot. She blushed in the shower as she again heard herself saying—never mind what!—to someone to whom she had only recently been introduced—a person she found it impossible to like, he was too conventionally handsome. Her most outrageous oration had been addressed directly to him. All too directly.

Why did she let herself drink so much. Why had she eaten a whole 15mg spansule of Deximil. She nearly fell down in the shower because her brain lurched heavily in an unexpected northeasterly direction.

Instead of telephoning Dr. Bitteschoen, as she had planned to do, she had stopped into a bar to have a drink with Max Lammergeier, even though they were planning to go to the same party that evening. She had managed to meet Tom within twenty minutes of the time that they had planned to eat dinner, to quarrel fitfully for a little while, drive home and change clothes all in good time to arrive fashionably late at the large and elegant party.

Dorothy told Tom, "We can't stay more than an hour. I have to get back home and read a little while before I go to bed *early*. Anyway, it isn't a bit stylish to stay all night at one of these parties; everyone ends up dancing without their shoes at the Fairmount and then running barefoot across the Bridge to have breakfast on some yacht in Tiburon."

Tom agreed. He had a headache and was feeling cranky. "Just don't give me no bad time when I come around and tell you that it's time to go home."

The party turned out to be wonderfully diverting, in Dorothy's opinion. Waiters plied the guests with strong drink and delicious hand-made Swedish kickshaws and tidbits. When Tom told her that it was eleven o'clock, Dorothy looked at him with her eyes all out of focus, a mad grin on her face.

"It really is, isn't it, Tom. It's eleven o'clock. Well, I'll just finish this drink and then we'll go. This isn't such a high-class party, after all. The waiters aren't wearing gloves. That one with the marvelous hair is going to go through all the rest of his life with a gooey canapé stuck to his left thumb."

Tom said, "Sure, Baby." He was feeling much better, and he was inclined to be indulgent towards Dorothy; she looked happy, and he could tell from the melodic lilt of her voice that she was having a good time and would not leave just then; she'd probably stay until the last possible moment. He asked her, "Do you have money enough for a cab?"

Dorothy said, "Don't be silly."

"All right," Tom said. "Don't say I never asked you." But by then, Dorothy was involved in a conversation with several other people, although she was clinging tightly to Tom's arm. When she let go of him to make some magniloquent gesture, he went away and got his coat and went home.

By midnight, Dorothy was introducing Dr. Bitteschoen to everyone.

"This is my father, Dr. Bitteschoen, who is also my first or third husband. He taught me everything I can't remember. He singlehandedly invented Singhalese-Dravidian-Tamil phonemics. He's really awfully bright."

Dr. Bitteschoen was happily drunk and having a splendid time. He was glad to see Dorothy having a good time, and he was accustomed to her American extravagances of speech. He was feeling so good that he hadn't been speaking English for many hours. Dorothy chatted and joked with him in elegant literary polite Berlinese. There were several other guests who were near his own age, Europeans with whom he had a fine time talking about the old days before the war. One of them had been in the Masaryk cabinet.

Dr. Bitteschoen escorted Dorothy to her front door in a taxi. When she saw a clock she panicked. It read 3:45 a.m. Dorothy somehow blundered her way into the house and into bed without breaking her neck or any of the frangible pottery in the hallway. She thought, "I've really *got* to find another place for those Peruvian things. If somebody else doesn't break them, I'm going to. I wonder what it is I've got against dogs?"

■ ■ ■

Roy was broke again. The part-time job had folded for the summer. Nobody had bought any poems from him for a long time. His belongings were stored away in the attics and cellars of his friends' houses. He was temporarily sleeping on the couch in the living room of a friend who had a big house and a big family, but Roy kept worrying about where he was going to stay next, because he couldn't expect his friend to house him much longer; Roy had already been there a couple of months.

Most days, around noon, he went out and asked a different one of his friends to feed him. Sometimes he was invited to stick around for supper as well. Some days he felt too ashamed to go ask anyone for lunch or to stay in the house where he was sleeping when meal times came around; at the same time he worried about the people who were helping him—he was adding to their already large burdens of responsibility.

Roy felt that what he had to do was write down what he knew and what he kept "discovering." But he was feeling cold and angry and afraid all the time. He was disgusted with himself, and with his unwillingess to try doing anything more to help himself get food and a place to live. He had begun writing a long prose book and he wanted to go on writing it. He didn't want any other job; and he felt, right then, that he couldn't do anything else: he had a job of writing to do and it was taking all the time and energy he could find to do it. "Now I'm doing my job," he told himself. "This is the only work I really believe in, the only harmless and necessary work I've ever done."

His friends told him, "It's all right, Roy, quit stoning yourself. Come around when you're hungry; we've always got some food, anyway—we may not have much else to help you, but we can give you something to eat." But Roy was alternately writing and raging at himself and wishing for independence from his own mad ambition and from his friends, and this made him feel bad because he loved his friends and they were helping him and he felt guilty about wanting away from them. He wanted a private life. He hated to be bothered and he hated bothering other people. He hated most of all to be continuously worrying about food and shelter and booze. He didn't get more than twenty or thirty pages of his long prose book written.

Roy had a tab at a little bar in North Beach. He had always eventually paid it off from time to time in the past, and the bartender was a friend. Roy brought in a certain amount of business with him; he had lots of friends and acquaintances and admirers who came every night to the bar to see Roy and talk with him.

People who were interested in poetry but who lived in other cities, thought about how great it would be to visit San Francisco and go to that bar to see Roy and all the poets and hear what they all said and watch them do all the funny things that people said that the happy artists do. Quite a number of people from out of town actually made the pilgrimage: hairy, goggle-eyed students from upstate junior colleges who traveled with guitars and girlfriends who had long blond hair and sleepy eyes. Most of these young persons were either manic and babbling from injections of methadrine or they were smiling and goo-goo eyed from blowing up too many catnip cigarets. There were shy, bespectacled crypto-faggot highschool teachers from Nevada, and there were sack-suited, crew-cut sharpies who had "temporarily" been working for the J. Walter Thompson Agency for the past eight years. There were lady verse-weavers and word-jewelers from the polite bedroom towns of the Peninsula. There were reporters from national magazines who had already grown large mustaches and small beards, who had almost finished paying for that extra color TV set and their second divorce and who actually had manuscripts to show Roy, and they drew maps to indicate the location of the little mining town in the northern Sierra where they were very soon going to hide themselves away from bill collectors and ex-wives and *Newsweek*. From there would shortly commence to pour streams of art & culture, because several of the guys had already bought or were building weekend places up there in the mountains. Wild poems, shocking plays, revolutionary symphonies and oil paintings and titanic sculpture and wiggy architecture would soon be issuing from the dark & secret heart of Stanislaus County.

Roy denounced and discouraged and enraged and blessed those who came to him, just as the spirit moved him. He couldn't figure out why they should lay the mantle of Elijah upon him, but since they were foolish enough to do so, he'd give them the straight replies that went with that costume. He told them that they were losers and phonies and self-deceivers. He told the highschool teachers that they could teach nothing unless they went to bed with their students; whether one at a time or in group orgies was a matter for opportunity and ingenuity to decide. He advised the magazine and advertising and TV people to go kill themselves, for they had so degraded and debased their souls that they could never be artists of any kind; their attempts at writing and the other arts were only going to cause them endless pain and suffering from which death would be the only release. He advised the young to rob and lie and cheat and steal until they had enough money to get away to Europe or South America in order to preserve their lives and sensibilities: America would kill and eat them if they weren't careful, if they didn't escape.

All these people who came to hear Roy bought a great number of drinks for themselves, for Roy, and for each other. (The more sensitive among them moved on to other bars or went home.) Some would become intoxicated and converted by Roy's exhortations and prophecies; they would hang around until closing time and then haul the raving poet to their home where he might give them personal instruction.

One month Roy decided to turn himself completely loose and see where he'd end up on any particular morning. He began a book of *aubades*, following the French form strictly at first, then breaking away into strange patterns of his own. He spent several days in a giant Spanish hacienda palace villa made of pink stucco and imported Moorish tiles; it was located near Pebble Beach and it had a marble swimming pool, but there were too many other bums hanging around the place; Roy felt there was too much of a distracting atmosphere.

One morning, just after waking up, Roy nearly fell headfirst into San Francisco Bay from the twenty-seventh floor of a Russian Hill apartment building. Another time, he awoke in a high, light room with yellow walls and a skylight. There were rare plants growing in pots and boxes; they produced strange and gorgeous flowers. Brilliantly colored tropical birds—some in cages, some chained to open perches, some flying at large among the plants and trees and vines—all whistled and sang and argued with the new day. Suspended from the ceiling, standing on pedestals or reclining on the floor were many works of contemporary sculpture. Disturbed by a draft or the wind from a gaudy wing, or by the proximity of a viewer, some of these sculptures moved, chimed, spun, whirred, blinked colored lights or waved colored glass reflecting jewels or muttered electronic stutters and groans and whines.

Roy never saw who lived in that place, and he couldn't remember how he got there. He looked around the room at all the wonders, then he discovered the way to the bathroom. Afterwards, he opened all the other doors in the place. One of them led into a bedroom. There was no one inside. The sun shone brilliantly through a window which was dressed in beautiful translucent curtains and brocade drapes. The large bed was neatly made up. On a chiffoniere there stood a picture in a silver frame; it was a photograph of an elderly couple; they were standing on the steps of the Capitol building in Washington, D.C. The man looked as if he might work there; he held a briefcase under one arm and was very well dressed. The woman was somebody's mother.

Roy went into the kitchen and found a note on the table; it was addressed to him. The swiftly written block-print letters read,

> Dearest Roy, Here is a dollar for ciggy-boos. I've got to
> drive Mama to La Jolla tomorrow, today I mean—early,
> anyhow. I'll see you when I get back tonight. Help yourself
> to whatever you want to eat or drink. Love, N.

Roy couldn't imagine who "N." was, or why she (he?) had left him a dollar. He helped himself to a quart of milk from the refrigerator. He drank it all from the carton because he didn't want to bother looking for a glass nor to bother washing it afterwards. The kitchen was beautifully new and clean; everything was carefully put away in drawers and cabinets.

Roy wrote a note on the back of N.'s note to him:

> Dear N., Thanks for the party. Thanks for the dollar. I'll see
> you later. Now I've got to go to work. Love, Roy.

Roy set the note on the table and put a jar of cardamom seeds on it so that it wouldn't blow away. He wondered whether the birds had been fed. He supposed that N. must have arranged with somebody to take care of them. N. seemed to be a thoughtful type. Then Roy wondered whether he himself might not have volunteered (while in his cups) to be the caretaker, the bird-watcher. He went back into the big room. The seed and water dishes were in reasonably good order and in case the water supply should run low, there was more to be had from the big glass aquaria which stood about the room. If the birds get thirsty, let them drink out of the fish bowls, Roy thought. If they get hungry they can eat flowers or the bugs and insects which doubtlessly afflict all these plants. Roy picked up his notebook and put on his dark glasses. He left the apartment and was surprised to find himself in the marble-lined corridor of an office building. He took an elevator down to the street level and walked out into the white foggy sunshine of the financial district.

■ ■ ■

Margaret Gridley telephoned to Dorothy from Eugene:

"Hi, Dotty, I'm coming to see you right away. I have to come down to the city and shop for some fashionable maternity garments."

"No!" Dorothy incredulously replied.

"It's all really true," Margaret drawled. "I'm coming on the electric fan company airplane. I'll meet you for lunch at Swann's Oyster Depot; I've got to eat nothing but protein from this moment forward."

"How's Herbert," Dorothy inquired.

"Fine. He shot this seven hundred pound bear in the wilderness behind our house. We've been living on it for weeks. I'll bring some for you and Tom."

Dorothy was laughing and choking and gasping. At last she was able to ask Margaret, "What did he really do?"

"I'm telling you," Margaret said. "Herbert brought back this animal. His mother fixed it all up for the deep-freeze. He gave lots of it to his relatives and to all his friends—about two hundred pounds of it."

"Margaret, you're making it all up!" Dorothy said.

"And we still have about three hundred pounds of it left and a lovely fur rug for Herbert's office or the spare bedroom...wouldn't you like to have a big bearskin rug?"

"No! I'm in a horrible rush, trying to fix my wonderful essay," Dorothy told her. "I have to get ready to go to the thing in Monterey and I don't have anything decent to wear and my hair is standing out all over my head and my shoes are all old and funny-looking..."

"Then we'll be able to go *everywhere*," Margaret exclaimed. "To all the stores. I'll help you. I'll stay three days. Is Tom all right?"

"He's fine. Dr. Bitteschoen got him appointed official photographer for the Conference."

"It's going to be quite a family party," Margaret said.

"Even pukey old Roy's going," Dorothy continued, "I suppose that Clifford Barlow made them ask him."

"Clifford Barlow? I thought he was in Iowa or someplace," Margaret said. "Are you going to talk to *him*? I wouldn't if I were you. He's bad for you."

"Clifford? Don't be ridiculous. He'll be too busy being the center of attention and the pompous expert. I'm not afraid of him—in fact, I have to see him and find out what he's been doing in Katmandu with that Sarah Gardner."

"Be sure to let me know," Margaret said. Her tone indicated a profound indifference. She disliked Sarah Gardner. "Have you read about my show?" Margaret asked.

"Oh, Margaret, where? I didn't know!" Dorothy replied.

"It's only the Whitney Museum in New York," Margaret told her. "I keep telling you that you *have* to read *The New Yorker* faithfully and entirely, every week. There were even a few sales..."

"Oh, Margaret!"

"I'll tell the world. It certainly helps right now. Young Wilberforce can have a decent debut."

"How do you know it's a boy?" Dorothy asked.

"Don't be silly," Margaret said. "I know what I'm doing. Herbert expects it."

"The big faggot," Dorothy cried.

"Isn't it so," Margaret said. "Well, I'll be there at noon tomorrow. Warn Tom and air out the guest room. I'll bring some gin. And the baby."

■ ■ ■

Roy got a postcard from somebody called Tom Prescott, who said he wanted to take Roy's picture. He proposed to meet Roy on a certain day in front of a North Beach bookstore. Roy appeared at the stated time. Tom Prescott was standing in front of the store; it was quite apparent that he was a photographer. He was wearing two cameras on leather straps around his neck. There was a battery pack on the ground beside him. There was a carrying bag for the flashlight over one of his shoulders and slung on the other shoulder was another case containing a collection of filters and lenses and a collapsible tripod and exposure meters and lens shades and an old Kodak folding camera which made postcard-sized photographs in case all the other equipment should fail to work.

The pockets of Tom's big Air Force jacket were full of more equipment—more light meters, lens dusters, cleaning tissues and fluids, a tape measure, pocket magnifying glasses, prisms, optical mirrors, and a square piece of fine black cloth to use as a hood when he wanted to look into the view finder on the big Kodak.

Tom Prescott was wearing a pair of blue whipcord officer's pants, a blue plaid wool shirt and a pair of Pivetta walking boots. His yellow hair was cut close to his big round head and his big red ears hung out on either side of it. He had very thick blond eyebrows growing across a heavy supraorbital ridge. He had a big crooked nose (it had been wrecked in a football game) and a big square jaw. No matter how often he shaved and washed it, his face always looked rocky and a little grubby.

Standing in front of the bookstore, Tom didn't seem to be too interested in the scene; he appeared merely to be a photographer standing around waiting for somebody. But he was holding a small camera with a very big lense and it was photographing all the people who came up or down the street; Tom was working the film winder and the shutter very fast and without looking at the camera and without (seemingly) focusing it. People who saw him were more interested in looking at all the paraphernalia that he had hanging from him and only a few of them were aware he was really taking pictures with the little camera he seemed to be adjusting or playing with.

When Roy came up to him, Tom said, "Let's go get some coffee. I have to reload my handgun and it's easier to talk if we sit down and have something for the nerves."

Roy thought that Tom was rather abrupt and commandeering, but he didn't want to argue. He was used to the curious arrogance of photographers and movie people. He watched and listened while Tom reloaded the little camera and told Roy all about the Cuban Revolution, which he had recently been photographing. Tom didn't drink much of his coffee; he kept talking to Roy and photographing the waiters and the man who was running the espresso machine and all the other customers and sometimes the people who were passing in front of the big plateglass window near which he and Roy sat. Sometimes he aimed a big portrait lens at Roy, but it seemed that Tom never worked the shutter of the camera that he happened to be looking through.

Roy thought that Tom was very cool and collected. Nobody seemed to realize that Tom was really photographing them; he moved very slowly and deliberately. He never spoke very loudly. While they sat inside the coffee shop, Tom shot up a whole roll of film with the little camera and reloaded it again. Occasionally he consulted a light meter with the same kind of gesture an old-time railroad man uses when he looks at his watch. Quite often Tom would reach the end of a paragraph or anecdote and stop talking. It didn't seem to embarrass him to sit silently for five minutes at a stretch.

Roy asked him about himself, where he was from, where he grew up and Tom answered at length, unhurriedly, with details, and with a pause at the end of each paragraph in case Roy should wish to make a comment or to change the subject. He told Roy about the Air Corps and about Darlene and their son, about football and traveling and his present project. Tom was traveling all around America in order to make photographs of writers and artists. He figured that he'd be able to sell some of the pictures to magazines or to submit the best ones in competitions—while the whole collection would make an interesting one-man show in a gallery.

Tom and Roy swapped stories about the people Tom had already photographed. They spent the rest of the day walking around the city together; Roy wanted Tom to see his favorite parks and buildings. At last Roy asked him, "Do you turn on? I'd like to get a little high and then go eat dinner."

Tom felt flattered. He hadn't been in town long enough to locate a connection, and he hadn't had any grass since he had left Los Angeles. He recognized it as a compliment from Roy that he'd asked him to turn on.

240

Lots of times, Tom's professional manner offended people. He was often described as a square by some of the younger people that he'd met in his recent travels. They tended to imagine that a man with so many cameras must have sold his ass to Henry Luce or the Government in order to buy them. Tom had had to do a lot of scuffling to buy his equipment; he still owed money on a lot of it. Although a few of his photographs were beginning to be published, there hadn't as yet been any real rush from editors and publishers to buy his work.

■  ■  ■

The Grand Mahatma says: "We sometimes learn—and it comes as a shock to us—that the gift we gave to somebody else wasn't ours to give, nor was it in our power to bestow it. For some time we had been congratulating ourselves on our own generosity; now, we realize, there wasn't really any gift nor was anything received, and the whole affair has been a great delusion from the start. Perhaps we might try to credit ourselves with having had good intentions for once in our lives—but this is only a hasty fumbling among the gravel in search of consolation...that piece of water-worn glass which isn't a gem stone."

■  ■  ■

As he came up the walk and into the small Gothic chapel, Clifford could hear the organ. He was both intrigued and annoyed. The organ was supposed to be reserved for him to practice on at this hour; who was this ham-handed type, messing around with the C Minor Passacaglia?

He found a man called Roy Aherne seated at the console. Roy was an aged freshman, newly graduated from the army. He had come to Bull Run College in order to have time to read a few books, write a novel, and meet some beautiful rich young lady who would take care of him for the rest of his life. The G.I. Bill was making all this possible for him; otherwise, he was as penniless as Clifford, who was at Bull Run on a meagre scholarship. Clifford was having to pose for art classes on campus and at the museum school downtown. He also had a job as a hasher in the college commons in order to help pay for his board and room and other necessities.

Clifford was upset by Roy's total ignorance of keyboard technique.

"Look at the little numbers beside the notes. They tell you where to put your fingers: put them there. You read music just fine, you understand the time" (Roy was playing again) "but read, right there, hey! Stop a minute! 5-1-4—5-1-4! you're trying to go 5-1-3 and right away you run out of fingers to do it—, see? Try again."

Roy laughed. He said, "I know, I know, I never learned right, and I'm too nearsighted to see the little numbers. I can just about see the notes from here. I have to do most of it by ear and fake the rest. My feet don't hit the right pedals, either. How do you learn how to do that?"

"You know where they are, if you think about it. Hit the black ones with your toe and the white ones with your heel; that way you can feel right where all the notes are if you practise a little bit. Try to play some easier Bach things to learn the pedal board. Memorize the score."

"Oh, I can see OK, it's just hard at that distance," Roy said.

Clifford kept trying to teach Roy from time to time, but Roy didn't make any progress. He didn't practice regularly; he said that he was too busy flunking all his courses and working on his book.

"I started too late," Roy told him. "I've got too many untrained reflexes. Just like trying to be a student in this beanery. . . If I was your age, maybe it would be different, maybe I'd be able to take it seriously."

■ ■ ■

Dorothy went to Reno to act as a witness in Margaret's divorce when it came on for trial in the Washoe County Courthouse. She had a hard time of it, trying to look like a respectable and responsible citizen. She had a hangover and all her nerves were frying in a bath of methadrine that she'd taken in order to get over her hangover fast. She was trying to be a good sport and help Margaret. She felt responsible for the marriage in the first place. But she hoped that Margaret would forget all the things that they'd been talking about the night before.

They couldn't sleep in Margaret's smelly motel room with its short twin beds and its *moderne* decor. They went to one of those low-ceilinged clubs which appear to have been carved out of solid red plush. The club had no external walls; a barrier of gas heat prevented whatever chill airs of evening from attacking the guests "inside" the place. Gambling machines clashed and tinkled. Voices of croupiers and dealers, powerfully amplified by expensive electronic equipment, gently but authoritatively penetrated the din. Somewhere in the red empyrean, above all the other sounds and voices, a velvet curtain of Muzak gently floated and billowed. The plush floor and walls and thickly upholstered furniture, coupled with the presence of a large crowd of people, was supposed to keep the noise level bearable. Theoretically it did.

Dorothy and Margaret drank gin and talked most of the night. They hadn't seen each other for several weeks and a great deal had happened within that span of time.

Margaret asked Dorothy, quite un-apropos of anything, "How did it happen that you married Clifford instead of Roy?"

Dorothy answered, quite candidly, "Clifford asked me first. Then he went to Ceylon and then Dr. Bitteschoen wanted me to be there. Besides, Clifford Barlow was famous and good-looking and sort of marvelous—I had made up my mind to marry Clifford long before I met Roy. When I first knew Clifford, I thought he was really something special."

"Were you preg that time you had appendicitis before you went to Ceylon?" Margaret asked.

"Of course. But it all went away by itself; I was sick in the hospital for only a little while and they took out my appendix, but the pregnancy took care of itself—I'm Rh negative or some delightful thing like that, I forget. Type B?"

"You really ought to have married Roy," Margaret said. "He's still cuckoo about you; I'm sure of it."

"Don't be insane," Dorothy said. "Roy's an old faggot."

"How did you get pregnant that time? Did you sit on the wrong toilet seat?"

Dorothy took a drink. She sighed and played with her glass. Then she told Margaret, "He didn't want to marry anybody, he wanted to run around writing poetry. Clifford was his oldest friend, he had to—oh, I don't know what all. Anyway, I had to marry Clifford like I said I would; it was a decision I had made and I had to believe in it."

"You never got pregnant by anybody else, did you," Margaret said.

There was a crash and a roar and a blare of music from one corner of the room. A four-bit machine was paying off: elderly ladies in capacious Capri pants were squealing and hopping arthritically up and down; strong men standing near the laboring machine slavered as a flood of silver coins gushed from the little door.

■ ■ ■

The Grand Mahatma says, "I live entirely for my own pleasure; this may explain why I have lived to be so old. The wicked must live through many lives in many worlds before they become fortunate enough to hear about the possibility of escaping from the fixed rounds of existence.

"But am I really wicked? I've certainly been illogical. And I've lived to see the beautiful, the talented and the wise disappear from all these many worlds: all the persons that we need most are gone. The least intelligent, the least virtuous and the least attractive remain here in this puddle where I chirp and paddle."

■ ■ ■

Roy told Dorothy, "You know, it used to bother me a lot when people would ask me, 'What do you write about?' or 'What's your new book about?'"

"You take everybody so seriously," Dorothy said. "What do you care about what all these fools ask or say?"

"Yeah . . . but this really monumental answer came to me while I was in the shower this morning," Roy said. "Listen," and at this point his voice assumed a portentous, theatrical tone: " 'I write of man's forward, endless, hurtling flight from the inexorable, implacable, incomprehensible mystery—' " Roy paused in mid-career, holding a forefinger in the air. "You have to imagine 'mystery' as being capitalized," he explained, then

continued: " 'Of God's infinite mercy and love and joy.' Isn't that great?''
Roy inquired, dropping his Papal tone. "I love 'implacable.' ''

Dorothy laughed. She was pleased to see him happy for once, but she
told him, "You won't be able to remember all that. And anyway, you know
what anybody's going to tell you if you hand them all that—they'll just
look at you and say, 'Huh?' or 'How very nice. Won't you take a little more
tea?' ''

■ ■ ■

Clifford and Roy sat together on the edge of a swimming pool in
Monterey. They were enjoying the sunshine and the spectacle of many
beautiful young persons disporting themselves in and about the pool.

Clifford said, "Anyway, I am right."

Roy said, "Oh, yes. OK. What else?"

"You'll have to find out for yourself, some day, that's all," Clifford said,
magisterially. "Now I'm going to swim the length of the pool underwater
and then I have to go play music."

"I guess I'll stick around while it's still warm," Roy said. "The fog will be
coming in, pretty soon."

"Don't get sunburned," Clifford told him. "Remember you don't have
any skin. I'll see you at my place for drinks, around six. Fare thee well,"
Clifford said, and then he dove into the pool.

Roy watched him zoom along under the green water like a sea lion, a
flickering blue-green shadow. Here we are, Roy thought, at the end of the
world at the end of our lives, both of us alone. But Cliff is right and I am
wrong and neither of us has Dorothy. He believes in his own righteousness and goes on leading and instructing—trying to force everybody else
into believing in their own righteousness—so that the entire universe will
be engaged in the production of right? Why not. The world has just about
exhausted itself producing wrongs and wickedness and evil. It's time for
a change. For a beginning, I must figure out a way to forgive Cliff for his
goofiness and bossiness and righteousness. How do you do that. But it
has to be done.

Roy stood up and adjusted his shorts. Shall I dive in, he wondered. The
water was very likely freezing cold. It has to be done, but there isn't really
any *doing* about it. There is only this feeling I have now, associated with
the idea of forgiving or the word is the feeling or the idea is the doing; let
it alone. It's a mess, it's all candy, like John Dryden sang:

> All, all of a piece throughout;
> Thy Chase has a Beast in View,
> Thy Wars brought nothing about;
> Thy Lovers were all untrue.
> 'Tis well an Old Age is out,
> And time to begin a New.

Roy dove into the pool. The water was exactly the right temperature.

■ ■ ■

Dorothy told Roy, "I'm having all kinds of trouble with dreams again. I keep remembering them in the morning and in the afternoon. The memories of what people did and said and what I did and said in the dream are as clear as other memories, so that I'm getting confused, now, about what have I really said or what really has happened."

Roy said, "It doesn't matter; it's all the same."

"You're a big help," Dorothy said. "I wonder if I ought to go see Max Lammergeier. But he always keeps telling me the same thing—as long as you're getting your work done, you're fine. *Naturally* I get my work done—compulsively, obsessively, just like I'm supposed to, every day. I'm going to marry Tom Prescott, we're desperately in love with each other, we're going to have a complete new life. Then I'm going to go right straight out of my head and Clifford will kill himself or me or Tom or somebody. What are we going to do?"

"Let's have a little more gin," Roy said. "You take too many of those funny pills. You ought to drink more."

Dorothy shouted, "More? My God, I'm practically an alcoholic already! And alcohol is composed exclusively of calories, and I'm grotesquely huge now. Anyway, I have some new pills that Ed Bancroft gave me—they aren't as fizzy as the old ones. Do you want to try one?"

"Sure. Anything for a change," Roy said. "I'll take it in the morning when I'm feeling sad."

■ ■ ■

Basil Johnson was called Beefy partly because of his first two initials—B.F., for Basil Frederick—and partly because of a natural steatopygia. When he was a boy, his friends called him King Freddy, because one day when they asked him, "Basil? What kind of a name is that?" Beefy all innocently told them what his mother had told him:

" 'Basil' is from an ancient Greek word that means 'king.' I named you that becasue I want you to grow up to be a king among men. You'll be called lots of other things because you're black, but you must always remember to be as great and noble as your name. Then no matter what people say about you, no matter how dark you are, the greatness and the beauty inside of you will shine through. Always try to remember that."

Beefy had a number of fights about his name, but he won most of them, and so he had a new name: Beefy. A very few of his oldest friends were allowed to call him "King." The dossiers which were kept on him by the FBI, the Treasury Department, Army Intelligence and the local police (among other agencies) listed "King Basil" as one of Beefy's official aliases. "We know all about him," a T-man said.

245

By the time Basil was nineteen, he was cutting records with a jazz group. He attended the university during the day. He had always enjoyed reading, and now he had discovered that it was easy for him to write essays and examination papers and the knowledge excited him. He was playing many different kinds of music with the campus orchestra. In his spare time, he used to get a kick out of trying to play on all the different orchestral instruments in the music department building. He studied harmony and counterpoint and orchestration with Mark Sanderson, who thought that Beefy was the best young musician he'd seen in years. Beefy studied very hard; he had to know all the things on paper that he could already do when he was working with a group of musicians.

The local narcotics squad arrested him not long after the beginning of his senior year at the university. The citizens of the Bay Area were convinced that all the university students were taking dope and fucking each other, right on the campus, which is State Property. The police imagined that they must do something about this dread condition which the newspaper said that everybody was worried about. Who was more likely to be the Big Connection and Mother on the university campus than this Negro kid musician who hung around with all the heads in the Fillmore? While they questioned Beefy, they said they were having an officer inspect his car. An officer came in, a few minutes later, to show Beefy several little brown seeds which, he said, had been found in Beefy's car—seeds of the hemp plant, source of the Killer Drug, marijuana! These little seeds would make it possible for the police to put Beefy away for a long time.

Beefy said, "Are you serious?" but he didn't see which one of them it was who slapped him very hard across the side of his head, it happened so fast.

"Talk respectful when an officer asks you something, Basil," one of them said.

Beefy asked, "Can I call my lawyer?"

"Maybe you can, later, after you've told us where you got all the pot and who you've been selling it to. You're going to tell us a lot, King Basil."

It was only by the merest fluke of chance that Beefy's father happened to visit the jail that day in order to see one of his clients. Everyone was embarrassed all around, and the police were extremely apologetic, there must have been some kind of mistake, and surely Mr. Johnson realized how important it was to follow every possible lead that might help them to apprehend the despicable criminals who were engaged in the monstrous narcotics traffic which was (as Mr. Hoover teaches us) all a part of the international communist conspiracy: dope is a means of undermining the moral fabric of America in order to make the country a pushover for the Russians and the Chinese. There was, of course, no charge pending against Basil, and it was quite clear that there had been a regrettable error in identification—Basil wasn't the boy whom they thought they had found, the one they thought would be able to help them.

Edwin Johnson said, "Well, Sergeant, Johnson is a very common name."

"I fell down the elevator," Beefy said. His nose was still bleeding. "Can we leave now, Papa?"

■ ■ ■

Roy wondered, "When am I going to quit trying to justify myself to all my friends and before all the world? I'm tired of explaining that writing is a full-time job, that whatever time I have left I like to use for relaxing and talking and drinking and then it's time to write again. Why don't I just go ahead and do what I want to do? They don't really care. And why am I afraid that everybody will stop loving me? Why should every man, woman, child, cat, dog, and seagull in the world love me? What did I ever do for them, that they are bound to give me their total, admiration and approval?"

Then he sighed and answered his own question. "Because I love all of them, every one. Why don't they be nice to me?" But he corrected himself immediately. "I don't really love them, I love their beauty. The trouble is that I don't love just one single person. If I really loved one, I wouldn't be interested in the judgments of all the others, nor would I be seeing all the others as judges: only as individuals who were as loving and gentle and kind as that love which I was experiencing. I wouldn't confuse them any more with my parents or with the police. And there, at last, is that. I've managed to realize eighteen million rare and wonderful things— maybe a few that nobody else has thought of before—but I've never really known that I'm a separate, adult individual and that my childhood is truly over and that I no longer am required to believe everything that I'm told, no longer obliged to obey the commands of my parents or wait for orders from some other superior officers."

■ ■ ■

Dorothy told Roy, "It's marvelous to have running water and electricity. Living in Asia is so hard all the time. And toilets that flush! I never want to go anywhere west of Hawaii again. Everything here is awful but I don't care, I'll get used to it again, soon: all the big cars and billboards and noise. But the American faces! You've no idea how funny we look, a boat-load of *Us*, a streetcar full of Americans: all the madness and bitterness and hatefulness that shows in our faces. At first I hated the blank sort of stare, the fake politeness and the smooth lazy hopelessness of India. Now I miss all those people—they were beautiful to look at, no matter how crazy or weird or dishonest they may have been. I can't *look* at Americans. Have some more gin."

Roy helped himself from the frosty bottle. "What really happened with you and Clifford? Why are you leaving him? You really broke with him before you ever met Tom, didn't you?"

247

"It's none of your business, Mr. Nosey. We found that we were mutually incompatible and mentally cruel to each other."

"Come on," Roy said.

"He's a liar and a phony and a kink and I hate him," Dorothy broke out. "He cares for nothing but running after other women. He was interested in me for the first week we knew each other, years ago, and he was interested again when we were first married. (He really wants a family, you know.) When I didn't get pregnant right away, he let me know that his real interests are music and scholarship and he had his schedule and I had mine—and of course, I was to take care of the household in accordance with his old-maid ideas, cook all the meals to conform to his nutty notions about proper diet and nutrition, practice music two hours a day so he could teach me that, too (although I admit I learned a lot about music that I didn't know—he can't play a flute, himself, but he knows exactly how it *ought* to be played), and he's right—he's always right."

"As usual," Roy said.

"But it's all fake, all false, all that he's really interested in is different women—everything else is window dressing," Dorothy went on. "He even fools himself, for hours at a time, about being a great intellectual and a great authority in his field—a great authority: he can certainly give orders, all right, he's great at that. I don't think that he realizes (or maybe he really does, which I don't want to think about; it would make him even worse than he is—or better—or something—I hate him!). Maybe he doesn't really know that he's a satyr, an insatiable wandering stiff cock and nothing more."

Roy said, "But that's a whole universe, too—of connections and highs and feelings and losses which makes all the rest worth anything. The learning and the arts are only momentary flashes of abstract, mental beauty. The *real* is our affections, our holding each other, our naked loving—"

"It's all because you're a man that you defend him," Dorothy cried. "It's what you really want, too—it's *all* of you: childish, self-indulgent, narcissistic—you don't love anybody but yourselves and each other—no woman's got a chance—all of you really *are* a bunch of dirty old faggots, that's the real truth. All your ideas and big muscles and mountain climbing are phony. All you want is to scare each other to death with your big cocks and how you can do it with more women than any other man—how you can coax and wheedle more dumb women to sleep with you than the other one can. You're all insufferable. Why don't you go home. I hate you."

Roy said, "Very well, I'll take my gin and go." He remained seated in his chair, holding onto his glass.

"Oh, don't go," Dorothy said. "Tell me about everything. How are Mark and Beth? How is Max?"

"Everybody's about the same," Roy said. "All of us are older. All of us ought to get out of town, I suppose. We're all such fixtures here. I wish I could travel for a while and see if there really is any more to the world than just USA."

"You'd love it in India," Dorothy told him. "You ought to go there, if anybody should. Get a job for a while and get some money and go. It isn't hard."

"I've already got a job," Roy wearily repeated. "I haven't got time to work for somebody else."

"Clifford Barlow says everybody must work. It's bad for people to have money, it spoils their natures. We must work very hard all day every day. Clifford always makes a garden, wherever he's living and he works very hard in it. The flowers are always beautiful and the tomatoes are superb. He talks to all the vegetables and flowers in order to make them grow *right*. They don't dare disappoint him."

■ ■ ■

The Grand Mahatma says, "They ask me all the time, 'Why is the world this way? Why is it all messed up?' And I shock them with my answer:

"Somebody's making a pile of money out of it, that's why. The present world is an extremely profitable enterprise being operated by a few extremely rich and powerful men and women. Karl Marx was a maniac: communism is another invention for keeping the yokels quiet and working on the inside of a gloomy factory fourteen hours a day instead of letting them make love and pick flowers and paint pictures and write poems and play music and take dope and build stately pleasure domes.

"You come around here asking me questions about the Soul and the Higher Consciousness—you're nothing but a potential dollar in the Gross National Product. You're no more than a possible casualty in some phony 'brush-fire' war against some fake brand of 'Under-developed' communist. You're nothing but a little row of figures in a ledger down at the Bank of America. Get away from me. I'm tired of looking at you and hearing your tiresome little voice.

" 'Why?' Why, indeed! Why not? Why shouldn't you get precisely what you deserve, whether it's a question of lives or worlds or answers?"

■ ■ ■

Roy was very happy. He had just received a letter from Dorothy. She sounded happy and excited about traveling and Tom was much better and she had been invited to teach at the university when they got back from wherever it was they finally decided to go.

He was glad that Dorothy was getting along so well. He took a certain amount of credit for introducing her to Tom. In a way, it repaired the blunder which he'd committed when he told her to go and marry Clifford. That had been a real mistake, Roy thought—no doubt Origen must have thought something very like that, just after he had performed his celebrated home-surgery act.

249

Roy walked under the plane trees in Golden Gate Park while the band played *Gems from "Zampa."* He was very nearly killed when he tried to cross the road near the aquarium; a large municipal bus was barreling along the narrow street between the giant head of Beethoven and the grand monument to Giuseppe Verdi: the driver was gazing dreamily at Robert Emmet's roaring effigy.

■ ■ ■

The Grand Mahatma says, "Say, I need help. I hurt. Isn't anybody going to come and help me? Isn't there any human being around here to give me a hand? I hurt! Why don't you get me a doctor? Why don't they take me to the hospital? Why don't they give me a shot of something? Say, what kind of outfit is this, anyway? I'M ALL IN THE DIRT AND ON FIRE OR SOMETHING, G E T   M E   O U T   O F   H E R E."

■ ■ ■

Dorothy and Tom drank hot chocolate and ate delicious whipped cream pastries in a famous Viennese coffee house. They had been to the American Express to pick up their mail, and afterwards they had retired to this mellow cave of dark mahogany and plush to read their letters by the light of the real crystal chandeliers. It was snowing outside. The Muzak inside was playing a series of Argentine tangos. Tom was humming along with the music,

*Adios, muchachos, compañeros de ma vida . . .*

He looked up, at last, and asked Dorothy, "Well, what's the dope?"

"Oh, it's only Mother," Dorothy replied. "She's fussing about the Blind Babies' Bargain Bazaar and she wants her piano."

*Kyoto*
30:VIII:66 − 28:V:67

PHILIP WHALEN was born in Portland, Oregon in 1923. From 1943 until 1946 he was in service with the US Army Air Corps as a radio operator and mechanics instructor. He attended Reed College, where he met Gary Snyder and Lew Welch, and graduated in 1951 with a BA in Language and Literature. He lived in San Francisco until the mid-1960s, working in a variety of jobs, including the post office and three summers as a lookout fireman in Mt. Baker National Forest, Washington. He met Allen Ginsberg and Jack Kerouac, participated in the Six Gallery reading on October 6, 1955, and was part of the San Francisco poetry Renaissance. In 1962 he received a Poets Foundation Award; in 1965 a grant-in-aid from the National Academy of Arts and Letters; and two grants from the Committee on Poetry, 1969-71. In 1963 *You Didn't Even Try* was begun in Mill Valley and completed in San Francisco. He lived in Japan from 1966-67, during which time *Imaginary Speeches for a Brazen Head* was composed. He returned to Kyoto in 1969 after a visit to the USA and remained there until 1971. In 1972 he moved to the Zen Center, San Francisco, and in 1973 was ordained *Unsui* (Zen Buddhist monk). In 1975 he served as *Shuso* (head monk) at Zenshinji, Zen Mountain Center, Tassajara Springs, California. From 1981 until 1982 he was the head monk at South Ridge Zendo, San Francisco. In 1984 he became the head monk at Dharma Sangha in Santa Fe, New Mexico. He has been a visiting poet at the Naropa Institute since 1975.

PAUL CHRISTENSEN wrote the essay on Philip Whalen's poetry for the volume on "The Beats" of the *Dictionary of Literary Biography* (Gale Research, 1979). The volume was edited by Ann Charters. He has published numerous essays on modern poets and poetics, and is the author of *Charles Olson: Call Me Ishmael* (Texas, 1979). A poet and editor of Cedarshouse Press, Christensen has been a professor of modern literature and creative writing at Texas A & M University, where he has taught since 1974. He lives in Bryan, Texas.

Two Novels *was set in 11 point Novarese.*
*Composition by Type for U, Cambridge, Massachusetts.*
*This book was printed on acid free paper and*
*the binding sewn for book longevity.*

*A first edition of 350 clothbound and 1200 paperbound copies*
*was printed by Thomson-Shore, Inc., Dexter, Michigan.*
*Fifty copies of the cloth edition are signed*
*and numbered by the author.*